PENGUIN  CLASSICS

THE GOLDEN LEGEND: SELECTIONS

JACOBUS DE VORAGINE was born about 1229. His name is spelt 'Varagine' in early records, suggesting that he came from the coastal town of Varazze near Genoa. A Dominican friar, he joined the Order in 1244 in Genoa and was subsequently prior in the convents of Como, Bologna, and Asti. From 1267 to 1277 and again from 1281 to 1286 he was prior of the Dominican Order of Lombardy. In 1292 he became archbishop of Genoa, in which capacity he was active in trying to make peace between the warring Guelf and Ghibelline factions. His major works were three volumes of sermons, a *Mariale*, a *Chronicle of Genoa* and *The Golden Legend*. The latter was probably compiled while he was at Bologna and Asti. He died in 1298, and was beatified by Pope Pius VIII in 1816.

The Golden Legend, a collection of saints' Lives and related material was one of the most widely copied and read books of the later Middle Ages. Over a thousand manuscripts of the Latin text survive, and it was frequently printed during the first century of printing. It was also translated into most European languages. Its extremely varied contents offer a broad range of stories and information, not all historically accurate, covering many aspects of medieval life and attitudes, and it is an invaluable work of reference for art historians interested in the medieval and Renaissance periods.

CHRISTOPHER STACE read Classics at Fitzwilliam College, Cambridge, and graduated with First Class Honours. He then taught at Christ's Hospital, and held the position of Senior Classics Master at Bradfield College from 1973 to 1997. He has translated a variety of classical authors: Euripides' *Bacchae* for the BBC, which was filmed on location in Greece, Plautus for Cambridge University Press (1981) and Sophocles for performances at the Royal Exchange Theatre, Manchester (*Philoctetes* in 1982; the two *Oedipus* plays in 1987). His most recent book was *Florence, City of the Lily* (1989), a celebration of his love of Italy, where he now spends part of every year.

RICHARD HAMER is ⊤ . . . . Literature at Christ Church, Ox . . .

JACOBUS DE VORAGINE

The Golden Legend:
SELECTIONS

Selected and translated by
CHRISTOPHER STACE

With an Introduction and Notes by
RICHARD HAMER

PENGUIN BOOKS

PENGUIN BOOKS

Published by the Penguin Group
Penguin Books Ltd, 80 Strand, London WC2R 0RL, England
Penguin Putnam Inc., 375 Hudson Street, New York, New York 10014, USA
Penguin Books Australia Ltd, 250 Camberwell Road, Camberwell, Victoria 3124, Australia
Penguin Books Canada Ltd, 10 Alcorn Avenue, Toronto, Ontario, Canada M4V 3B2
Penguin Books India (P) Ltd, 11 Community Centre, Panchsheel Park, New Delhi – 110 017, India
Penguin Books (NZ) Ltd, Cnr Rosedale and Airborne Roads, Albany, Auckland, New Zealand
Penguin Books (South Africa) (Pty) Ltd, 24 Sturdee Avenue, Rosebank 2196, South Africa

Penguin Books Ltd, Registered Offices: 80 Strand, London WC2R 0RL, England

www.penguin.com

Published in 1998

035

Translation copyright © Christopher Stace, 1998
Introduction and Notes copyright © Richard Hamer, 1998
All rights reserved

Set in 9.5/12 pt PostScript Monotype Garamond
Typeset by Rowland Phototypesetting Ltd, Bury St Edmunds, Suffolk

Printed and bound in Great Britain by Clays Ltd, Elcograf S.p.A.

ISBN-13: 978-0-14-044648-7

www.greenpenguin.co.uk

CONTENTS

The Golden Legend:
SELECTIONS

INTRODUCTION

The Golden Legend, or, to give it its Latin name, *Legenda Aurea*, was without doubt one of the most widely disseminated books throughout Europe from its completion in about 1266 until the end of the Middle Ages. Some knowledge of its nature and contents and the underlying assumptions of its readers is therefore of importance for anyone who wishes to understand that period. It is also specifically useful, if not essential, for students of the history of art, since so many depictions of the saints and events relating to the liturgical feasts in paintings, stained glass and other media are based on material derived from it directly or indirectly. In addition, it is a treasure-house of stories and information, history and myth which the modern reader will find both interesting and entertaining. For all these reasons we believe it should be made more easily accessible than it has hitherto been, and hence the present translation of a substantial part of it has been undertaken.

This claim for its significance for the study of art history is forcefully supported by the work of one of the greatest of art historians, Emile Mâle. In his *L'Art religieux du XIIIe siècle en France*, first published in 1898, but in its latest revised version (available in English translation) still regarded as fundamental for this subject, he devoted a chapter to 'the saints and *The Golden Legend*', saying that he uses the *Legend* as his 'principal guide' for this aspect of iconography; and the rest of the book is peppered with references to it.[1] During this chapter he summarizes the accounts of many saints while discussing their treatment by the artists; and in view of the huge numbers of portrayals of saints and of incidents in their lives in stained glass, sculpture and paintings in churches and cathedrals, and in manuscript illustrations and separate paintings, it seems surprising that the full texts of these Lives have not become more widely available since he wrote.

The author, or to be more precise 'compiler', of *The Golden Legend* was the Dominican friar Jacobus de Voragine. This spelling of his name goes back a long way, and is perhaps a mistake or even a joke, suggesting the word *vorago*, 'whirlpool', but his name appears as 'Varagine' in the earliest records, meaning 'from Varazze', a town on the Italian coast twenty-two miles west of Genoa, whence he, or perhaps his family, came. He was born about 1229, entered the Dominican Order in Genoa in 1244, and became prior in succession in the convents at Como, Bologna and Asti, and it was probably at the last two of these that he wrote *The Golden Legend*, between 1259 and 1266. In the following year he became prior of the Order in Lombardy until 1278 and then again from 1281 to 1285. In 1292 he became archbishop of Genoa, an office which he had previously declined, and in this capacity was actively engaged in peacemaking between the local feuding families representing Guelfs and Ghibellines. He died in 1298 and was beatified by Pope Pius VIII in 1816.

In his *Chronicle of Genoa*, probably written between 1295 and 1297, Jacobus listed his six major works: the *Chronicle* itself, *The Golden Legend*, a *Marialis* and three volumes of sermons. In addition to these, Giuseppe Monleone, who has written far the fullest and best account of his life and work, records eleven minor works.[2] Thus Jacobus was a productive writer throughout his life despite what must have been a busy career involving much administration.

This volume contains a representative selection of Lives from *The Golden Legend*, and indeed the Lives given are in some cases abridged according to principles laid out in the Translator's Note (p. xxxvii). In the following paragraphs, describing the whole of the original work, I shall necessarily sometimes have to refer to passages not included in the Lives selected for this volume.

The Golden Legend as it left the hands of Jacobus comprised a prologue and 177 chapters, consisting of Lives of saints and accounts of the main liturgical feasts, arranged in the calendar order of the Church year. The chapters range from a few lines in length to many pages; in the former case, Jacobus simply gave all the information available to him, and in the latter he made selective use of his sources, combining and abbreviating them as seemed appropriate. The general pattern was for each chapter to consist of an 'etymology', a narrative account, a series of miracles and the citation of appropriate devotional material; but often one or more of these components was omitted. The penultimate chapter, not included in this selection, differs from the remainder and consists of a very brief account of St Pelagius followed by a lengthy ecclesiastical history of the Lombards. Perhaps because of this, a number of early copies of the whole work are named *Historia*

Lombardica, though it may equally be because its compiler lived and worked mostly in Lombardy.

The etymologies with which many Lives begin must appear to us one of the strangest features of *The Golden Legend*. They consist of an explanation, often entirely fanciful, of the meaning of the name of the saint, linking it as far as possible to his particular significance and characteristics; thus 'Nicholas comes from *nicos*, which is "victory", and *laos*, which means "people", that is, *Nicholas* as though "victory of the people"'; 'George comes from *geos*, which is "earth", and *orge*, which is "to till", as if "tilling the earth", that is, "his flesh"'; 'Bartholomew ... comes from *bar*, "son", and *tholos*, "suspending", and *moys*, which is "water", whence "son of the one who suspends waters", that is to say "of God", who raises the minds of the doctors on high, so that they can pour down the waters of doctrine. It is a Syrian name and not Hebrew.' These may well seem no more nor less appropriate to the saints to which they are applied than to most other saints, but at that time it was believed that names signified in a profound way the nature of the person or object they belonged to, so that in the case of a saint it would be particularly important to seek the underlying meaning. In each of these examples I have given only the first quarter of the etymology, which then goes on to offer alternatives which appear to be no more helpful or convincing. They are therefore almost all left out of the Lives translated in this volume.

The Lives Jacobus selected for his legendary were simply those generally celebrated in the liturgical calendar of the time, and Jacobus was up-to-date in that the latest Lives included are those of Dominic (d. 1221, canonized 1234), Francis (d. 1226, canonized 1228), Elizabeth of Hungary (d. 1231, canonized 1235), and the Dominican Peter Martyr (d. 1252, canonized 1253). In the last of these a miracle is attributed to the year 1259.

This raises the question of the date of composition. It is clear from the dates just mentioned that *The Golden Legend* cannot have been completed in its final form before 1259, though it could have been in progress by then. The date of the earliest surviving dated manuscript, Munich clm 16109, is 1265. (The next earliest dated manuscript, of 1273, was at Metz, MS 1147, but it was destroyed during the war in 1944.) Many manuscripts, including several of the earliest to survive, contain no statements confirming their precise dates. The Life of St Elizabeth is absent from a number of these early manuscripts, including the 1265 Munich manuscript referred to (which also lacks several other Lives that are in other manuscripts); it is therefore possible that this Life was added somewhat later to the main corpus. Some have suggested that Jacobus may not himself have been responsible for 'St Elizabeth', partly on these grounds and partly because its nature and style are said to be different from the main bulk of the work; but, as will appear shortly, his Lives are taken from a variety of sources and there are others of which one could say the same. For example, 'St Barnabas' is very unlike the more typical Lives such as 'St Andrew', 'St Nicholas' and 'St George', and there is no reason to suppose that it is not original. In the case of 'St Elizabeth', it is very probable that Jacobus would feel, or have had suggested to him, that such an important recent saint should be included, and it would not be surprising that he should then turn to the most readily available account, the official documentation for her canonization, since she did not appear in his main sources, and this alone would account for difference of style and structure. In fact, all the thirteenth-century Lives are found in many *Golden Legend* manuscripts written within his lifetime; if such significant additions were being made to his work in so many manuscripts, it would be odd if he himself were not responsible and should have allowed somebody else to undertake them. So the main composition probably took place between 1259 and 1265, when a 'complete' version was available for the Munich manuscript, with some additional material being added later.

A span of several years would not be unlikely for compilation of a work of this scale. *The Golden Legend* runs to 857 pages in the only 'modern' edition of the Latin text, edited by T. Graesse and first published in 1846.[3] Jacobus is, however, modest in what he says about both the book and his own labour, describing himself as a 'compiler' rather than claiming any greater creative status. In the listing of his works in his *Chronicle of Genoa* referred to above, writing of himself in the third person, he says simply: 'He compiled legends of the saints in one volume' – neither hinting at the scale of the work nor supplying it with a name. This deficiency was soon made good by others, and his work had acquired the epithet *aurea* by the end of the century.

In the same passage he goes on to acknowledge three major sources he relied on throughout the work, and the existence of others, 'adding many things in these legends from *Ecclesiastical History*, *Tripartite History* and *Scholastic History*, and from chronicles by various authors'. These three named works were by Eusebius, Cassiodorus and Peter Comestor respectively. In his text he generally acknowledged his many citations with care, and, as the Abbé J.-B. M. Roze recorded in the introduction to his French translation, he refers to more than 120 sources.[4] These range from the Acts of the Apostles onwards, and include such major figures as Bede, Ysidore, Orosius, Augustine and Jerome; there are also fleeting citations from more remote sources, even from Mahomet.[5] It is worth remarking that Jacobus appears scarcely if at all to have used one of the most important and large works of the time, the massive *Mirror of History* by the Dominican Vincent de Beauvais. Vincent (d. 1262) wrote this encyclopaedic work between 1247 and 1259, and it contains much material on the saints, very often in almost identical words to the accounts in *The Golden Legend*, so it might have been thought Jacobus had used this convenient source. It seems, however, that the similarity is explained by their use of the same sources; by its nature Vincent's work was highly derivative, and it is not surprising that both he and Jacobus should have turned to the obvious main authorities.

But when Jacobus says he is 'adding many things', one needs to ask what he regarded as the basis to which he was adding. It has, in fact, for some time been recognized that a substantial proportion of *The Golden Legend* was closely derived from works by two Dominicans, Jean de Mailly's *Summary of the Deeds and Miracles of the Saints* (a lengthy work, despite its title) and Bartholomew of Trent's *Afterword on the Deeds of the Saints*. Ernst Geith has demonstrated, by printing parallel passages from these works and *The Golden Legend*, how closely Jacobus followed them, merely abbreviating them somewhat and mildly paraphrasing.[6] Geith reports that sixty-one of the legends are derived entirely from Jean de Mailly, and another thirty-eight partially. Further, in an article published in 1958, L. Boyle showed that the Life of St Clement is closely based on the account in the official Dominican Lectionary issued under the direction of Humbert of Romans, provincial prior of Paris. This dates to 1259, though it was probably first drafted from about 1246, the final version being commissioned in 1254. It is highly probable that other chapters are taken from the same source, though this has not yet been investigated.[7] Whether Jacobus would have had access to earlier stages of this work is not known; but even if he did not see it before 1259, he would have had time to make substantial use of it. Thus Jacobus in most cases used whichever of these three works seemed best as the basis of his own chapter, adding to them and amending them more or less substantially according to the three main sources previously referred to, and sometimes also making use of other works, which were in truth not all 'chronicles', but of varied types.

Medieval authors were often thorough in giving references to their sources, though not always quite accurate, at least in literary cases; the English poet

Layamon, for example, claimed that he used 'the English book that Bede made', and two other books, whereas his long poem *Brut* was in fact an adaptation almost entirely based on the Anglo-Norman poet Wace, whom he did not name. Chaucer made fun of the system by his purported source 'Lollius' in *Troilus and Criseyde*, as did Malory with his frequent assertions 'as the Frensshe booke maketh mencioun'. Jacobus was appropriately scholarly in this respect. Not only does he specify the origin of any quotation within his chapters, but he also often names the ultimate sources for a Life at the beginning of the chapter, or at the end of the etymology. Thus for 'St Andrew', 'The priest and deacons of Achaia or Asia wrote his passion as they saw it all with their own eyes'; for 'St Nicholas', 'The doctors of Argos wrote his legend; but elsewhere one reads that the patriarch Methodius wrote it in Greek and John the Deacon translated it into Latin and added much'; for 'St John', 'Miletus bishop of Laodicaea wrote his Life, which Isidore in *The Rise and Life or Death of the Holy Fathers* abbreviated'; for 'St Matthias', 'His Life, which is read in the churches, Bede is believed to have written'; for 'St Gregory', 'Paul the Lombard, historiographer, wrote his Life, which John the Deacon afterwards very diligently compiled'. These forms of words do not, of course, necessarily mean that Jacobus had the cited work in front of him, and in many cases clearly he did not, but he used the major sources referred to above and repeated the details of these other references from them.

That he did not himself make direct use of all his cited sources is confirmed when he mentions an uncertainty about the source of some information, as happens when he writes near the end of 'St Mary Magdalene': 'Hegesippus – or according to some sources Josephus – is in general agreement with this version of events.' If either of these authors had been to hand, he would have been able to check. And to confirm this, in 'St James the Less' we find: 'Hegesippus relates, as we read in the same *Ecclesiastical History* . . .', and again, in 'St John', this time quoting Clement from the same source.

Sometimes, however, Jacobus turns to a single Life for his material, in which case he says so. Thus he writes concerning his chapter on 'St Paula', 'the blessed Jerome composed [her] Life in these words', and then proceeds to copy Jerome's version exactly.

When quoting from any of these sources, Jacobus was often careful to give specific references, and particularly so for the Bible; the fact that these are sometimes inaccurate in such details as chapter numbers may be the result of subsequent scribal error, to which numbers were particularly liable. For example, if one compares the figures in the various manuscripts of the Dominican Jean de Vignay's French translation and the English 1438 translation with those in the Latin original, it is quite astonishing to discover how many numbers of all sorts are wrong. This is very largely attributable to the Roman numeral system, in which it is easy to miscount the repeated letters 'x' or 'i'; also 'x' and 'v' can look similar in some scripts, and even 'l' and 'i' are sometimes confused.

If Jacobus had really directly used most of the sources cited, he would clearly have had to have access to an excellent library. Certainly one would expect the Dominican houses to have at least good reference collections, but presumably not on the scale that the whole list of sources supplied by Roze would imply. But if, as seems probable, he was working mostly from the rather more limited number of main sources described above, that might well be within the range of an individual house; and presumably someone of his status would be able to borrow or have copies made.

It may be helpful at this point to give a brief account of the Dominicans and of friars in general. The Dominican Order, officially known as *Ordo Praedicatorum*, was formed under St Dominic about 1215–18, and was committed to poverty. As preachers, Dominicans were particularly concerned with the purity and correctness of the faith, as one result of which they early began to engender a considerable amount of intellectual activity. Dominic himself proposed that the earliest centres of their activity should be set up in university towns, including Paris and Oxford. Dominicans were also in the forefront of missionary enterprise and in the suppression of heresy, and were therefore prominent among inquisitors, which, as the *Oxford Dictionary of the Christian Church* observes, was 'not calculated to increase their popularity', and indeed it is no great surprise to find that the inquisitor St Peter Martyr, whose Life is not included in this selection, was assassinated, as was the Franciscan inquisitor Conrad of Marburg, the spiritual mentor of St Elizabeth. The Franciscan Order, or Order of Friars Minor, was founded by St Francis of Assisi in 1209 and was likewise dedicated to poverty, preaching and missionary work. Not surprisingly, there was a certain competitiveness between the two Orders at times, but one notes the inclusion in the chapter on St Dominic of a story particularly calculated to encourage mutual respect. It is perhaps worth observing that friars are not the same as monks, and, for example, do not have abbots, though many who should know better have tended to confuse the two; for instance, Matthew Lewis, whose best-selling Gothic novel *The Monk* (published in 1796) led to his acquiring the nickname 'Monk' Lewis, seems from that novel to have been entirely unaware that there was any difference. In fact, since the friars in due course set up Houses to act as their bases and became in many cases wealthy, monks tended to regard them with hostility as upstart competition, as did many priests, and we find them treated with great disdain by a number of writers, including Chaucer and Langland.

In stressing the closeness of *The Golden Legend* to its sources, and even its use of their very words, it may be felt one is detracting considerably from the achievement of its writer, asserting his status as a 'mere' compiler or 'harmless drudge'. Jacobus has sometimes been praised or blamed for aspects of his style, but on the above assessment he can neither be praised nor blamed for the brisk clarity of the narrative sections, the vigour and occasional drama of some of the dialogue, or the complex and sometimes turgid orotundity of a number of the passages of pious exaltation, except to the extent that it was he who selected them. And it is worth pointing out that the style of the large proportion of the book which deals with the main narratives and miracles is lucid and vivid and much to be admired, whoever is ultimately responsible for it.

The huge success of the book, as evidenced by its widespread dissemination and use, and its 'defeat' in these terms of any possible rivals, is probably largely because it supplied just the right sort and amount of required information. This was the opinion of A. Dondaine, whose knowledge of and contribution to the study of hagiographic writings in this period was considerable. He believed, however, that the work of Jean de Mailly already contained most of what is to be admired in Jacobus's work, and that Mailly was therefore entitled to most of the credit, but that Jacobus, by his adjustments of the contents in adding the liturgical feasts and in reducing the number of saints' Lives (not least by omitting many French ones) produced the 'one volume' which was seen as most convenient by its immediate recipients.[8] Its reputation therefore snowballed, and as a result it was copied widely and effaced the memory of its predecessors. Somewhat ironically, those very Lives that Jacobus had elected to omit often appeared later on among the Lives that were added to different versions; for example, the Parisian Carmelite Jean Golein restored many of these French Lives, taking them from Vincent de Beauvais and adding them to Vignay's translation, whence they passed into the French version in Flanders, and so to Caxton in England.

Emile Mâle adopts what one might consider the most practical and sensible position on this issue when he writes:

Jacob of Voragine was doing nothing original when he wrote his famous *Legenda Aurea* at the end of the thirteenth century. His book was simply a popularisation of the lectionary, and even followed its plan. His compilation is not in the least original; here and there he merely completed the stories of the lectionary by referring to the original texts and adding new legends. *The Golden Legend* became famous in all of Christendom because it made available to everyone the stories that until then had scarcely ever been found outside liturgical books; barons in their chateaux and merchants in the back of their shops could henceforth savour these fine stories at their leisure.[9]

While knowledge about Jacobus's use of sources has been increased since he wrote this by recent research, and with the proviso that the movement of these stories from the monasteries and friaries may have taken a little longer than Mâle implies, there is much truth in this summary. Elsewhere he makes an important chronological point when he remarks that 'the glass painters of the thirteenth century had already made most of their windows before Jacob of Voragine composed his book. But all of *The Golden Legend* was to be found in lectionaries and in the *Speculum historiale* of Vincent of Beauvais.'[10]

In fact, many writers of the later medieval period use the term *Golden Legend* to refer to collections of saints' Lives in general, no doubt on the assumption that they are either Jacobus's work, or based on or closely similar to it; and sometimes recent writers do the same thing, more probably by inadvertence, attributing to Jacobus Lives or passages which are in reality not in *The Golden Legend* itself. Mâle points out that one of the most famous stories about St Nicholas, in which he restored to life three children who had been murdered, cut up and put into a salting tub by an innkeeper, was widely used by artists, and is to be found in many church windows going back to the thirteenth century, and yet for some reason Jacobus did not include it; Mâle suggests that he may have considered it 'somewhat doubtful', but perhaps it was simply not in the source he used.[11] However, it is precisely this story which is most often used for illustrations in manuscripts at the beginning of this Life, including the surviving French illuminated manuscript copies of Vignay's translation; and doubtless the illustrators assumed that this incident was included in the text.

From the modern point of view, and perhaps for his contemporaries also, Jacobus has one particular admirable quality: when he finds an inconsistency, improbability or apparent error in his material, he applies his mind to it with common sense. When he finds himself combining two or more incompatible accounts of some matter, he says so, and either opts for one or reconciles the differences. Thus in 'St Bartholomew':

Opinions are divided over the manner of Bartholomew's martyrdom. St Dorotheus, for example, says he was crucified ... St Theodorus says he was flayed. Again, in many books, one reads that he was merely beheaded. But these discrepancies can be explained if we assume that he was crucified, then before he died, taken down from the cross and flayed, to prolong his suffering, then finally beheaded.

Likewise at the end of 'St Hilary' Jacobus expresses doubts about a miracle involving a Pope Leo 'because no chronicle has any record of a Pope Leo at this period'. At the end of 'St Barnabas' he undercuts a detailed narration of some three or four pages by concluding 'The blessed Dorotheus, however, says: "Barnabas first preached Christ in Rome, then became bishop of Milan."' In 'Sts Gervase and Protase' he points out that the appearance of Celsus is incompatible with what is said in 'St Nazarius', and in the same Life he says that it is not clear whether a blind man mentioned by Augustine who had recovered his sight was the same blind man as had already been referred to two paragraphs before. In 'St Paul' we encounter a lady called Plantilla, but 'According to Dionysius her name was Lemobia, but perhaps she had two names.' Or, we might think, perhaps one of his sources had got it wrong. At the end of 'The Seven Sleepers' Jacobus notes some incorrect mathematics: 'But there are grave doubts about the statement that the saints slept for 372 years, because they rose from the dead in AD 448, and Decius's reign lasted only one year and three months, ending in AD 252. So in fact they slept for only 196 years.'

Traces of healthy scepticism are to be found in other places, as in 'St Matthias' in which a story is told of Judas, which turns out to be very like Oedipus: 'The story thus far is found in the apocryphal history mentioned above. Whether or not the tale is worth repeating must be left to the reader's judgement, though it should probably be rejected as fancy...' Again, in 'St Andrew', following a story of a miracle by Andrew, Jacobus comments: 'That is the traditional account of how Matthew was freed from gaol and regained his eyesight. But I find it hard to credit. For surely it would diminish the stature of St Matthew to suppose that the great evangelist could not obtain for himself the favour Andrew won for him with such ease.' Jacobus also notes with some suggestion of reservation that very much the same story is told of two saints, Andrew and Bartholomew: 'One reads nearly the same story about the blessed Andrew.' He was not, of course, the only writer to regard some stories with doubt, but his attitude appears to differ somewhat from that of Vincent de Beauvais to a story in 'The Assumption of the BVM'; whereas Jacobus expresses a reservation which he attributes to his source, Jerome, Vincent writes: 'This story is considered to be apocryphal, but it seems to be worthy of pious belief.'

With regard to his selection of the material, Jacobus was largely governed by the general plan of his work. But within this he often had to make decisions about what to retain from his main sources, what to add from others, and which source to use. The general pattern of his chapters has been described above. For the shortest lives which run to only a few lines, such as 'St Praxed', 'The Four Crowned Martyrs' and 'St Petronilla', he simply supplied all available information, which was almost none. 'St Praxed' is as inaccurate as it is brief, as can be seen from the implausibility of the link with Timothy at the date given, and consists of only the following two sentences:

The virgin Praxed was the sister of blessed Potentiana, and they were sisters of Sts Donatus and Timothy, who were instructed in the faith by the apostles. And after they had buried the bodies of many Christians during a savage persecution and given their resources to the poor, they finally rested in peace about AD 165 under Mark and Anthony the Second.

It may seem surprising that saints of whom so little was known should be included in the Church calendar, but so it was; and, furthermore, churches were dedicated to these saints, so that a preacher at such a church would on their festival days be required to say at least something. Browning's famous poem *The Bishop orders his tomb at St Praxed's* refers to the fine church dedicated to her in Rome, its size being quite out of proportion to the surviving knowledge of her. For the majority of the saints Jacobus supplies a lively and full narrative, sometimes including lengthy passages of dialogue between persecutors and their victims. These are followed by accounts of miracles, in some cases a large number of them; they are usually fairly short, and range from the impressive to the trivial. For a specimen of the latter we could cite a miracle in 'St Benedict' where the saint drove away a blackbird which was fluttering around his head by making the sign of the cross. There are, of course, miracles which would now be considered likely to have a natural explanation, such as numerous cases in which the apparently dead are brought to life, when one would presume the victim was merely unconscious.

Many others are more truly impressive, and there is no doubt that they were all widely believed; indeed, their presence in these highly regarded legendaries would have fortified their acceptance.

The dissemination of *The Golden Legend* was rapid, and copies of it were to be found right across Europe, no doubt especially wherever the Dominicans had a base. The earliest surviving dated manuscript known to have been in England during the thirteenth century, Cambridge University Library MS Ff.V.31, of 1299, contains only 123 of the chapters, but Cambridge, Peterhouse, MS 132 from Ramsey Abbey is complete and of similar or possibly earlier date, as is MS HM 3027 in the Huntington Library in San Marino, California, which came from Fountains Abbey in Yorkshire and lacks only a few of the original chapters; others must certainly have been in England at that time. The earliest dated manuscript surviving anywhere was, as we have seen, of 1265, and there are several other dated manuscripts from the next twenty years or so. From a grand total of surviving manuscripts recorded by Barbara Fleith for the whole medieval period of over a thousand,[12] more than seventy can be reliably dated to the thirteenth century by codicological means (that is, by studying their handwriting and other physical features, or by identifying them with records in early lists, etc.).

By the end of the Middle Ages *The Golden Legend* had been translated into most European languages, including French, English, Dutch, Low German, High German, Alsatian, Provençal, Catalan, Italian, Czech and Polish, in some cases more than once. Furthermore, copies both in Latin and in the vernaculars are very frequent among the earliest printed books.

From early on, Voragine's compilation was regarded not only as a complete unit but as one which could be used as a basis either for selective collections, as in the Cambridge manuscript referred to above, or for adding to. In the latter case the most common practice was for the inclusion of one or more saints of special interest to the institution or region where the new volume was produced, most obviously by the insertion of local saints. But there were also additions of what seemed to the writers important exclusions from the original, involving such major figures as St Polycarp, or of festivals that were growing in importance, such as the Conception, or of new saints, notably Thomas Aquinas (d. 1277). Graesse in his edition includes an appendix of sixty-one additional chapters from various copies, and Fleith lists hundreds of saints added in different Latin manuscripts.[13] And as will be seen, in England *The Golden Legend* was substantially used by the authors of several specialized collections, while in northern France in the fifteenth century it was used in conjunction with other sources to produce several new composite legendaries, consisting of Lives compiled from earlier versions containing sections closely copied from different sources rather in the manner of Jacobus himself.

This widespread proliferation shows that *The Golden Legend* became easily the dominant collection of saints' Lives, and it had spread well beyond the Dominican users for whom it was in the first instance doubtless compiled. Many of the surviving manuscripts are plain, unadorned and reasonably formal, intended as decent but usable copies for reference and study in such centres as Dominican houses; others are more informally written, perhaps made by their writers for their own use, and often not so convenient or legible; a third category suggests a change of perception, in that from an early stage there appear a few fine illuminated copies appropriate to noble or even royal owners. From the middle of the fourteenth century this became particularly prevalent in France, where such copies of the most common French translation, that of Jean de Vignay, were regarded as a standard component of any major private library. Several copies survive from the royal collections of this time, and from those of the dukes of Berry, Burgundy and Orleans and other noble houses. There are also a number of more modest French manuscripts from this period; and in England during the fifteenth century all surviving copies of the 1438 English translation come into this category. Several of these English copies were products of the London book trade, and some seem to have been in private hands, including one that belonged to John Burton, a London mercer, and was left by him to his daughter for her lifetime and after that to the prioress and convent of Holywell. But one or two others were apparently always intended for monastic use, such as a copy of which the first half is now at Gloucester Cathedral and which was probably either at Gloucester or Glastonbury, both Benedictine houses, before the Dissolution.

The influence of *The Golden Legend* was extensive in England from an early stage. During the latter part of the thirteenth century a long verse legendary in English, now called *The South English Legendary*, was in process of composition. A study by Manfred Görlach has shown that the earliest parts of it were unaffected by *The Golden Legend*, but that as soon as the latter became available the author(s) began to make use of it.[14] *The Golden Legend* was also a major source for many other English works containing saints' Lives, including John Mirk's *Festial*, Osbern Bokenham's *Legendys of Hooly*

Wummen, the *Scottish Legendary*, and a number of separate single Lives and shorter collections. It also seems clear that Chaucer not only knew *The Golden Legend*, but directly used it as his source for the first part of *The Second Nun's Tale*, the story of St Cecilia, which even includes the etymology. It is of course not impossible, as some scholars have suggested, that he used an intermediate version in which this source had already been combined with another which became the latter part of his *Tale*, but it seems rather unlikely. In any case, anyone as well read as Chaucer is likely to have been acquainted with, if not to have read extensively, *The Golden Legend*. Langland too knew the work, and referred to it by the name *Legendas sanctorum* in *Piers Plowman*, B-text, passus XI.160.

By the fifteenth century a need was felt for a straightforward English translation, and one called the *Gilte Legende* was made in 1438 by an anonymous translator, who refers to himself as 'a synfulle wrecche', but about whom nothing else is known. Basically he translated the *Légende dorée*, itself a close French translation of the original which Jean de Vignay had made in Paris about a hundred years before. Vignay's translation contained inaccuracies which generally survive in *Gilte Legende*, although the translator can be shown to have done a certain amount of checking against a Latin copy.[15] Also a few chapters were added, 'St Malchus', which is a direct translation of Jerome's life of that saint, 'St Alban', the first British martyr, both in their correct positions in the text by calendar date, and at the end of the legendary 'Conception of the BVM', and, oddly it may seem, two Old Testament stories, 'Adam and Eve' and 'The Five Wiles of Pharaoh'. The inclusion of 'St Alban' suggests, but no more, that the translator may have been a monk at the abbey of that name, which had a strong tradition of engendering new versions of its patron saint's Life; for example, one of the abbots commissioned a verse Life from John Lydgate, the poet and monk of Bury St Edmunds. Three surviving manuscripts of *Gilte Legende* contain a number of additional Lives, mostly of English saints, on the pattern of the many legendaries in other countries which made this sort of local addition. Several, but not all, of these additions are shared by all three of these manuscripts, which indicates some sort of common policy, but who was responsible or what the exact principle of selection was is not clear.

The final stage in England was the printing of *The Golden Legend* in 1483 by William Caxton, seven years after his introduction of printing to his homeland. This was reprinted once by Caxton in 1487, and subsequently by his successors Wynkyn de Worde, Pynson and Notary, demonstrating a continuing demand. This version was very substantially Caxton's own work, as he tells us in his Prologue:

I have submysed myself to translate into Englysshe the Legende of Seyntes which is callyd Legenda Aurea in Latyn, that is to saye the Golden Legende ... Ageynst me here myght somme persones saye that thys Legende hath be translated tofore, and trouthe it is. But for as moche as I had by me a Legende in Frensshe, another in Latyn, and the thyrd in Englysshe, whiche varyed in many and dyvers places, and also many hystoryes were in the two other bookes whiche were not in the Englysshe book, and therfore I have wryton one oute of the sayd thre bookes, which I have ordryd otherwyse than the sayd Englysshe Legende is whiche was so tofore made.

This account by Caxton of his procedure raises the question why on earth he gave himself the labour of translating it when one of his 'Legendes' was in English, since his own reason quoted above seems insufficient. However that may be, he did in fact for the most part translate it from the French, and it has been shown that he really did make use of all three, not merely for adding Lives from other versions, but making corrections and improvements from one or another as he went along. The French version he used was a copy of the expanded Vignay version which had been compiled in Flanders. This contained numerous additional Lives, many of which were of saints from northern France and Flanders; and although some manuscripts of this version survive, it seems that he used a printed version of about 1472, perhaps from Bruges, within the area where he had spent a good deal of his earlier life. In this version the contents are arranged in a quite different order from that of the original, and it is on the whole this order that Caxton follows, despite the implication in the last sentence of his own statement quoted above that he had devised his order himself.

The actual English manuscript used by Caxton no longer exists, but one very like it does, and it is now in the British Library (MS Add. 35298). It is one of the expanded versions of the *Gilte Legende* already referred to, and its closeness to the missing one is shown by the similarity of the additional English Lives printed by Caxton, both in subject matter and in detail. Lastly, whatever Latin text, whether printed or manuscript, was the third 'Legende' Caxton referred to has not been identified and is probably also lost. If what Caxton says is true about 'the two other bookes' containing many histories not in the English one, this must also have been an expanded version. It perhaps contained a 'St Hugh of Lincoln', and possibly a 'St Rocke', 'whiche lyf is translated oute of Latyn into Englysshe by me, William Caxton'.

Perhaps the most surprising difference between Caxton's *Golden Legende* and its predecessors is that, having followed his French source in placing at the beginning the chapters on the liturgical festivals, Caxton then inserts fourteen chapters from the Old Testament, ranging chronologically from 'Adam' to 'Judith', thus in this respect departing entirely from the general pattern and intention of the previous legendaries. He gives no indication of his motive for doing this, but it has been suggested that, publication of a translation of the Bible not being permissible at that time, he intended to print as much biblical material as he could get away with.

This account of the influence and availability of *The Golden Legend* in Britain is intended both to show the sort of international interdependence there was in the transmission of books and ideas during the later Middle Ages and to exemplify the direct demand there continued to be for access to the work itself, as well as its contribution to the creation of other works throughout a very long period.

Having thus looked at the characteristics of *The Golden Legend*, its more immediate antecedents and sources, and a range of its descendants, it is time to consider the whole nature of the genre and the reasons for its importance. From the very earliest period of the Christian era there was naturally intense interest in the teaching, writing and expounding of Christian doctrine and in those responsible for such work, especially since in a number of cases they courageously paid for their convictions with their lives, thus becoming 'witnesses' both in spreading the doctrine and in setting an example by their actions (the word 'martyr' means literally 'witness'). Some information is given about the lives of the earliest Christian saints after the Crucifixion in the 'Acts of the Apostles' and the rest of the New Testament. After that, a number of accounts of individual saints were written during the ensuing centuries, and other information survived either in general historical writings and documents or more uncertainly in the form of oral traditions. Often a saint's Life would be written by one of those who had known him, and despite the localized interest this might imply, such Lives could spread throughout Christendom. Typical of a Life which became widely known is *The Life of St Martin* by Sulpicius Severus. Even when a Life was written by a former associate of a saint, it was often patterned closely upon other existing Lives, to the extent that sometimes the new Life seemed more dependent on these than on the life of the saint purportedly being written. There were various reasons for this, among which were the desire to relate and even possibly equate the new saint to previously established saints, and the importance of stressing certain appropriate standard motifs rather than the relatively more humdrum (if to us more interesting) details of the subject's own life.

Naturally general histories, especially those with an ecclesiastical bent, would contain a good deal about individual saints. This applies to such works as Bede's *Ecclesiastical History of the English People*, as well as to other types of work, such as Pope Gregory's *Pastoral Care*. Bede was also among the first of those who thought that a collection of such Lives, in this case of martyrs, would be desirable, and he seems to have written the first *Martyrology*. Although this work does not survive as he wrote it, it appears to be closely behind the earliest that do, such as that of Usuardus and the now somewhat incomplete Anglo-Saxon *Martyrology*. The practice of following the order of the Church year was obviously a useful one, and is adopted in these cases, as it was later in the Anglo-Saxon period when Abbot Ælfric used the Lives of saints and the liturgical feasts as the material for his various series of Homilies. He shares with Jacobus a critical approach to his sources, though this is related more to the importance of avoidance of 'error' than to reconciling differences and questioning apparent absurdities; thus: 'Heretics have written falsehoods in their books about the holy man who is called George. Now we will tell you what is the truth about him, so that their heresy may not harm anybody.'[16] Ælfric included a number of English saints, taken from various sources such as Bede, and, in the case of 'St Edmund', from Abbo of Fleury; this interesting example of the Life of an English saint written by a Frenchman and used as the source for an English Life by so distinguished an author is a powerful reminder of the international nature of the dissemination of and interest in saints' Lives. In 'St Edmund', Ælfric refers *en passant* to Sts Sebastian and Laurence, thus relating his subject to foreign and internationally famous saints; he also shows his concern that the English should have confidence in their land by observing: 'The English race is not lacking in the Lord's saints, when there lie in England such saints as this holy king and the blessed Cuthbert, and St Audrey at Ely . . .'[17]

The patriotic character of the English, doubtless no more pronounced than that of any other nation, also led to a number of individual saints' Lives being written in Anglo-Saxon times, such as 'St Mildred' and 'St Guthlac', who was particularly well-favoured with one Life in prose and two in verse. But it was not all patriotism; there are also poems on St Andrew

(Old English 'Andreas'), St Juliana, St Helen (Old English 'Elene'), and a rather breathless run-through of the Twelve, now called *The Fates of the Apostles*.

Sets of Lives following the order of the Church calendar would continue to be useful, but collections might well come to be made for other purposes, and one of the most famous in the Middle English period is the collection called the Catherine Group, consisting of Lives of St Catherine, St Margaret and St Juliana, and apparently written in the first place for the edification of a group of anchoresses (religious women living apart and following a 'rule', but not formally part of any Order) who were living in a remote part of Herefordshire near the Welsh border. But there was developing at this time a trend towards very large works of reference, and it became an age of encyclopaedic volumes, such as the *Mirror of History* of Vincent de Beauvais already referred to, in whose massive work of some 3000 pages it has been estimated that about 900 relate to saints' lives, and some much larger legendaries from which, in their turn, *The Golden Legend* and its immediate sources derived.

While the immediate objective of Jacobus was undoubtedly to supply a reliable and comprehensive reference work for Dominican and other preachers, he would, of course, have had no objection to the use of his work for other pious purposes and activities, such as reading and study, or of its contents for the creation of further compilations or writings which would help to disseminate his material in different ways. To our more secular and sceptical age, while it may seem right that any efforts should be made to fortify the Christian faith and morality and to clarify and illuminate certain fundamental theological points, it is not easy to understand the reason for the popularity of some of these figures, since many of their lives seem incredible or even in a few cases absurd. Friedrich Heer summarizes well a difference in general outlook between Christians then and now when he writes:

Popular religion gave great prominence to the battle between Heaven and Hell, between flesh and spirit, yet the two were intimately linked, two faces of one reality. The battles of a parish priest or a monk with the devil were no different from his battles with an enemy in the next village or monastery. God and the Evil One, the blessed saints and the wicked demons, were just as close and familiar as the animals and implements which made up the routine of daily life.[18]

To later ages this battle may be seen as internal, so the quasi-physical manifestations of it which are so often illustrated in the Lives may seem naïve and unnecessary. We are perhaps better in tune with the more directly allegorical method sometimes practised, as in the early thirteenth-century English sermon *Sawles Warde*, in which the soul is portrayed as a housewife supported by her servants the four cardinal virtues but beset by dangers from equally allegorical external characters. The best-known work in this allegorical mode is the secular *Roman de la Rose*, which Chaucer translated into English.

One might wonder what relevance many of the stories in these saints' Lives had to Christians of the thirteenth century and after. A substantial number of them (more than have been included in the selection in this book) were about the victims of the two great Roman persecutions of early Christians, a situation which one might think was scarcely likely to recur. Nevertheless, it must be remembered that the Albigensian heresy had flourished not long before this time, and that and other heresies had been regarded as a real threat and had had adherents in many parts of Europe. The Albigensian Crusade ended only in 1218, and the continuing Crusades in the Near East had increased awareness of a large and powerful non-Christian world there and in Africa, so that such tales may not have seemed quite so irrelevant as we might assume.

One feature of these stories of martyrs is the description of the horrifying tortures to which many of them were subjected, though one cannot assume that in all cases the particular tortures were applied to the saints to whom they are attributed. In some cases these are turned into a comic account of the failure of the persecutors to force the victims to abandon their faith, and even of their inability to kill them by the ingenious and complicated means attempted, as for example in 'Sts Cosmas and Damian' and 'Sts Dionysius, Rusticus and Eleutherius'. This failure ends when the tyrants abandon their subtleties and order instead straightforward beheadings. Persecuting tyrants are mocked by all sorts of means, including the miraculous destruction of their temples and idols and the contemptuous verbal defiance offered by their victims, even by small children; in 'St Quiricus and His Mother Julitta' the governor is rebuked by the three-year-old Quiricus in words beginning with the elegantly but untranslatably stylish '*Tuam, praeses, miror insipientiam*' (Your stupidity, sir, amazes me!). This grotesque combination of the gruesome and the comical, while calculated to appeal to the basic emotions of sympathy for the martyrs and contempt for their torturers, must have been effective, or the pattern would scarcely have been so often repeated with only minor variations.

Within these tales one is often confronted by an attitude to martyrdom which can at its extreme seem unpleasant, even insane. St Peter's reaction to the martyrdom of his wife seems almost to amount to unholy glee, and, in another way, his treatment of his daughter, described in 'St Petronilla', seems quite intolerable; and the disappointment of Barlaam and others at not becoming martyrs appears positively unbalanced, as does the pleasure of various saints when their conversion of those around them leads to the immediate slaying of these new converts. But such a reaction on our part is totally inappropriate; the willingness, even desire, to make the ultimate sacrifice is something which we can accept in other contexts and must allow to medieval Christians, even though the number of examples with which we are confronted, and sometimes the manner of their expression, can provoke distaste and incomprehension.

There are also numerous accounts of women who are subjected to pressure to marry against their wills, either because they wish to live in chastity and dedicate themselves to God, or because they want to marry a Christian and object to a proposed pagan husband; others are expected simply to submit to the lust of some tyrant. In some of these Lives the saints were forced to work in a brothel or subjected to tortures of a sexual type. The intention of such stories is again to enlist the horrified sympathy of the audience for the victim, and the description of these particularly unpleasant examples, by giving some variety, at least avoids a too obvious repetitiveness, and in some cases furnishes a memorable emblem for the saint, such as St Catherine's wheel. There are many accounts of this kind, such as 'St Juliana', 'St Agnes', 'St Catherine'. It has been surmised that the motif of the refusing bride may have been used to illustrate the oppression felt by women as a result of their lack of power over their own destinies, which was implicit in many of the social and political arrangements of the times, but in the absence of any outright statement of such an intention it is not safe to assume that there was one. The general theme of a virgin subjected to the lust of a powerful man is, of course, a frequent literary motif, and one such from a non-Christian source is the story of Virginia, derived ultimately from Livy, which appears in the *Roman de la Rose*, Boccaccio's *De claris mulieribus*, Chaucer's *Physician's Tale* and Gower's *Confessio Amantis*; another version is to be found in Shakespeare's *Measure for Measure*.

An interest in stories of unusual situations can be exemplified by Lives in which, for sound (though, in the case of St Theodora, somewhat reprehensible) reasons, women spend much of their lives in monasteries disguised as monks, during the course of which they seem particularly liable to attract the undesirable attentions not of other monks but of lecherous young women, with disastrous results. There are also in these stories many women saints of other types, such as the reformed prostitutes St Mary of Egypt and St Thais, who illustrate the possibility of God's forgiveness of sinners, and are in that regard comparable to the reformed St Paul, St Elizabeth, who renounced the trappings of her royal status and ministered to the sick in the most difficult and unpleasant of conditions, and so on. That there are many and varied women saints' Lives in *The Golden Legend* was for the good reason that there were many women saints, and while obviously they might have been appropriate for the female members of congregations to identify with in a general sense, they would have been included by no means only for that purpose. The stories associated with them are no more dramatic or extreme than those of some of the male saints, or indeed those which relate to whole families, such as 'St Eustace'.

In sum, there was much sound theological and moral guidance within these Lives, both the more biographical and historical ones and the more allegorical and fanciful. Such stories as those dealing with the possibility of redemption even for a person who has made a deal with the Devil, as in 'St Basil, Bishop', make a point as serious as any that can be made in a more literal Life. This mixture and variety is an essential characteristic of legendary as a *genre*, and despite the instances of repetitiveness and improbability which may concern the modern reader, these stories must have been a source of keen interest as well as potential moral improvement to their hearers.

Christopher Stace's selection of a substantial proportion of the Lives from *The Golden Legend* for his translation has been made in such a way as to demonstrate this variety and eliminate most of the repetitiveness; and, while concentrating on the narrative passages, he has supplied enough of the other elements of the original to give a fair impression of the totality of Jacobus's book. He has also captured the various styles of the original, and in the lively and lucid narrative sections he reproduces the vitality and colloquial effects which are such an attractive feature of the original *Legenda Aurea*.

The following Bibliography is highly selective, but it shows the considerable and increasing interest there has been in *The Golden Legend* during the last hundred years. Graesse's edition of a century and a half ago has done invaluable service, but its deficiencies have long been recognized. In notes to their translations R. Benz, J. J. A. Zuidweg, M. Plezia and now Christopher Stace have supplied numerous corrections to his text, and these significantly help to establish what the original said; however, copies of the first three of these are not easily accessible, and a new edition of the Latin text based on good early manuscripts is much needed. A major move towards this possibility has been the work of Barbara Fleith, whose assembly of information on the surviving manuscripts and their contents (published in 1991) is a substantial advance on what was previously available. Books and articles continue to be written on general aspects of hagiography and also on separate Lives and collections, and the international nature of this interest is exemplified by the contributors and contents of two volumes of papers from conferences organized by Brenda Dunn-Lardeau on aspects of *The Golden Legend*. But many of the medieval legendaries and related works have yet to be printed at all or studied in detail, so that knowledge of the sources of *The Golden Legend* is still incomplete. Equally there is no available edition of many of the later medieval translations and other derivatives, though work is in progress on some of them. There is much scope for further research, both on its sources and on works derived from it. For the present it is hoped that this volume will help to bring this highly interesting work to a wider audience.

Richard Hamer

Notes

1. Mâle, E., *L'Art religieux du XIIIe siècle en France*, Paris, 1898; trans. Marthiel Mathews, *Religious Art in France: The Thirteenth Century*, Princeton, 1984.

2. Monleone, G., *Iacopo da Varagine e la sua Cronaca di Genova dalle origini al MCCXCVII*, Fonti per la storia d'Italia 84–5, Rome, 1941.

3. Graesse, T., *Jacobi a Voragine Legenda Aurea vulgo Historia Lombardica dicta ad optimorum librorum fidem recensuit*, Dresden, 1846 (2nd edn Leipzig, 1850; 3rd edn Breslau, 1890; 3rd edn re-issued in Osnabrück, 1965).

4. Roze, J.-B. M., *La Légende dorée de Jacques de Voragine nouvellement traduite en français*, Paris, 1902.

5. Boureau, A., *La Légende dorée: Le Système narratif de Jacques de Voragine*, Paris, 1984.

6. Geith, K.-E., 'Jacques de Voragine: Auteur indépendant ou compilateur?' in Dunn-Lardeau 1993, pp. 17–32.

7. Boyle, L., 'Dominican Lectionaries and Leo of Ostia's *Translatio S. Clementis*', *Archivum Fratrum Praedicatorum*, 28 (1958), 362–94.

8. Dondaine, A., 'Le dominicain français Jean de Mailly et la *Légende dorée*', *Archives d'histoire dominicaine*, 1 (1946), 53–102.

9. Mâle, *Religious Art in France*, p. 272.

10. *ibid.* p. 476, n. 32.

11. *ibid.* pp. 286–7.

12. Fleith, B., *Studien zur Überlieferungsgeschichte der lateinischen Legenda Aurea*, Brussels, 1991.

13. *ibid.* pp. 437–49.

14. Görlach, M., *The Textual Tradition of the South English Legendary*, Leeds Texts and Monographs, New Series 6, Leeds 1974.

15. On these two versions, see Knowles, C., 'Jean de Vignay, un traducteur du XIVe siècle', *Romania*, 75 (1954), pp. 353–83; Hamer, R., *Three Lives from the Gilte Legende*, Heidelberg, 1978, pp. 14–23; and Hamer, R., and Russell, V., 'A critical edition of four chapters from the *Légende dorée*', *Mediaeval Studies*, 51, 1989, pp. 130–204.

16. Skeat, W. W., ed., *Ælfric's Lives of Saints*, volume 1, Early English Text Society, Original Series 76 and 82, Oxford 1881 and 1885, p. 306.

17. *ibid.*, volume 2, Early English Text Society, Original Series 94 and 114, Oxford 1890 and 1900, pp. 314–35.

18. Heer, F., *The Medieval World*, trans. from the German by Janet Sondheimer, London, 1962, p. 38.

BIBLIOGRAPHY

Latin Text

Graesse, T., *Jacobi a Voragine Legenda Aurea vulgo Historia Lombardica dicta ad optimorum librorum fidem recensuit*, Dresden, 1846 (2nd edn Leipzig, 1850; 3rd edn Breslau, 1890; 3rd edn re-issued Osnabrück, 1965).

Translations

Benz, R., *Die Legenda Aurea des Jacobus de Voragine aus dem lateinische übersetzt*, Jena, 1917, 9th edn Heidelberg, 1979.

Brunet, M. G., *La Légende dorée de Jacques de Voragine*, 2 vols., Paris, 1843.

Laager, J., *Jacobus de Voragine, Legenda Aurea, Heiligenlegenden*, Zurich, 1982; 3rd edn 1990. (Selections)

Leturmy, M., *Jacques de Voragine, La Légende dorée*, Paris, 1956. (Adaptation)

Lisi, C., *Jacobus de Voragine, Leggenda Aurea*, Florence, 1952.

Macías, J. M., *Santiago de la Vorágine, La Leyenda dorada*, 2 vols., Madrid, 1982.

Nickel, R., *Jacobus de Voragine, Legenda Aurea, Lateinisch/Deutsch*, Stuttgart, 1988. (Selections)

Plezia, M., and Pleziowa, J., *Jakub de Voragine, Zlota Legenda, Wybor*, Warsaw, 1955. (Selections)

Roze, J.-B. M., *La Légende dorée de Jacques de Voragine nouvellement traduite en français*, Paris, 1902; re-issued in 2 volumes without the original Introduction, Paris 1967.

Ryan, W. G., *Jacobus de Voragine, The Golden Legend, Readings in the Saints*, 2 vols., Princeton, 1993.

Ryan, G., and Ripperger, H., *The Golden Legend of Jacobus de Voragine, translated and adapted from the Latin*, New York, 1941.

Wyzewa, T. de, *Le bienheureux Jacques de Voragine, La Légende dorée, traduite du latin d'après les plus anciens manuscrits*, Paris, 1925.

Zuidweg, J. J. A., *De duizend en een nacht der Heiligenlegenden, de Legenda aurea van Jacobus de Voragine*, Amsterdam, 1948. (Selections)

Other Studies and Reference Works

Attwater, D., *Penguin Dictionary of Saints*, Harmondsworth, 1965.

Boureau, A., *La Légende dorée: Le Système narratif de Jacques de Voragine*, Paris, 1984.

Boyle, L., 'Dominican Lectionaries and Leo of Ostia's *Translatio S. Clementis*', *Archivum Fratrum Praedicatorum*, 28 (1958), 362–94.

Cross, F. L., and Livingstone, E. A., *The Oxford Dictionary of the Christian Church*, 2nd edn, Oxford, 1974.

Delehaye, H., *Les Légendes hagiographiques*, Brussels, 1907; trans. D. Attwater, *The Legends of the Saints*, New York, 1962.

Dondaine, A., 'Le dominicain français Jean de Mailly et la *Légende dorée*', *Archives d'histoire dominicaine*, 1 (1946), 53–102.

'Saint Pierre Martyr', *Archivum Fratrum Praedicatorum*, 23 (1953), 66–162.

Dunn-Lardeau, B., and Coq, D., 'Fifteenth- and Sixteenth-century Editions of the *Légende dorée*', *Bibliothèque d'humanisme et renaissance*, 47 (1985), 87–101.

Dunn-Lardeau, B., ed., *Legenda Aurea: Sept siècles de diffusion*, Montreal, 1986.

ed., 'Legenda Aurea – la Légende dorée (XIIIe–XVe siècle)', *Le Moyen Français*, 32, 1993.

Ellis, F. S., ed., *The Golden Legend*, 3 vols., Kelmscott Press, 1892.

ed., *The Golden Legend or Lives of the Saints as Englished by William Caxton*, 7 vols., London, 1900.

Farmer, D. H., *The Oxford Dictionary of Saints*, Oxford, 1978.

Fleith, B., *Studien zur Überlieferungsgeschichte der lateinischen Legenda Aurea*, Brussels, 1991.

Gaiffier, B. de, '*L'Historia apocrypha* dans la *Légende dorée*', *Analecta Bollandiana*, 91 (1973), 265–72.

Geith, K.-E., 'Jacques de Voragine: Auteur indépendant ou compilateur?' in Dunn-Lardeau, 1993, pp. 17–32.

Görlach, M., *The Textual Tradition of the South English Legendary*, Leeds Texts and Monographs, New Series 6, Leeds 1974.

'Middle English Legends, 1220–1530', *Hagiographica*, 1 (1994), 429–85.

Hamer, R., *Three Lives from the Gilte Legende*, Heidelberg, 1978.

Hamer, R., and Russell, V., 'A Critical Edition of Four Chapters from the *Légende dorée*', *Mediaeval Studies*, 51 (1989), 130–204.

Heer, F., *The Medieval World*, trans. from the German by Janet Sondheimer, London, 1962.

Knowles, C., 'Jean de Vignay, un traducteur du XIVe siècle', *Romania*, 75 (1954), 353–83.

Mâle, Emile, *L'Art religieux du XIIIe siècle en France*, Paris, 1898; trans. Marthiel Mathews, *Religious Art in France: The Thirteenth Century*, Princeton, 1984.

Monleone, G., *Iacopo da Varagine e la sua Cronaca di Genova dalle origini al MCCXCVII*, Fonti per la storia d'Italia 84–5, Rome, 1941.

Nagy, M. von, and Nagy, C. de, *Die Legenda Aurea und ihr Verfasser Jacobus de Voragine*, Berne, 1971.

Reames, S. L., *The Legenda Aurea: A Re-examination of its Paradoxical History*, Madison, 1985.

Skeat, W. W., ed., *Ælfric's Lives of Saints*, volume 1, Early English Text Society, Original Series 76 and 82, Oxford 1881 and 1885.

Vauchez, A., 'Jacques de Voragine et les saints du XIIIe siècle dans la *Légende dorée*', in Dunn-Lardeau, 1986, pp. 27–56.

Vidmanová, A., 'Autour de l'auteur de la *Vie de sainte Elisabeth*', in Dunn-Lardeau, 1993, pp. 33–48.

Wolpers, T., *Die englische Heiligenlegende des Mittelalters*, Tübingen, 1964.

TRANSLATOR'S NOTE

Like all recent translators of *The Golden Legend* I have used the only modern
Latin edition, that of T. Graesse (1846). (For details of this and of all the
works referred to in what follows, see the main Bibliography of this volume
on pp. xxxiii–xxxv.). Unfortunately Graesse's text, based on fifteenth- and
sixteenth-century editions, is less than satisfactory, and his apparatus criticus
almost non-existent. When the Latin he gives is plainly corrupt, or makes
no sense, I have had recourse to variant readings listed in the translation of
Richard Benz. He took these variants from one of the two earliest manuscripts
available, Munich clm 13029; or, where that text is corrupt or suspect, from
the oldest German and Italian manuscripts; or, in the last resort, from early
printed editions. I have also made use of the variants listed by J. J. A.
Zuidweg, which come from a fifteenth-century edition of the *Legend*, and,
in the case of the Lives of St George and The Seven Sleepers of Ephesus,
from two manuscripts of the thirteenth and fourteenth centuries. I have
also used the readings of a fifteenth-century manuscript cited by M. Plezia.
Where the sense of a passage was still in doubt, I have looked for help in
other hagiographies and relevant literature, and have on several occasions
been guided by the 1483 translation of William Caxton, whose narrative is
often tantalizingly different from that transmitted in Graesse, and who clearly
had access to sources not available to modern editors.

Of complete modern versions, I am most indebted to those of Abbé
J.-B. Roze and William Granger Ryan. The earlier translation of Ryan and
Ripperger seems to me vitiated by its mannered style, and its cavalier omission
of problematical passages. The Spanish version of Fr Jose Manuel Macias
is useful, because complete, and illustrated by charming Venetian woodcuts,
but ranks more as a paraphrase than a translation. Rainer Nickel's little
selection is fine, as far as it goes, and has a short bibliography and 'afterword',
as well as textual notes; and Jacques Laager's selection, enlivened by sixteen

miniatures in colour, contains notes which, although all too few and brief, are very welcome.

Unfortunately, explanatory notes (help e.g. with the construction of the text; with citations from other authors; with the correction of misinformation) are few and far between in editions of the *Legend*, and the translator needs much more help than he can get from the pages of a single book. I have had the good fortune to be advised by the medievalist Richard Hamer, and have profited at every stage from his criticism and direction. He has brought to our joint enterprise not only enormous learning, but also wit and good humour, without which my task would have been less enjoyable, and the result immeasurably poorer.

In this selection I have concentrated on the lives of the saints, and omitted the treatises on the festivals of the Christian year, interesting as they are. I have also omitted almost all of the (usually fanciful) etymologies which preface some twenty of the seventy-one Lives included, and have generally, for reasons of space, chosen to end the narrative at the saint's death, denying the reader, for example, the florid effusions of Ambrose and lengthy lists of posthumous miracles. There is also a small number of minor omissions in the body of the text (signified, in the usual way, by an ellipsis), usually where a theological comment, or some pious ejaculation, hinders the flow of the narrative. Biblical quotations have, where necessary, been completed within square brackets.

The saints' Lives are here presented in the traditional chronology of their feast-days through the Church year, and so, in the cases of Ambrose, Basil, Margaret, Theodora, Eustace, and Chrysanthus and Daria, my order differs from that given in Graesse. The numbering of the Psalms may cause difficulty: from Psalm 10 to 147, the Hebrew numbering (followed by e.g. the Book of Common Prayer, Authorized Version, Revised Version and the Jerusalem Bible) is one ahead of the Greek and Vulgate numbering. Where Psalms are referred to in this translation, the Greek and Vulgate number is given first, and the Hebrew in brackets after.

The Golden Legend:

SELECTIONS

ST ANDREW, APOSTLE

30 November

St Andrew and certain others of the apostles were called by our Lord on three different occasions. He called them first of all to make his acquaintance, and this happened one day when Andrew was standing with his teacher John and another disciple, and he heard John say: 'Behold, the Lamb of God [who takes away the sin of the world]' [John 1:29]. Immediately he and the other disciple went and saw where Jesus lived, and stayed with him all day. Then Andrew found his brother Simon and took him to Jesus. The next day they returned to their work as fishermen.

Later Jesus called them a second time to be his friends. This was the time when crowds of people were thronging round him on the shore of Lake Genesareth, also called the Sea of Galilee, and Jesus got on to Simon and Andrew's boat. Then, after they made a huge catch of fish, he called James and John, who were in another boat, and they followed him, and then again returned to their work.

After that he called them a third and final time, this time to be his disciples. Jesus was walking beside the same lake, and he called them from their work and said: 'Follow me, and I will make you fishers of men' [Matt. 4:19]. They left everything and followed him, and never returned to their work again. But there was still another occasion on which Jesus called Andrew and others of his disciples to be his apostles, and this is described in Mark, Chapter 3. 'He called to him those he himself wanted, and they came to him and he made his companions twelve in number.'

After the Lord's ascension and the dispersion of the apostles, Andrew preached the word in Scythia, and Matthew in Murgundia[1] or Ethiopia. The inhabitants of the region utterly rejected Matthew's preaching; they tore his eyes out, bound him, and threw him into prison, intending to put him to death a few days later. Meanwhile an angel of the Lord appeared to Andrew and ordered him to go to Matthew in Murgundia. When Andrew replied that he did not know the way, the angel told him to go to the coast and board the first ship he could find. This Andrew did and, with the angel as his guide, and helped by a favouring wind, he reached the city where Matthew was imprisoned. He found the gaol open; when he saw Matthew's plight he wept bitterly, and in answer to his prayer the Lord restored Matthew's sight, which the wicked pagans had taken from him. Matthew then left the area and went to Antioch. Andrew remained in Murgundia, where the local people, furious at Matthew's escape, seized him and dragged him through the streets with his hands tied. As the blood poured from him, he prayed for his persecutors, and by his prayer converted them to Christianity. He then set out for Achaea.

That is the traditional account of how Matthew was freed from gaol and regained his eyesight. But I find it hard to credit. For surely it would diminish the stature of St Matthew to suppose that the great evangelist could not obtain for himself the favour Andrew won for him with such ease.

Against his parents' wishes, a young man of noble birth had become a follower of the apostle, and his parents set fire to the house in which he was living with St Andrew. The flames were already leaping to a great height when the young man took a bottle of water, sprinkled it on them and put out the fire. 'Our son has turned into a sorcerer!' the parents cried, and they stood a ladder against the wall to gain entry into the house. But God robbed them of their sight and they were suddenly so blind they could not even see where the ladder was. Then they heard someone shout: 'You are wasting your time. Can you not see that God is fighting on their side? Give up now, or his anger might fall upon you.' Many people who witnessed this were converted; as for the youth's parents, fifty days later they were both dead and buried within an hour of each other.

A woman who had married a murderer fell pregnant, but was unable to give birth. She said to her sister: 'Go and pray to our mistress Diana for me.' But when her sister prayed, it was the Devil who answered her. 'I can do nothing for you,' he said. 'Why pray to me? Go to Andrew the apostle: he will be able to help your sister.' So she went to him and took the apostle to her sister, who was at death's door. 'You brought this suffering on yourself,' the apostle told her. 'You were wrong to marry, wrong to conceive, and you have called upon demons. But repent, believe in Christ, and the child will come.' The woman believed, was delivered of a stillborn child, and her pains stopped.

Once an old man named Nicholas went to Andrew and said: 'Master, I

4

am seventy years old and all my life I have been a slave to lust. From time to time I have read the Gospel and prayed to God to grant me the gift of continence. But the sin had become an addiction, and almost immediately I was overcome with desire and went back to my evil ways. One day, on fire with lust and forgetting that I had a copy of the Gospel on me, I went to a brothel, and as soon as the whore set eyes on me she said: "Get out, old man, get out! Don't touch me! Don't even come near me! There is something supernatural about you, I can see it. You are an angel of God, I know you are!" I was amazed by what she said until I remembered I had the Gospel with me. So pray for me, holy man of God, and let your prayers win my salvation!'

When he heard this tale, St Andrew began to weep, and he knelt in prayer from terce until nones. When he finally rose to his feet, he refused to eat anything and said: 'I will not eat until I know if the Lord will take pity on this old man.' After he had fasted for five days, a voice came to him, saying: 'Andrew, your prayer is granted. But just as you have mortified your body by fasting, so Nicholas, too, must fast and suffer in order to win his salvation.' This the old man did. For six months he fasted on bread and water, and subsequently, full of good works, he died a peaceful death. And the voice came to Andrew again, saying: 'Through your intercession Nicholas, whom I had lost, is restored to me.'

A Christian youth came to St Andrew and told him in great confidentiality: 'My mother is so enamoured of my looks that she has tried to get me to sin with her. Because I refused to listen, she has gone off to the judge and means to gain revenge by accusing me of the crime. Pray for me, please: save me from a death I do not deserve! I would rather say nothing in my defence and forfeit my life than shame my mother in this way!' The young man was duly summoned to stand trial, and Andrew went with him. The youth's mother was insistent: she accused her son of having tried to violate her, and the son, though asked several times if this were true, answered not a word. Then Andrew said to the mother: 'You cruel, cruel woman. You would let your only son die, and all because of your own lust!' The woman told the judge: 'This is the man my son took up with after he could not have his way with me.' The judge was incensed at this, and ordered the youth to be put in a sack, smeared with pitch and thrown into the river. Andrew he ordered to be held in prison until he could think of a suitably cruel method of execution. But as Andrew prayed, there came a fearful clap of thunder which terrified everyone present, and a mighty earthquake threw them all to the ground. The woman was struck by lightning, frizzled up, and crumbled into pieces. All who witnessed this begged the apostle to pray for them and save them, and when he did so, everything became still again. At once the judge was converted, and his whole household became Christians with him.

When the apostle was in the city of Nicaea, the people told him that along the road outside the city gate seven demons lived, and they were killing everyone who passed by. The apostle ordered these demons to appear before him, and they came in the form of dogs. He told them to be gone, to go somewhere where they could not harm anyone. Instantly they vanished, and all the townsfolk who witnessed this were converted to Christianity.

When Andrew came to the gate of another town, he happened upon a funeral procession in which a young man was being carried to his grave. The apostle asked what had happened to the youth and was told that seven dogs had set upon him in his bedroom and killed him. In tears the apostle exclaimed: 'I know, Lord! These were the demons I banished from Nicaea.' And he said to the father: 'What will you give me if I bring your son back to life?' The father replied: 'Nothing is dearer to me than my son. I will give you him.' Andrew said a prayer and the youth at once got up and became one of his followers.

A band of men, forty in number, were travelling by sea to receive instruction in the faith from Andrew, and the Devil raised a tempest and they were all drowned. But when their bodies were washed ashore, they were taken to the apostle, and he at once brought them to life again. They spread the story of what had happened to them, and this is why in the hymn traditionally addressed to St Andrew, we find the words: *'Quaterdenos iuvenes / submersos maris fluctibus / vitae reddidit usibus'* ['Forty young men / who were drowned at sea / he restored to life']. Master John Beleth remarks, in his account of the feast of St Andrew, that the saint was dark-skinned, with a thick beard, and of slight build.

While Andrew was in Achaea, he filled the area with churches and converted large numbers of people to the Christian faith. Among those to whom he taught the faith and gave new life through holy baptism was the wife of the proconsul Aegeus. When Aegeus heard of this, he went to Patras and tried to force the Christians there to sacrifice to the idols. Andrew went to meet him and said: 'You have aspired to be a judge of men on earth. But what you should do is acknowledge your judge who is in heaven, acknowledge and worship him, and utterly renounce these false gods of yours.' Aegeus replied: 'So you are Andrew. You are the one who preaches the doctrines of the superstitious sect which the Romans have been ordering us to wipe out.' Andrew said: 'The emperors of Rome have not yet learnt that the Son of God came on earth, and he taught that idols are demons and their worship is an offence against God. And God, being offended, turns from those who sin in this way and will not hear their prayers, and because he will not hear them, they become ensnared by the Devil and are deluded by him until finally, stripped of everything, their souls leave their bodies, taking nothing but their sins with them.' Aegeus said: 'It was for talking nonsense like that that your Jesus was nailed to a cross.' Andrew replied: 'He suffered the agony of the cross willingly, and for our salvation, not through any guilt of his own.' 'He was betrayed by one of his own disciples,' Aegeus retorted, 'imprisoned by the Jews and crucified by Roman soldiers. How can you say he "willingly" suffered crucifixion?' In reply Andrew proceeded to demonstrate by five arguments that Christ had suffered of his own free will. Firstly, Christ foresaw his passion, and told his disciples about it beforehand, when he said: 'Behold, we are going up to Jerusalem [and the Son of Man shall be betrayed]' [Matt. 20:18]. Secondly, when Peter tried to dissuade him from this course, he was angry and said: 'Get thee behind me, Satan [thou art an offence to me]' [Matt. 16:23]. Thirdly, he made it plain that he had the power both to suffer death and to rise again, when he said: 'I have power to lay down my life and to take it up again' [John 10:17]. Fourthly, he knew in advance who his betrayer would be, when he gave him the bread dipped in wine, yet he made no effort to avoid him. And lastly, he chose the spot where he knew Judas would come to betray him. Andrew assured the proconsul that he himself had been present on each of these occasions. He also added that the cross was a great mystery. 'The cross is no "mystery",' Aegeus said; 'it is a punishment. However, if you refuse to obey my orders, I shall give you a taste of this mystery yourself!' Andrew said: 'If I feared the agony of the cross, I would not be preaching the glory of the cross. So let me tell you about its mystery, and perhaps you will believe in it, and worship it and win your salvation.'

Andrew then proceeded to explain to Aegeus the mystery of redemption, and to prove, by a further five arguments, how fitting and indeed necessary it had been. Firstly, since the first man brought death to the world through the wood of a tree, it was fitting that the second Adam should banish death by suffering on the wood of a cross. Secondly, since the first sinner had been formed of purest earth, it was fitting that the one who reconciled us with God should be born of a pure virgin. Thirdly, because Adam had stretched out greedy hands to gather forbidden fruit, it was fitting that the second Adam should stretch wide his innocent hands upon the cross. Fourthly, since Adam had tasted the sweetness of forbidden fruit, it was fitting that Christ should atone for this by tasting the bitterness of gall. Fifthly, for Christ to grant us his own immortality, it was fitting that he should take upon himself our own mortal nature. For if God had not become a mortal, man could not have become immortal.

Aegeus said: 'Teach this nonsense to your own kind! Now do as I tell you and offer sacrifice to the almighty gods.' But Andrew said: 'Every day I offer to Almighty God a spotless lamb, and when all the people have eaten it, this lamb remains alive and whole.' When Aegeus asked him how this was possible, Andrew said he would tell him, but only if he became a disciple of Christ. 'I shall torture you,' Aegeus said, 'and force you to tell me'; and angrily he ordered him to be imprisoned. Next morning, Andrew was brought before the tribunal, and the proconsul again asked him to offer sacrifice to the idols. 'If you refuse to obey me,' he said, 'I shall have you hung from a cross, since you value the cross so highly!' When he threatened Andrew with many other cruelties, the saint replied: 'Give me the direst punishment you can think of! The more steadfastly I endure these torments for my King, the more I shall win his favour.' Aegeus then had him flogged by twenty-one men, and after the flogging tied hand and foot to a cross, so that his suffering should be prolonged. As Andrew was being led to the cross, the townsfolk crowded around him, shouting: 'This man is innocent! He is condemned to die without just cause!' But the apostle pleaded with them not to oppose his martyrdom. Then, seeing his cross in the distance, Andrew greeted it, saying: 'Hail, holy cross, sanctified by the body of Christ and adorned with his limbs as with rarest pearls! Before the Lord was lifted up on you, with what dread you inspired mankind! But now you have received heaven's love, with what joy and thanksgiving we welcome you! I come to you in confidence, rejoicing, so that you may take to yourself in triumph a disciple of him who hung upon you. For I have always loved you and longed to embrace you. Dear cross, glorified and beautified by the limbs of our Lord! How long I have yearned for you, how fervently loved you, how constantly sought you, and now at last you await me, the answer to my soul's prayer! Take me from the world of men and restore me to my Master, so that he, who redeemed me through you, may through you receive me again!' So saying, he took off his clothes and handed them to the executioners, and they hung him on the cross as they had been ordered. He survived for two days, and as he hung there he preached to twenty thousand people. Then, as the crowd threatened to kill Aegeus, saying that a holy, gentle and pious man like Andrew should not be tortured so cruelly, Aegeus had to come and take him down from the cross. Seeing him, Andrew said: 'Why have you come, Aegeus? If it is to ask my pardon, you shall have it. But if it is to take me down from here, I tell you I shall not come down alive. For I can already see my King awaiting me!' When Aegeus's men tried to release him, they could not even reach up to him; their arms immediately became limp and useless. But as he hung there, Andrew, seeing that the people wished to free him, said the following prayer, which is quoted by Augustine in his book *On Penitence* [*De vera et falsa poenitentia*, c. 8]: 'Let me not go down alive, Lord! It is time for you to entrust my body to the earth. I have carried it so long now; you entrusted it to me, and I have watched over it and toiled so hard that now I long to be relieved of this duty, and freed from this burdensome garment I wear. I remember how hard I laboured to carry its heavy weight, to master its self-will, to nurse its infirmities, to curb its wantonness! You know, Lord, how often it fought to distract me from the pure joys of contemplation, how often it strove to rouse me from the repose of that delicious peace, how much pain it caused me and how often. Most loving father, I have fought these attacks so long, and when I could, with your aid, I have overcome them. But I beg you, most just and loving judge, leave this body in my charge no longer! I give back what you entrusted to me. Commend it to another, and burden me with it no longer! Let the earth keep it till it rise again, then release it so that you may receive the reward of its labours. Commit it to the earth so that I no longer have to watch over it, and it will not hamper and hinder me as I strive so eagerly to come to you, who are the source of life, of unfailing joy!'

When he had finished praying, a brilliant light came down from heaven and encircled him for a full half-hour, so that no one could even see him. Then, as the light faded, Andrew gave up the ghost. Maximilla, the wife of Aegeus, took the body of the holy apostle and gave it honourable burial. As for Aegeus, before he could even get back to his house he was seized by a demon and died in the street with everyone looking on.

There is also the story that from St Andrew's tomb a flour-like manna and a fragrant oil issued, and that the local inhabitants could tell from this how good the next year's harvest would be. If there was only a trickle, the harvest would be poor; if it was plentiful, then the harvest, too, was plentiful. This may have been true in the past, but it is generally believed now that the saint's body was transported to Constantinople . . .

ST NICHOLAS

6 December

Nicholas, a citizen of Patras, was born of rich and devout parents. His father Epiphanes and his mother Johanna brought him into the world in the first flower of their youth, and thereafter led a life of continence. On the day of his birth Nicholas stood up unaided in the bath while being washed. After that he took his mother's breast only twice a week, once on Wednesdays and Fridays. When he grew up, he avoided the pleasures of other young men and preferred to spend his time visiting churches, and whatever he could learn there of Holy Scripture he made sure to remember.

After his parents died he began to wonder how he might use his great riches, not to win any praise for himself, but rather for the glory of God. Now it happened that one of his neighbours, a nobleman who had fallen on hard times, was about to prostitute his three young daughters, hoping by this shameful business to raise enough money to support his family. When the saint learnt of this he was appalled at the thought of such a crime: he wrapped a sum of gold in a piece of cloth and threw it into the nobleman's house one night through a window, then stole away again. When the nobleman got up next morning, he found the gold and, thanking God, he arranged the marriage of his eldest daughter. Not long afterwards the servant of God did the same thing again. The nobleman, again discovering the gold and loudly singing the praises of his unknown benefactor, decided to sit up and keep watch, in order to discover who it was who had rescued him from his poverty. After a few days Nicholas threw double the amount of gold into his house; but the noise woke the nobleman and he gave chase as Nicholas ran off, shouting after him: 'Stop! Don't sneak away! I want to see you!' And, as he redoubled his efforts to catch him, he saw that it was Nicholas. Immediately he fell to the ground and tried to kiss his feet, but Nicholas stopped him, and made him promise never to reveal his secret until after his death.

Later, when the bishop of Myra died, his fellow bishops met to appoint his successor. Now among them was one particular bishop of great authority, whose opinion was extremely influential. He urged the others to give themselves up to fasting and prayer, and that very night he heard a voice telling him to station himself at the doors of the church at daybreak, and to consecrate as bishop the first man he saw coming to church, whose name would be Nicholas. He recounted this to the other bishops and, urging them to devote themselves to prayer, he went to his post in front of the church doors to keep watch. At daybreak, miraculously directed by God, Nicholas came to the church before anyone else. The bishop stopped him and asked: 'What is your name?' With dove-like simplicity, he bowed his head and replied: 'Nicholas, a servant of your holiness.' So the bishops took him into the church and, though he struggled hard to resist them, installed him on the bishop's throne. But in all he did subsequently Nicholas displayed the same humility and gravity of manner: he passed whole nights in prayer; he mortified his body; he shunned the company of women; he was humble in his attitude towards others; he was an effective preacher, ardent in exhorting men to good, severe in his denunciation of evil.

It is also stated in one chronicle that Nicholas took part in the Council of Nicaea.[1]

One day some sailors, in great peril at sea, tearfully offered up this prayer: 'Nicholas, servant of God, if what we hear of your power is true, grant that we may feel it now!' Immediately a figure appeared, looking just like the saint, and said: 'You have called me, and here I am.' And he promptly set about helping the crew with the sails and cables and the rest of the tackle, and all at once the storm abated. When later the sailors made their way to his church, though they had never seen him in the flesh before, they recognized him instantly. So they thanked God and the saint for their deliverance, but Nicholas told them it was due to God's mercy and their own faith, and not to any merits of his own.

At one time a serious famine was ravaging the whole region, and no one had food to eat. Now the man of God, hearing that some merchant ships loaded with corn had put into harbour, immediately set out there, and asked the sailors to come to the aid of the starving by supplying a minimum of a hundred measures of corn from each vessel. They replied: 'We dare not, father. It was measured out in Alexandria, and we must deliver the full amount to the emperor's granaries.' The saint said: 'Do as I tell you, and I promise you, by the power of God, that your cargo will not be found wanting when the emperor's steward inspects it.' They did as he ordered, and delivered to the emperor's officials exactly the same amount as they had taken on board at Alexandria. They told everyone of this miracle, and praised and glorified God for his servant Nicholas. As for the corn they had given him, Nicholas distributed it to everyone according to their need, and miraculously provided not only enough food for two whole years, but grain for sowing as well.

Now in the past this whole region had worshipped idols, and the people had long held in particular veneration an image of the infamous goddess Diana. Even in the time of St Nicholas some countryfolk still adhered to this abominable superstition and performed pagan rites to Diana beneath a sacred tree. In an attempt to stamp out these rites the saint had the tree cut down. This infuriated the Ancient Enemy, who made up a magic oil[2] which could burn even in water or on stone. Then, taking on the appearance of a nun, he put out in a little boat and drew alongside a band of pilgrims who were travelling by sea to meet Nicholas. 'I would have liked to go with you to see the saint,' he told them, 'but I cannot. So please, would you take this oil to his church as an offering and, in memory of me, anoint the walls of the building with it?' He then vanished. And suddenly they saw another boat, full of honest souls, and among them someone very like St Nicholas, who said to them: 'Ah! What has that woman said to you? What has she brought you?' They told him the whole story and he said: 'That was the shameless goddess Diana! And to prove the truth of what I tell you, throw that oil into the sea!' They did as he said and a great tongue of flame leapt up from the water and, as they watched, the flames burnt away for hours with supernatural vigour. They completed their journey, and when they found the servant of God, they exclaimed: 'You really are he! You are the one who appeared to us out at sea and saved us from the snares of the Devil!'

Around this time a certain tribe had rebelled against the Roman Empire and the emperor sent three princes, Nepotianus, Ursus and Apilio, to quell them. They were compelled by contrary winds to put in at the port of Andriaca, and St Nicholas invited them to dine with him, hoping to get them to restrain their troops from the usual thieving on market days. Meanwhile, during the saint's absence, the Roman consul was bribed to condemn three soldiers to death by beheading. When Nicholas heard the news, he asked his three guests to join him as quickly as they could, and when he reached the place of execution, he found the condemned men already kneeling with their heads covered and the executioner brandishing his sword above them. Ablaze with zeal, Nicholas charged at him, dashed the sword from his hand, freed the three soldiers and took them home unharmed. Then he hurried to the consul's residence and, finding the door locked, he forced it open. Presently the consul came hurrying to greet him, but Nicholas rebuffed him. 'Enemy of God!' he cried. 'Subverter of the law! How dare you look me in the eye when you have committed so heinous a crime!' And he continued to hurl abuse at the man until finally, yielding to the princes' pleas, he acknowledged the consul's repentance and good-naturedly forgave him. Then, after receiving the saint's blessing, the emperor's envoys resumed their journey, subdued the enemy without bloodshed, and were given a splendid welcome by the emperor on their return.

But certain of their countrymen were jealous of the princes' success, and bribed the imperial prefect to accuse them of treason before the emperor. When the emperor heard the prefect's charge, he flew into a rage and had the princes thrown into prison, with orders that they should be executed that night without the formality of a hearing. The princes, learning what had happened from their guard, tore their clothing in despair and began to weep bitterly. Then one of them, Nepotianus, recalling that Nicholas had saved the three innocent soldiers from execution, urged the others to pray for his protection. In answer to their prayers, St Nicholas appeared that night to the emperor Constantine. 'Why have you been so unjust?' he demanded. 'Why have you arrested these three princes and sentenced them to death, when they have done no wrong? Get up now, quickly, and have them released at once, or I will ask God to start a war in which you will be overthrown, and your corpse will be the prey of wild beasts!' The emperor replied: 'Who are you that dare burst into my palace and talk like this?' Nicholas replied: 'I am Nicholas, bishop of Myra.' He also terrified the prefect in the same way, appearing to him in a vision. 'You fool!' he said. 'You senseless man! Why have you consented to the murder of innocent men? Hurry now, make sure to set them free, or your body will be riddled with worms and your house collapse in ruins!' The prefect replied: 'Who are you to threaten me like this?' 'I am Nicholas,' the saint replied, 'bishop of Myra.' Immediately both emperor and prefect awoke and recounted to each other their dreams. They sent at once for the prisoners. 'What is this sorcery of yours,' the emperor demanded, 'that you send such dreams to delude us?' They replied that they were no sorcerers and had not deserved to be sentenced to death. The emperor then asked them: 'Do you know a man called Nicholas?' When they heard his name, the princes stretched their hands to heaven in prayer and asked God, through the merits of St Nicholas, to save them from the peril that threatened them. And when the emperor learnt from them about the life and miracles of Nicholas, he said: 'Go free, then, and thank God for saving you through the intercession of Nicholas. But take the saint some jewels as gifts from me, too, and ask him to threaten me no more, but to pray constantly to the Lord for me and my kingdom.'

A few days later they prostrated themselves at the saint's feet and exclaimed: 'You are a true servant of God, a true worshipper and lover of Christ!' And when they told him all that had happened, Nicholas raised his hands to heaven and thanked God from the bottom of his heart and, after instructing them fully in the faith, he sent them back home.

Now when the Lord decided to take Nicholas to him, the saint prayed that he might send him his angels, and, with his head still bowed in prayer, he saw them approaching him. He recited the Psalm '*In te Domine speravi*' ['In thee, O Lord, have I trusted' (Psalm 30 (31))], and when he reached the words: '*In manus tuas Domine commendo spiritum meum*' ['Into thy hands, O Lord, I commend my spirit' (v. 5)], he breathed his last, and at his passing, the heavenly choirs were heard. This was in the year of our Lord 343.

When he was buried in his marble tomb, a stream of oil flowed from his head and a stream of water from his feet, and holy oil still issues from his body today and heals many sick people. Nicholas's successor was a good man, but he was expelled from his see by the jealousy of his rivals. While he was in exile, the holy oil stopped flowing, but as soon as he was recalled it began to flow again. Long after this the Turks destroyed Myra. Then, one day, forty-seven soldiers from Bari happened to come to the city, and with the aid of four monks they opened up the tomb of St Nicholas, removed his bones, which were swimming in oil, and took them back to the city of Bari. This was in the year 1087 . . .

3

ST AMBROSE

7 December

Ambrose, son of Ambrose the prefect of Rome,[1] was sleeping in his cradle in the atrium of his father's palace one day, when suddenly a swarm of bees came and covered his face and mouth so completely that it seemed as if they were flying in and out of a hive. After a while they flew up into the air so high that they could scarcely be seen by the human eye. This was observed by Ambrose's father, who declared: 'If this child lives, he will be something of importance.' Later, when Ambrose had grown to adolescence and seen his mother and his sister, a consecrated virgin, kissing the hands of priests, he offered his own hand in jest to his sister, assuring her that she should do the same for him. But she pushed him away, thinking that he was a mere child and did not know what he was saying.

He was educated at Rome and pleaded as a barrister in the law courts with such brilliant success that the emperor Valentinian appointed him to govern the provinces of Liguria and Emilia. So he went to Milan, where, since the see was vacant, the people were assembled to elect a new bishop. But there was a fierce dispute between Arians and Catholics over this appointment, and Ambrose hurried to the cathedral to stop them quarrelling. As soon as he arrived, however, a child's voice suddenly rang out, crying: 'Ambrose must be bishop!' Everyone present shouted their agreement and unanimously acclaimed Ambrose as their bishop. When he took in what had happened, Ambrose tried to frighten the people into changing their minds: he left the cathedral, took his place on the tribunal and, contrary to his usual custom, ordered several prisoners to be put to the torture. But the people were not to be put off and kept crying: 'Let your sins be on us!' Deeply disturbed, Ambrose went back home and tried to establish himself as a teacher of philosophy, but the people insisted that he give up this idea. He then made a show of bringing public prostitutes to his house, in the hope that, when they saw this, the people would change their minds about his election. But this, too, was unsuccessful and the people kept shouting: 'Let your sins be on us!' Finally Ambrose decided to flee to Rome in the middle of the night. He did so and, thinking he was going in the direction of Pavia, he in fact found himself next morning at the Porta Romana in Milan. There he was discovered by the people, who subsequently kept him under guard. A report of all this was dispatched to the emperor Valentinian, who was delighted to learn that judges appointed by him should be so sought after as candidates for the priesthood. The prefect Probus, too, was delighted that his own words had proved to be prophetic. For when he gave Ambrose his commission as he set out for Milan, he had said to him: 'Go, then, and act not like a judge but like a bishop.' While a response to the report was still awaited, Ambrose again made off; but again he was found and, because he was still a catechumen, he was baptized, and eight days later enthroned as bishop. Four years after this, when he went to Rome and his sister, the consecrated virgin, kissed his right hand, he said to her with a smile: 'There, you are kissing a bishop's hand, just as I said you would.'

Ambrose had gone off to another city to ordain a bishop whose election the empress Justina and other heretics were opposing, because they wanted one of their own faction to be ordained instead. An Arian girl, one more impudent than the rest, climbed the pulpit and grabbed hold of Ambrose's vestment, intending to pull him over to where the women were standing so that they could give him a beating and drive him ignominiously out of the church. Ambrose told her: 'Though I may be unworthy of the high office of bishop, you should not lay hands on a priest, no matter who he is. You ought to have feared God's judgement and the penalty you may have to pay.' Events proved him right. The next day the girl died, and Ambrose, repaying her insult with kindness, accompanied her body to the grave. The whole affair caused great consternation among the people.

After this Ambrose returned to Milan, where he had to endure the constant intriguing of the empress Justina, who tried to rouse the people against him by bribery and the promise of honours. So there were many who were striving to force him into exile, and one of them, a particularly desperate individual, was so bitterly hostile towards the bishop that he rented a house near the cathedral and there kept a chariot and team of four horses at the ready so that, if Justina gave the word, he could seize Ambrose and carry him off into exile at a moment's notice. But God willed otherwise, for on the very day he was intending to abduct the bishop, he was himself taken from that same house, in the same chariot, and driven into exile. But

Ambrose, again repaying evil with good, made sure to supply the exile with money and the other necessities of life.

It was Ambrose who was responsible for ordering the chants and offices used in the church of Milan.

At that time in Milan there were many who were possessed by demons and who shouted at the top of their voices that it was Ambrose who was tormenting them. Justina and many of the Arians, who lived together, claimed that Ambrose was bribing people to say they were troubled by unclean spirits, whereas they were in fact being tormented by Ambrose. Then, quite suddenly, one of the Arians there was himself seized by a demon, and he sprang into the midst of the throng and cried: 'May all those who do not believe Ambrose be tormented as I am tormented!' The Arians, mortified at this, threw the man into a pond and drowned him. There was another heretic, a shrewd debater and a die-hard Arian, who utterly refused to be converted to orthodoxy. Then, while listening to Ambrose preaching, he saw an angel whispering in his ear the text of the sermon he was delivering to the people. As a result of this vision, he became a defender of the faith he had previously been persecuting.

There was a soothsayer who summoned demons and sent them to do harm to Ambrose, but the demons came back and told him that not only could they not reach the bishop himself, but they were unable even to get near the doors of his house, because a raging fire surrounded the whole building and they were scorched even if they remained at a distance. When later this soothsayer was put to the torture by a judge for his crimes, he cried out that the torments he suffered at the hands of Ambrose were worse.

A man possessed by a demon was released by his demon on entering Milan, but when he left the city it entered him again. When the demon was asked about this, he confessed it was because he was afraid of Ambrose.

Another man, whom Justina had bribed to do her bidding, made his way into Ambrose's bedroom one night to kill him with a sword, but the instant he lifted it to deliver the blow, his hand withered . . .

A man possessed by a demon began to cry out that it was Ambrose who was tormenting him. 'Be silent, Devil,' Ambrose told him. 'It is not Ambrose who torments you, but your own envy, because you see men ascending to the heights from which you fell in such ignominy. Ambrose knows no pride.' And at once the possessed man was quiet.

Once Ambrose was walking through the city, when a man happened to take a fall and lay sprawled on the ground, and a passer-by, seeing this, burst out laughing. Ambrose told him: 'You are standing now, but be careful you don't take a fall yourself!' No sooner had he spoken these words than the man fell to the ground and regretted having laughed at the other man's misfortune.

One day Ambrose went to the residence of Macedonius, the chief minister, to intercede for an accused man, but he found the doors closed and was unable to gain admission. 'One day,' he said, 'you will come to my church and not get in. The doors will be wide open, but even so you will not be able to enter.' Some time afterwards Macedonius, in fear of his enemies, fled to the church for sanctuary, but even though the doors were open, he was unable to find a way in.

Ambrose lived a life of such asceticism that he fasted every day except Saturdays, Sundays and major feast-days. His generosity was such that he gave away everything he possessed to churches and the poor, and kept nothing for himself. He was so full of compassion that, when someone confessed a sin to him, he would weep so bitterly that the sinner, too, was compelled to weep. And he was so humble and hard-working that he wrote out all his books in his own hand, unless prevented from doing so by infirmity. He was of such an affectionate and sweet disposition that when he heard of the death of some holy priest or bishop, he would weep almost inconsolably. When he was asked why he wept so over the passing of these holy men, who had gone to heaven, he replied: 'Do not think I am weeping because they have gone. No, it is because they have gone before me, and because it is so hard to find someone worthy of taking their place.' His courage was so unflinching that, far from condoning the errors of emperor or princes, he quite openly and fearlessly condemned them.

When a man who had committed a terrible crime was brought before him, Ambrose declared: 'This man should be handed over to Satan for the mortification of his flesh, in case he dares to perpetrate such crimes again hereafter.' At that very moment, while the words were still on his lips, the Unclean Spirit began to tear the man apart.

We are told that once, when St Ambrose was on his way to Rome, he stayed in a villa in Tuscany as the guest of an enormously wealthy man and questioned this man with great interest about his life. His host replied: 'My lord, my life has been fortunate, unbelievably so. Look, I have an abundance of riches; I have armies of slaves and servants; I have always had exactly what I wanted. There has been no adversity in my life, no unhappiness at all.' Hearing this, Ambrose was deeply disturbed. He told his travelling companions: 'Get up, and let us flee from here as quickly as we can! The Lord is not in this house. Hurry, my sons, hurry, make no delay, or God's vengeance may overtake us here and implicate us all in the sins of this household!' So they fled, and had not gone far when the earth opened up and swallowed the rich man together with all his possessions, so that no vestige of the place remained. As he watched, Ambrose said: 'See, brothers, how merciful God is when he allots us adversity here on earth, and how hot his anger is against those who enjoy nothing but prosperity.' It is said that a yawning ravine marks the spot, even to this day, as witness to the truth of this story.

Ambrose saw that greed, the root of all evils, was increasing more and more among men, and especially among those who were in positions of high authority, men who would sell anything at a price; and this was true also of some who exercised the sacred ministry. This caused him great anguish, and he earnestly prayed to be released from the misery of this world. When it was vouchsafed to him that his wish was granted, he joyfully revealed to his brothers that he would be with them only until Easter Sunday. A few days before he retired to his sickbed he was dictating an exegesis of the forty-fourth psalm, when his secretary suddenly saw a slender tongue of fire covering Ambrose's head, then gradually slipping into his mouth, as if it were returning home. The saint's face immediately turned white as snow, but soon afterwards regained its normal colour. That day Ambrose stopped his reading and writing and was unable to complete his exegesis of the psalm. A few days later his condition grew worse. The count of Italy, who was in Milan, called the leading citizens together and warned them that, if such an important man were to die, there was a danger that all Italy might be imperilled, and he asked them to go to the man of God and beg him to obtain from the Lord just one more year of life. When Ambrose heard their request, he replied: 'I have not lived among you in such a way that I would be ashamed to live on, nor, since our Lord is good, am I afraid to die.'

Meanwhile four of Ambrose's deacons met together to discuss who might be the best man to succeed him as bishop. They were some distance from the room in which the saintly Ambrose lay dying, and they all nominated Simplicianus, whispering their choice so softly that they could scarcely hear each other; yet from far away on his deathbed Ambrose cried out three times: 'He is old, but he is good!' When they heard this cry, the deacons fled in terror, and after Ambrose's death, they chose none other than Simplicianus.

On his deathbed Ambrose saw Jesus coming towards him with a smile of joy upon his face. Honoratus, bishop of Vercelli, who was awaiting news of Ambrose's death and had fallen asleep, heard a voice crying to him three times: 'Get up! He is soon to depart!' Honoratus got up, made haste to Milan, and was in time to give Ambrose the sacrament of the Lord's body. A moment later Ambrose extended his arms in the shape of a cross and breathed his last, while still uttering a prayer. He flourished around AD 379 · · ·

4

ST LUCY, VIRGIN

13 December

Lucy, a virgin of Syracuse, came of noble family. Hearing the fame of St Agatha spread through all Sicily, she went to visit her tomb with her mother Euthicia, who for four years had suffered from an incurable haemorrhage. Now it happened that they arrived during mass, when the Gospel was being read, and it was the story of the Lord curing the woman suffering from the same complaint as Euthicia. Lucy said to her mother: 'If you believe this story, then you must also believe that Agatha is always in the presence of him for whose name she suffered, and if you touch her tomb with faith, you will instantly be restored to health.' So when everyone else had gone, the mother and daughter remained at prayer beside the tomb. Soon Lucy fell asleep, and in her sleep she saw Agatha surrounded by angels and adorned with precious jewels, and she heard her say: 'Lucy, my sister, virgin consecrated to God, why do you ask of me what you can grant your mother yourself? Why, through your faith she has already been cured!' Lucy awoke and said to her mother: 'Mother, you are cured! I beg you now, in the name of her who has healed you by her intercession, do not speak to me again of a husband! Distribute among the poor whatever you were to give me as dowry.' Her mother replied: 'First close my eyes, then you may do what you want with what is yours.' 'What you give me at your death,' Lucy told her, 'you will give because you cannot take it with you. Give it to me while you still live and you will have your reward.' When they returned home, every day they took something they owned and sold it to ease the plight of the poor, until one day Lucy's betrothed came to hear that her fortune was being given away and asked her nurse what was going on. She answered him warily, telling him that Lucy had found a better estate somewhere and she wanted to buy it in his name, and that was why she had decided to sell some of her possessions. Fool that he was, he took this to refer to some business transaction, and began to assist them in the disposal of their property. But when everything had been sold and given to the poor, he dragged Lucy before the consul Paschasius and accused her of being a Christian, and of violating the laws of the Caesars.

When Paschasius ordered Lucy to sacrifice to his gods, she replied: 'The sacrifice that is pleasing to God is to visit the poor and help them in their need; and since I have nothing else to offer, I will offer him myself.' Paschasius said: 'You can save that nonsense for fools like yourself. It will get you nowhere with me. I abide by the laws of the emperors.' Lucy said: 'You keep the laws of your masters, and I shall keep the law of my God. You fear the emperors, I fear God. You would not offend them, I take care not to offend God. You wish to please them, I wish to please Christ. So do what you think best for yourself, and I will do what I think best for me.' Paschasius replied: 'You have wasted your inheritance on corrupt people; you have been led astray and you talk like a whore!' 'I have put my inheritance where it is quite safe,' Lucy told him. 'And I know nothing of those who are truly corrupt, men who corrupt both body and mind.' Paschasius said: 'Who are these people who corrupt the body and mind?' Lucy replied: 'Minds are corrupted by people like you, who urge souls to abandon their Creator. Bodies are corrupted by all who put bodily pleasures before joys that are eternal.' Paschasius said: 'You will find less to say when I have you flogged!' Lucy retorted: 'The word of God will never be silenced.' 'Then you are God?' Paschasius asked. Lucy replied: 'I am the handmaid of God.' He said: "When you stand before kings and leaders [do not worry about what to say: it will not be you who speak, but the Spirit will speak in you]" [Mark 13:9–11].' 'So,' Paschasius said, 'you have the Holy Spirit in you?' 'Those who live chaste lives,' Lucy replied, 'are the temples of the Holy Spirit.' 'I will have you taken off to a brothel and prostituted,' Paschasius told her. 'You will soon lose this Holy Spirit of yours!' Lucy said: 'The body can only be defiled if the heart consents. If you have me used against my will, the reward for my chastity will be greater, and my martyr's crown will be assured. You can only force me to do this: I will never do it willingly. My body is ready for any torture you can inflict. Why delay? Begin, you son of the Devil! You long to cause me pain, so do your worst!'

Paschasius then summoned procurers. 'Invite the whole city to come and use her,' he told them. 'I want her ravished to death!' But when his men tried to drag her away, the Holy Spirit made her so heavy that they could not move her from the spot. Paschasius called in a thousand men and had them tie her hands and feet together, but still they were quite unable to move her. Then he added the pulling power of a thousand pairs of oxen, but still the holy virgin could not be moved. He sent for sorcerers to use their spells on her, but the result was still the same. 'What evil power is at work?' he cried in disbelief. 'How can it be that a thousand men cannot move a single girl?' 'This is no evil power,' Lucy told him. 'It is the holy power of Christ. If you add another ten thousand, they will not make the slightest difference.' Now Paschasius had heard it said that urine had the power to banish witchcraft, so he had urine thrown all over her. When even this failed to dislodge her, he went berserk: he built a huge fire around her and had pitch and resin and boiling oil poured over her. Lucy cried: 'God has granted me this delay in my martyrdom so that I might free believers from their fear of suffering and silence the mockery of unbelievers!' Then the consul's friends, seeing how distraught he was, plunged a dagger into Lucy's throat. But she had by no means lost the power of speech, because she said: 'I have news for you: peace has been restored to the Church! Today Maximianus has died and Diocletian has been driven from his kingdom. And just as the city of Catania has my sister Agatha as its protectress, so I am to be patroness of the city of Syracuse!'

While Lucy was speaking, ambassadors from Rome suddenly arrived. They arrested Paschasius and took him back with them in chains to Caesar, for Caesar had heard that he had been plundering the whole province. When he arrived in Rome, he appeared before the Senate, and was convicted and executed. As for the virgin Lucy, she never moved from the spot where she was stabbed, and she did not breathe her last until priests came to bring her the body of the Lord and everyone present gave the final Amen. There, at that same spot, she was buried, and a church was built in her honour. She suffered in the time of the emperors Constantine and Maxentius, around AD 310.

5

ST THOMAS, APOSTLE

21 December

Thomas was in Caesarea when the Lord appeared to him, saying: 'Gundo-forus, king of India, has sent his vizier, Abbanes, to look for a man skilled at architecture. Come, and I will send you to him!' Thomas replied: 'Lord, send me anywhere you will except India!' 'You need have no fear,' the Lord told him. 'I will protect you. And when you have converted the Indians, you will come to me with the palm of martyrdom.' Thomas said: 'You are my Lord, and I am your servant. Your will be done.' And while the vizier was walking through the market place, the Lord said to him: 'Young man, what is it you want?' He replied: 'My master has sent me to hire some skilled architects, so that he can have his own palace built in the Roman style.' Then the Lord introduced Thomas to him, assuring him that he was highly skilled in such matters.

They set sail, and in the course of their voyage put in at a city where the king was celebrating his daughter's wedding. He had made a proclamation that everyone should be present at the wedding or incur his displeasure, so Abbanes and Thomas went to the palace. Now a young Hebrew girl with a flute in her hand was greeting each of the guests with words of welcome, and when she saw the apostle, she knew he was a Hebrew, too, because he ate nothing and gazed fixedly towards heaven. When the girl sang before him in Hebrew: 'There is but one God, the God of the Hebrews, who created all things, and laid the foundations of the seas', the apostle pressed her to sing the same words again. But a waiter, seeing he was neither eating nor drinking but simply staring heavenwards, struck the apostle on the cheek. Thomas said: 'Better that you receive a punishment of short duration now, and gain pardon in the life to come. I will not get up from here until dogs bring in the hand that struck me.' The waiter went off to draw water from a well, and a lion killed him and drank his blood. Then dogs tore his body apart, and one of them, a black one, brought his right hand into the middle of the banqueting hall. When the guards saw this, they were horrified, and the young Hebrew girl, recalling the apostle's words, dropped her flute and fell down at his feet . . .

At the king's request Thomas blessed the bride and bridegroom. 'Lord,' he said, 'give these young people the blessing of your right hand and sow in their hearts the seeds of life.' When the apostle left them, the young man found in his hand a palm branch heavy with dates. Both bride and groom ate the fruit, then fell asleep and dreamt the same dream. In it a king arrayed in precious jewels embraced them and said: 'The apostle has blessed you, so that you may both share in eternal life.' They woke and told each other their dream, and the apostle came to them, saying: 'My king has just appeared to me and has brought me here to you through closed doors, so that, with my blessing to help you, you can preserve the purity of your bodies. Chastity is queen of all virtues and the fruit of eternal salvation. Virginity is the sister of the angels, the crown of all good things, the conquest of evil passions, the reward of faith, the triumph over the Devil, the sure pledge of eternal joys. Lust breeds immorality, immorality begets defilement, from defilement comes guilt, and guilt in turn brings disgrace.' While Thomas was speaking these words, two angels appeared, who said to them: 'We have been sent to be your guardian angels. If you follow the apostle's advice carefully, we will present all your petitions to God.' Then Thomas baptized them and instructed them fully in the faith. Some time afterwards the bride, whose name was Pelagia, took the veil, consecrated her life to Christ, and suffered martyrdom; and Dionysius, her husband, was ordained bishop of that city.

Thomas and Abbanes finally arrived in India and reached the court of the king. The apostle drew up the plans for a magnificent palace and received a vast treasure in payment, and, when the king went off to visit another province, he distributed the entire amount to the people. For two whole years, while the king was absent, the apostle preached with great fervour and converted countless numbers to the faith. But when the king came back and learnt what Thomas had done, he threw him and Abbanes into the depths of a dungeon, intending later to take his revenge by flaying them and burning them alive. Meanwhile Gad, the king's brother, died, and a sepulchre of unparalleled magnificence was built for him. But on the fourth day after his death he came to life again: everyone was dumbfounded, and, as people fled in horror, he remarked to his brother: 'The man you intended to flay and burn at the stake is a friend of God, and all the angels wait upon him! As they led me into paradise, they showed me a wonderful palace built of gold and silver and precious stones, and, when I admired its beauty, they told me: "This is the palace Thomas built for your brother." I exclaimed: "If only I could be a doorkeeper in such a place!" And they replied: "Your brother has proved unworthy of it. If you want to live there, we shall ask the Lord to bring you to life again, so that you can buy it from your brother and give him back the money he thinks he has lost."' So saying, Gad ran to the dungeon where Thomas was kept prisoner, asked him to forgive his brother, took off his chains, and begged him to accept the gift of a costly mantle. But the apostle said: 'Do you not know that those who desire power in heaven desire nothing earthly, nothing material?' As Thomas left the dungeon, the king met him and, prostrating himself at his feet, begged his forgiveness. The apostle told him: 'God has been generous in revealing to you his secrets. Believe in Christ and be baptized, so that you may share in the eternal kingdom!' The king's brother said to Thomas: 'I have seen the palace which you built for my brother, and I have been told that I can buy it.' 'That depends upon your brother,' answered the apostle. The king said: 'The palace is mine! The apostle can build you another; or, failing that, then you and I can live in it together.' The apostle told them: 'There are countless palaces in heaven, palaces made ready for the chosen from the beginning of time, and they are bought by faith and acts of charity. Your riches may precede you there, but there is no way that they can follow you.'

A month later the apostle got all the poor people of the region together and, when they were assembled, he separated the sick and the infirm from the rest, and said a prayer over them. The faithful among them answered Amen, whereupon there came a great flash from heaven, which for a full half-hour bathed the apostle and those with him in such a brilliant light that everyone thought they had been struck by lightning. But Thomas got to his feet and said: 'Get up! My Lord has come down as lightning and cured you!' And when they got to their feet, they were all healthy again, and they glorified God and his apostle.

Then Thomas began to teach them and to expound to them the twelve degrees of virtue. The first is believing in a God who is one being and yet three persons in one; and he gave them three easy examples to show them how these three could still be one. Man has only one wisdom, yet it is composed of intelligence and memory and reason. By reason, he said, we discover new facts; by memory we avoid forgetting them; and by intelligence we grasp whatever it is that is shown or explained to us. Similarly there are three parts to a vine: the stock, the leaves and the fruit – three elements, but a single vine. And in one human head there are four senses: sight, taste, hearing and smell – a plurality of senses, but still one head. The second degree of virtue is receiving baptism; the third, abstaining from fornication; the fourth, the avoidance of greed; the fifth, the control of gluttony; the sixth is living a life of penitence; the seventh, persevering in good works; the eighth, the practice of liberal hospitality; the ninth, seeking out and actively doing the will of God; the tenth, seeking out what is not God's will and avoiding it; the eleventh, practising charity towards friends and enemies alike; and the twelfth, being scrupulous in observing all these things. After the apostle had finished preaching, nine thousand men were baptized, not to mention the children and women.

After this Thomas left for Upper India, where he won great renown for his countless miracles. He also kindled the fire of faith in Syntice, a friend of Migdomia, the wife of Carisius, a cousin of the king. This caused Migdomia to ask Syntice: 'Do you think I might see the apostle?' Then, on Syntice's advice, Migdomia changed out of her rich clothing and mingled with the poor women to whom Thomas was preaching. He began to expatiate on the misery of this life and said, among other things: 'This life of ours is a miserable one, subject to so much misfortune, and so transitory, that just when we think we have it in our grasp, it slips away and escapes us!' Thomas then proceeded to exhort them all to open their hearts to the word of God, which he compared to four different things: first to eye ointment, because it brings light to the eyes of our understanding; secondly to medicine, because it purges and cleanses our emotions of all carnal love; thirdly to sticking plaster, because it heals the wounds of our sin; and lastly to food, because it gives a delightful taste of the things above. And just as these things do no good to a sick person unless he takes them in the proper way, so the word of God cannot benefit a languishing soul unless it is heard with devotion. While the apostle was preaching, Migdomia was converted, and from that moment she never went near her husband's bed again. Carisius went to the king about this and had the apostle thrown in prison. There Migdomia visited him and begged him to pardon her for being the cause of his imprisonment. He consoled her kindly and assured her that he endured all his suffering gladly. Carisius then asked the king to send the queen, his wife's sister, to Migdomia, to see if she could get her to relent. But when she did so, the queen was herself converted by the very person she had sought to subvert; and when she saw all the miracles the apostle was performing, she said: 'Any who see all these signs and wonders and do not believe are accursed of God!' Thomas then spoke briefly to everyone present on the importance of three things, namely, loving the Church, honouring priests, and gathering together regularly to hear the word of God.

When the queen returned, the king demanded: 'Why have you been so long?' She answered: 'I thought Migdomia was stupid, but in fact she is very wise. She took me to the apostle of God and had me learn the way of truth. Those who do not believe in God are the stupid ones!' And she told him she would never sleep with him again. The king was speechless with rage and said to Carisius: 'While I was trying to win back your wife for you, I lost my own, and she is giving me even more trouble than yours is giving you!' He then had the apostle brought before him, his hands tied, and ordered him to make the two women return to their husbands. But the apostle proceeded to demonstrate, by three examples, that as long as they both persisted in the error of their ways, their wives should not do so. The examples he used were those of the king, the tower and the spring. 'Since you are a king,' he said, 'you will have no dirty servants working for you; they must all be clean, manservants and maids alike. How much more true this is of God! Do you not think he loves only the chastest, cleanest servants? Why should you blame me if I preach that God likes in his servants what you like in yours? I have built a soaring tower and you tell me, the builder, to pull it down again? I have dug a deep pit and brought a spring flowing up from the depths and you tell me to stop it up?'

At this the king flew into a rage. He had some iron plates heated until they were red hot, and made the apostle stand barefoot on them. But immediately, at God's command, a spring burst from the ground and cooled them. Then, on the advice of his brother-in-law, the king had Thomas thrown into a fiery furnace, but it cooled so quickly that next day the apostle emerged absolutely unharmed. Carisius said to the king: 'Make him sacrifice to the Sun God, and he will incur the wrath of this God of his who keeps saving him from death!' But when they tried to make him sacrifice, Thomas told the king: 'You are greater, surely, than the things you make. So why do you refuse to worship the true God and worship a man-made image instead? You think, as Carisius does, that my God will be angry with me when I have worshipped your god. But it is your god he will be more angry with, and he will destroy him. So I will worship yours, and if, when I do, my God does not destroy him, I will sacrifice to him. But you must believe in my God if he destroys yours.' 'Must?' the king retorted. 'How dare you speak to me as if you were my equal!' But the apostle, speaking in Hebrew, ordered the demon inside the idol to destroy it utterly as soon as he knelt down before it. As he did so, Thomas said: 'I kneel in worship, but what I worship is not this idol; what I worship is not made of metal; what I worship is not a graven image. No, I worship my Lord, Jesus Christ, in whose name I command you – you, the demon hiding inside it – to destroy the idol!' At once it melted away like wax. This made all the priests howl with terror, and the high priest of the temple, raising his sword, ran the apostle through with the cry: 'I will avenge this insult to my god!' As for the king and Carisius, when they saw that the people meant to avenge the apostle and burn the high priest alive, they fled, whereupon Christians carried away the apostle's body and gave it honourable burial . . .

6

ST ANASTASIA

25 December

Anastasia was the daughter of a noble Roman family. Her father Praetextatus was a pagan, while her mother Fausta was a Christian, and she was brought up in the Christian faith by her mother and St Chrysogonus. When she was given in marriage to a young man named Publius, she pretended to be sick and in this way avoided having to share his bed. Then Publius discovered that Anastasia dressed herself up as a poor woman and, with only a single maid, went around visiting Christians in prison and ministering to their needs; so he kept her locked up and even denied her food, hoping that this would kill her and he could then live a life of debauchery with the aid of her great wealth. Anastasia, thinking that she was dying, wrote pitiful letters to Chrysogonus, which he answered with words of consolation. But meanwhile her husband died and she was set free.

Anastasia had three very beautiful maids, who were sisters: one was called Agape, one Chionia and the other Irene. Now they were all Christians, so when a certain prefect began to made advances towards them, they refused absolutely to gratify him, and he had them confined in a tiny room where cooking utensils were kept. There went the prefect, consumed with lust, and determined to have his way with them. But he suddenly lost his wits and, thinking he had the three girls in his arms, began hugging and kissing the pots and pans, the kettles and other vessels. After he had had enough, he left the room – a sorry sight, covered all over in black, his clothes in tatters. When the slaves who had been waiting for him at the door saw him in this state, they thought he had turned into a demon and gave him a sound beating, then ran off and left him. The prefect went off to the emperor to lodge a complaint, but everyone who met him set about him, thinking he had gone mad: some beat him with staves, some spat in his face, some threw handfuls of mud and dust at him. But his eyes were closed, and he could not see how terrible he looked (he thought he was dressed in white like everyone else), so he was at a loss to understand why people who had always shown him such respect were all mocking him in this fashion. But when they told him and he finally realized what a dreadful state he was in, he could only think that the three girls had worked some spell on him, and gave orders that they should be brought before him and stripped, so that at least he might have the satisfaction of seeing them naked. But when they came, their clothes clung to them so tightly that no one could begin to remove them. The prefect was flabbergasted, and fell suddenly into a deep sleep and snored so loudly that he could not be woken, even when he was shaken and slapped. The three virgins finally won the crown of martyrdom. As for Anastasia, the emperor gave her to another prefect, and told him he could marry her if he first made her sacrifice to the gods of Rome. This prefect took her into his bedroom, but the moment he tried to embrace her he was at once struck blind. He consulted the gods to see if he could be cured, but they replied: 'Because you have caused Anastasia such pain, you have been handed over to us, and from this moment you will be tortured for ever with us in hell!' And as he was being taken back home, he died in the arms of his servants.

Then Anastasia was handed over to yet another prefect, who was ordered to keep her under close arrest. But hearing that she was enormously wealthy, he told her in secret: 'Anastasia, if you want to be a Christian, do as your Lord commanded! He said: "He who does not renounce all his possessions [cannot be my disciple]" [Luke 14:33]. So give me all you possess and go wherever you want, and you will be a real Christian.' But she answered him: 'God said we should sell all we have and give it to the poor, surely, not to the rich. Since you are rich I would be acting contrary to God's command if I gave you everything.'

Anastasia was then thrown into an appalling dungeon to be starved to death, but for two months she was fed on bread from heaven by St Theodora, who had already won her crown of martyrdom. Finally Anastasia, along with two hundred other virgins, was sent off to the island of Palmaria,[1] where many Christians had been banished for their faith. After only a few days the prefect there called them all to appear before him and had Anastasia tied to a stake and burnt alive. The others he executed in a variety of ways. Among those put to death was a man who had been robbed of his wealth several times over because of his faith, and he kept repeating: 'At least you cannot take Christ from me!' Apollonia buried St Anastasia's body in her garden and built a church there in her honour. Anastasia suffered martyrdom in the reign of Diocletian, who came to power in around AD 287.

7

ST JOHN, APOSTLE AND EVANGELIST[1]

27 December

John, the apostle and evangelist, the disciple whom Jesus loved, was called in the purity of his youth. After Pentecost, when the apostles went their separate ways, John set out to Asia where he founded many churches. The emperor Domitian, hearing of his reputation, had him brought to Rome and thrown in a vat of boiling oil before the Latin Gate. But John emerged unharmed, just as he had always escaped all fleshly corruption. Seeing that this had failed to stop John preaching, the emperor exiled him to the island of Patmos, where, living a solitary life, he wrote the Apocalypse.

That same year, Domitian was assassinated because of his intolerable cruelty, and all his decrees were revoked by the Senate; and so it came about that John, who had been exiled on Patmos unjustly, returned in great honour to Ephesus, and a vast crowd of the faithful ran to meet him, shouting: 'Blessed is he who comes in the name of the Lord!' Just as he was entering the city, he encountered the funeral procession of a woman named Drusiana, who had loved the apostle deeply and had been longing for his arrival there. Her parents and the widows and orphans of the city cried out: 'Look, St John! This is Drusiana we are carrying out for burial. She always followed your teachings and cared for us all. More than anything she longed for your return, and she used to say: "If only I could see the apostle before I die!" Now you have come back and she was not able to see you.' John told them to put down the bier and uncover the corpse. 'Drusiana,' he said, 'may my Lord Jesus Christ raise you to life again! Up you get, go home, and prepare me a meal!' At once she rose and hurried away to do as the apostle had told her, and clearly she believed she had merely been woken from sleep, not dead and brought to life again from the dead.

The next day, the philosopher Crato called the people together in the main square, intending to show them how they ought to despise the world. He had induced two very wealthy young brothers to sell all their property and to buy some precious jewels with the proceeds. These jewels they were then to smash in pieces in front of all the people. Now it happened that the apostle was crossing the square, and he called the philosopher over and condemned this contempt for the world he was teaching. His argument was threefold: firstly, such behaviour was applauded by the world, but condemned by the judgement of heaven; secondly, it cured no vice, and as such was as useless as a medicine which cured no disease; thirdly, such contempt for riches was virtuous only if someone gave his riches away to the poor. As the Lord said to the young man: 'If you wish to be perfect, go and sell all you have and give it to the poor' [Matt. 19:21]. Crato replied to John: 'If God is truly your master, and he wants these stones to be sold and the money given to the poor, then make them perfect again: mend for God's glory what I have broken for worldly acclaim.' St John gathered up the fragments of the stones in his hands and prayed, and suddenly they were perfect again, as before, and at once the philosopher and the two brothers believed, and they sold the gems and gave the money to the poor.

Two other young men of noble family did the same, sold everything they had, gave the money to the poor and followed the apostle. But one day they saw their former servants dressed in the smartest and costliest clothes, while they themselves had only a single cloak between them, and they began to feel sorry for themselves. St John, who realized from their downcast expressions what they were thinking, had some sticks and stones brought up from the seashore, and turned them into gold and precious stones. At the apostle's command the two youths went off to show them to all the goldsmiths and jewellers they could find, and after a week they returned with the news that the experts had declared that they had never seen gold so pure or stones so precious. John said to them: 'Go and buy back the land you have sold, because you have lost the riches of heaven! Flourish now, and your bloom will only wither! Be rich for a time, and you will beg for all eternity!' The apostle then went on to speak at length against riches, suggesting six arguments which ought to keep us from an inordinate desire for wealth. The first was taken from Scripture: he told the story of the rich glutton, whom God rejected, and the pauper Lazarus, whom God chose. The second was from nature: man comes into the world naked and penniless, and so he must leave it. The third was drawn from creation: the sun and moon and stars, the rain and air, are common to all men, and their benefits are free to everyone, so everything else should be freely shared. The fourth was the curse of wealth: the rich man becomes the slave of his money and of the

Devil: of money because he does not possess his wealth, instead his wealth possesses him; and of the Devil because, according to the Gospel, the man who loves money is the slave of Mammon. The fifth was the anxiety caused by wealth: rich people fret day and night over how to make more money, and worry endlessly about keeping what they already have. The sixth was the ruin brought about by riches. Two evils are involved in its acquisition: it leads to pride in this world and eternal damnation in the next; and with eternal damnation comes the loss of two blessings: God's grace now and eternal glory in the future.

While St John was arguing in this vein against riches, a young man who had been married only thirty days previously was carried out for burial. His mother, his widow and the rest of the mourners threw themselves at the apostle's feet and begged him to bring him back to life in the name of God, as he had done with Drusiana. For some time the apostle wept and prayed, until the dead man rose to life again and John commanded him to tell his two young followers what a dire penalty they had incurred, and what glory they had lost. This he did, and he spoke at length of the glories of paradise and the punishments of hell he had witnessed. 'You poor fools,' he said. 'I have seen your angels weeping and the demons leaping for joy!' He also told them that they had lost the eternal palaces where the choicest banquets were laid, places abounding in every delight, the seats of everlasting bliss. He further told them of the eight pains of hell, which are listed in these two verses:

> *Vermes et tenebrae, flagellum frigus et ignis,*
> *Daemonis aspectus, scelerum confusio, luctus.*

['Worms and darkness, the scourge, ice-cold and burning fire, / the sight of the Devil, remorse, and endless lamentation.']

Then the man who had been brought back to life joined the other two young men, who fell at the apostle's feet and begged him to pray for heaven's pardon. He replied: 'Do penance for thirty days, and during that time pray that the sticks and stones revert to their former state.' They did as he told them, and when the thirty days were up, he said to them: 'Go and take those sticks and stones back where you got them.' As soon as they did so, the sticks and stones became as they had been before, and the two young men were again blessed with all the virtues they had previously possessed.

When St John had preached throughout the whole of Asia, the idol worshippers stirred up a revolt among the people and dragged him to the temple of Diana to try and force him to offer sacrifice. John proposed to them the following alternative: if they could destroy the Church of Christ by calling on Diana, he would himself sacrifice to the idols. But if he destroyed the temple of Diana by calling on Christ, then they should believe in Christ. The majority of the people agreed to this, and when everyone was clear of the temple, the apostle prayed, the temple collapsed in ruins, and the image of Diana was smashed to pieces. But Aristodemus, the high priest of the temple, worked the people up into such a passion that the two sides were getting ready to do battle. The apostle said to him: 'What can I do to persuade you?' Aristodemus replied: 'If you want me to believe in your God, I will give you poison to drink, and if it does you no harm, then I shall know that your Lord is the true God!' The apostle said: 'Then do so.' 'First,' the high priest added, 'I want you to see others die when they drink it, so that you can see how deadly it is.' Aristodemus hurried off to the proconsul and got him to release two condemned criminals. In front of everyone he gave them the poison, and the moment they drank it they dropped dead. The apostle then took the cup and, fortifying himself with the sign of the cross, drank the poison and was none the worse. And everyone there began to praise God.

But Aristodemus said: 'I am still not convinced. But if you bring the two dead men back to life again, then I shall have no more doubts and I shall believe.' The apostle took off his tunic and handed it to him. 'Why have you given me this?' asked Aristodemus. The apostle replied: 'To shake you from your unbelief!' 'You really think,' said the priest, 'that your tunic will make me believe?' The apostle told him: 'Go and lay it over the two dead men, and say: "The apostle of Christ has sent me to raise you to life in the name of Christ."' Aristodemus did so, and at once the two men came to life again. The high priest and the proconsul were converted. The apostle baptized them, together with their families, in the name of Christ, and they subsequently built a church there in honour of St John.

St Clement says, as it is reported in the fourth book of *Ecclesiastical History* [III, 23] that the apostle once converted a handsome, but wilful, young man and entrusted him to the care of a certain bishop. But after a time the youth left the bishop to become the leader of a band of robbers. When the apostle came back and asked the bishop to return what he had left with him in trust, the bishop, thinking he was referring to money, was quite nonplussed. The apostle said to him: 'It is that young man I want, the one I was so anxious that you should look after.' 'Reverend father,' the bishop replied, 'he is dead, at least so far as his soul is concerned. He lives on the mountain with bandits. He is their leader.' When the saint heard this, he tore his clothes and beat himself about the head, and cried: 'A fine guardian of a brother's soul you proved!' In haste he had a horse saddled and rode fearlessly off towards the mountain. When the young man spotted him, he was so ashamed of himself he jumped on his horse and rode off as fast as he could. But the apostle, forgetting his years, spurred his horse to a gallop and gave chase, shouting after the fugitive: 'Why are you running from your father – from an un-armed old man? Don't be afraid, my son! I will answer to Christ for you. I will die for you gladly, I promise, just as Christ died for us all. Come back, my son, come back! It is the Lord who has sent me to you.' The youth, hearing these words, was overwhelmed with remorse, and he turned back and wept bitterly. The apostle fell at his feet and, as if his repentance had already cleansed him, began to kiss his hand. By fasting and prayer he obtained God's pardon for the young penitent, and later even ordained him as bishop.

In the aforementioned *Ecclesiastical History*, and in the gloss on the second canonical epistle of John, we read that when John was at Ephesus and went to the baths to wash, catching sight of the heretic Cerinthus there, he made a hasty retreat, shouting: 'Everyone out, quick, before the whole place comes down on top of us! Cerinthus, enemy of the truth, is bathing here!'

Cassian, in his *Conferences*, tells the story of how St John was once given a live partridge by someone and, as he held it and stroked it gently, a youth, amused at the sight, called out to his friends: 'Look at this old man playing with his little bird! He is just like a child!' John, knowing intuitively what he was thinking, called the youth over and asked: 'What have you got in your hand?' The youth said it was a bow, so John asked him what he used it for. The youth replied: 'To shoot birds and animals.' 'How?' asked the apostle. So the youth bent the bow and strung it, and held it at the ready. But when the apostle said nothing, he unstrung it again. 'My son,' said the apostle, 'why have you unstrung the bow?' 'Because,' came the answer, 'if I kept it strung too long, it would become too slack to fire the arrows.' To this the apostle replied: 'Humans have just the same frailty: a man would find less strength for contemplation if he were always at full stretch and did not occasionally give way to his weakness. Take the eagle: it flies higher than any other bird and stares straight at the sun, yet its nature is such that it has to come down to earth again. So, too, the human spirit which relaxes a while from its contemplation can return refreshed each time and with renewed zeal to ponder the things of heaven.'

According to Jerome, St John lived on in Ephesus until he was extremely old and he could only get to church if he were almost carried there by his disciples. He could hardly speak, but each time they stopped for a rest, he would repeat: 'My dear sons, love one another!' At length his disciples, puzzled by this, asked: 'Master, why do you always say the same thing?' 'Because it is the Lord's commandment,' John replied, 'and if you obey him in that alone, it is enough.'

Heliandus[2] tells us that when John was on the point of writing his Gospel, he told his flock to fast and pray that his words might be worthy of his subject. And there is a story that, when he withdrew to the lonely place where he was going to write his holy Gospel, he prayed that, while at work, he might not be troubled by either wind or rain. And the elements in that region are said to have respected the apostle's wishes, and still do so to this very day.

According to Isidore, when John was ninety-eight years old, that is, in the sixty-seventh year after the Lord's passion, the Lord appeared to him with his disciples and said: 'Come to me, my beloved: it is time for you to feast at my table with your brothers!' John rose and was about to go, when the Lord added: 'You will come to me on Sunday.' When Sunday arrived, all the people gathered in the church that had been built in his name, and John preached to them at cockcrow, exhorting them to be steadfast in the faith, and zealous in carrying out the commandments of God. Then he had them dig a square grave near the altar and throw the earth outside the church. He went down into the grave and, with arms outstretched to God, said: 'Lord Jesus Christ, you have called me to your feast: here I am, and I thank you for deigning to invite me to your table. You know that I have longed for you with all my heart!' When he had said this, he was surrounded by a light so brilliant that he was lost to human sight. Then, when the light faded, the grave was found to be full of manna. This manna is still produced there to this day, and it covers the floor of the grave, looking rather like the fine grains of sand at the bottom of a spring . . .

8

ST THOMAS OF CANTERBURY

29 December

While he was at the court of the king of England, Thomas of Canterbury saw things going on which were contrary to religion, so he left the court and went to serve the archbishop of Canterbury, who made him his arch-deacon. But at the archbishop's insistence he accepted the post of royal chancellor, an office in which he could employ all his mental faculties, which were exceptional, in thwarting the attacks of wicked men upon the Church. And the king held Thomas in such affection that after the death of the archbishop he wanted to raise him to the see of Canterbury in his place, and, though Thomas resisted stubbornly, under an order of obedience he finally agreed to shoulder this burden. Quite suddenly he changed and became another man – an ascetic, who mortified his flesh by fasting and wearing a hair-shirt. In fact, he wore not only a hair-shirt, but also under-breeches of haircloth that reached down to his knees. But he took pains to hide his asceticism, and, always aware of the obligations of his position, he would wear the sort of clothing and outer ornaments to suit whatever company he was in. Every day he would go down on his knees and wash the feet of thirteen poor people, feed them, and send them away with four silver pieces each.

The king tried hard to bend Thomas to his will and asked him to follow his predecessors in sanctioning certain practices limiting the freedom of the Church. But Thomas would not hear of this, and consequently incurred the wrath of the king and his barons. One day, however, Thomas and his fellow bishops were put under intolerable pressure by the king, who even threatened him with execution; and, misled by the partial advice of certain influential men, he gave his verbal assent to the king's wishes. But then, seeing how the souls of the faithful would be imperilled by what he had done, he immediately subjected himself to even crueller mortifications, and would not allow himself to celebrate mass again until the pope considered that he deserved to be restored to grace. When the king subsequently demanded that he confirm this verbal assent in writing, Thomas boldly refused him, and, holding aloft his cross of office, he left the court, while the ungodly barons shouted: 'Arrest the thief! Hang the traitor!' Then two influential barons who were Thomas's trusted friends came to him in tears and assured him, on oath, that many of their colleagues were plotting to kill him. So the man of God, fearing more for the Church than for himself, took flight. He went to France, where in Sens he was welcomed by Pope Alexander, and was recommended by him to the monastery at Pontigny. The king responded by sending a request to Rome that envoys come and settle the matter, but he was flatly refused, and this enraged him still further against the archbishop. So he confiscated all Thomas's property and that of all his kin, and condemned the entire family to exile, regardless of station, sex, rank, age or condition. Meanwhile Thomas prayed daily for his king and country; and it was revealed to him that he would return to his church and there win the palm of martyrdom and join Christ in glory. Finally, in the seventh year of his exile, he was allowed to return to England, and was received there by everyone with the greatest respect.

Some days before Thomas's martyrdom a young man had died, but then miraculously come back to life. This young man said that he had been taken to the highest company of saints in heaven, and there, among the apostles, he had seen an empty throne. When he had asked whose throne it was, an angel had told him that it was reserved for an illustrious English priest.

A priest who used to celebrate mass every single day in honour of the Blessed Virgin was reported for this to the archbishop. Thomas summoned him and suspended him from office on the grounds that he was a simpleton and insufficiently educated. Now it happened that the saint's hair-shirt needed repairing, and he had hidden it beneath his bed ready to bring out when he had time to mend it. Then Blessed Mary appeared to the priest and said: 'Go to the archbishop and tell him that the one for whose love you said all those masses has mended his shirt. It is under the bed, and she has left with it the red silk thread she used to mend it. And say she is sending you to him to tell him that he must lift the ban he has imposed on you.' When Thomas heard this and found, to his amazement, that his shirt had been mended exactly as predicted, he lifted the priest's suspension, and told him to keep the whole affair a secret.

Thomas continued to defend the rights of the Church as before, and the king could neither cajole him nor threaten him into yielding. He refused to move one inch. So finally the king sent armed soldiers to the cathedral, and they loudly demanded to know where the archbishop was. Thomas went to confront them. 'Here I am,' he said. 'What is it you want?' They answered: 'We have come to kill you. You have to die.' He replied: 'I am ready to die for God, in the defence of justice and the freedom of the Church. So if it is me you want, I forbid you, in the name of Almighty God and under threat of anathema, to do any harm at all to anyone else here. I commend myself and the cause of the Church, to God, to the Blessed Virgin Mary, to St Denis and all the saints.' When he had spoken these words, the assassins rushed at him with their swords, aiming blows at his venerable head. They split open his skull and dashed his brains on to the pavement of the church. Such was the martyrdom of St Thomas, in the year of our Lord 1174 . . .[1]

9

ST HILARY

13 January

Hilary, who was to become bishop of Poitiers, was born in Aquitania, and rose like the brilliant morning star to outshine all others. Earlier on he had had a wife and daughter, but, layman though he was, he led the life of a monk. Eventually, because of his holiness of life and the extent of his learning, Hilary was elected to the see of Poitiers, and he defended not only his own city but the whole of France against the heretics. As a result, on the advice of two heretical bishops, Hilary, together with Eusebius, bishop of Vercelli, was sent into exile by the emperor, who himself supported the heretics. Later, when the Arian heresy was spreading everywhere, the emperor gave his permission for all the bishops to come together and define the truths of the Christian religion. Hilary attended this council, but the two aforementioned bishops, finding themselves no match for his eloquence, persuaded the emperor to order him to return to Poitiers. When he reached the island of Gallinaria, which was infested with snakes, the snakes all fled at the very sight of him. He fixed a stake in the middle of the island as a marker and forbade all snakes to pass it, and it worked – it was as if the other half of the island were sea and not dry land at all!

Back at Poitiers, by the power of prayer Hilary restored to life a child who had died without baptism. For some time he lay by the child in the dust on the ground until finally both of them got up together, the old man from his prayers and the child from death.

Apia, his daughter, wanted to be married, but Hilary spoke to her of the virtues of chastity and persuaded her rather to dedicate herself to God. Seeing that she was now resolved, but afraid that she might subsequently weaken, he prayed earnestly that the Lord might take her to him and allow her to live no longer. And so it happened, for a few days later Apia died, and Hilary buried her with his own hands. Then Apia's mother, seeing what the bishop had done for her daughter, asked him to obtain the same favour for her. Hilary did so, and, by his prayers, sent his wife on before him to the kingdom of heaven.

At that time Pope Leo, who had been led astray by the Arian heresy, called a council of all the bishops, which Hilary attended, though he had not been invited. Hearing of his arrival, the pope gave instructions that no one should rise when he entered or offer him a seat. Hilary duly entered and the pope said to him: 'So you are Hilary, the Gallic cock!' [Latin *gallus* = either 'a cock' or 'a Gaul'] 'I am no Gaul,' replied Hilary, 'though I am from Gaul. That is to say, I was not born in Gaul: I am a bishop there.' The pope replied: 'Well, so you are Hilary of Gaul; and I am Leo, judge and apostolic bishop of the See of Rome.' 'Well,' retorted Hilary, 'so you are Leo; but you are not the Lion [Latin *leo* = "lion"] of Judah, and if you sit in judgement, it is not on the judgement seat of God.' At this the pope rose in indignation. 'Wait here a moment,' he told Hilary. 'When I come back, I will punish you for your insolence.' 'And if you do not come back,' Hilary asked, 'who will answer me in your place?' 'I will be back in a moment,' the pope replied, 'and then I shall soon humble that arrogance of yours!'

The pope went off to answer a call of nature, but he suffered an attack of dysentery: all his intestines spilled out and he died a most wretched death. Meanwhile Hilary, noticing that no one rose to greet him, calmly sat upon the ground, quoting the Psalm *'Domini est terra'* ['The earth is the Lord's' (Psalm 23 (24))]. Instantly, by God's will, the ground where he sat began gradually to lift, until the saint was on a level with the other bishops. Then news came of the pope's miserable death, and Hilary rose and confirmed all the bishops in the Catholic faith before sending them back home to their dioceses. But there is some doubt about the authenticity of this miraculous death of Pope Leo: firstly, because the *Ecclesiastical History* and the *Tripartite History* make no mention of it; secondly, because no chronicle has any record of a Pope Leo at this period; and thirdly, because, as Jerome states: 'The Holy Roman Church has always been without stain, and will remain, for all time to come, untainted by any heresy.' It is, however, a possibility that there was a pope of this name at the time, not one canonically elected, but one who had used force to secure the papacy. Or perhaps Pope Liberius, who sided with the heretical emperor Constantine, was also known as Leo.

Finally, after performing many miracles, the blessed Hilary, now feeble with old age, learnt that his end was near. He summoned Leontius, a priest whom he loved dearly, and instructed him, as night came on, to go outside and tell him what he heard. Leontius did so, and came back to tell him that all he had heard was the noise of the crowds in the city. He kept watch at the bishop's bedside, awaiting his death; but then, around midnight, Hilary told him to go out again and bring him back news of anything he heard. This time Leontius said he heard nothing; then suddenly a bright light enveloped Hilary, a light so dazzling that the priest could not look; and as the light gradually faded, so the saint passed to his Lord. Hilary flourished about AD 340 in the reign of Constantine . . .

10

ST ANTHONY, ABBOT[1]

17 January

When Anthony was twenty years of age, he heard the following text read in church: 'If you wish to be perfect, go and sell everything you have and give it to the poor' [Matt. 19:21]. He sold all his possessions, gave the money to the poor, and adopted the life of a hermit. He faced countless temptations at the hands of demons. Once, when by the strength of his faith he had overcome the demon of incontinence, the Devil appeared to him in the form of a black boy, bowed low before him and admitted defeat. Anthony, in answer to his prayers, had been granted the power to see this demon of incontinence, who was waylaying young people, and when he saw him in the form just described, he said: 'Now I have seen you in your vilest form, I shall never fear you again.'

Another time, when he was living in the seclusion of a tomb, a troop of demons assaulted him so violently that his servant, thinking he was dead, carried him off on his shoulders. The local people, too, all gathered round him and mourned him as dead; but then, in the middle of their lamentations, Anthony suddenly revived, and had his servant carry him back to his tomb. There he lay, prostrated by the pain of his wounds, but by sheer strength of will he challenged the demons to another battle. In response they appeared to him in the forms of savage wild beasts, and tore him again with their teeth, horns and claws. Then, suddenly, a miraculous light shone out in the tomb, which put all the demons to flight, and Anthony was immediately well again. Realizing that Christ was present, he said: 'Where were you, Jesus? Dear Lord, where were you? Why were you not here earlier to help me and heal my wounds?' The Lord replied: 'I was here, Anthony. But I was waiting to see you do battle. Now that you have fought so valiantly, I shall spread your fame throughout the world.'

Anthony's religious fervour was so great, in fact, that when the emperor Maximian was persecuting the Christians, he used to follow the martyrs about, hoping himself to merit the reward of martyrdom with them, and was deeply saddened each time his wish was not granted.

When he went into another part of the desert, he found a silver dish and said to himself: 'How can this have got here? There is no trace of any people in the neighbourhood. It is too big for a traveller to have dropped without noticing. No, this must be your work, Satan! But you will never change my will!' As soon as he spoke these words, the dish vanished in a cloud of smoke. Later he found a huge sum of real gold, but he fled away from it as if it had been a raging fire, taking refuge in the mountains, where he stayed for twenty years, winning great renown for his countless miracles.

Once, in a trance of ecstasy, Anthony saw the entire world covered with snares, all interconnected with each other, and cried: 'Ah, who shall escape them?' And he heard a voice reply: 'Humility!' Another time he was lifted on high by the angels, and demons appeared and tried to stop him passing them, accusing him of all the sins he had committed since his birth. But the angels said: 'Those sins you are not allowed to name, because they have already been wiped out by Christ's mercy. But if you know of any he has committed since he became a monk, name them!' And when the demons could prove nothing against him, Anthony was carried aloft and set down on the ground again without interference.

Anthony tells the following story about himself: 'I once saw an exceedingly tall demon, who brazenly claimed to be the "Power and Wisdom of God", and he said: "What do you want me to give you, Anthony?" But I spat in his face and threw myself upon him, calling on the name of Christ, and immediately he vanished.' Another time the Devil appeared to him as a giant, and he was so enormous that his head seemed to touch the sky. When Anthony asked him who he was, he said he was Satan, then added: 'Why do monks fight against me so, and Christians curse me as they do?' Anthony replied: 'They are right to do so: you never cease to torment them with your wicked scheming.' 'It is not I who torment them,' Satan retorted. 'It is they who trouble each other. For I am reduced to nothing, now that Christ reigns everywhere.'

An archer once saw the blessed Anthony making merry with his brethren and took exception to this. Anthony told him: 'Put an arrow in your bow and shoot!' The archer did as he was asked, but when the saint told him to do it a second and a third time, he said: 'If I keep on at this rate, my bow is going to break!' Anthony replied: 'It is the same with God's work: if we overstretch ourselves, we are soon broken. So it is best to relax from our austerities from time to time.' And the archer went on his way, having learnt a valuable lesson.

Someone asked Anthony: 'What rules must I observe to please God?' Anthony replied: 'Wherever you go, keep God always before your eyes; in all you do, be guided by the testimony of the Holy Scriptures; and when you settle in a place, do not be in any hurry to move elsewhere. Observe these three rules and you will be saved.' And when an abbot once asked him for his advice, Anthony told him: 'Do not trust in your own righteousness; master your appetite and your tongue; and do not cry over spilt milk.' Another saying of Anthony's was: 'Just as fish die if they stay on dry land, so monks who spend too much time out of their cells and keep company with worldly people are weakened in their resolution to lead a life of solitude.' And another: 'The man who leads a life of solitude and silence avoids three sources of conflict: from hearing, from speaking and from sight. He will have only one thing to fight against, and that is his own heart.'

Some monks came with an old man on a visit to Abbot Anthony, and he told them: 'You have found a good companion in this old man.' Then he asked the old man: 'Father, have you found these monks good men?' 'Yes,' he replied, 'they are good men, but the house where they live has no door, so anyone who wants can walk right into the stable and untie their donkey.' By this he meant that whatever was in their hearts was immediately on their lips.

Abbot Anthony also said: 'Bodily disturbances are of three sorts: one caused by nature, one by an excess of food and one by the Devil.'

A monk had renounced the world, but not entirely, because he still kept some of his possessions with him. Anthony told him to go and buy some meat, but when he had done so and was on his way back with the meat, he was attacked and mauled by dogs. Anthony said to him: 'This is what happens to those who renounce the world, but want to hold on to their money: they are attacked by demons and torn to pieces.'

At one stage Anthony wearied of his life in the desert and prayed: 'Lord, I want to be saved, but my thoughts will not allow me.' He got up and went out and saw a man sitting at work who then rose from his work and began to pray. It was an angel of the Lord, and he told Anthony: 'Do the same, and you will be saved.'

One day the brethren had asked Anthony what would happen to their souls, and in answer the next night a voice called to him and said: 'Get up, go out and look!' He did so, and lo and behold, he saw a huge terrifying creature whose head reached the clouds; there were beings with wings trying to fly heavenwards, and the creature stretched out his hands and was stopping them. Others flew upwards without difficulty, and these he was unable to hold back. Anthony heard shouts of great joy mingled with cries of grief and realized that he was witnessing the heavenward passage of souls, and that this was the Devil trying to stop them. Some souls, the guilty ones, he did hold back, but he was powerless to halt the ascent of the holy ones, and this made him groan in anguish.

One day, when Anthony was working with his brethren, he looked up to heaven and saw a terrible vision. He fell on his knees and begged God to avert this evil that was coming, and when the monks asked him about it, weeping and sobbing he told them that the world was threatened by a wickedness unparalleled in history. 'I saw,' he told them, 'the altar of God surrounded by a great herd of horses, and they were trampling everything beneath their hooves. The Catholic faith is destined to be torn apart by a terrible storm, and men will trample like beasts on the holy things of Christ!' Then the voice of the Lord was heard, saying: 'They will abominate my altar.' Two years later the Arian heresy broke out: the Arians split the Church, defiled baptistries and churches, and slaughtered Christians on the altars like so many sheep.

A certain eminent Egyptian called Ballachius, who was an Arian, was persecuting the Church of God, stripping nuns and monks naked and whipping them in public. Anthony wrote to him the following warning: 'I see the wrath of God coming upon you. Stop persecuting Christians now, or his anger will fall on you, for he is threatening you with imminent destruction.' The wretch read this letter, laughed at it, and with a curse flung it to the ground. He had the monks who had delivered it beaten soundly and sent back to Anthony the following reply: 'You rule your monks with a rod of iron. Soon you will feel the severity of my discipline!' Five days later he was mounting his horse, the gentlest of beasts, when it bit him, threw him to the ground, and gnawed and mangled his legs so badly that within three days he was dead.

Some of the brethren asked Anthony one day to tell them the secret of salvation. He said: 'You know what the Lord said: "If anyone strikes you on one cheek, then offer him the other" [Matt. 5:39].' But they said: 'That is too much to ask.' He replied: 'Then at least bear the one blow patiently.' 'We cannot do that either,' they objected. 'Then at least,' Anthony said, 'let yourself be struck, rather than be the aggressor.' But they replied: 'Even that is too much.' Then Anthony said to his disciple: 'Go and make up a tonic for these brothers: they are too frail by half!' Then he told the brothers: 'All you need do is pray.' All this can be read in the *Lives of the Fathers*.

Finally, in the hundred and fifth year of his life, the blessed Anthony kissed his monks farewell and died in peace. This was in the reign of Constantine, which began around AD 340.

11

ST SEBASTIAN

20 January

Sebastian was a devout Christian, a native of Narbonne and a citizen of Milan. He was esteemed so highly by the emperors Diocletian and Maximian that they gave him the command of the First Cohort, and had him wait upon them constantly. Sebastian served as an officer for one reason only: it meant he could have access to the Christians he saw being tortured and strengthen their resolution if they were beginning to weaken. Now Marcellianus and Marcus, twin brothers of the noblest family, were about to be beheaded for the faith, and their parents visited them to try to persuade them to relent. First their mother came, with her hair dishevelled and her clothes torn, and, uncovering her breasts, she cried: 'Ah, my dear, dear sons, I am beset by misery unheard of, by grief unbearable! Ah me, I am losing my sons, and they are running gladly to their death! If the enemy were taking them from me, I would pursue their captors through the turmoil of war! If they were condemned to imprisonment, I would break in to them at the cost of my own life! Here is a novel way of dying, when the victim begs the executioner to strike, when he prays for his life to end, and beckons death to come! Here is a new kind of grief, a new misery, when one's young sons forfeit their youth willingly, and parents are forced to live on in a pitiable old age!'

As she spoke, the old father arrived, helped along by his slaves. His head was covered in dust and he cried aloud to heaven: 'My sons go willingly to their death and I have come to bid them farewell! Ah me! What I had intended for my own funeral, I must use for my sons'! Oh, my sons, stay of my old age, twin lights of my life, why are you so in love with death? Come here, all you young people, and weep for the death of my young sons! Come, old men, and mourn my sons with me! Fathers, draw near, and see that you never suffer grief like mine! Weep, eyes, blind me with your tears, and let me not see my sons put to the sword!' The father had just finished speaking, when the young men's wives arrived, holding up their own children for their husbands to see, and with loud wails they cried: 'To whose care are you leaving us? Who will be a father to these children now? Who will divide all your possessions? Alas, what iron hearts you have! You scorn your parents, reject your friends, cast off your wives, disown your children, and of your own free will deliver yourselves to the executioners!'

In the face of all this, the hearts of the two men began to soften. Then St Sebastian, who was present, stepped forward and said: 'Most valiant soldiers of Christ, do not let these pitiful appeals rob you of an eternal crown!' And he said to the parents: 'Do not fear, they will not be separated from you. They are going before you to prepare you a dwelling among the stars. For ever since the world began, life has duped those who put their hope in it, deceived those who sought it, mocked those who trusted it. It affords security to no one, but proves false to all. It counsels the thief to steal, the cantankerous to bluster, the liar to cheat. It drives a man to crimes, forces him into wickedness, urges him to commit injustice. But this persecution which we suffer in this life flares up today and tomorrow comes to nothing; it burns hot today and tomorrow cools; one hour we face it, the next it is gone. But the suffering of eternity constantly is renewed in order to pierce more keenly; it is increased to burn more fiercely; its fires are stoked to make the pain last for ever. Let us therefore kindle in ourselves now a passionate desire for martyrdom! The Devil thinks he is the victor in this, but when he tries to catch us, he is himself caught; when he seeks to hold us fast, he is himself held; when he would vanquish us, he is himself vanquished; when he tortures us, he is tortured; when he slits our throats, he is slain himself; and when he mocks us, it is he who is an object of derision!' . . .

While St Sebastian was speaking in this vein, Zoe, the wife of Nicostratus, in whose house the two Christians were being detained, fell at his feet: she had lost the power of speech, but was clearly begging the saint's forgiveness. Sebastian said: 'If I am the servant of God, and the things this woman has heard me say are true and she believes, let him who opened the mouth of Zacharias his prophet open her mouth, and let her speak!' Immediately the woman could speak again and she cried: 'Blessed be the words of your mouth, and blessed be all who believe what you have said! For I have seen an angel holding a book before you in which everything you have said was written.' Hearing this, her husband fell at St Sebastian's feet, begging forgiveness. Sebastian then freed the martyrs from their chains and invited them to go free. But they answered that they would not hear of forgoing the victory they had won. The Lord had endowed Sebastian's words with such grace and power that not only did he strengthen Marcellianus and Marcus in their determination to be martyred, but he also converted to the faith their father, whose name was Tranquillinus, their mother and many others of the household, all of whom the priest Polycarp baptized.

Now Tranquillinus was suffering from a serious illness; but the moment he was baptized, he was cured. Chromatius, the prefect of the city of Rome, was also very ill, and he asked Tranquillinus to bring him the man who had cured him. So the priest Polycarp and Sebastian went to the prefect and he asked them to make him well. Sebastian told him that he must first renounce his idols and give him permission to destroy them, and that was the only way he could be cured. The prefect replied that his slaves should do this, and not Sebastian himself, but Sebastian objected. 'No,' he said. 'They are too frightened to destroy their gods; and if they did, and the Devil chose to harm them, the infidels would be sure to say that they had been punished for doing violence to the gods.' So Polycarp and Sebastian set to and demolished more than two hundred idols. They then said to Chromatius: 'Now we have smashed the idols, you ought to be cured. But since you are not, it is clear that either you have not yet renounced your heathen beliefs, or there are some idols you are holding back.' The prefect then confessed that he had a room in which all the stars of heaven were plotted in their courses; his father had spent more than two hundred pounds of gold in equipping this room, and by consulting it he could foretell all future events. Sebastian told him: 'As long as you keep that room as it is, your ill health will continue.' So the prefect agreed to dismantle it, but his son Tiburtius, a youth of great promise, came forward and said: 'I cannot bear to see such a splendid piece of work destroyed. But far be it from me to do anything to hinder my father's recovery. I shall have two furnaces fired, and if my father is not cured when the room is destroyed, these two Christians will be roasted alive!' 'Very well,' Sebastian replied. 'So be it.' And while the laboratory was being demolished, an angel appeared to the prefect and told him that Jesus had cured him. Instantly Chromatius was well again, and he ran after the angel, trying to kiss his feet. But the angel would not let him, as he had not yet been baptized. So the prefect himself, his son Tiburtius and fourteen hundred persons of his household were baptized. Nicostratus's wife Zoe was subsequently seized by the heathen, subjected to cruel tortures, and finally died a martyr. On hearing of this, Tranquillinus exclaimed: 'The women are winning their crowns before us! Why do we go on living?' And a few days later he himself was stoned to death.

St Tiburtius was given the choice of either burning incense to the heathen gods, or walking barefoot over live coals. So he made the sign of the cross and walked boldly in his bare feet over the glowing coals, exclaiming: 'I feel as if, in the name of our Lord Jesus Christ, I were walking over a bed of roses.' The prefect Fabianus rejoined: 'Everyone knows it is Christ who has taught you this witchcraft!' 'Silence, you poor fool,' Tiburtius told him. 'You are not worthy to utter a name so holy, a name so sweet!' Enraged at this insult, the prefect had him beheaded.

Marcellianus and Marcus were tied to a stake, and there they sang the words '*Ecce quam bonum et quam iucundum habitare fratres in unum*' ['Behold how good and how pleasant it is for brothers to dwell together in unity!' (Psalm 132 (133): 1)] 'Pitiful fools!' the prefect yelled at them. 'Give up this madness and save yourselves!' But they replied: 'We have never been more content! How happy we should be if you could leave us here like this, while our souls remain in our bodies!' The prefect then ordered his men to run them through with their spears, and so the two brothers finally achieved their martyrdom.

After this the prefect made a formal report to the emperor Diocletian about Sebastian. The emperor summoned the saint and said: 'I have always treated you as one of the most important men of my court, yet all this time you have secretly been working against me, and against the gods.' Sebastian replied: 'No, it has been for your salvation that I have honoured Christ; it has been for the preservation of the Roman Empire that I have worshipped God who is in heaven.' Diocletian then had him tied to a tree in the middle of an open field, and told his archers to use him for target practice. They hit him with so many arrows that he looked like a hedgehog, and they left him there for dead. But within a few days he recovered and was standing on the steps of the palace, and reproaching the two emperors for the terrible things they were doing to the Christians. 'Is this not Sebastian,' they exclaimed, 'whom we had shot to death?' Sebastian answered them: 'The Lord saw fit to bring me to life again so that I could confront you and reproach you with all the atrocities you are committing against the servants of Christ.' One of the emperors then ordered him to be beaten with clubs until finally he breathed his last. He then had his body thrown into the sewer so that he could not be worshipped by the Christians as a martyr. Next night St Sebastian appeared to St Lucina, told her where his body lay, and asked her to bury it near the remains of the apostles. This was duly carried out. Sebastian suffered under the emperors Diocletian and Maximian, whose reign began in about AD 287 . . .

12

ST AGNES, VIRGIN

21 January

Agnes was a virgin of uncommon discernment, as Ambrose, who wrote the story of her martyrdom, attests. At the age of thirteen she vanquished death and won life. Though she was young in years, she had the wisdom of old age; her body was that of a child, but her heart was precociously mature; she was fair of face, but fairer still for her faith.

One day she was returning from school, when the prefect's son saw her and fell wildly in love with her. He promised her jewels and untold riches if she would consent to be his wife, but Agnes replied: 'Be gone from me, you fuel of iniquity, you fodder of sin, you food of death! I have been claimed already by another lover!' She then began to sing the praises of her lover and future bridegroom, listing five qualities that brides particularly seek in their spouses-to-be, namely, nobility of lineage, physical beauty, abundant wealth, courage combined with strength, and all-surpassing love. She added: 'I love one far nobler than you, and of higher lineage, whose mother is a virgin, whose father has never known a woman; the angels serve him; the sun and the moon wonder at his beauty; his riches never fail, his wealth never grows less; his fragrance brings the dead to life, his touch strengthens the infirm; his love is chaste, his touch holy; in his embrace I am wholly virgin.' Then, summarizing her lover's matchless excellence, she said: 'Whose lineage could be loftier, whose strength mightier, whose beauty greater, whose love sweeter? Who could be better endowed with every grace?' Next she enumerated five gifts which her betrothed had given her, and gives to all his other brides, namely, he espouses them with the ring of faith; he clothes them and adorns them with an infinite variety of virtues; he marks them with the blood of his passion; he binds them to himself with the bond of love; and enriches them with the treasures of heavenly glory. 'He has placed his ring on my right hand,' she said, 'and put a necklace of precious stones about my neck; he has clothed me in a robe of gold weave, and adorned me with priceless jewels; he has placed a sign upon my face so that I may take no lover other than him; and his blood has embellished my cheeks. Already I am wrapped in his chaste embraces, already his body is united with mine. He has shown me incomparable treasures and promised that they will be mine if I remain true to him.'

When he heard this the young man went almost out of his mind. He returned home and threw himself on to his bed; and it was clear to doctors from his pathetic sighing that he was lovesick. His father found the girl and explained the situation to her, but she remained firm: she told him she could never violate the agreement she had already made with her betrothed. The prefect tried to find out who this betrothed might be, this person about whose power she made such extravagant claims. Then someone told him it was Christ whom Agnes called her lover, and the prefect, in an attempt to undermine her resolve, first tried gentle persuasion, then had recourse to violent threats. 'Do whatever you wish,' Agnes told him. 'You will never get what you want from me.' And she treated his attempts to threaten or cajole her with equal derision. The prefect replied: 'Choose one of two things: either sacrifice to the goddess Vesta along with her virgins, if you are so enamoured of virginity; or go to a whorehouse and ply your trade as a whore!' (Since Agnes was of the nobility, the prefect could not use force on her. His charging her with being a Christian was merely a pretext.) Agnes replied: 'I will not sacrifice to your gods, nor shall anyone defile me. I have an angel of the Lord to keep my body from harm.' The prefect then had her stripped and taken naked to a brothel. But the Lord made her hair grow so long that it covered her better than any clothing could have. When she entered the house of shame, she found an angel waiting, who filled the whole place with a piercing radiance and held out to her in readiness a robe of burning white. So the brothel became a place of prayer, and anyone who showed reverence to the heavenly light went away a purer man than he had come in.

The prefect's son came to call with other young friends, and he invited them to take their pleasure with her first. In they went, but they were immediately terrified by the brilliant light and, shamefaced, came out again. Calling his friends miserable cowards, he angrily went in to Agnes himself, but when he tried to touch her, he, too, was enveloped in the same flood of light; and because he had not honoured God, the Devil throttled him and he expired. When the prefect learnt of this, he went straight to Agnes, weeping inconsolably, and questioned her in great detail about the cause of his son's death. Agnes said: 'The Devil, whose will your son wanted to carry out, got him in his power and killed him. His friends ran in terror at the miracle they had witnessed and they escaped unharmed.' 'You will only convince me that you have not done all this by witchcraft,' the prefect told her, 'if you can bring my son back to life by prayer.' So Agnes prayed, and the young man recovered and went about publicly preaching Christ. At this, the priests of the temples began to stir up trouble among the people. 'Away with this witch!' they shouted. 'Away with this sorceress who warps men's minds and bewitches their souls!' Now the prefect, after witnessing the miracle Agnes had performed, would have set her free, but, fearing that he might be exiled, he put his deputy in charge and, sad though he was that he could not save her, left the area.

This deputy, whose name was Aspasius, had Agnes thrown into a roaring fire, but the flames divided down the middle, utterly consuming the rioting crowds on either side, but leaving Agnes completely untouched. Finally Aspasius had her stabbed in the throat; and so it was that her bridegroom, in dazzling white and radiant with love, hallowed Agnes as his bride and martyr. It is believed that Agnes suffered in the time of Constantine the Great, whose reign began in AD 309 . . .

13

ST VINCENT

22 January

Vincent was noble by birth, but nobler still for his faith and religious fervour. He was a deacon to blessed Valerius, bishop of Saragossa, and because Vincent was more eloquent than he, the bishop entrusted all his preaching to him, while he devoted himself to prayer and contemplation. On the orders of the governor, Dacian, these two were sent to Valencia, thrown into gaol and kept in close confinement there. When Dacian judged that they must be on the point of starving to death, he had them brought before him and, seeing they were both in the best of health and spirits, he angrily burst out: 'What have you to say for yourself, Valerius, you who defy the decrees of the emperors on the pretext of religion?' The blessed Valerius began to make a mild reply, but Vincent said to him: 'Reverend father, do not whisper to the man as if you were afraid! Speak out loudly and clearly! Or if, holy father, you want me to, I will answer our judge myself.' Valerius replied: 'My dearest son, I have long since appointed you as my spokesman: now I entrust to you the task of defending the faith which we uphold.' Vincent then turned to Dacian and said: 'All you have said amounts to a demand that we should deny our faith. But you should know that, according to the Christian way of thinking, it is a wicked blasphemy to renounce the worship of God.'

This reply angered Dacian, who ordered the bishop to be sent into exile. But he determined to make an example of Vincent, whom he considered an arrogant and presumptuous youth, and to punish him in a way that would strike fear into the hearts of others. So he ordered him to be stretched on the rack and torn limb from limb. When his whole body had been broken, Dacian said: 'Tell me, Vincent, what do you think of your body now?' But Vincent replied with a smile: 'This is the answer to my prayers!' The governor was infuriated, and began to threaten him with every sort of torture if he did not give in. But Vincent cried out: 'I count myself blessed! The more you try to frighten me, the more you comfort me! So begin, you poor fool, do your worst, do whatever your evil nature bids you! You will see that with God's help I have more power to resist pain than you to inflict it!' At this the governor began to shout; he screamed abuse at his torturers and laid about them with cudgels. Vincent said to him: 'What is this, Dacian? You yourself avenging me on my tormentors?' The governor now flew into the wildest rage. 'You useless fools!' he shouted at his men. 'What is wrong with you? You have managed to break adulterers and parricides down, tortured them into telling you everything they know, but this Vincent has withstood every cruelty you can devise!' The torturers then forced iron combs deep into Vincent's ribcage, so that the blood streamed from every part of his body and his entrails could be seen between his broken bones. 'Have pity on yourself, Vincent!' Dacian said. 'You are young and handsome; you can be free again to enjoy your youth and save yourself from further torments.' But Vincent retorted: 'You venomous tongue of the Devil! It is not your tortures I fear: I dread only this show of pity! The more furious I see you become, the greater is my joy. Do not hold back, I beg you! I want you to torture me as cruelly as you know how, then to admit that my victory is total and complete.' He was then taken down from the rack and pushed towards a glowing gridiron. Vincent, reproaching his torturers for their slowness, hurried on to his next ordeal. Of his own free will he climbed on to the gridiron and was there roasted, seared and scorched, while iron hooks and red-hot plates were driven into every part of his body. As his blood spattered the fire, he was wounded time and time again; then salt was thrown on to the fire to make the flames hiss and leap into his wounds and burn him even more cruelly. Then the torturers abandoned his limbs and drove their hooks deep into his entrails until the intestines spilled out of his body. But during all this Vincent lay motionless, with his eyes turned to heaven, and prayed to the Lord.

When Dacian's men reported this to him, he cried: 'What? Still defeated? Well, now let him live on, let us prolong his agony! Shut him up in the darkest dungeon. Make him a bed of all the sharpest splinters and fragments of brick you can find. Tie his feet to a stake and make him lie there. Leave him without a soul to comfort him. And when he is dead, bring me word.'

Swiftly his cruel servants obeyed their still more cruel master. But at this moment the King for whose sake the soldier was suffering turned his agony into glory. For suddenly the darkness of the dungeon was dispelled by a brilliant light; Vincent's bed of torture became a bed of the sweetest smelling flowers; his fetters fell from his ankles; and holy angels were at his side offering their comfort. When he walked on the bed of flowers and joined the singing of the angels, the sweetness of the melody and the wonderful fragrance of the flowers was wafted far and wide, and the guards, terrified by what they witnessed through chinks in the wall of Vincent's cell, were instantly converted to the faith.

Dacian, hearing what had happened, was beside himself. 'What more can we do to him?' he cried. 'We are beaten! Very well. Take him out of his cell and lay him on a couch with the softest bedding. We will only make him more of a martyr if he dies under torture. As soon as he recovers, he can be put to the torture again.' So Vincent was carried to a soft bed, but after resting there for a short while, he suddenly breathed his last. This was around the year AD 287, in the reign of Diocletian and Maximian.

When Dacian received the news, he was badly shaken, and it pained him to have been beaten in this fashion. 'Even if I could not conquer him alive,' he said, 'I can still punish him when he is dead. That way I shall appease my wrath and have the final victory!' So on Dacian's orders Vincent's body was exposed in an open place to be devoured by birds and beasts. But instantly a phalanx of guardian angels surrounded it and prevented any beasts from coming near. Finally a crow, a naturally greedy bird, attacked all the other birds, even those bigger than itself, and, beating its wing at them, drove them off; and when a wolf appeared, it chased him away, pecking at him and cawing loudly. Then it turned its head and seemed to fix its gaze on the saint's body, as if it were staring in wonder at the angels guarding it.

When all this was reported to Dacian, he remarked: 'I believe I shall never defeat him, even in death!' So he gave orders for Vincent's body to be tied to a great millstone and cast into the sea, so that what had not been eaten by wild beasts on land should at least be devoured by the monsters of the deep. Sailors therefore took the body out to sea and flung it over the side. But the corpse returned to the shore more quickly than the sailors in their boat. Subsequently it was discovered by a lady and certain others to whom the saint had appeared, and they gave it honourable burial . . .

14

ST JOHN THE ALMSGIVER

23 January

John was patriarch of Alexandria, and one night, deep in prayer, he saw a most beautiful girl standing by him, wearing a crown of olives on her head. Startled at this apparition, he asked her who she was, and she replied: 'I am Pity. It was I who brought the Son of God down from heaven. Take me as your bride and you will prosper.' Knowing that the olive crown signified mercy, from that day on John became so compassionate towards others that he was called 'Eleymon', which means 'Almsgiver'. He always called the poor his 'masters', and that is why the hospitallers to this day refer to the poor by that name. He therefore got all his servants together and said to them: 'Comb the city and draw up a list of my masters – every last one of them.' When they failed to understand him, he said: 'Those you call the poor, the beggars – those I tell you are our masters, our benefactors, because they are the ones who can really help us to win the kingdom of heaven.'

In order to get people to give alms, he used to tell them the following tale: once upon a time, in Constantinople, some poor men who were warming themselves in the sun began to compare the virtues of those who gave them alms, and they were united in singing the praises of the good and condemning the wicked. Now there was a certain tax collector named Peter, a very rich and powerful man, but absolutely lacking in compassion towards the poor, whom he would drive away in furious indignation if they called at his door. None of the poor could be found who had ever received any alms at his house. Then one of them said to the rest: 'What will you give me if I can get alms from him today?' So they made a bet with him, and he went off to Peter's house and asked for alms. Now Peter happened to have been out and was returning home, and when he saw the poor man at his door, having no stone to throw at him, he seized one of the loaves of bread his servant was carrying and angrily hurled it at the beggar. He caught it, ran straight back to his companions and showed them the alms the tax collector had given him. Two days later Peter lay desperately ill and saw himself standing before the Judgement Seat. There was a huge pair of scales and some blackamoors were weighing up his evil deeds in one balance pan, while on the other side stood creatures clad all in white, lamenting the fact that they could find nothing to put in on their side to redress the balance. Then one of them said: 'Truly we have nothing except a single loaf of bread which he gave to Christ two days ago – and that against his will.' But when they put the loaf into the pan, it seemed to Peter that it all but balanced all his sins on the other side. And the creatures told him: 'You must add something to this loaf, or the blackamoors will get you!' Then Peter woke up and, discovering he was well again, exclaimed: 'I cannot believe it! If a single loaf which I threw at a beggar in anger could bring me so much good, how much more good would it do me if I gave all I had to the poor?' Then one day, when he was walking along the street dressed in his finest clothes, a man who had been shipwrecked asked him for something to cover himself with. Peter immediately took off his costly cloak and gave it to him. The man went straight off and sold it. When the tax collector, returning by the same route, saw his cloak hanging up for sale, he was plunged into such gloom that he could not eat, and he said to himself: 'I wanted the poor man to have something to remember me by, but I was not worthy even of that.' But while he was sleeping, he saw a figure who shone more brightly than the stars; the figure had a cross on his head, and he was wearing the cloak Peter had given to the poor man. He asked him: 'Why are you weeping, Peter?' And when Peter told him, he said: 'Do you recognize this cloak?' 'I do, Lord,' Peter said. And the Lord said to Peter: 'I have been wearing this ever since you gave it to me, and I am grateful for your kindness, because I was freezing with cold and you clothed me.' When Peter awoke, he began to bless the poor. 'As God lives,' he exclaimed, 'I will not die until I have become one of them!' He gave everything he had to the poor, then summoned his notary. 'I want to tell you a secret,' he said, 'but if you do not keep it and do as I tell you, I shall sell you to the heathen!' He gave him ten pounds of gold and said, 'Go to the holy city and buy yourself what you want; then sell me to some Christian there, and give whatever I fetch to the poor.' The notary refused, but Peter told him: 'If you do not obey me, I shall sell you to the heathen!' So the notary did as he said: he took him, dressed him in filthy clothes and sold him off as one of his slaves to a silversmith for thirty pieces of silver, then distributed the money among the poor. As a slave, Peter did all the most menial tasks and was regarded as the lowest of the low; his fellow slaves subjected him to regular beatings and even called him a half-wit. But the Lord appeared to him often, and consoled him by showing him the clothing and all the other things he had given to the poor.

Meanwhile the emperor and all the citizens of Constantinople had been mourning the loss of such a distinguished man. Then one day some of Peter's former neighbours came from Constantinople to visit the holy places and they were invited to the house by Peter's master. While they sat at dinner, they whispered to each other: 'How like Peter the tax collector that slave is!' And then, as they all studied his features closely, one of them cried: 'It is Peter, it really is! I'll go and get him!' But Peter realized what was afoot and slipped away. Now the doorkeeper was deaf and dumb, and anyone wanting to go in or out had to use sign language. But Peter used no signs: he spoke to him and told him to open the door. The doorkeeper heard him at once and could suddenly speak again, and he answered Peter and opened the door for him. Then he went back inside and, to the great surprise of the company, told them what had happened. 'The slave who did the cooking has gone, he has run away. But he must be a servant of God, because when he said to me: "Open up, I tell you!" a flame shot from his mouth which touched my tongue and ears, and at the same moment I could hear and speak!' They all leapt to their feet and ran after Peter, but they were unable to find him. Then, because they had treated a holy man so vilely, every member of the household did penance.

A monk named Vitalis decided to test St John to see how ready he would be to listen to gossip and be misled into thinking ill of him. So he went into the city and drew up a list of all the public prostitutes. He then went to call on them one by one and said to each of them: 'Grant me this one night and abstain from fornication.' Then he would enter the woman's house, find a secluded corner and spend the whole night on his knees praying for her; and next morning he would leave, asking her to say nothing to anyone. But one of them did let out what he was up to, and directly, in answer to the old monk's prayer, she began to be tormented by a demon. Everyone said to her: 'God has punished you as you deserve. You told a lie. That good-for-nothing monk called on you to commit fornication, and for no other reason!'

Each evening Vitalis used to tell anyone who happened to be listening: 'I have to go now, a certain lady is expecting me.' Many people were critical of his behaviour, but he would reply: 'Have I not a body, like everyone else? Or is God angry only with monks? Monks are men, just like the rest!' Some of them said: 'Take yourself a wife, father, but take off that monk's habit, and put an end to all the gossip!' But, pretending to be angry, he retorted: 'Be off! I will not listen to you. If people choose to take offence, then let them! Let them beat their heads against the wall! Has God appointed you to be my judges? Leave me alone, and mind your own business! I will answer for myself!' All this he said as loudly as he could, but when people complained to John, God hardened John's heart so that he did not believe the accusations. Meanwhile Vitalis begged to God to reveal to someone after his death the truth about what he had been doing, and that those who had been so ready to defame him should not be punished for it. In the end he managed to convert many of the women he had visited, and persuaded several of them to enter a convent.

One morning, when he was leaving the house of one of these women, he met one of her customers on the way in. This man promptly boxed the monk's ears and cried: 'You good-for-nothing! When will you ever mend your filthy ways?' 'Believe me,' Vitalis told him, 'I will fetch you such a blow that the whole city will hear and come running!' And indeed soon after the Devil, in the form of a Moor, did strike him in the face and said: 'This is from Abbot Vitalis!' And the man was immediately tormented by a demon, and tormented so savagely that everyone ran when they heard his cries. But he repented, and was delivered from the demon's power by Vitalis's prayers. And when the man of God was near to death, he wrote down and left the following words of warning: 'Never judge in haste!' After his death, when the women finally revealed the truth about what he had done, everyone glorified God, and St John most of all, who remarked: 'Would that I myself had received the blow that he received!'

A poor man in the garb of a pilgrim came to John and begged him for alms. John called his steward and said: 'Give him six gold pieces.' The poor man took them, then went off, changed his clothes, and returned to the patriarch and begged him for alms again. John called his steward and told him: 'Give him six gold pieces.' When he had handed them over and the beggar had left, the steward told John: 'I did as you asked me, father, but that man had alms from you twice today. He simply changed his clothes!' But John pretended to be unaware of the deception. The poor man then changed his clothes again, and came a third time to John and begged alms. The steward nudged John and gestured that this was the same man. In response St John said: 'Go and give him twelve gold pieces. This may be the Lord Jesus Christ testing me, to see if I tire of giving before he tires of taking!'

A certain dignitary once wanted to use some money belonging to the Church in a commercial venture, but the patriarch absolutely refused to allow it, intending as he was to distribute the money among the poor. After a heated argument the two men parted in anger. As the day drew to a close, the patriarch sent his archpriest to the man with a message: 'My lord, the sun is going down.' When he heard this, the dignitary burst into tears, went to John and begged his forgiveness.

A nephew of John's had been grossly insulted by a shopkeeper. He was deeply offended, and went to the patriarch and complained to him, but nothing John said could console him. 'How,' the patriarch asked, 'could anyone have dared contradict you or answer you back? Believe me, my son, humble as I am, I shall do something to that shopkeeper today that will amaze all Alexandria!' When he heard this, the youth was placated, because he imagined his uncle would have the man soundly flogged. John, seeing how cheered his nephew was, embraced him and kissed him, and said: 'My son, if you truly are the nephew of someone of my humility, then prepare to be flogged and insulted by all and sundry! The test of true kinship is not flesh and blood, but strength of character.' Then he quickly sent for the shopkeeper and exempted him from all rents and taxes. Everyone who heard about this was astonished, and then they understood what John had meant when he said that he would do something to the shopkeeper that would 'amaze all Alexandria'.

The patriarch heard that as soon as an emperor was crowned there was a custom that masons took four or five pieces of differently coloured marble, presented themselves before the new emperor and asked: 'Of what sort of marble or metal does your majesty wish his tomb made?' This custom John followed, and he gave orders for the building of his tomb, but he insisted that it should remain unfinished until his death. He also ordered that, whenever he was officiating with his clergy at some festivity, someone should go up to him and say: 'Lord, your tomb is unfinished. Have it completed: you do not know at what hour the thief might come.'

A rich man, seeing that blessed John had only the coarsest of bedclothes to lie on, since he had given all the rest away to the poor, bought an extremely costly coverlet and gave it to him. But John, feeling the weight of it, was unable to sleep a wink all night, because he kept thinking that three hundred of his 'masters' could be kept warm with the money that had been spent on the coverlet. All night he groaned and kept saying to himself: 'How many of them have lain down without supper; how many lie soaked with rain out in the square; how many with their teeth chattering with the cold? And you eat a hearty supper of fish and lie in your great bed with all your sins, and warm yourself under a coverlet that cost thirty pieces of silver! No! The lowly John shall never sleep under this again!' So, as soon as morning came, he sold the coverlet and gave the proceeds to the poor. But the rich friend got to hear of this, and bought the coverlet back and gave it to John, asking him not to sell it again, but to keep it for his own use. John accepted it, but again had it sold and the proceeds distributed among the poor. The rich man heard what he had done, and once again went off, bought it back and gave it to John, and this time he said: 'We shall see who tires first: you of selling it or I of buying it back!' So in this delightful way, the saint, as it were, kept cropping his rich friend's wealth; and he told him that, if someone robbed the rich with the intention of helping the poor, he was guilty of no sin, because he was doing both parties a service: the rich because he was saving their souls, and the poor because of all the money he was able to give them.

Blessed John, always trying to persuade people to be more charitable, used to tell the story of St Serapion. Serapion had only just given his cloak to a pauper when he met another pauper who was suffering from the cold. He gave this one his tunic, and then sat down half-naked with his Gospel book in his hand. A passer-by asked him: 'Father, who has robbed you of your clothes?' And Serapion, waving his Gospel book, said: 'It was this.' On another occasion, when he saw another pauper, he even sold his Gospel book and gave the proceeds to him, and when he was asked where his Gospel book was, he replied: 'The Gospel commands us: "Go and sell all you have and give the money to the poor." All I had was my Gospel book, so I did what it said and sold it.'

A man came begging for alms and St John ordered that he be given five pence, but the man was indignant that the saint had given him no more, and began to curse him and insult him to his face. John's servants wanted to rush at the beggar and give him a sound thrashing, but the saint would not let them touch him. 'Let him be, brothers,' he told them. 'Let him curse me. Look, I am sixty years old now: all that time my life has been a reproach to Christ. What right have I to resent one insult from this man?' And he had his purse brought out and put down in front of the beggar, so that he could take from it as much as he wanted.

Now during mass, as soon as the Gospel had been read, people were in the habit of leaving church and engaging in idle chatter outside. So once, after the reading, the patriarch left church with them and sat down among them. They all expressed their surprise at this, but he said to them: 'My children, the shepherd's place is with his flock. Either go back in yourselves, and I will go with you and proceed with the mass, or stay out here, and I will, too.' He did this repeatedly, until finally he taught the people to stay in church.

A young man had run away with a nun, and the clergy, expressing to St John their outrage at this, suggested that the youth should be excommunicated, because he had lost two souls, his own and the nun's as well. John calmed them down. 'Not so, my sons, not so!' he said. 'Allow me to show you that you yourselves are guilty of two sins. Firstly, you are breaking the Lord's commandment: "Judge not that ye be not judged"; and secondly, you do not know for certain that they are still living in sin and have not repented.'

Often, when John was at prayer, he would become rapt in ecstasy and could be heard arguing with God. 'Very well, good Lord Jesus,' he would say, 'let us see who does more: you in giving to me, or I in giving your gifts away.'

At the end of his life, when John had a raging fever and realized that his death was near, he said: 'I thank you, Lord, that you have heard my prayer – a wretched sinner beseeching your goodness – that when I died, no more than a single penny should be found on me. That penny I now want given to the poor.'

His venerable body was laid in a tomb in which the bodies of two other bishops had been buried, and by a miracle they made room for St John and left him space between them.

A few days before his death, a woman came to John who had committed a sin so terrible that she dared not confess it to anyone. So St John told her at least to write her confessions down on a piece of paper (because she knew how to write), seal it and bring it to him, and he would pray for her. She agreed to this, wrote down her confession, carefully sealed it and handed it over to St John. But a few days later the saint fell ill and died. When the woman heard the news, she thought she would be humiliated and disgraced, because she was sure that John would have given her confession to someone else and it was now in the hands of another person. So she went to St John's tomb, and there, dissolving into tears, cried: 'Ah me! I thought I could avoid my disgrace, but now I am disgraced before the world!' She wept bitterly and begged St John to reveal to her where he had put her confession, and suddenly the blessed John came forth from his tomb, dressed in all his pontifical finery and flanked by the two bishops who lay at rest with him. 'Why do you disturb us like this?' he asked the woman. 'Why will you not allow me and these two saints to rest in peace? Look, our vestments are all wet with your tears!' And he held out to her the confession, still sealed as it had been before, and said: 'There is your seal. Open the document and read it.' She did as he said and found that her sin had been wiped out, and in its place she read these words: 'Because of my servant John, your sin is wiped away.' So she gave heartfelt thanks to God, and John retired to his sepulchre with the two bishops. John flourished around AD 605, in the reign of the emperor Phocas.

15

ST IGNATIUS

1 February

Ignatius was a disciple of John the Evangelist and bishop of Antioch. He is said to have written a letter to the Blessed Virgin which went as follows: 'To Mary the Christ-bearer, her servant Ignatius sends greetings. I appeal to you for strength and consolation, I who am a novice in the faith and a disciple of your servant John, for I have learnt many things about your son Jesus, wondrous things, things I have been dumbfounded to hear. Now I long with all my heart to hear from you the truth about what I have been told, for you were always so close to Jesus, and shared his secrets. Farewell, and may the other neophytes who are with me be strengthened in the faith by you, and through you, and in you.' The Blessed Virgin Mary, the Mother of God, replied to Ignatius as follows: 'To Ignatius, my beloved fellow disciple, the lowly handmaid of Christ Jesus sends greetings. The things you have heard and learnt from John about Jesus are true. Believe them, cling to them, hold firm to the vow you have made to Christ and base your life and works upon it. I will come with John to visit you and those with you. Stand firm and act courageously in the faith. Do not give way in the face of persecution, however cruel, and may your spirit be strong and rejoice in God your Saviour. Amen.'

Now the blessed Ignatius was held in such a very high regard that even Dionysius, the disciple of the apostle Paul, who was a distinguished philosopher and accomplished theologian, cited Ignatius's words as authoritative confirmation of his own teachings. In his work *On the Divine Names*, he tells us that there were some who objected to the use of the word '*amor*' ['love'] in a theological context, maintaining that '*dilectio*' ['charity']¹ was more appropriate. Dionysius, wishing to demonstrate that '*amor*' could rightly be used in any spiritual context, says: 'The divine Ignatius writes: "My love ['*amor*'] has been crucified."'

There is a story in the *Tripartite History* that Ignatius once heard angels singing antiphons on a mountainside, and as a result he introduced the rule that antiphons should be sung in church and that the psalms should be intoned in the manner of the antiphons.

St Ignatius had been praying for a long time for the peace of the Church, not out of fear for himself, but for what might happen to the weaker brethren. Now the emperor Trajan, whose reign began in AD 100, on his return from a victorious campaign was threatening to put all Christians to death, so Ignatius went to confront him and openly declared that he was a Christian. Trajan had him bound in chains and handed him over to ten soldiers with orders to take him to Rome, and he warned Ignatius that he would be thrown to wild beasts and eaten alive. On his way to Rome Ignatius wrote letters to all the churches, strengthening them in the faith of Christ. In one of these, which was addressed to the church in Rome, as the *Ecclesiastical History* attests, he pleaded with his brother Christians not to do anything to prevent his martyrdom. 'From Syria to Rome,' he writes, 'by land and sea, I have been fighting with wild beasts night and day. I have been chained and shackled to ten leopards – the soldiers set to guard me and take me to Rome. The kinder I am to them, the more savage they become. But I learn all the time from their cruelty. Ah, when will they come, those beasts that await me, that will be my salvation? When will they be unleashed; when will they be allowed to glut themselves on my flesh? I will invite them to devour me, beg them not to be afraid to touch my body, as they have been sometimes with others. And if they do hold back, what is more, I will resort to violence, I will throw myself at them! So pardon me, please, my brothers, I know what is best for me. Let them burn me, crucify me, throw me to wild beasts; let them crush my bones, tear my whole body limb from limb, rack me with every torture the Devil has invented, if only my prize is to be with Christ!'

When he got to Rome and was brought before Trajan, the emperor said to him: 'Ignatius, why are you stirring all Antioch to rebellion and converting my people to Christianity?' Ignatius replied: 'Would that I could convert you, too, so that you might possess the greatest, the most lasting kingdom of all!' 'Sacrifice to my gods,' Trajan told him, 'and you shall be chief of all the priests.' Ignatius said: 'I will not sacrifice to your gods, nor have I any ambition for high office. You can do whatever you wish with me, but you will not change me in the slightest.' So Trajan called to his men: 'Lay bare his shoulders and scourge him with leaded thongs! Rip open his sides with iron hooks and chafe the wounds with jagged stones!' But, as they did all these things to him, Ignatius stood unmoved. Trajan said: 'Bring live coals and make him walk on them barefoot!' But Ignatius declared: 'Neither searing fire nor scalding water can quench my love for Christ Jesus!' 'This must be sorcery,' Trajan burst out, 'if you can suffer such torture and not give in!' 'We Christians are no sorcerers,' Ignatius told him. 'Our law condemns sorcerers to death. You are the sorcerers, you who worship idols!' Trajan called out to his men: 'Lay open his back with your hooks and pour salt in the wounds!' Ignatius said: 'The sufferings of this world are as nothing compared with the glory that is to come.' 'Now pick him up!' Trajan commanded. 'Bind him in iron chains to a stake and keep him in the depths of my dungeon. Let him go without food or drink for three days – then throw him to the beasts to be eaten alive!'

When the three days were up the emperor and Senate and the whole people gathered together to see the bishop of Antioch fighting with the beasts. 'Since Ignatius is so arrogant and obdurate,' Trajan said, 'tie him up and let two lions loose on him, so there will be nothing left of him at all!' St Ignatius then addressed the crowd of spectators: 'Men of Rome, all you who witness this spectacle! I tell you, my labours have not been in vain. It is not for doing evil, but for serving God, that I suffer this.' Then, as recounted in the *Ecclesiastical History*, he added: 'I am the wheat of Christ: let me be ground by the teeth of these beasts to become pure bread!' When the emperor heard this, he commented: 'The endurance of these Christians is remarkable! What Greek would endure so much for his god?' Ignatius replied: 'It is not through my own strength that I have been able to endure this, but through the help of Christ.' He then began to provoke the lions, goading them into attacking him and eating him. The two savage beasts leapt at him, but they merely suffocated him: nothing would induce them to touch his flesh. Seeing this, Trajan was absolutely astonished; and he left the amphitheatre with the orders that if anyone wanted to remove the corpse, he should not be prevented from doing so. So Christians carried off the martyr's body and gave it honourable burial. Later, when Trajan received a letter from Pliny the Younger, in which he expressed a high regard for the Christian whose execution the emperor had ordered, he greatly regretted the things he had done to Ignatius and issued the order that, while any Christians who fell into the hands of the authorities should be punished, they were no longer to be hunted down.

There is also the story that St Ignatius, in the midst of all the tortures inflicted on him, never stopped calling on the name of Jesus Christ. When the torturers asked him why he kept repeating it over and over again, he told them: 'I have this name written on my heart, so I cannot stop invoking it!' After his death, those who had heard this remark were curious to find out if it was true, so they removed his heart from his body, cut it in two, and there found the name 'Jesus Christ' inscribed in letters of gold. This miracle converted many unbelievers to the faith . . .

16

ST BLAISE

3 February

Blaise was so highly esteemed for his sweetness of disposition and holiness that the Christians of Sebaste, a city in Cappadocia, elected him as their bishop. But after succeeding to the episcopate, he was compelled by the persecution of Diocletian to seek refuge in a cave, and there he lived the life of a hermit. Birds brought him food, and crowds of wild animals visited him and would not leave him until he laid his hands on them in blessing. And if any of them were sick, they would go immediately to him and went away well again.

One day the governor of that region sent his soldiers out hunting, and when they had met with no success elsewhere, they chanced upon St Blaise's cave. There they found a great gathering of wild animals crowding about the hermit, but try as they might they were unable to catch a single one. In astonishment they reported this to their master, and he at once sent out more troops with orders to bring this hermit before him, together with any other Christians they might find. That very night Christ appeared three times to Blaise, saying: 'Get up and offer sacrifice to me!' Then the soldiers arrived. 'Come out!' they called. 'The governor wants you!' St Blaise replied to them: 'Welcome, my sons! Now I see that God has not forgotten me!' He went with them, and along the way he preached to them continually and performed numerous miracles, which they all witnessed.

On one occasion a woman brought him her son, who was dying because he had a fishbone stuck in his throat. She put the child down at the saint's feet and tearfully begged him to make the boy better. St Blaise laid his hands on him and prayed that this child and all others who petitioned God in his name should be blessed with healing. And immediately he was well again. Another woman, a poor widow, had nothing in the world but a pig, and now a wolf had seized it and carried it off. She begged St Blaise to get her pig back, and he smiled and said: 'Don't worry, woman, you will get your pig back.' Whereupon the wolf at once returned and gave the widow back her pig.

As soon as Blaise set foot in the city he was clapped in gaol on the orders of the governor. The next day the governor had him brought before him, and when he saw him, he greeted him with the most fulsome flattery: 'Greetings, Blaise,' he said, 'friend of the gods!' 'And to you, your Excellence!' replied Blaise. 'But do not call them gods, call them demons, because they will be consigned to the eternal fire along with all those who honour them!' The governor angrily gave orders for him to be beaten with cudgels and thrown back in gaol. But Blaise said to him: 'You fool! You hope to destroy my love of God by these punishments, when I have him within me to give me strength?' Now the poor widow whose pig Blaise had rescued came to hear of his plight, and she killed the pig and brought its head and trotters to the saint, together with a candle and some bread. He thanked her, ate the food and said to her: 'Offer a candle every year in the church which bears my name and all will go well with you, and with all who do the same.' The widow faithfully did as he said, and thereafter enjoyed the greatest prosperity.

In due course the prefect had Blaise taken out of gaol, but he was still unable to persuade him to worship his gods, so he ordered him to be hung from a beam and his flesh ripped open with combs of iron, then to be put back in gaol. Seven women followed the saint as he was taken off and collected the drops of his blood. They were immediately arrested and told they must offer sacrifice to the idols. They replied: 'If you want us to worship your gods with proper reverence, have them taken down to the lake so they can be washed and cleaned up before we worship them.' This delighted the governor, who quickly took up their suggestion. But the women seized the idols, threw them out into the middle of the lake and cried: 'Now we shall see if they really are gods!' When the prefect heard of this, he was beside himself with rage. Beating his breast, he called to his servants: 'Why did you not hold on to the gods and prevent them from being thrown into the middle of the lake?' 'What the women said to you about washing them was a lie,' they replied. 'They tricked you so that they could throw them into the lake.' And the women told him: 'The true God cannot be tricked. If your idols had really been gods, they would have foreseen what we were going to do.' In a fury the governor called to his men to prepare some molten lead and combs of iron, and had seven red-hot breastplates placed on one side and on the other seven linen shifts. He then told the women that they must make their choice. One of the women, who had two small children with her, ran forward boldly, seized the linen shifts and threw them into the fire. The children cried to their mother: 'Do not leave us behind, dearest mother! You have filled us with the sweetness of your milk, now fill us with the sweetness of the kingdom of heaven!' So the prefect ordered the women to be hung up and their flesh torn with the iron combs; and their flesh was a radiant white like snow, and milk instead of blood flowed from their wounds. And as they struggled to endure these torments, an angel of the Lord came to them to strengthen and comfort them. 'Do not be afraid!' he told them. 'The good workman, who begins his work well and brings it to a successful end, wins a blessing from his master. He is rewarded for the work he has done, and the wage he receives is joy!'

Then the governor had them taken down and thrown into a furnace, but miraculously its fire was quenched and they emerged unscathed. The governor exclaimed: 'Stop this witchcraft of yours and worship our gods!' But the women replied: 'Finish what you have begun! We have already heard our call to the heavenly kingdom!' So he sentenced them to be beheaded. They knelt, and as they waited for their execution to be carried out, they worshipped God, saying: 'O God, you have brought us out of darkness into this glorious light; you have chosen us to be sacrificed in your name; receive our souls, we pray, and grant that we may attain life eternal!' Then their heads were cut off, and they joined their Lord in heaven.

After this the governor had Blaise brought before him and asked him: 'Are you going to worship the gods or not?' 'Godless man!' Blaise replied. 'I do not fear your threats! Do what you will. My body is wholly yours: I surrender it to you!' The governor gave orders for him to be thrown into the lake, but Blaise made the sign of the cross over the water and at once it became as hard as dry land. 'If your idols are really gods,' he cried to the governor's men, 'then show me their power and walk over the water to me!' Sixty-five men stepped into the lake and were instantly drowned. Then an angel of the Lord came down and said to him: 'Come out, Blaise, and receive the crown God has ready for you!' Blaise stepped out of the lake, and the governor demanded: 'Are you absolutely determined not to worship the gods?' Blaise replied: 'Poor fool! I tell you, I am a servant of Christ. I do not worship demons!' So the governor gave the order for him to be beheaded, and Blaise prayed to the Lord that anyone who had trouble with his throat or any other malady and begged his intercession should be heard, and at once made well again. In answer a voice came to him from heaven, announcing that his prayer would be granted. And then, together with the two small children mentioned above, St Blaise was beheaded. His martyrdom occurred around AD 283.

17

ST AGATHA, VIRGIN

5 February

Agatha, a native of Catania, was a girl of noble birth and exceptional beauty, and from her childhood she had always been devoutly religious. But Quintianus, the consul of Sicily, a low-born lecher, a miser and idolater, was determined to get her in his grasp: being of lowly birth, he hoped to gain respect by marrying this noble girl; being a lecher, to possess her; being a miser, to rob her of her wealth; and, being an idolater, he wanted to make her sacrifice to his gods.

So he summoned her, and when she was brought before him, finding her quite unshakeable in her purpose, he handed her over to a prostitute called Aphrodisia and her nine daughters (who were all in the same business) and gave them thirty days in which to win her over and somehow get her to change her mind. By one moment promising her happiness and the next terrifying her with their threats, they were confident that they could seduce her from the path of virtue. But Agatha said to them: 'My soul is built on solid rock and founded in Christ: your words are like wind, your promises no more than rain, your threats as ineffectual as water! No matter how they beat against my house, its foundations are secure, and it will not fall!' But even as she spoke, she wept; day in, day out she wept and prayed earnestly that she might win the palm of martyrdom. And Aphrodisia, seeing that she remained unmoved, told Quintianus: 'You could sooner soften stone or change iron to lead than sway this girl, or turn her heart from Christ!'

Then Quintianus had Agatha brought before him and said: 'What is your background?' She replied: 'I am of noble birth, and my family is a distinguished one, as all my relatives can bear witness.' Quintianus said: 'If you are noble, why do you choose to live the life of a slave?' She replied: 'It is because I am the slave of Christ.' Quintianus said: 'If you say you are noble, how can you talk of being a slave?' She replied: 'The slavery of Christ is the highest nobility.' Quintianus said: 'Make your choice. Either sacrifice to my gods or be put to the torture.' Agatha replied: 'May you live like the gods you worship! May your wife be a second Venus, and you another Jupiter!' At this Quintianus had her struck in the face: 'Watch your tongue!' he said. 'How dare you insult your judge!' Agatha replied: 'I am surprised at a man of sense calling such creatures gods! How can you, when you do not want your wife to be like them? How can I be insulting you if I wish that you live the life of the gods? If your gods are good, I have wished you nothing but good; but if in reality you find their promiscuity disgusting, then you think as I do, as a Christian.' 'Enough of this!' Quintianus snapped. 'Either sacrifice to my gods, or I shall have you tortured and put to death!' Agatha replied: 'If you set wild beasts on me, they will become tame when they hear the name of Christ. If you burn me at the stake, angels will bring dew from heaven to quench the flames. If you beat me, no matter how cruelly, and torture me, the Holy Spirit is by my side, and with his help I shall laugh at whatever you do!'

Because she had defied him publicly, the consul ordered that Agatha be taken off to prison; and to prison she went with great joy, even triumphantly, as if she had been invited to a banquet; and as she went she called upon the Lord to watch over her suffering.

The following day Quintianus said to her: 'Deny Christ and worship my gods!' When she still refused, he had her tied to the rack and tortured. Agatha said: 'In the midst of all these sufferings, I feel only joy, like someone who hears good news, who meets a long-lost friend, or finds some boundless treasure. Wheat cannot be stored in the granary before it is properly threshed and separated from the chaff, and so it is with me – my soul will never enter paradise with the palm of martyrdom unless you have my body flailed by the executioners!' In fury Quintianus ordered them to torture her by crushing her breasts, and when she had suffered in this way for many hours, he finally ordered that her breasts be cut off. 'Impious, cruel, odious tyrant!' Agatha cried. 'How could you do this? Are you not ashamed to take from a woman what your own mother gave you to suck? No matter: I have other breasts you cannot harm, breasts that give spiritual nourishment to all my senses, and them I dedicated long, long ago to God.' Then he had her taken back to prison with strict orders that no doctor should visit her, and nobody should give her bread or water.

Around midnight an old man came to her, led by a boy holding a torch; he was carrying various medicines and said: 'Though that monstrous consul has caused you terrible pain, you caused him more with the answers you gave. He has torn your breasts, but he that tore them will shed tears in plenty! I was there when you were being tortured and I saw then that your breasts could be healed.' Agatha said to him: 'I have never used medicines for my bodily ailments; it would be shameful to lose now what I have preserved so carefully for so long.' 'Your modesty?' the old man said to her. 'My daughter, you need have no fear on that account: I am a Christian, like you.' Agatha replied: 'Indeed, how could I fear for my modesty? You are an old, old man, and my body has been so cruelly treated that no one could feel any desire for me now. But thank you, sir, for your concern.' He asked: 'Then why do you not allow me to heal you?' Agatha replied: 'Because I have Jesus Christ as master, who can cure me with a single word and make me completely better. If he chooses, he can heal me in a moment.' With a smile the old man said: 'And I am his apostle, and he has sent me to you to tell you that you are whole again.'

Immediately the apostle vanished and St Agatha, falling to the ground, gave thanks to God, and, as she did so, discovered that all her wounds were healed and her breasts had miraculously been restored to her! The prison was filled with a light so blinding that the guards fled in terror, leaving the doors open, and some of her fellow prisoners urged her to escape. 'God forbid,' she said, 'that I should flee, and by so doing lose the crown that will reward my suffering, or bring punishment down on the heads of my guards.'

After four days Quintianus commanded her to worship his gods, or suffer even more terrible consequences. Agatha told him: 'Your threats are foolish and vain; worse, they pollute the very air with their wickedness! You poor fool, how could you think I would worship images of stone and renounce the God of heaven, who healed me?'

Quintianus said: 'Who healed you?' Agatha replied: 'Christ, the Son of God.' 'How dare you utter that name again,' Quintianus cried, 'the name I loathe above all others!' Agatha said: 'As long as I live, the name of Christ will be in my heart and on my lips.' 'Very well,' Quintianus said. 'Let us see if Christ will heal you this time!' He had his men put red-hot coals down on the ground and scatter broken tiles on them; then he ordered them to strip Agatha naked and push her back and forth over this bed of fire.

But while this was going on, there was suddenly an almighty earthquake. This shook the whole city so violently that the palace collapsed and killed two of Quintianus's counsellors. The whole population ran to the consul complaining that this was a punishment for his cruelty to Agatha.

Then Quintianus, afraid partly because of the earthquake and partly because the people were rioting, had Agatha taken back to prison. There she began to pray: 'Lord Jesus Christ,' she said, 'you brought me into the world and have guarded me from my infancy; you have saved my body from defilement and kept my heart from love of earthly things; you have enabled me to overcome my sufferings and given me the strength to endure them: receive my soul now and grant me your mercy!' When she had finished praying, she cried aloud and gave up the ghost.

All this took place around the year 253 in the reign of the emperor Decius.

While the faithful were anointing Agatha's body with spices for burial and placing it in a sarcophagus, a young man clad in silk, accompanied by more than a hundred other youths (strangers who had never been seen before in those parts, all of them most handsome and splendidly dressed in white tunics), came up to the body and placed over it a marble tablet, then immediately disappeared from view. On the tablet was the inscription: 'A saintly and generous soul, an honour to God and the saviour of her country.' (In other words, St Agatha was a holy soul; she gave herself freely up to martyrdom, honoured God, and saved her native land from pagan tyranny.) When the story of this miraculous tablet got about, even pagans and Jews began to venerate Agatha's tomb.

As for Quintianus, while he was hurrying off to Agatha's house to see what he could lay his hands on, the two horses pulling his chariot suddenly began to gnash their teeth and run wild. One turned on him and bit him; the other lashed out and kicked him so hard he was pitched into a river. His body was never recovered.

A year after the death of St Agatha a volcano near the city of Catania erupted and belched out a torrent of fire, which came down the mountainside like a mighty flood, melting rocks and scorching the land until, with a terrible roar, it was on the point of devouring the city. The countryfolk came crowding down from the mountainside, ran to St Agatha's tomb, seized the veil which covered the tomb, and placed it right in the path of the advancing flames. The veil halted the fire at once: the flames stopped dead and came no further. This miracle took place on St Agatha's very birthday . . .

18

ST AMAND

6 February

Amand, who was born of noble parents, became a monk while still a youth. One day he was walking through the monastery and came upon a huge serpent, and by the power of prayer and with the sign of the cross he made it go back to its lair never to come out again. He then went to the tomb of St Martin, where he stayed for fifteen years, wearing only a hair-shirt, and existing on a diet of water and barley bread. After this he went to Rome and tried to spend a night in prayer in the church of St Peter, but the custodian there disrespectfully threw him out. Then, at the command of St Peter, who appeared to him as he was sleeping outside the door of the church, he went to Gaul to reprimand King Dagobert for his crimes; but the king indignantly banished him from his kingdom. Now Dagobert was childless, and when after some time his prayers were answered and he was granted a son, he began to consider whom he should ask to baptize the child, and it occurred to him that Amand was the man to do it. He therefore sent men to search for Amand, and when he was brought before him, he fell at the saint's feet and begged him to forgive him and to baptize the son whom the Lord had granted him. Amand willingly agreed to his first request, but, afraid of becoming too involved in worldly affairs, refused his second and went away again. But in the end he gave way to the king's entreaties and agreed to do as he asked. And during the baptism, when nobody else gave the proper response, the infant said: 'Amen.'

After this Dagobert had Amand elevated to the see of Maastricht. But when Amand realized that the vast majority of the people there took no heed of his preaching, he went to Gascony. There, a jester who was poking fun at Amand's preaching was suddenly seized by a demon, and, tearing at his own flesh with his teeth, he confessed that he had wronged the man of God. A moment later he died a miserable death.

One day a fellow bishop saved the water in which the saint had washed his hands and subsequently used it to cure a blind man.

Another time Amand, at the instigation of the king, was about to build a monastery in a certain place, when the bishop of a nearby city, resenting this intrusion, sent his men to kill him, or at least to drive him elsewhere. They tried to trick Amand by asking him to go with them, promising they would show him the best site for his monastery. The saint knew in advance of the mischief they intended, but, because he so longed for martyrdom, he went with them until they reached the top of the mountain where they planned to kill him. But quite suddenly a storm broke out, and the mountain was enveloped in such a violent downpour that they could not even see each other. Thinking they were about to die, they fell to the ground begging the saint's pardon and beseeching him to let them escape with their lives. Amand said a prayer, and in a moment the weather was utterly calm and serene again. The bishop's men at once went back home, and St Amand escaped unharmed to perform many other miracles before finally dying a peaceful death around the year AD 653, in the reign of the emperor Heraclius.

19

ST JULIANA

16 February

Juliana was betrothed to Eulogius, the prefect of Nicomedia, but she refused to marry him unless he accepted the faith of Christ. So her father had her stripped and beaten, then handed her over to the prefect. 'My dearest Juliana,' the prefect said to her, 'why have you so misled me? How can you refuse me like this?' She replied: 'If you worship my God, I will agree to marry you. But otherwise you will never be my husband.' 'My dear, I cannot do that,' the prefect told her, 'because the emperor will have me beheaded.' 'If you are so afraid of a mortal emperor,' Juliana retorted, 'how can you expect me not to fear an emperor who is immortal? Do whatever you want: you will never change my mind.'

So the prefect had her severely flogged, then hung her up by her hair for twelve hours on end while molten lead was poured over her head. When none of this harmed her in the slightest, he bound her in chains and shut her in a dungeon. There, the Devil came to her in the likeness of an angel. 'Juliana,' he said, 'I am an angel of the Lord, and he has sent me to you to tell you that, to save yourself from endless torture and a horrible death, you must sacrifice to the gods.' Juliana wept when she heard this. 'O Lord my God,' she prayed, 'do not let me perish! Show me who this is who is offering me such wicked advice!' And a voice was heard, telling her to lay hold of her visitor and force him to confess his true identity. So she held him tightly, and when she asked him who he was, he told her that he was a demon and that his father had sent him to lead her astray. Juliana asked: 'And who is your father?' 'Beelzebub,' he replied, 'who sends us out to do all sorts of evil, and has us cruelly beaten whenever we let Christians get the better of us. I know I shall pay dearly for failing to outwit you like this!' Among other things he admitted that he was most effectively kept at bay by the Christians when they were celebrating the mystery of the Lord's body, and likewise when they were preaching or praying. Juliana then tied his hands behind his back and gave him a sound thrashing with the chain she had round her, until the Devil cried out and pleaded with her: 'Mistress, have pity!'

At this point the prefect commanded that Juliana should be removed from the dungeon, so out she came, dragging the demon in chains behind her. 'Juliana! Mistress!' the demon begged her. 'Do not mock me any more, or I shall never have the power to lead anyone astray again! Christians are supposed to be merciful, yet you show me no mercy at all!' But she dragged him right across the market place and ended by throwing him in a privy.

When Juliana was finally brought before the prefect, he had her stretched on a wheel until all her bones cracked and the marrow shot out. But an angel of the Lord smashed the wheel in pieces and healed her in a moment. Everyone who witnessed this miracle was converted, and subsequently suffered martyrdom. Five hundred men and one hundred and thirty women were beheaded on the spot. Juliana was then placed in a cauldron full of molten lead, but the lead cooled and seemed to her no warmer than bath water. The prefect cursed his gods for being incapable of punishing a young girl who was bringing such disgrace upon them. He then ordered Juliana to be beheaded. While she was being taken off to her place of execution, the demon to whom she had given the beating appeared in the form of a young man and shouted loudly: 'Show her no mercy! She has vilified your gods, and last night she gave me a wicked beating! So give her what she deserves!' Juliana opened her eyes a little to see who was saying all this, and the demon cried: 'Help! Help! I think she wants to catch me and tie me up again!' and promptly vanished. After Juliana had been beheaded the prefect was drowned in a storm at sea together with thirty-four of his men, and when the sea threw up their bodies on the shore, they were devoured by wild beasts and birds of prey.

20

ST MATTHIAS,
APOSTLE

24 February

Matthias was the apostle who took the place of Judas, but first let us briefly consider the birth and origins of Judas himself.

According to one history, which is admittedly apocryphal, there was a man in Jerusalem called Ruben, otherwise known as Simon, of the tribe of Dan (or, according to Jerome, of the tribe of Issachar), who was married to a woman named Cyborea. One night, after they had paid each other their conjugal dues, Cyborea fell asleep and had a dream which, groaning and sobbing with terror, she related to her husband. 'I dreamt I was giving birth to a child,' she told him, 'a son so wicked that he would cause the ruin of all our people!' 'What a ghastly dream!' Ruben exclaimed. 'You must never tell a soul about this. You must have been the victim of some demonic delusion!' 'If I find I have conceived and bear a son,' she warned him, 'we shall know for certain that this was a genuine revelation, and not a delusion at all.' In due course a son was born, and his parents were full of foreboding and began to wonder what to do with the child. They were horrified at the thought of killing him, but determined not to raise him to bring ruin on their people; so they put him in a wicker basket and set him adrift at sea, and the waves carried him to an island called Scarioth (from where Judas subsequently took his name Iscariot). Now the queen of this island, who was childless, had gone down to the seashore for a walk and, seeing the basket bobbing about in the waves, had it fetched and opened. In it she discovered a handsome baby boy and, with a sigh, she said: 'Ah, if only I could have a bonny child like this! What a comfort to know there would be someone to succeed to my kingdom!' So she had the child nursed in secret and meanwhile pretended to be pregnant. Then, when she judged the time right, she announced that she had given birth to a son, and the news spread through the length and breadth of the kingdom. The king was absolutely jubilant at the birth of his son and so were all his people, and the boy was brought up in a style befitting a prince. But not long afterwards the queen conceived a child of the king's, and in due course gave birth to a son. When the boys grew up, they often played together, and Judas would tease and bully the king's son and frequently made him cry. This upset the queen, especially since she knew he was not her real son; but though she beat him time and time again, Judas continued his bullying. In the end the truth came out, and it became known that Judas was not the queen's child but a foundling. When Judas himself found out, he was utterly humiliated, and he crept up on the king's son – the one he had thought was his brother – and murdered him. Then, fearing he might be condemned to death for this crime, he took up with some men who had come to pay the king tribute money and fled to Jerusalem. There he attached himself to the court of Pilate, who was governor, and, since like attracts like, Pilate soon found that Judas and he saw eye to eye and became very fond of him. Eventually he made Judas chief minister of his court, and his power there was absolute.

One day Pilate was looking down from his palace into an orchard and he was seized with such a craving for the fruit he saw growing there that he thought he would faint. This orchard belonged to Ruben, Judas's father, but neither knew of the other's existence, because Ruben thought Judas had perished at sea, and Judas had no idea who his father was or where he lived. Pilate called for Judas and told him: 'I want that fruit so badly that if I cannot have it, I shall die!' So Judas hurried off, vaulted into the orchard, and quickly picked some apples. But while he was there, Ruben suddenly appeared and caught him in the act. They began to argue heatedly; this led to insults, the insults led to fighting, and they were both hurt in the exchange. In the end Judas struck Ruben at the base of his neck with a stone and killed him. He then made off with his apples and told Pilate what had happened. Day waned, and as night came on Ruben's body was discovered, and it was thought he had died suddenly of natural causes. Pilate subsequently made over all Ruben's possessions to Judas, and in addition gave him Cyborea, Ruben's wife, to marry. Then one day Judas heard his wife sighing deeply and he begged her to tell him what was the matter. 'Alas,' she replied, 'I am the unhappiest of women! I drowned my baby boy in the sea and then found my husband dead, and now, in the midst of all my sorrow and absolutely against my wishes, Pilate has added the crowning misery and made me marry you!' And when she told him all about her baby son and Judas related all his adventures, it became clear that Judas had married his own mother and killed his own father. He was overwhelmed with remorse, and at his mother's suggestion went to our Lord Jesus Christ and begged forgiveness for his sins. (The story thus far is found in the apocryphal history mentioned above. Whether or not the tale is worth repeating must be left to the reader's judgement, though it should probably be rejected as fancy rather than accepted as fact.)

The Lord made Judas his disciple and later chose him to be an apostle, and he was so close to him and so fond of him that he entrusted all money matters to the very man who later was to betray him. For it was Judas who carried the disciples' money, and he was thus able to steal the offerings that were given to Christ. At the time of the Lord's passion, when Judas deplored the fact that the ointment worth three hundred *denarii* had not been sold, it was only because then he could have stolen that, too. Then he went off and sold his master for thirty pieces of silver, and since each piece was worth ten *denarii*, he made good his loss of three hundred *denarii* for the ointment (or, as some say, he always stole a tenth of everything that was given to Christ, and so he sold his master for a tenth of what he had lost on the ointment, i.e. three hundred *denarii*). However, he instantly regretted doing so, and took back the money and went away and hanged himself, and as he hung on the tree, his stomach burst asunder and all his entrails spilled out. But nothing issued from his mouth, because it was not fitting that a mouth that had kissed the glorious lips of Christ should be so foully defiled. However, it was perfectly fitting that the entrails which had conceived Christ's betrayal should burst apart and pour out, and that the throat through which the traitor's voice had issued should be throttled by a halter. Also he died hanging in the air, because he had offended both the angels in heaven and men on earth, so it was right that he should be kept from the regions inhabited by angels and men, and left in mid-air with the demons for company.

In the time between the Ascension and Pentecost, the apostles were gathered in the upper room, and Peter, aware that they were now fewer than twelve, which was the number the Lord had chosen to preach the faith of the Trinity in the four corners of the earth, rose to his feet and addressed his brother apostles: 'Brothers,' he said, 'we must appoint someone in Judas's place, someone to bear witness with us to the resurrection of Christ, because the Lord told us: "You will be my witnesses in Jerusalem and in all Judaea and in Samaria and to the very ends of the earth" [Acts 1:8]. And since a witness can only bear witness to what he has seen, we must choose one of those who have constantly been with us, and seen the Lord's miracles and heard his teaching.' So they brought forward two of the seventy-two disciples:

Joseph, who was called 'the Just' because of his holiness of life, the brother of James, son of Alpheus; and Matthias, of whom we are told nothing more than that he was chosen as an apostle, which is praise enough. They then said a prayer: 'Lord, you know the hearts of all men. Show us which of these two you have chosen to take over the ministry and apostolate forfeited by Judas.' They then cast lots and the lot fell on Matthias, so he was counted as one of the twelve . . .

The apostle Matthias was subsequently assigned to Judaea, where he preached zealously, and after performing many miracles died a peaceful death. In some manuscripts, however, we read that he was crucified and went up to heaven wearing the martyr's crown. His body is said to have been buried in a tomb of porphyry in the church of Santa Maria Maggiore in Rome, where his head is displayed to the faithful.

According to another legend, which is preserved at Trier,[1] we read among other things that Matthias was of the tribe of Judah and was born in Bethlehem of illustrious parents. As to his education, he quickly gained a profound knowledge of the Law and the Prophets, turned his back on all frivolous pastimes, and by the maturity of his character triumphed over all the temptations of youth. He directed all his inclinations towards virtue and was of exceptional intelligence, always ready to show compassion, in prosperity unassuming, in adversity resolute and fearless. He strove to practise what he preached, and to illustrate in his own actions the principles of his teaching. During the time he was preaching in Judaea, he gave sight to the blind, healed lepers, exorcized demons, made the lame walk and the deaf hear, and brought the dead back to life. When he was taken before the high priest and arraigned on a number of charges, he replied: 'I will not waste words rebutting the charges you are making against me – "crimes" as you call them – for to be a Christian is no crime; it is the highest glory.' The high priest asked him: 'If we give you time to reconsider, will you relent?' 'God forbid,' Matthias said, 'that, having found the truth, I should recant and abandon it!'

Matthias was extremely learned in the Law, pure of heart, of high intelligence, expert at solving problems in Holy Scripture, far-sighted in his judgement and a gifted speaker. While he was preaching the word of God in Judaea, the marvels and miracles he performed converted many to the faith. But this incurred the jealousy of the Jews, and they brought him before the council. Two false witnesses, the ones who had brought the accusations against him, were the first to begin stoning him, and Matthias insisted that the stones they threw should be buried with him as evidence against them. During the stoning he was beheaded with an axe, according to the Roman custom, and as the axe fell, he raised his hands to heaven and gave up his soul to God. The same legend adds that his body was translated from Judaea to Rome and from Rome to Trier.

In yet another legend we read that Matthias went to Macedonia and preached there. He was given a poisoned drink, which blinded everyone who drank it, but Matthias invoked the name of Christ, drank it and was none the worse. This poison had blinded more than two hundred and fifty people, but by laying his hands upon them, one by one, Matthias restored their sight. The Devil now appeared to them in the shape of a young child and persuaded them to kill the saint for putting an end to their religion. Matthias was right under their noses, and they looked for him for three days and still could not find him. But on the third day he came out into the open and said: 'Here I am!' They tied his hands behind his back, put a noose round his neck, and manhandled him cruelly before shutting him in prison. There demons appeared, gnashing their teeth at him, but they could not get at Matthias because suddenly, in a great blaze of light, the Lord was with him, and he lifted him from the ground, loosening his bonds, and with sweet words of comfort opened the prison door. So Matthias escaped and began to preach the word of the Lord yet again. Some still obstinately refused to listen and he told them: 'I warn you, you will go down to hell alive!' Instantly the earth yawned open and swallowed them, and the rest were converted to the Lord.

ST GREGORY

12 March

Gregory was of senatorial stock; his father was named Gordianus and his mother Silvia. While still in his youth he attained the highest level of philosophic learning and was also possessed of enormous wealth; but still he thought of abandoning all this and giving himself up to the religious life. For some time, however, he put off this conversion and thought he might serve Christ better if, in appearance at least, he remained a layman and performed the duties of an urban prefect. But a host of worldly affairs so utterly engrossed him that his attachment to earthly things ceased to be a pretence and became a reality.

After the death of his father Gregory had six monasteries built in Sicily and established a seventh in his own home, within the walls of Rome, which he dedicated to St Andrew the Apostle. There, abandoning his silken robes glistening with gold and gemstones, he would cover himself in the coarse habit of a monk. In a short time he attained to such a degree of sanctity that even in the earliest days of his conversion he could be numbered among the most perfect of Christians. Indeed, some idea of his perfection can be gauged from the preface he wrote to his *Dialogues*, where he says: 'My poor spirit, crushed by the weight of its present occupations, recalls how different life was in the monastery, how it let the world flow past beneath it, how it rose high above all the things of life; that it had been accustomed to think of nothing but the things of heaven; that even while still restrained in the body, it could transcend the limitations of the flesh in contemplation; and it was in love with death, which most people regard as such a painful thing, because it was the doorway to life and the reward for all its labours.' Finally he inflicted such austerities on his body that his stomach was weakened and he scarcely stayed alive: he suffered fainting fits (called '*syncope*' by the Greeks) during which he experienced such difficulty in breathing that for hours at a time he seemed near to death.

One day Gregory was sitting in the monastery where he was abbot, writing, when an angel of the Lord came to him disguised as a shipwrecked sailor and tearfully asked him to have pity. Gregory had six silver pieces given to him and off he went, but he returned the same day and said that, in comparison with all he had lost, what he had been given was little. Gregory gave him the same sum as before, but the sailor came back a third time and begged insistently and loudly for more alms. When Gregory was told by the steward of his monastery that there was nothing left to give except the silver dish on which Gregory's mother used to put the vegetables she sent him, he immediately gave instructions for this to be given to the castaway, who eagerly took it and went happily away. But the castaway was an angel of the Lord, as he afterwards revealed to the saint.

One day, while St Gregory was crossing the forum in Rome, he noticed some young slaves up for sale. They were all of splendid physique, and had handsome faces and dazzling blond hair. So he asked the dealer where he had got them, and he replied: 'From Britain. All the natives there have the same fair colouring as these do.' Then he asked if they were Christians. 'No,' the dealer told him, 'they are all in the grip of pagan cults.' Gregory gave a deep groan. 'Alas,' he said, 'how sad that the prince of darkness should still possess such glorious faces!' Then he asked the name of their race. 'They are called Angles,' the man replied. 'They are well named,' Gregory said. ' "Angles" sounds like "angels", and their faces are angelic.' Then he asked the name of their province, and the man replied that their people were called the Deiri. 'They are well named,' Gregory remarked, 'because they must be saved from God's ire [Latin: '*de ira*'].' And when he asked the name of their king, the dealer told him he was called Aelle. 'Aelle, too, is well named,' Gregory said, 'for the Alleluia must be sung in his kingdom.'

Gregory went straight to the supreme pontiff and earnestly and insistently pleaded with him to send him to convert the British people. This request the pope finally granted. But when he was already on his way there, the people of Rome, greatly perturbed at his departure, went to the pope and expressed their displeasure. 'You have offended St Peter,' they protested, 'and you have destroyed Rome. Yes, you have sent Gregory away!' These accusations alarmed the pope, who dispatched messengers to recall the saint. Gregory, after travelling for three days, had made a stop, and while his companions were resting he was reading a book, when a locust alighted on him and forced him to pause. And when he considered the name of this creature, he realized it was telling him that he should stay in that locality [Latin: *locusta* = locust, here derived from *locus* = place and *stare* = stay]. The realization came to him in a flash of inspiration, so he urged his companions to press on with all speed. No sooner had they gone than the pope's couriers appeared, and he was compelled to return with them, reluctant though he was to do so. The pope subsequently removed him from his monastery and ordained him as his cardinal deacon.

One day the Tiber overflowed its banks and rose so high that its waters poured over the city walls and caused the collapse of many houses. The river carried a great number of serpents and a huge dragon down to the sea, but they drowned in the waves and were thrown up on the shore, and the whole atmosphere was polluted with the stench of their rotting bodies. A terrible pestilence ensued, called the bubonic plague, and people claimed that they could actually see arrows falling from heaven and striking victims down. Pope Pelagius was the first to be stricken by the plague, and he died almost at once. Then the disease ran amok through the whole population, and wreaked such havoc that many families were wiped out and houses stood empty throughout the city.

But since God's Church could not be left without a leader, the people unanimously elected Gregory as pontiff, though he did all he could to resist them. When the time came for him to be consecrated, the plague was still ravaging the populace, so he preached a sermon to the people, organized a procession, ordered the singing of litanies, and urged everyone to show more perseverance in their prayers. While the entire population of the city was at prayer, however, the plague raged among them to such deadly effect that ninety men died in a single hour; but Gregory, undeterred, continued to urge them to keep praying and not to stop until God's mercy drove the plague from the city.

After the procession Gregory planned to flee from Rome, but since guards were posted at the gates day and night to look out for him, he was unable to get away. Finally he disguised himself and got some merchants to put him in a wine barrel and smuggle him out of the city on a waggon. When in due course he reached a wood, he looked for a cave to hide in, and for three days lay low. Meanwhile the people were out searching for him everywhere, when a brilliant shaft of light streamed from heaven and hung over the spot where Gregory was hiding, and on it a hermit saw angels ascending and descending. So in no time the people caught him, and, against his will, he was taken back to Rome and consecrated as supreme pontiff. Gregory's reluctance to be elevated to a position of such pre-eminence can clearly be seen in his writings. In his letter to the patrician Narsus he says: 'When you describe the profound joys of contemplation, you cause me to grieve afresh for my own ruin. It reminds me of all the inward happiness I have lost, while outwardly, without deserving it, I have risen to the loftiest pinnacle of power. Truly I am so unhappy that I can scarcely speak of it! So do not call me "Naomi" [Hebrew: 'my beautiful one'], call me "Mara" [Hebrew: 'my bitter one'], because of the bitterness I feel [Ruth 1:20].'[1] Elsewhere he wrote: 'If you love me, weep when you learn that I have been raised to the rank of bishop, because I myself weep without ceasing, and ask you to pray to God for me.' In the preface to his *Dialogues* he writes: 'Because of my pastoral duties my soul has to concern itself with the affairs of worldly men, and, after knowing the beauty of inward quiet, finds itself besmirched by the dust of earthly business. So I consider what I have to endure and what I have lost. And when I contemplate what I have lost, my burden grows heavier. For here I am tossed by the waves of a mighty sea, and in the vessel of my spirit I am battered by raging storm winds; and when I recall my former life, I look back, I see the shore behind me and I sigh.'

But the plague was still ravaging Rome, and Gregory ordered the traditional procession to do the rounds of the city at Eastertide to the singing of litanies, and an image of Blessed Mary Ever Virgin was carried in great reverence at its head. (This, they say, is the image in the church of Santa Maria Maggiore in Rome, which was painted by St Luke, a doctor by profession, but also an excellent artist, and it is alleged to be a perfect resemblance of the Virgin in every detail.) Miraculously all the pollution and noisome vapours yielded before her, as if fleeing from her and unable to bear her presence, and in her wake she left a supernatural calm, and the air was pure again. Also, the story goes that angel voices were heard round the image singing '*Regina coeli, laetare, alleluia, / Quia quem meruisti portare, alleluia, / Resurrexit, sicut dixit, alleluia!*' ['Queen of Heaven, rejoice, alleluia, / Because he whom you were meet to bear, alleluia, / Has arisen as he promised, alleluia!'], to which St Gregory instantly added: '*Ora pro nobis Deum, rogamus, alleluia!*' ['Pray to God for us, we beg you, alleluia!']. Then, above the castle of Crescentius, St Gregory saw an angel of the Lord wiping a bloody sword and replacing it in its sheath, and he realized that this meant the end of the plague. And so it turned out. Thereafter, the castle of Crescentius was called the Castle of the Angel.

At a later date Pope Gregory sent Augustine, Mellitus, John and others as missionaries to England, as he had so long been determined to do, and by his prayers and merits the natives were converted to the faith.

St Gregory was possessed of such humility that he would not allow anyone to praise him. Witness his reply to Stephen, a bishop who had written him congratulatory letters: 'In your letters you pay me great compliments – far more than I in my unworthiness deserve to hear – though it is written: "Praise no man while he lives." However, though I did not deserve to hear such things, I beg you to pray for me that I may become worthy of them, and that, if you have ascribed to me virtues which I do not possess, I may henceforth possess them because you said that I did.' Likewise he wrote in a letter to the patrician Narsus: 'When in your letters to me you seek to match the man to his great office, and use such grandiose and bombastic rhetoric, I assure you, dearest brother, you are calling a lion what is, in fact, no more than a monkey: you are as wide of the mark as people who call mangy little kittens "Leopard" or "Tiger"!' Likewise in a letter to Anastasius, patriarch of Antioch: 'When you call me "mouth of the Lord" and refer to me as a "luminary", because you say my preaching benefits so many people and has the power to enlighten them, I confess you raise in me the most serious doubts about your judgement. For when I consider who I am, I can detect no trace of any of the virtues you name; then again, when I consider who you are, I do not think that you can be lying. So, when I am inclined to believe what you say, my frailty forbids me; when I am inclined to dispute what is said in my praise, your holiness contradicts me. But I beg you, your Grace, let some good come to us out of this disagreement, and if what you say about me is not so, let it be so because it is you who say it.' All titles which sounded high-flown or privileged he utterly rejected: hence his response to Eusebius, patriarch of Alexandria, who had called him 'universal pope': 'At the head of the letter you have sent me you have taken it upon yourself to address me by the grandiose title of "universal pope". I beg your dear holiness not to do this again, because paying another more honour than reason demands only robs you of your own. For I have no wish to be dignified by titles, but rather by uprightness of character, and I cannot regard as an honour anything which exalts me at the expense of my brothers. So let there be an end of expressions which inflate vanity and offend one's love for others.' Similarly when John, bishop of Constantinople, applied to himself this vainglorious title and, by fraudulent means, won from the Synod the right to be called 'universal pope', St Gregory wrote, among other things,

94

the following about him: 'Who is this man who, in defiance of the precepts of the Gospel and canonical decrees, presumes to lay claim to a new title for himself; who seeks to be "universal" so that he alone can reign supreme?'

He refused to have his bishops speak of his 'commands'. Hence he says in a letter to Eulogius, bishop of Alexandria: 'Your Grace writes to me saying "as you have commanded". Please never let me hear that word "command" again, because I know who I am and I know who you are. In point of status you bishops are my brothers, but in holiness my fathers.' Also, because of his extraordinary humility Gregory would not let women call themselves his 'handmaids'. Hence he wrote to Rusticana, a patrician lady: 'There was one thing in your letter to which I took exception, something which might be said once, perhaps, but was said time and time again: "your maidservant". When I took on the duties of bishop, I became the servant of all: why then do you speak of yourself as my "maidservant"? Even before assuming the office of bishop I was yours to command. So I beg you, by Almighty God, do not ever let me find that word in your letters again!'

St Gregory was the first pope to style himself 'servant of the servants of God', and he established the use of this title among his successors. So humble was he that he was unwilling to have his books published in his lifetime. In comparison with those of other writers he considered them worthless. Thus he wrote to Innocent, governor of Africa: 'You have expressed the wish to have my exegesis of Job sent to you, and I am delighted by your interest. But if you want to nourish your soul on the most exquisite food, read the treatises of your compatriot, the blessed Augustine. Do not set my bran beside his fine flour! Indeed, I do not wish anything I may chance to have said to become common knowledge during my lifetime.' We also read in a book translated from Greek into Latin that a holy monk named John came to Rome to visit the churches of the apostles, and when he saw the blessed Pope Gregory walking through the city centre, he wanted to meet him and pay him due reverence. But blessed Gregory, seeing that the monk was about to prostrate himself, quickly fell to the ground before him and would not get up before the monk had done so first. This is another illustration of his profound humility.

So great was his generosity in almsgiving that he supplied the needs not only of the local people, but also of those far removed, for example the monks of Mount Sinai. He kept a written record of the names of all the needy, and was liberal in providing for them. He founded a monastery in Jerusalem and ensured that the servants of God who lived there were sent all the necessities of life. He also used annually to donate eighty pounds of gold for the daily expenses incurred by three thousand nuns. And every day he would invite pilgrims to his table. One day one of these pilgrims came to dine, and Gregory was about to pour water over his hands as a gesture of humility; he turned to pick up a jug, turned back a moment later, and found that the pilgrim had vanished. For some time Gregory was puzzled by what had happened, but that same night the Lord spoke to him in a vision: 'On other occasions you have received me in my members, but yesterday you received me in person.'

Another time he told his steward to invite twelve pilgrims to dinner, and the steward hurried to carry out his orders. But when they were all seated together, the pope looked up and counted thirteen: he called the steward and asked him why, contrary to his instructions, he had presumed to invite thirteen guests. The steward counted the guests and, finding there were only twelve, said: 'Believe me, father, there are only twelve.' Then Gregory noticed that a guest who was seated nearby kept changing his appearance: one moment he was a youth, the next he was a venerable old man with white hair. So when dinner was over, he took him into his private chamber and asked him to be good enough to tell him his name. The man replied: 'Why do you ask my name, which is a name of wonder?[2] However, I am that castaway to whom you gave the silver dish on which your mother used to put the vegetables she sent you, and be assured of this: from the very day on which you gave it to me, the Lord destined you to become the head of his Church and the successor of the apostle Peter.' Gregory said: 'How did you know that the Lord destined me to govern his Church?' 'Because I am his angel,' came the reply, 'and the Lord sent me back to you so that I may protect you always, and all that you seek through me you may obtain from him.' And in that moment he vanished.

At that time there was a hermit, a man of great holiness, who had left everything for God and possessed nothing except a cat, which he would stroke and fondle on his lap, and treat almost as if it were his wife. This hermit in prayer asked God to deign to reveal to him, who for love of him possessed no earthly riches, the soul with whom he might hope to share a dwelling place in heaven. Then one night it was revealed to him that he might hope to dwell with Gregory, the Roman pontiff. At this the hermit groaned aloud, considering that his voluntary poverty had been of little benefit to him if his reward was to share eternity with a man who enjoyed such an abundance of earthly riches. Day in, day out, he ruefully compared his own poverty with Gregory's wealth, until one night he heard the Lord saying to him: 'It is not the possession of wealth that makes a man rich, but the lust for riches. So how dare you compare your poverty with Gregory's riches, when you clearly show every day that you love that cat of yours, which you sit there stroking, more than he loves all his wealth – wealth which so far from prizing, he actually despises and gives away freely to all and sundry!' So the hermit gave thanks to God, and, whereas at first he had thought sharing a place in heaven with Gregory would be scant reward for his piety, he now prayed that one day he might become worthy of dwelling in heaven with such a man.

When Gregory was falsely accused before Emperor Maurice and his sons of doing away with a certain bishop, he wrote a letter to the emperor's secretary in which he said: 'There is one small thing you might bring to the attention of my lords: if I, their servant, had wished to become involved in killing Lombards and causing them harm, then today the Lombard people would have no king, no duke, no counts: it would be a ruined nation! But because I fear God, I would be afraid to cause the death of any man.' His humility was such that, supreme pontiff though he was, he called himself the emperor's servant, and the emperor his lord. And witness his innocence, which was such that he refused to countenance the death of his own enemies.

When the emperor Maurice was persecuting Gregory and the Church of God, Gregory wrote to him, among other things, the following: 'Because I am a sinner, I believe that the more cruelly you persecute me, the more you win the approval of God Almighty, so badly do I serve him.'

One day a man dressed in a monk's habit stood fearlessly before Maurice, brandished a sword in his right hand, and predicted that the emperor would die by the sword. Terrified, Maurice stopped persecuting Gregory and earnestly begged him to pray that God would punish him for his wrongdoings in this life and not defer his punishment until the Last Judgement. Then one day Maurice saw himself standing before the judge's tribunal, and the judge was calling out: 'Bring Maurice forward!' The attendants seized him and set him before the judge. The judge said: 'Where do you wish me to pay you back for the wrongs you have done in this world?' Maurice replied: 'Punish me here, my lord, and not in the world to come!' At once a voice from heaven commanded that Maurice, his wife, sons and daughters should be handed over to a soldier named Phocas to be put to death. And so it happened. Not long afterwards a soldier called Phocas put the emperor and his whole family to the sword, and himself succeeded to the throne.

When Gregory was celebrating mass one Easter Sunday in Santa Maria Maggiore and pronounced the words: '*Pax Domini*' ['The peace of the Lord (be with you)'], an angel of the Lord gave the loud response: '*Et cum spiritu tuo*' ['And with thy spirit']. In memory of this, the pope celebrates a Station Mass on Easter day in Santa Maria Maggiore, and when he intones the *Pax Domini*, in memory of this miracle there is no response.

Once, when the Roman emperor Trajan was hurrying off to war, a widow came up to him in tears and said: 'Please, I beg of you, avenge the blood of my son! He has been killed unjustly!' Trajan promised to do so, if he returned home safely. 'And who will help me,' the widow replied, 'if you are killed in battle?' Trajan said: 'Whoever is emperor after me.' 'And what good will it do to you,' the widow asked, 'if someone else redresses my wrongs?' 'None whatsoever,' Trajan agreed. 'Then would it not be better,' said the widow, 'for you to redress my wrong yourself and receive the reward for it yourself than to leave it to someone else?' Trajan was moved to pity, got down from his horse, and saw to it there and then that the young man's death was avenged.

There is also a story that one of Trajan's sons, while racing his horse through the city at a reckless speed, ran into the son of a widow and killed him. When the widow tearfully explained to Trajan what had happened, he handed over to her the son who was responsible in place of her dead son, and gave her a generous endowment as well.

One day, long after the death of Trajan, Gregory was crossing Trajan's Forum and was reminded of the emperor's clemency when giving judgement. He went to the basilica of St Peter and there wept bitterly for the emperor's pagan beliefs. A voice from heaven answered him: 'I have fulfilled your petition, and spared Trajan eternal punishment. But henceforth you must take care not to offer prayers for a soul that is damned.' John Damascene, too, in one of his sermons, relates that Gregory, while praying earnestly for Trajan, heard a voice from heaven saying: 'I have heard your voice, and I pardon Trajan.' This fact is attested, he adds in the same sermon, by both East and West.

On this subject some have said that Trajan was restored to life and subsequently obtained grace and earned pardon, and so won glory and was not finally consigned to hell, nor condemned to eternal punishment by an irrevocable sentence.[3] Others have said that Trajan's soul was not simply absolved from guilt and condemnation to eternal punishment, but that this punishment was suspended for a certain time, that is to say until the Day of Judgement. Others again say that his punishment, in terms of its place and method, was assessed only conditionally, in other words until the prayers of St Gregory, through the grace of Christ, won Trajan a commutation in these respects. Others, like John the Deacon, who compiled this legend of the saint, say that Gregory did not pray, but only wept; that the Lord frequently takes pity and grants what man may long for, but does not presume to ask, and that Trajan's soul was not delivered from hell and placed in paradise, but simply freed from the torments of hell. The soul (as John says) can be in hell, and yet, through the mercy of God, not feel the torments of hell. Yet others say that eternal punishment consists of two kinds of pain: the pain of sensation and the pain of loss (meaning privation of the sight of God). As to the first pain, Trajan's punishment was remitted, but as to the second, it was upheld.

The story is told that the angel who spoke to Gregory also said: 'Because you pleaded for a damned soul, you must choose one of two punishments: either to be tormented in purgatory for two days, or to be laid low for the rest of your life with sickness and pain.' Gregory preferred to be racked with aches and pains for the rest of his life rather than to be tormented in purgatory for two days. So from that time he was constantly fighting fevers, troubled by gout, racked with griping pains all over, or prey to the most excruciating stomach-aches. In this connection he wrote in one of his letters: 'I suffer so much from gout and other pains that my life is a most terrible punishment to me. Every day I faint with the pain and sigh with longing for the release of death.' In another letter he says: 'Sometimes the pain is slight, sometimes unbearable, but never so slight that it goes away, nor so unbearable that it kills me. So every day I am at death's door, yet death always repulses me. I am so poisoned by noxious humours that living is a torment, and I wait longingly for death, which I think is the sole remedy for my miseries.'

There was a woman who used every Sunday to bake altar-breads and present them to Gregory. One day, during the celebration of mass, when Gregory held out to her the body of the Lord, with the words: '*Corpus Domini Jesu Christi proficiat tibi in vitam aeternam*' ['The body of our Lord Jesus Christ preserve you unto everlasting life'], the woman let out a hoot of laughter. Gregory immediately withdrew his hand from her mouth, placed the conse-crated particle on the altar, then asked the woman, in front of the whole congregation, why she had dared to laugh. She replied: 'Because you were calling the bread, which I made with my own hands, the "body of the Lord"!' Gregory prostrated himself and prayed forgiveness for the woman's incredulity, and when he rose again he found that the particle of bread had turned into flesh, in the shape of a finger. The woman's faith was instantly restored. Then Gregory prayed a second time, saw the flesh turn to bread again, and handed it to the woman, who made her communion.

Some princes asked Gregory to supply them with a precious relic, and he gave them a fragment of St John the Evangelist's dalmatic, but, suspecting that the relic was worthless, they indignantly returned it to him. St Gregory said a prayer, asked for a knife and stabbed at the cloth, and blood streamed at once from the cuts he had made. So Gregory demonstrated, by means of a miracle, how precious the relic really was.

A rich Roman left his wife and as a result was excommunicated by the pope. He was greatly aggrieved by this, but, being unable to flout the authority of the supreme pontiff, sought the aid of sorcerers. These sorcerers promised to use their spells to make a demon enter the pope's horse and drive it so wild that anyone who rode it would be in peril of his life. So when Gregory was riding by one day, the sorcerers sent a demon into his horse and tormented the animal so cruelly that no one was able to hold it. But it was revealed to Gregory that a demon had entered into his horse, and, by making the sign of the cross, he delivered it from the madness that had seized it; what was more, the sorcerers were struck permanently blind. They subsequently admitted their guilt, and later attained the grace of baptism. Gregory refused to restore to them their power of sight, in case they might take up their sorcery again; but he did order that they should be cared for at the expense of the Church.

We also read in the book which the Greeks call *Lymon*[4] that the abbot who ruled St Gregory's monastery reported to the saint that one of his monks had in his possession three pieces of silver. So, to instil fear into the rest of the community, Gregory excommunicated the monk. Later, when the guilty monk died, Gregory was not told, and when he found out, he was incensed that the monk had died without absolution and wrote a prayer as his epitaph, in which he released the dead man from the bond of excommunication. He gave the prayer to one of his deacons with orders to read it over the grave of the dead brother. This the deacon did, and the following night the dead monk appeared to the abbot and declared to him that he had been until now held in prison, but that yesterday he had been set free.

Gregory was responsible for instituting the offices and chants of the Church, and he also established a school for cantors: for this he had two houses built, one beside the basilica of St Peter, the other near the Lateran church. There to this very day are preserved, with fitting veneration, the couch on which the saint reclined when teaching and the rod with which he threatened the choristers, together with an original antiphonary in his own hand. To the canon of the mass he added the words: *'diesque nostros in tua pace disponas atque ab aeterna damnatione nos eripi et in electorum tuorum jubeas grege numerari'* ['and grant us thy peace in our day, order us to be saved from eternal damnation, and to be numbered in the flock of thine elect']. Finally, full of good works, the blessed Gregory departed this life, having been pope for thirteen years, six months and ten days. On his tomb the following verses are inscribed:

> *Suscipe terra tuo corpus de corpore sumptum,*
> *Reddere quod valeas vivificante Deo.*
> *Spiritus astra petit, leti nil iura nocebunt,*
> *Cui vitae alterius mors magis ipsa via est.*
> *Pontificis summi hoc clauduntur membra sepulchro,*
> *Qui innumeris semper vixit ubique bonis.*

['Receive, earth, the body taken from your body / For you to give back when God revives it. / The spirit climbs to the stars, no powers of hell shall harm / One for whom death itself is the way to the other life. / In this tomb are enclosed the remains of the supreme pontiff / Who was always and everywhere known for his countless good works.']

Gregory died in the year AD 604, during the reign of Phocas . . .

ST LONGINUS

15 March

Longinus was a centurion who with other soldiers stood at the foot of the Lord's cross, and at Pilate's command pierced the Lord's side with a spear. Then, when he saw the miracles which followed his death, the eclipse of the sun and the earthquake, he believed in Christ. But, according to some, the chief factor in his conversion was more personal: either because of some disease, or because of his age, Longinus was all but blind, but when Christ's blood ran down his spear on to his hands, and he then got some of it in his eyes, he could instantly see quite clearly. He subsequently gave up soldiering and was instructed in the faith by the apostles at Caesarea in Cappadocia. The next twenty-eight years he led the life of a monk, and converted many to the faith by his teaching and example. Finally he was arrested by the governor and ordered to offer sacrifice to the idols, and, when he refused, the governor had all his teeth torn out and his tongue cut off. But Longinus had not lost the power of speech: he got hold of an axe and smashed all the idols in pieces and cried: 'Now we shall see if they are gods or not!' The demons came out of the idols and entered the governor and his aides, who went berserk and, barking like dogs, fell at Longinus's feet. 'Why do you live in idols?' Longinus demanded. They replied: 'We can only live where Christ's name is never heard and the sign of the cross is never seen!' Now the governor, while ranting and raging, had lost his eyesight, and Longinus told him: 'Believe me, you cannot be healed until you have killed me. As soon as I am dead, I will pray for you and God will restore your body and soul to health.'

So the governor had Longinus beheaded at once; then he went over to where his body lay and fell down before it, weeping with remorse. Instantly his sight and sanity were restored to him, and he devoted the rest of his life to good works.

ST BENEDICT

21 March

Benedict was born in the province of Nursia and subsequently sent to Rome to study the liberal arts; but while still young he abandoned his studies and decided to lead a solitary life. His nurse, who loved him dearly, went with him until they came to a place called Enfide. There, while bread-making one day, she managed to break a sieve she had borrowed to sift grain, putting it down rather clumsily on the table, and it fell in two pieces. When Benedict saw her weeping, he picked up the two pieces and with a prayer joined them together again, so the sieve was as good as new.

After a while he ran away from his nurse and found a cave where he stayed for three years, unknown to anyone except a monk called Romanus, who kindly provided him with the necessities of life. Since Benedict's cave was almost inaccessible, Romanus used to climb above it, tie loaves of bread to a long rope, and lower them to the mouth of the cave. He also attached a bell to the rope so the holy man should know when to come out and take the bread. But the Ancient Enemy, envying the one his charity and the other his food, threw a stone and broke the bell. But even so Romanus continued to look after the hermit. And subsequently, when a certain priest was preparing his dinner on Easter Sunday, the Lord appeared to him and said: 'While you are making a delicious meal for yourself, on the mountainside nearby a servant of mine is dying of hunger.' The priest left at once, and after a lengthy search he found the hermit and said: 'Come, let us eat this meal together: it is Easter Day.' 'It must indeed be Easter,' Benedict replied, 'if I am blessed with visitors like you.' (For, far removed from civilization as he was, he did not know that it was Easter Sunday.) The priest said: 'I assure you, today is the day of the Lord's resurrection, so you should not be fasting. That is why God has sent me to bring you food.' So, after saying grace, they ate the meal together.

One day a blackbird started flying round Benedict's head, fluttering so close to his face that he could have reached out and caught it, but he made the sign of the cross and the bird immediately made off.

Then the Devil brought to his mind the image of a woman he had seen at some time past, and so inflamed him with passion that he was close to giving way to his desire and abandoning the life of a hermit. But suddenly, through God's grace, he became himself again. He stripped off his clothes and threw himself among the thorns and briars which covered the place, and rolled about in them until he had torn his body from head to toe. In this way he drew out the sins of his soul through the wounds he inflicted on his body. And so he mastered his weakness, and quenched the flames of sexual passion. After this he was never again tormented by bodily desires.

His fame grew, and when the abbot of a nearby monastery died, the whole community of this monastery came to Benedict and begged him to become their new abbot. For a long time he refused, maintaining that he was not suited for life in a community such as theirs. But eventually he was won over and consented. However, when he insisted that their rule should be applied with greater severity, they cursed themselves for having appointed a man so punctilious that he found their own licences offensive. Seeing that under Benedict they were not allowed the slightest latitude, and exasperated at having to give up all the little indulgences to which they had become accustomed, they mixed some poison in a glass of wine one evening and gave it to Benedict as he was retiring. But no sooner had he made the sign of the cross than the glass shattered, just as if it had been hit by a stone. So immediately realizing that the drink had contained a deadly poison, because it could not withstand the sign of the cross, he got up and said calmly: 'May Almighty God have mercy on you, brothers! Did I not tell you I was not suited to your way of life?'

Then he went back to his cave in the wilderness, where he became more and more famous for the miracles he worked, and so many people flocked to join him that he founded no fewer than twelve monasteries. Now in one of them was a monk who was quite unable to stay at prayer for any length of time, and while the other monks were praying, he would sneak out and give himself up to other, more earthly pursuits. When the abbot of this monastery told St Benedict, he went to observe this monk, and saw him being dragged out of chapel by a black imp, who had hold of him by the fringe of his habit. He called to the abbot and a monk called Maurus: 'Can you not see who it is who is pulling him along?' And when they replied: 'No', he said: 'Let us pray, then, so that you can see him, too.' When they had prayed, Maurus did see the imp, though the abbot still could not. Next day, after prayers, St Benedict found the monk outside the chapel, and as punishment for his neglect he struck him with his staff. From that day on the monk never strayed from his devotions, and the Devil, smarting as if he himself had received the beating at the hands of the saint, never again dared to interrupt his meditations.

Three of these monasteries were at the summit of a lofty mountain, and since the monks had to fetch their water by a long and laborious descent, they often pleaded with St Benedict to move them elsewhere. So one night, with a young monk as his companion, he climbed the mountain and, after lengthy prayers, placed three rocks on the ground in a particular spot as markers. Next morning, when he went back to the monastery and the monks again begged him to move them, he said: 'Go and find the place where I left three rocks and dig up the ground between them. You will have your water: God will make it spring from that spot.' Off they went and found the rocky ground already oozing water, so they dug a hole there and soon saw it filled. Even today the spring produces so much water that it cascades all the way down to the foot of the mountain.

One day a man happened to be clearing the brambles from around the monastery with a bill hook and the blade came out of the haft and fell to the bottom of a deep lake. The workman was inconsolable, but the saint plunged the haft in the water of the lake and at once the blade floated up to join it again.

On another occasion, when a young monk called Placidus went out to draw water, he fell into the river and was swept away by the current, and in no time at all he had been washed to the foot of the mountain. But the saint, who was in his cell, saw all this in a vision, called Maurus, told him what had happened and made him run to rescue the lad. Waiting only to receive the saint's blessing, Maurus hurried off and, thinking he was on dry land, in fact ran over the surface of the stream until he reached Placidus and, holding him by the hair, pulled him out of the water. When he got back to Benedict and told him what had happened, the saint said that the miracle had come about not through any virtues of his own, but as a reward for Maurus's obedience.

A priest named Florentius, who was jealous of the saint, actually went so far as to put poison in a loaf of bread and send it to the saint as alms. The saint accepted the gift gratefully, then threw it to a crow, whom he used to feed from his own hands. He said: 'In the name of Jesus Christ, take this bread and drop it where no one can reach it.' The crow, his beak wide open and wings spread, began to fly around the loaf and squawk, as if trying to indicate that he wanted to obey the saint, but could not. Again and again the saint said: 'Pick it up, don't be afraid. Pick it up and do as I told you.' Finally the crow picked up the bread, flew away and after three days returned and let the saint feed him grains of corn, as before. Then Florentius, seeing that he could not harm the body of the master, tried instead to destroy the souls of his disciples. He smuggled seven girls into the garden of the monastery, and had them frolic and sing and dance naked to excite the monks to lecherous thoughts. The saint saw this going on from his cell, and, fearing that the brothers might yield to temptation, took some of his followers with him and went off to find another place to live. As for Florentius, he was standing on a balcony watching Benedict's departure and congratulating himself, when the balcony collapsed and he fell to his death. So Maurus ran after the saint and called out joyfully: 'Come back! The man who wanted to harm you is dead!' When the saint heard this, he sighed deeply, not only for the death of his enemy, but also because a follower of his had taken such pleasure in announcing his death. So he imposed a penance on Maurus and continued on his journey. But though he went to live in a different place, the same Enemy pursued him.

When he reached Monte Cassino, he turned the temple of Apollo there into an oratory of St John the Baptist, and converted the local inhabitants from their pagan beliefs. But the Devil could hardly endure this, and he repeatedly appeared to the saint in the most hideous forms imaginable, his eyes shooting flames as he vented his rage: '*Benedicte, Benedicte!* ['Blessed one']' he called. But when the saint made no reply, he cried: '*Maledicte, maledicte, non Benedicte!* ["Accursed one, accursed, not blessed"] Why do you persecute me so?'

Then one day, when the brothers were trying to raise a larger stone from the ground to use in a building, they found that, however many of them made the attempt, they were simply not strong enough to lift it. Along came the saint, who gave the brothers his blessing and up it came without the slightest difficulty – which proved that the Devil himself had been sitting on it and preventing it from budging. And when the brothers were raising the wall of their church, the Ancient Enemy appeared to the saint and told him he was going straight to visit the brothers at their work. So Benedict immediately sent word to them. 'Brothers,' he said, 'be on your guard! An evil spirit has come amongst you!' Scarcely had this message been delivered when the Devil smashed down the wall, crushing a young novice to death. But the saint had the novice's mangled limbs brought to him in a sack, and, with a prayer, brought him to life again and sent him back to building the wall.

Now there was a devout layman who each year used to visit St Benedict, and on his journey, as a discipline, he had made a habit of fasting. One day, on his annual pilgrimage, he was joined by another traveller. The hour was late, and the stranger, offering to share the provisions he was carrying with him, said: 'Come, my friend, let us eat something, or we shall faint by the wayside.' When he replied that he would not break his fast until his journey's end, the stranger for a time fell silent. Then, after a while, he repeated his offer, but the answer was still the same. Time went by and finally, after they had covered a considerable distance, they were both exhausted. So, when they came upon a verdant meadow with a spring of water and the stranger suggested again that he have something to eat and rest for a while, this time the pilgrim found his offer and the sight of the meadow too tempting to resist. And as soon as they reached their destination, St Benedict said to the pilgrim: 'Ha! The Enemy tried to have his way with you, brother, and twice he failed. But the third time he won!' In shame the pilgrim fell at his feet and confessed his sin.

Totila, king of the Goths, took it into his head to find out if the saint had the gift of second sight, so he dressed up one of his guards in his own robes and sent him in regal magnificence to the monastery. But as soon as he saw the man, St Benedict said: 'Take it off, my son, take it off! That robe you are wearing is not yours.' Immediately the soldier fell to the ground in awe, terrified at having tried to fool a man with such powers.

A clerk who was possessed by the Devil was brought to St Benedict to be healed. When the saint had exorcized the Devil, he said to the clerk: 'Off you go, but eat no more meat and never take holy orders. For the day you do so, the Devil will gain control over you.' For some time the clerk heeded this warning, but then, annoyed that others much younger than himself were becoming ordained, he forgot what the saint had said and entered holy orders. Immediately the Devil who had left him took possession of him again and plagued him unceasingly until he drove him to his death.

A certain man sent a boy with two flagons of wine for the saint, but this boy delivered only one of them, having hidden the other by the roadside. The saint accepted his gift with thanks, but as the boy was about to leave, he gave him a warning: 'My son, do not drink from the flagon you have hidden! Lay it carefully on its side and you will see what is in it.' Blushing with shame, the boy took his leave and hurried back to see; and no sooner had he laid the flagon on its side than a deadly snake slithered out.

One evening, when the saint was having supper, it happened to be the turn of a monk who was the son of a distinguished public figure to serve him at table and to hold a light for him. This monk, considering himself too good for such a menial task, thought: 'Who is this man, that I should have to serve him at table and hold a light for him as if I were his servant? Why should I wait on him?' In a flash the saint said: 'Open your heart, brother, open your heart! What is it you wish to say?' And he called the others together, told them to take the lamp from the young monk, and ordered the young monk to go back to his cell and sit in silence.

In the days of King Totila, there was a Goth named Galla, a heretic of the Arian persuasion, who was so crazed with hatred for members of the monastic orders that he killed every single clerk or monk that crossed his path. Now one day, in his insatiable greed, Galla was looting the home of a peasant and was torturing him with quite inhuman cruelty, when the poor man, unable to stand any more pain, declared that he had put himself and all his goods under the protection of St Benedict. Galla took him at his word, and this won the peasant a stay of execution. Galla stopped torturing him, but tied his hands tightly together, and, making him walk in front of his horse, told him to take him to this Benedict who had undertaken to protect his goods. So the peasant led Galla to Benedict's monastery, where he found the saint sitting, reading, outside the door of his cell. He turned to Galla and pointed him out: 'Look, there he is – Father Benedict, the monk I told you about.' As soon as he set eyes on him, Galla stormed and raged, his black heart seethed with hatred, and, sure that the saint would try to make him renounce his heresy, he began shouting at him: 'Come on, on your feet! This peasant entrusted his goods to you. Well, he has been robbed! You see if you can get them back!' The saint stopped his reading and looked up; first he eyed Galla, then he turned his attention to the farmer. And the very moment his gaze fell on him, a miracle! The thongs which bound his hands sprang apart: no human hands could have untied them with such incredible speed. And Galla, awestruck at seeing a man who had been securely tied up suddenly stand free, fell to the ground at St Benedict's feet, and, bowing his neck in humility, begged him for his prayers. The saint, without interrupting his reading, called his brethren and asked them to take Galla into the chapel for a blessing. When Galla came back, Benedict warned him that he must put an end to his cruel ways. As he left the monastery later, Galla made a promise: because the saint had freed the peasant so miraculously, without even laying a hand on him but with the merest glance, he undertook never to rob him again.

Once there was a terrible famine in Campania. Food was so scarce that every family was threatened, and soon in the monastery of St Benedict there was no grain left; almost all the bread had been eaten, and one day no more than five loaves could be found to feed the brethren. But the saint, seeing them all looking miserable, gave them a mild rebuke for being so faint-hearted, and, in an effort to lift their spirits, said: 'Why are you so concerned? Today there is little, true, but tomorrow you will have more than you can eat.' And the next day two hundred measures of flour were found in sacks at the door of St Benedict's cell. But whom God prompted to put them there has never been discovered. Witnessing this miracle, the brethren gave thanks to God for his bounty, and learnt never to give up hope, even in the direst extremity.

There is also a story about a boy suffering from elephantiasis: his symptoms were so acute, in fact, that his hair was falling out, all his flesh was bloated, and he had a perpetual, gnawing hunger that no amount of eating could satisfy. Nevertheless, when his father brought him to St Benedict, he was cured in an instant – it was as if he had never been ill – and as a result both father and son thanked God unceasingly. The boy subsequently lived a happy life, dedicating himself to the service of others until the day he fell asleep in the Lord.

One day the saint sent off some of his monks to build a monastery somewhere, and told them he would visit them on such-and-such a day to tell them exactly how he wanted it built. Now the night before he was due to make this visit he appeared in a dream to the monk he had made abbot there and to his provost, and explained to them in minute detail the layout he required. But they were not convinced by this vision, and they continued to wait for the saint to arrive in person. Finally, however, they went back to him and said: 'Father, we waited for you to come, as you promised us, but you never did.' He replied: 'Why are you saying this? Did I not appear to you and describe what I wanted in every particular? Be off with you now, and do everything as you were told.'

Not far from Benedict's monastery there lived two nuns of noble birth who were simply unable to curb their tongues, and often angered their superior by their loose talk. When the superior reported this to the man of God, Benedict gave them the following ultimatum: 'Either hold your tongues, or I will excommunicate you.' He did not actually impose the sentence of excommunication, he merely threatened to do so. But the nuns did not change their ways, and a few days after this they died and were buried in the church. When masses were celebrated there, at the point where the deacon pronounced the customary words: 'Let anyone who is not in communion leave the church', the woman who had been the nurse of these two nuns, and who always made an offering on their behalf, saw them rise out of their tombs and leave the church. When St Benedict was informed of this, he gave an offering of his own for the two dead nuns and told his clergy: 'Go and make this offering for them and their excommunication will be over.' This was done, and the nuns were never again seen to leave the church when the deacon said the customary words.

A monk who had left the monastery to visit his parents without St Benedict's blessing died on the day he reached his home. But the earth refused to receive his body, and the same thing happened when he was buried a second time. So his parents went to find St Benedict and asked him if he would give their son his blessing. Benedict took a consecrated wafer and told them: 'Go and place this on his body, and bury him a third time.' They did so, and this time the earth kept the corpse and never rejected it again.

A monk who could face life in the monastery no longer pestered the man of God so insistently that Benedict, in annoyance, permitted him to leave. Scarcely had the monk set foot outside the monastery when he came upon a dragon, his jaws wide open and ready to devour him. 'Quick! Quick!' he cried. 'This dragon is going to devour me!' The monks hurried to help him, but could find no dragon anywhere, so they took him back, shivering and shaking with terror, to the monastery, and he promised faithfully never to leave again.

Once a terrible famine was ravaging the whole country, and St Benedict had given everything he could find to the needy, until there was nothing left in the monastery except a small amount of oil in a glass jar. Then, when a pauper came begging, he ordered the cellarer to give away even this. The cellarer heard the saint's order clearly enough, but he decided to disobey it, because there would be no oil left for the brothers. When Benedict discovered what had happened, he had the jar of oil thrown out of the window rather than have anything left in his monastery as the result of disobedience. The jar was duly thrown out of the window and landed on some great blocks of stone, but the glass did not break and not a drop of oil was spilled. So he had it fetched and gave it all to the man who had asked for it. Then, having taken the cellarer to task for his disobedience and lack of faith, he gave himself up to prayer, and instantly a large storage jar which stood nearby became full of oil – so full, in fact, that it was seen to overflow on to the floor.

On one occasion Benedict had gone down the hill from the monastery to visit his sister, and when he was sitting at table, she asked him to stay the night with her. He would not even listen to such a suggestion, so she lowered her head into her hands in prayer, and when she lifted it again, there was such lightning, such mighty claps of thunder and such a torrential downpour of rain that the saint could not possibly have set foot outside the house, though moments ago the night had been remarkably clear and still. Plainly her floods of tears had altered the stillness of the air and drawn down rain from heaven! In distress Benedict exclaimed: 'May God forgive you, sister! What have you done?' She replied: 'I begged you to stay, and you would not listen to me. So I prayed to the Lord and he heard me. Now go back if you can!' So it came about that they spent the whole night together in mutual edification, talking of spiritual matters.

One night, while St Benedict was at his window in prayer, he saw a light descending which spread with such brilliance that it dispelled the darkness all around. Suddenly the whole world was gathered and brought before his eyes, as if beneath a single ray of the sun, and there he saw the soul of Germanus, bishop of Capua, being carried up to heaven. He later found out that the bishop had died at that very hour.

In the year in which the saint was to die, he announced the day of his death to his community. Six days before this, he ordered his tomb to be opened, and soon afterwards he was in the grip of a fever which grew worse from day to day. On the sixth day he had himself carried into the oratory and there prepared himself for his death by receiving the Lord's body and blood. Then he stood up, his failing limbs supported on either side by his brethren, and raised his hands to heaven in prayer, and while still praying he breathed his last. The same day that St Benedict departed this life and went to Christ, two monks had the same vision, one of them in his cell, the other a considerable distance away: they saw a shining pathway strewn with rich cloths and glittering with innumerable lamps which rose from St Benedict's cell eastwards up to heaven. Above this a man of venerable appearance and radiant aspect stood, and he asked them if they knew whose pathway it was that they saw before them. When they answered that they did not know, he told them: 'This is the pathway by which Benedict, beloved of God, is to ascend to heaven.' St Benedict was buried in the oratory of St John the Baptist, which he had built himself over a ruined altar to Apollo. He flourished around AD 518, in the time of Justin the Elder.

24

ST MARY OF EGYPT

2 April

Mary of Egypt, called Mary the Sinner, lived a life of the greatest austerity in the desert for forty-seven years. She entered the desert around AD 270, in the reign of Claudius.

Now an aged priest named Zosimas had crossed the Jordan and was traversing a vast desert in the hope of finding some holy father there, when he saw a figure walking about naked, with a body blackened and burnt by the sun. This was Mary of Egypt, and she immediately took flight, while Zosimas chased after her as quickly as he could. Finally Mary said to him: 'Father Zosimas, why are you pursuing me? Forgive me, I cannot turn my face to you because I am a woman, and naked. But hand me your cloak so that I can look at you without shame.' Zosimas was astonished to hear her call him by name; he gave her his cloak and threw himself to the ground, asking her for her blessing. 'Father,' she replied, 'it is rather you who should give the blessing, for you are invested with the dignity of priesthood.' When Zosimas realized that she knew not only his name, but that he was a priest, his wonder grew, and he now insistently begged her to bless him. But Mary said: 'Blessed be God, redeemer of our souls!' And as she stretched out her hands in prayer, he saw her lifted a short way above the ground. The old man then began to wonder if she might be an evil spirit, and only pretending to pray. But she said: 'May God forgive you for thinking that I, a sinful woman, might be an unclean spirit.'

Zosimas then begged her earnestly, in the Lord's name, to tell him about her life. But she replied: 'Forgive me, father, but if I tell you the sort of person I am, you will flee in terror as if you had seen a serpent. Your ears will be defiled by my words, and the air will be contaminated with their filth.' But Zosimas kept pressing her until finally she told him: 'I was born in Egypt, and at the age of twelve I went to Alexandria. There, for seventeen years, I lived as a public prostitute, and never refused anyone who wanted me. But one day some of the local people were sailing up to Jerusalem to venerate the holy cross, and I asked the ship's crew to let me go with them. They asked me if I had the fare, and I told them: "Brothers, I have no fare to offer you: but you can take my body instead." So they took me on board, and had my body as payment.

'When I reached Jerusalem and went with the others to the church to venerate the holy cross, I got as far as the doors when suddenly, as if by an invisible force, I felt myself pushed back, and was prevented from going inside. Again and again I got to the threshold of the doorway, and each time suddenly, to my shame, I was repulsed. Yet all the others were able to enter quite freely, and felt nothing stopping them. Then I came to my senses and, realizing that this was happening because of the enormity of the sins I had committed, I began to beat my breast and to weep bitterly, and to heave deep sighs from the depths of my heart. Then, as I lifted my head, I saw before me an image of the Blessed Virgin Mary. In floods of tears I began to pray to her to win pardon for my sins and permit me to enter the church to venerate the holy cross, promising that I would renounce the world and henceforth live a life of chastity. After I had prayed, inspired with faith in the name of the Blessed Virgin, I went yet again to the doors of the church and this time entered without any hindrance.

'When I had venerated the cross with sincere devotion, somebody gave me three silver pieces, with which I bought three loaves, and I heard a voice telling me: "If you cross the Jordan, you will be saved." So I crossed the Jordan and came to this desert, where I have stayed for forty-seven years without setting eyes on any man. The three loaves I brought with me have become hard as stone over the years, but for forty-seven years now have sufficed me as food. My clothes fell off me in tatters long ago, and for seventeen years of my life in the desert here I was troubled by bodily temptations; but now, by God's grace, I have conquered them all. There, I have now told you everything about me, and I beg you to pray for me to God.' The priest prostrated himself on the ground and blessed the Lord in his handmaid. 'I also beg you,' she said, 'to come back to the Jordan on the day of the Lord's Supper, and to bring with you a consecrated host. I will meet you there and receive the Lord's body from your hand, for, since the day I came here, I have never received communion.'

The old man returned to his monastery, and the next year, as the day of the Lord's Supper drew near, he took a consecrated host and journeyed to the bank of the Jordan. He saw the woman standing on the other bank, and, making the sign of the cross over the river, she walked across it and joined him. The old priest watched her in amazement, then fell in humility at her feet. 'Do not kneel!' she told him. 'You have on your person the Lord's sacrament, and you are radiant with priestly dignity. But I beseech you, father, be good enough to come to me again next year.' After making her communion, she made the sign of the cross a second time over the waters of the Jordan, walked across and made her way back into the solitude of the desert.

Old Zosimas returned to his monastery, and the following year went back to the place where he had first conversed with Mary. There he discovered that she had died. He fell to weeping, but did not dare to touch her. 'How gladly I would bury this holy woman's body,' he said to himself, 'but I fear it may displease her.' As he was wondering what to do, he noticed something written in the earth near Mary's head, and it said: 'Bury Mary's little body, Zosimas. Return her dust to the earth, and pray for me to the Lord, at whose command I left this world on the second day of April.' So the old man knew for certain that Mary had ended her days as soon as she had received the Lord's sacrament and gone back into the desert; and that this same tract of desert which Zosimas had struggled to cover in thirty days she had crossed in a single hour, and after that had departed to the Lord.

He tried to dig her a grave, but was unable to. Then he saw a lion coming meekly towards him, and he said to it: 'This holy woman has instructed me to bury her body here, but I am old, and I have no spade, and I cannot. So, please, dig me a grave, so that we can bury her most holy body.' At once the lion began to dig, and soon fashioned a grave of suitable size. Then, its work finished, it went away again, meek as a lamb, and the old priest returned to his monastery, glorifying God.

25

ST GEORGE

23 April

George was a native of Cappadocia and a tribune in the Roman army. One day he came to Silena, a city in the province of Libya. Close by this city was a vast lake, as big as an inland sea, where a pestilential dragon had its lair.[1] The people had often risen in arms against it, but the dragon always put them to flight, and would venture right up to the city walls and asphyxiate everyone with its noxious breath. So the citizens were compelled to feed it two sheep every day, in order to allay its fury, otherwise it would make straight for the city walls and poison the air, causing a great many deaths. But in time, since their flocks were not large, the supply of sheep began to run out, and the citizens decided to give the dragon one sheep and one human being. The names of the victims were drawn by lot, and no one of either sex was excluded. But in due course nearly all the young folk were eaten up, and one day the lot fell upon the only daughter of the king, and the people seized her to feed her to the dragon. The king was heartbroken. 'Take my gold and silver,' he cried. 'Take half my realm, and let my daughter go, save her from this dreadful death!' But the people rounded on him in fury. 'It was you who issued this decree, your majesty, and, now all our children are dead, you want to save your own daughter? If you do not sacrifice your daughter, and do what you forced all the rest of us to do, we will burn you alive, you and all your household!' At this, the king began to weep for his daughter. 'Woe is me!' he cried. 'My sweetest child, what am I to do about you. What can I say? Can I no more hope to see your wedding day?' Turning to the people, he said: 'I beg you, grant me a week's grace in which to mourn my daughter.' This the people agreed to, but at the end of the week they came back and demanded angrily: 'How can you destroy your subjects just for your daughter's sake? We are all dying from the breath of the dragon!' Then the king, seeing that he could not save his daughter, dressed her in all her regal finery and, embracing her, said tearfully: 'Alas, my sweetest daughter, I thought to see you rear royal children at your bosom, and now you are going to be devoured by the dragon! Alas, my sweetest child, I hoped to invite all the nobility to your wedding, to deck the palace with pearls, to hear the music of timbrels and trumpets, and now you are going to be devoured by the dragon!' He kissed her and let her go with a final word: 'Oh, my daughter, would I had died before you, rather than lose you in this way!' She then fell at her father's feet, asking his blessing, and, when in a flood of tears he had blessed her, she set off towards the lake.

Now St George happened to be passing that way, and when he saw her weeping, he asked her what was the matter. 'Good youth,' she replied, 'mount your horse with all speed and flee, or you will share my fate and die as I must.' 'Do not be afraid, my child,' George told her. 'But tell me, what are you waiting here for, and why are all these people watching?' 'Good youth,' she replied, 'I see you have a noble heart, but do you want to die with me? Make haste and flee!' George told her: 'I shall not move from here until you tell me what is the matter.' So then she told him the whole story, and George said: 'My child, do not be afraid, for in the name of Christ I will help you.' 'You are a brave knight,' she replied. 'But do not perish with me. It is enough that I die, for you cannot save me, you would only die with me.' While they were talking, the dragon suddenly lifted its head from the lake. Trembling, the young girl cried: 'Flee, good lord, make haste and flee!' But George mounted his horse, armed himself with the sign of the cross, and bravely went to meet the dragon as it came towards him. Brandishing his lance and commending himself to God, he dealt the beast such a deadly wound that he threw it to the ground. He called to the princess: 'Throw your girdle round the dragon's neck! Do not be afraid, child!' She did as he told her, and the dragon followed her as meekly as a puppy. She led it into the city, but when the people saw it, they began to run for the mountains and hills, crying: 'Help! We are all done for!' But St George waved at them to come back. 'Do not be afraid,' he told them. 'The Lord has sent me to free you from the tyranny of the dragon. Only believe in Christ and be baptized, every one of you, and I will slay your dragon!'

So the king and all the people were baptized and St George drew his sword and slew the dragon, and gave orders that it should be carried outside the city walls. Four pairs of oxen dragged the beast out of the city and left it on a broad open plain. That day twenty thousand were baptized, not counting women and children. The king built a large and splendid church there in honour of Blessed Mary and St George, and from its altar there still issues a natural spring whose waters cure all illnesses. The king also offered

St George a vast sum of money, but the saint refused to accept it, and ordered it to be given to the poor. He then gave the king four brief rules of life: to cherish the Church of God; to honour priests; to be scrupulous in attending mass; and always to be mindful of the poor. With that he kissed the king farewell and left. We read in some sources, however, that when the dragon was rushing towards the girl to devour her, George actually armed himself with a cross, and then attacked and killed the dragon.

At this time, during the principate of Diocletian and Maximian, the prefect Dacian started such a vicious persecution of the Christians that within a single month seventeen thousand won the crown of martyrdom, and, as a result, threatened with torture of every kind, many Christians gave in and offered sacrifice to the idols. When he saw this, Saint George was grief-stricken; he gave away all his possessions, laid aside his soldier's uniform and dressed as a Christian. Then he ran out into the midst of the crowds and cried: 'All the gods of the heathen are demons! It was our Lord who made the heavens!' The prefect angrily rejoined: 'How dare you presume to call our gods demons! Tell me, where do you come from, and what is your name?' George answered him: 'My name is George, and I come from a noble family of Cappadocia. With Christ's help I conquered Palestine; but I have left everything in order to be more free to serve the God of heaven.' The prefect saw that he could not sway him, and ordered him to be put to the rack and torn limb from limb with iron hooks. Brands were thrust against his sides to sear his flesh, and where his entrails showed through, the prefect had salt rubbed in the wounds. But that same night the Lord appeared to George in a great blaze of light and tenderly comforted him: so blissful was this vision and so sweet the words he spoke that George thought nothing of his pain.

Dacian saw he could not conquer his prisoner by torture, so he summoned a sorcerer and told him: 'The Christians are laughing at our tortures. They must be using some magic of theirs! They show utter disrespect for the worship of our gods!' The sorcerer replied: 'If I cannot overcome his magic, then you can have my head.' He then worked his sorcery, called on the names of his gods, mixed poison in some wine and gave it to blessed George to drink. But the saint made the sign of the cross over the cup and drained it without suffering the slightest harm. So the sorcerer mixed a stronger poison with the wine, but again, after making the sign of the cross, George drank it without coming to any harm. When he saw this, the sorcerer fell at once at the saint's feet, tearfully begged his pardon, and asked to become a

Christian (soon after, in fact, the prefect had him beheaded for this). The following day Dacian had George tied on a wheel fitted all round with sharp, two-edged swords, but the wheel instantly fell apart, and George was found to be quite unhurt. In a rage the prefect ordered him to be plunged into a cauldron of molten lead, but George made the sign of the cross, got in and, with God's help, found it no hotter than a refreshing bath. Seeing that he could break George through neither threats nor tortures, Dacian now thought to win him over by persuasion. 'George, my son,' he said, 'you can see how indulgent our gods are. They put up with your blasphemy so patiently, and still they are ready to forgive you, if you will turn to them. So come, my dearest son, do as I advise you: abandon your superstition and sacrifice to our gods, and win great honours from them and from ourselves, too.' With a smile George replied: 'Why did you not use persuasion in the first place, rather than trying to break me with tortures? Very well, I am prepared to do what you want.' Dacian, fooled by George's assurance, was delighted: he had the herald call the whole people together to see George, who had resisted so long, finally give in and offer sacrifice. The whole city was decked out as for a festival, and there was general rejoicing, as George entered the temple to offer sacrifice, and all the people stood by in happy anticipation. But instead of sacrificing, George knelt and prayed for the Lord to destroy the temple and all its idols, and destroy it so completely that, for the glory of God and the conversion of the people, absolutely nothing was left of it. At once fire fell from heaven and burnt the temple, its idols and priests, to a cinder, and the earth gaped open and swallowed up the remains . . .

When Dacian learnt what George had done, he had him brought before him. 'You evil man!' he cried. 'What sorcery is this of yours? How could you commit so heinous a crime?' George replied: 'It is not as you think, my lord. Come along with me and see me sacrifice again!' Dacian retorted: 'I know what you are up to! You want to have the earth swallow me, too, as you made it swallow the temple of my gods.' 'Poor wretch,' George said, 'tell me, how can your gods help you, when they could not help themselves?' The prefect now flew into a mad rage. 'I am finished! I shall die!' he told his wife Alexandria. 'I cannot bear to see this man get the better of me!' 'Cruel, murderous tyrant!' she replied. 'Did I not often tell you to stop persecuting the Christians, because their God was fighting on their side? And now let me tell you this: I myself wish to become a Christian.' Dumbfounded, the prefect cried: 'No! This is too much to bear! Have you, too, been seduced by them?' So he had her hung up by her hair and cruelly beaten with scourges. While she was being beaten, she said to George: 'George, hero of the true faith, what do you think will become of me? I have not yet been reborn in the waters of baptism.' George answered: 'Do not be afraid, my daughter; the blood you shed will be your baptism and your crown.' Then, with a prayer on her lips, Alexandria breathed her last . . .

The following day George was condemned to be dragged through the length and breadth of the city and then beheaded. He prayed to the Lord that whoever implored his aid might have his prayer granted, and a heavenly voice came to him, saying that his wish would be fulfilled. When he had finished praying, he was beheaded, and thus he accomplished his martyrdom in the reign of Diocletian and Maximian, which began around the year of our Lord 287. As for Dacian, when he was returning to the palace from the place of execution, fire fell from heaven and consumed him and all his attendants with him . . .

26

ST MARK, EVANGELIST

25 April

St Mark the Evangelist was a Levite by race and a priest, and by baptism a son of Peter the Apostle, by whom he was instructed in the faith. Mark accompanied St Peter to Rome, and when Peter preached the Gospel there, the faithful at Rome asked St Mark to put it down in writing, so that all believers could have a permanent record of the Gospel. Mark wrote this account faithfully, just as he had heard it from the lips of his master St Peter. Peter examined it carefully, saw it was true in every detail, and recommended its acceptance by all believers.

Seeing that Mark was steadfast in the faith, Peter sent him to Aquileia, where he preached the word of God and converted countless multitudes of Gentiles to the faith of Christ. There is also a story that he wrote his Gospel there, and, to this day, the manuscript is on view in the church at Aquileia, and preserved with due devotion. Finally the blessed Mark converted to the faith a citizen of Aquileia called Hermagoras, and took him to Peter in Rome to be consecrated as bishop of Aquileia. Hermagoras duly took up his office as bishop, and ruled the church at Aquileia with great distinction until he was captured by infidels and crowned with martyrdom.

Next Mark was sent by St Peter to Alexandria, and was the first to preach the word of God there. According to Philo, that most sagacious of Jews, as soon as Mark arrived in Alexandria, vast numbers of people were united in faith and devotion and the practice of continence. Papias, the bishop of Hierapolis, too, sings the evangelist's praises in the most exalted language. And Peter Damian says this of him: 'God endowed him with so much grace in Alexandria that all who flocked together to learn the rudiments of the faith very soon, by the practice of continence and adherence to a wholly godly way of life, attained a degree of perfection that was almost monastic. Mark urged them to these heights not only by performing extraordinary miracles and by the eloquence of his preaching, but also by his own outstanding example.' The same author adds later: 'And it came about that after his death he was brought back to Italy, so that the land in which it had been granted him to write his Gospel might have the honour of possessing his sacred relics. Blessed art thou, O Alexandria, empurpled by his glorious blood! Happy art thou also, Italy, enriched by the treasure of his body!'

Mark is said to have been a man of such humility that he cut off his thumb so that no one could ever consider him worthy of elevation to the order of priesthood. But God's will and the authority of St Peter prevailed, and the latter consecrated Mark as bishop of Alexandria. As Mark entered Alexandria, his sandal broke and came apart, and he saw in this a spiritual meaning. 'Truly,' he said, 'the Lord has made my path lighter, and Satan will not be able to stand in my way, for the Lord has freed me from the works of death.' And, seeing a cobbler at work mending some old shoes, Mark handed him his sandal to mend. But while he was working on it, the cobbler cut his left hand badly and exclaimed: 'One God!' Hearing this, the man of God commented: 'Truly the Lord has indeed prospered my journey!' And he mixed some earth with his spittle and spread the paste over the man's wound, and it was instantly healed. Seeing what great powers Mark possessed, the cobbler took him into his house and asked him who he was and where he came from. Mark told him quite openly that he was a servant of the Lord Jesus. The cobbler said: 'I would like to see him!' And Mark replied: 'I will show him to you.' So he began to preach the Gospel of Jesus to him, and subsequently baptized him and his whole household.

Now the men of that city heard that some Galilean had arrived, who was pouring scorn on their idol worship, and they began to plot his downfall. Mark got wind of this, so he ordained Anianus, the man whose hand he had healed, as bishop in his place, and left for Pentapolis, where he stayed for two years before returning again to Alexandria. On the rocks along the seashore, at a place called Bucculi, he had built a church, and he found the numbers of the faithful had greatly increased there. So the priests of the temples began to try to seize him, and on Easter Sunday, when the blessed Mark was celebrating mass, they all met at his church, threw a noose round his neck and hauled him through the city chanting: 'Let us drag the bull [Latin: *bubalus* = 'wild ox'] to the butcher's [*loca bucculi*]!' Strips of his flesh were scattered all over the road and the stones were wet with his blood. After this he was shut up in prison and there he was comforted by an angel. And the Lord himself visited him and strengthened him, saying: 'Peace be with you, Mark, my evangelist. Do not be afraid, for I am with you to deliver you!' Next morning they threw a rope round his neck again and dragged

him roughly this way and that, shouting 'Drag the bull to the butcher's!'
While Mark was being hauled along the road, he gave thanks and said: 'Into
your hands, O Lord, I commend my spirit.' And as he uttered these words
he suddenly gave up the ghost. This was in the reign of Nero, which began
around AD 57. The heathens were going to burn his body, but suddenly a
whirlwind blew up, hail beat down, there was deafening thunder and great
flashes of lightning, so that everyone was desperately trying to take shelter,
and the saint's body was left untouched. Christians then smuggled it away
and buried it with great reverence in the church . . .

ST MARCELLINUS,
POPE

26 April

Marcellinus governed the church of Rome for nine years and four months. At the order of Diocletian and Maximian he was arrested and ordered to offer sacrifice. This he refused to do, but when, as a result, he was threatened with all sorts of tortures, fearing the pain he would have to bear, he put two grains of incense on the altar as an offering to the gods. This brought the infidels great joy, but caused the faithful even greater sadness. However, under a weak head the members rise in strength and make light of the threats of princes. On this occasion the faithful came in numbers to the pope and roundly condemned him. In response Marcellinus offered himself to be judged by an assembly of bishops. 'God forbid,' they said, 'that the sovereign pontiff should be judged by any man! No: consider your own case as your conscience directs you, and pronounce your own judgement.' By now the pope was regretting his weakness, and was full of remorse, so he abdicated; but the whole assembly of the faithful re-elected him. When the emperors heard about this, they had him arrested a second time, and when he utterly refused to offer sacrifice, they sentenced him to be beheaded, and renewed their persecution of the Christians with such vigour that in one month seventeen thousand were put to death. Just before Marcellinus was beheaded, he declared himself unworthy of Christian burial, and excommunicated anyone who might presume to bury him. So for thirty-five days his body remained unburied. Then St Peter the Apostle appeared to Marcellus, Marcellinus's successor, and said: 'Brother Marcellus, why do you not bury me?' Marcellus replied: 'Were you not buried long since, my lord?' The apostle said: 'So long as I see Marcellinus unburied I consider myself unburied.' 'Do you not know, my lord,' Marcellus said, 'that he placed anyone who dared bury him under a solemn curse?' Peter replied: 'Is it not written that he who humbles himself shall be exalted? That was the text you should have borne in mind. So go now, and bury him at my feet.' Marcellus at once went off and did exactly as St Peter had told him.

ST JAMES THE LESS,
APOSTLE

1 May

James the Apostle was called 'James of Alphaeus' (meaning 'son of Alphaeus'), 'brother of the Lord', 'James the Less' and 'James the Just'. He is called 'James of Alphaeus' not only because his father was Alphaeus, but also because of the meaning of the name. Alphaeus means 'learned', or 'example', or 'fugitive', or 'thousandth'.[1] He was rightly called 'James of Alphaeus', therefore, because he was learned through revealed knowledge; he was an example through his teaching of others; a fugitive from the world, because he so despised it; and 'thousandth' because of his reputation for humility.

He is called 'brother of the Lord' because he is said to have looked very like Jesus, so much so, in fact, that they were regularly mistaken for each other. This is why, when the Jews set out to arrest Christ, to avoid arresting James instead, they waited until Judas identified Christ to them with a kiss; for Judas could easily distinguish Christ and James because of his long-standing friendship with them. This physical similarity is also attested by Ignatius in his letter to John the Evangelist. 'If you will permit me,' he writes, 'I would like to go up to Jerusalem to see the venerable James, called "the Just", who, they say, so resembled Christ Jesus in his appearance, his way of life and his manner that he might have been his twin brother born of the same mother. If I see James, they say, I shall see a perfect likeness of Jesus himself.' Or he is called the 'brother' of the Lord because he and Jesus, who were the children of two sisters, were also thought of as being the descendants of two brothers, Joseph and Cleophas.[2] He is not called the brother of the Lord because he was the son of Joseph, Mary's spouse, by another wife, as some would have it, but because he was the son of Mary, the daughter of Cleophas, and this Cleophas was a brother of Joseph, Mary's spouse (though Master John Beleth states that Alphaeus, father of this James, was the brother of Joseph, Mary's spouse. This, however, is not thought to be correct, for the Jews called any males related by blood on both sides 'brothers'). Or he may be called the brother of our Lord because of his pre-eminence, and his exceptional holiness, in recognition of which he, rather than any of the other apostles, was ordained bishop of Jerusalem.

He is called James 'the Less' to distinguish him from James, son of Zebedee. For though he was born before James, son of Zebedee, he was called to be an apostle after him. This is the origin of the custom, in many religious houses, of calling the one who came forward first the 'greater', and the one who entered later the 'less', even if he is older or of greater holiness.

He is called 'the Just' by merit of his pre-eminent holiness, for according to Jerome the people so revered him for his sanctity that they vied with each other merely to touch the hem of his garment. Hegesippus, who lived not long after the apostles, writes of his sanctity as it is reported in ecclesiastical histories:[3] 'The leadership of the Church was assumed by James, brother of our Lord. James has universally been called "the Just", from our Lord's day right up to the present time. He was holy from the moment he was born: he drank neither wine nor strong liquor; he never ate meat; no razor ever touched his head; he never anointed himself with oil, never bathed, and wore only a plain linen garment. He knelt so often in prayer that his knees were as calloused as the soles of his feet. For his tireless and unrivalled rectitude, he was called "the Just", and "Abba", which means "bulwark of the people" and "rectitude". He alone among the apostles, because of his exceptional sanctity, was permitted to enter the Holy of Holies.'

James is also said to have been the first of the apostles to celebrate mass. Because of his perfect holiness the apostles bestowed on him the honour of being the first among them to celebrate mass in Jerusalem after the Lord's ascension, and this was even before he was ordained bishop, since we read in the Acts of the Apostles that even before James's ordination the disciples were persevering in the doctrine of the apostles and in the communion of the breaking of bread, which is taken to mean the celebration of mass. Or perhaps this is said of James because he was first to celebrate mass wearing pontifical vestments, as Peter was later first to celebrate mass in Antioch, and Mark in Alexandria. James was all his life a virgin, as Jerome attests in his *Against Jovinian*. According to Josephus, and also Jerome in his work *On Illustrious Men*, when the Lord died on the day before the Sabbath, James vowed he would not eat again until he saw Christ risen from the dead. And on the day of the resurrection, when James had still not tasted food, the Lord appeared to him and said to those who were with him: 'Lay the table and put out some bread.' Then he took the bread, blessed it and gave it to

James the Just, saying: 'Rise, my brother, eat, for the Son of Man has risen.'

On Easter Day in the seventh year of his episcopate, when the apostles were in Jerusalem, James asked them all what miracles the Lord had worked through them among the people, and each gave his account. Then James and the other apostles preached in the temple for seven days before Caiaphas and others of the Jews, and they were on the point of consenting to baptism, when suddenly a man came into the temple and shouted: 'Men of Israel, what are you doing? Why are you letting yourselves be deceived by these sorcerers?' And he stirred up the people to such a pitch that they wanted to stone the apostles. The man climbed up the steps to where James stood preaching and threw him to the ground below, and from that day on James always had a heavy limp. This happened to him in the seventh year after the Lord's ascension.

In the thirtieth year of James's episcopate the Jews, seeing that they could not put Paul to death because he had appealed to Caesar and been sent to Rome, turned the full fury of their persecution on James, and looked for an occasion to kill him. Hegesippus relates (and the same is found in the *Ecclesiastical History*), that the Jews went together to find him and said: 'We appeal to you: disabuse the people of their error in thinking that Jesus is the Christ! We beg you to persuade all those who are gathering to celebrate the Passover that they are wrong about Jesus. Do this, and we all promise to do as you say; and we and all the people will testify that you are a just man and no respecter of persons.' They then set James on the pinnacle of the temple and shouted: 'Most just of men, to whom we all owe our obedience, tell us clearly your opinion. The people are mistaken about Jesus who was crucified, are they not?' James replied in ringing tones: 'Why do you question me about the Son of Man? Behold, he is seated in the heavens on the right hand of God the Almighty, and he shall come to judge the living and the dead!' The Christians were overjoyed to hear this, and listened to him eagerly; but the Pharisees and scribes said: 'We were wrong to give him this chance of testifying to Jesus! Let us climb up there and throw him to the ground! That will frighten the people! They will be less ready to believe him, then!' And they all cried out together at the top of their voices: 'What? What? Even James the Just is in error!' They then climbed to the pinnacle and threw him off, and when they had done so, they shouted: 'Let us stone James the Just!' and began to hurl stones at him. But despite his heavy fall, James was so far from being dead that he turned over, raised himself to his knees and said: 'I beg you, Lord, forgive them, for they know not what they do.' Whereupon one of the priests, a son of Rahab, cried: 'Stop this, I entreat you! What are you doing? It is for you that this just man is praying, and you are stoning him!' But one of them snatched up a fuller's pole, aimed a mighty blow at James's head and dashed his brains out. This is Hegesippus's account of James's martyrdom. James departed to the Lord in the reign of Nero, which began in AD 57, and was buried where he died, close by the temple ...

29

ST PETRONILLA [1]

31 May

Petronilla, whose life was written by St Marcellus, was the daughter of Peter the Apostle. Because of her exceptional beauty her father cursed her with a fever, from which she suffered constantly. Then one day, when the disciples were reclining at table with Peter, Titus asked him: 'You can cure every kind of sickness, so why do you let Petronilla suffer so?' 'Because it is for her own good,' Peter told him. 'But in case you think I cannot cure her and am merely making excuses,' he added, turning and speaking to his daughter, 'get up, Petronilla, be quick now, and wait upon us!' At once Petronilla was well again, and she got up and served them at table. But as soon as she had finished, Peter said: 'Now go back to your bed, Petronilla!' And she did, and immediately she was stricken with the fever again. But later, when Peter was sure that she had achieved perfection in the love of God, he cured her completely.

Now a count named Flaccus had been smitten by her beauty, and in due course he called on Petronilla to ask her to be his wife. 'Why have you come with all these armed soldiers to call on an unarmed girl?' she asked him. 'If you want me for your wife, have some honest married women and chaste young girls come to fetch me in three days' time, and I will go with them to your house.' While the count was busy making these preparations, Petronilla began to devote herself to fasting and prayer; she then received the Lord's body, took to her bed, and after three days departed this life.

Realizing that he had been tricked, Flaccus now turned his attention upon Felicula, a friend of Petronilla's, and told her that she must either marry him or sacrifice to the idols. Felicula refused to do either, and the prefect, after keeping her in gaol for a week without food or drink, stretched her on the rack and put her to death, then threw her corpse into the sewer. But St Nicomedes retrieved her body and buried it. In consequence Flaccus had Nicomedes arrested and, when he refused to offer sacrifice, he was scourged to death with leaded whips. His body was cast into the Tiber, but his deacon, a man called Justus, recovered it and gave it honourable burial.

30

ST BARNABAS,
APOSTLE

11 June

Barnabas was a Levite and a native of Cyprus. He was one of the seventy-two disciples of the Lord, and is singled out for the warmest praise on many counts in the Acts of the Apostles, for he was very disciplined and orderly, both in himself and in his relations with God and his neighbours.

Firstly,[1] he was orderly in his own person in relation to the three appetites: the rational, the concupiscible and the irascible. First, his rational appetite was irradiated by the light of knowledge; hence we read in Acts 13 [v. 1]: 'Now there were in the church that was at Antioch prophets and teachers, among them Barnabas and Simeon . . .' Second, his concupiscible appetite was free from the taint of earthly attachments; hence we read in Acts 4 [vv. 36–7] that Joseph, surnamed Barnabas, sold a plot of land he possessed and brought the money and laid it at the feet of the apostles. The gloss comments: 'He shows that we should rid ourselves of what we avoid touching, and, by laying his money at the feet of the apostles, he teaches us that gold is a thing to be trampled underfoot.' Third, his irascible appetite was strengthened by his extraordinary rectitude, and this enabled him to show courage in tackling arduous tasks, perseverance in anything that demanded physical endurance, and resolution in suffering adversity. That he was willing to undertake arduous tasks is shown by his acceptance of the mission to convert the vast city of Antioch, and also by Acts 9 [v. 26–7], where we read that when Paul went to Jerusalem after his conversion and wanted to join the apostles, and everyone was fleeing from him like sheep from a wolf, it was Barnabas who had the courage to fetch him and lead him to them. He showed perseverance where physical endurance was required, because he mortified his body and subjected it to fasting; hence we read in Acts 13 [v. 2] of Barnabas and certain others that: 'They ministered to the Lord and fasted.' That he also showed resolution in adversity the apostles attest when they say: '[It seemed good unto us, being assembled with one accord, to send chosen men unto you] with our well-beloved

Barnabas and Paul, men that have hazarded their lives for the name of our Lord Jesus Christ' [Acts 15: 25f.].

Secondly, he was orderly in his relations with God because he deferred to God's authority, his majesty and goodness. First, that he deferred to God's authority is clear from the fact that he did not simply assume the office of preacher, but wished to receive the charge on the authority of God, as is shown in Acts 13 [v. 2]: 'The Holy Spirit said: "Separate me Barnabas and Saul for the work whereunto I have called them."' Second, that he deferred to God's majesty is shown by Acts 13 [14: 12ff.]: for when certain people wanted to attribute divine majesty to him and offer sacrifices to him as to a god, calling him Jupiter, as being the senior, and calling Paul Mercury, as being both wise and eloquent, Barnabas and Paul at once tore their garments and cried: 'Sirs, why do ye do these things? We also are mortal men as you are, and preach unto you that you should turn from these vanities unto the living God . . .' Third, he deferred to God's goodness; for, as we read in Acts 15 [v. 1ff.], when some Jewish converts sought to restrict and diminish the goodness of God's grace (by which, and not by the Law, we are freely saved), asserting that grace without circumcision was by no means sufficient, Paul and Barnabas stoutly opposed them and demonstrated that the goodness of God's grace alone, without the Law, was indeed sufficient. Further, they referred this question to the apostles and prevailed upon them to write letters to the churches refuting the heresy of these people.

Thirdly, Barnabas was orderly in his relations with his neighbours, because he nourished his flock by word, by good works and by example: first, by word, because he diligently preached the Gospel, as we read in Acts 15 [v. 35]: 'Paul and Barnabas continued in Antioch, teaching and preaching the word of the Lord, with many others.' The results of his diligence can also be seen in the great numbers he converted in Antioch, and it was there that the disciples were first called 'Christians'. Second, he nourished his flock by example, because his life was a mirror of sanctity to everyone, and a model of holiness. In all he did he was a courageous, energetic man, a man of piety and a man of action; he was conspicuous for his moral rectitude; he was abundantly blessed by every grace of the Holy Spirit; and he was outstanding in his devotion and in every kind of virtue. These four qualities are attested in Acts 15 [11: 22−4]: 'They sent forth Barnabas that he should go as far as Antioch' and 'he exhorted them all that with purpose of heart they would cleave unto the Lord; for he was a good man, filled with the Holy Spirit and with faith.' Third, he nurtured his flock by his good works in two ways, for there are two sorts of good works, or works of mercy, namely the temporal, which consists of ministering to temporal needs, and the spiritual, which consists of pardoning offences. Barnabas practised the first kind when he took alms to the brethren who were in Jerusalem. We read in Acts 11 [vv. 28–30] that in the reign of Claudius there was a severe famine, as Agabus had prophesied, and 'the disciples, every man according to his ability, determined to send relief unto the brethren which dwelt in Judaea. Which also they did, and sent it by the hands of Barnabas and Paul.'

And he performed a spiritual work of mercy when he forgave John, who was surnamed Mark, the offence he had caused him. For when this disciple deserted Barnabas and Paul, but subsequently came back and repented his action, Barnabas pardoned him and took him back again as a disciple, whereas Paul refused to take him back, and this was the cause of a rift between Paul and Barnabas. Each of them acted for good reasons and with laudable intentions: Barnabas took John Mark back because of his mild, forgiving nature; whereas Paul refused to because of his passion for rectitude. As the gloss on Acts 15 [v. 38] says: 'Since John Mark, when in the front line of battle, had proved lukewarm, Paul rightly spurned him, for fear that the resolve of others might be undermined by the influence of his example.' But this rift between Paul and Barnabas was not caused by any ill feeling between them: it was inspired by the Holy Ghost, so that they would separate and thus preach to more people, which is exactly what happened.

When Barnabas was in the city of Iconium, his cousin, this same John Mark, had a vision in which a radiant figure appeared to him and said: 'Be steadfast, John, for soon you shall be called John no longer, but "the Sublime".' When John related this to Barnabas, he replied: 'Be sure to tell no one about what you have seen. For the Lord appeared to me last night, too, and said: "Be steadfast, Barnabas, for you will win eternal rewards because you left your people and laid down your life for my name."' After Paul and Barnabas had been preaching for some time in Antioch, an angel of the Lord appeared to Paul, too, and said: 'Hurry to Jerusalem, for certain of your brethren are expecting you there.' So, since Barnabas wanted to head for Cyprus to visit his parents, while Paul wanted to hurry away to Jerusalem, at the inspiration of the Holy Spirit they went their separate ways. When Paul told Barnabas what the angel had said to him, Barnabas replied: 'The Lord's will be done! For my part, I am going to Cyprus, and I shall end my days there and see you no more.' He wept and fell humbly at Paul's feet and the latter, moved by compassion, said: 'Do not weep. This is the

Lord's will. The Lord appeared to me, too, in the night and said: "Do not prevent Barnabas from going to Cyprus, since he will bring many there to the light, and there finally win martyrdom." '

After this Barnabas left for Cyprus with John and took with him the Gospel of St Matthew, and, holding this over the heads of the sick, through God's power he healed a great number of people. As they were leaving Cyprus, they came upon Elymas, the sorcerer whom Paul had for a time deprived of his sight. Elymas opposed them and forbade them to enter Paphos. Then one day Barnabas saw men and women running about naked to celebrate some feast, and in outrage at this he cursed their temple, and suddenly a section of it fell to the ground, crushing a large number of the heathen. Finally Barnabas went to Salamis, and there Elymas the sorcerer incited a general uprising against him. The Jews seized Barnabas and, after subjecting him to repeated assaults, dragged him off and handed him over to the chief magistrate for punishment. But when it was discovered that Eusebius, an important and powerful relative of Nero, had arrived in Salamis, they were afraid he would take Barnabas from them and let him get away. So they put a noose round his neck, hauled him out of the city gate, and there without more ado burnt him alive. But not even then were the impious Jews satisfied, for they put his bones in a leaden casket, and were going to hurl it into the sea. But John, his disciple, got up in the night with two friends, rescued the relics and laid them to rest in a secret burial chamber. There, according to Sigbert, they remained hidden right up to the times of the emperor Zeno and Pope Gelasius, that is until AD 500, when Barnabas himself revealed their location and the relics were finally discovered. The blessed Dorotheus, however, says: 'Barnabas first preached Christ in Rome, then became bishop of Milan.'

ST BASIL, BISHOP

14 June

Basil was a venerable bishop and distinguished doctor of the Church. His Life was written by Amphilochius, bishop of Iconium. Basil's exceptional holiness was revealed in a vision to a hermit named Ephrem, who in an ecstatic trance saw a pillar of fire, its tip reaching up to heaven, and heard a voice from above, saying: 'Basil is a mighty pillar of fire, as great as this you see before you.' So he went into the city on the feast of the Epiphany to see the great man, and, when he saw Basil dressed in his white vestments advancing in solemn procession with his clergy, he said to himself: 'I can see I have wasted my time. This man is surrounded by every sort of honour: he cannot possibly be the holy man I took him for. We who have borne the heat and burden of the day have never had rewards such as this. How can this man, showered with honours and with such a crowd of attendants, be a "pillar of fire"? I cannot believe it!' But Basil knew in spirit what the hermit was thinking, so he had him brought before him. When Ephrem stood before the bishop he saw a tongue of fire darting from his mouth. 'Truly Basil is great,' he said. 'Truly Basil is a pillar of fire; truly the Holy Spirit speaks through his mouth!' And he pleaded with the bishop: 'My lord, I beg you, grant that I may speak Greek.' 'What you ask is no easy matter,' Basil replied. But he prayed for him, and Ephrem at once began to speak Greek.

Another hermit saw Basil in procession wearing all his pontifical robes, and despised him because he thought in his heart that the bishop was revelling in all the pomp and ceremony. But suddenly a voice spoke to him, saying: 'You take more pleasure in stroking your cat's tail than Basil does in outward ornament.'

The emperor Valens, a supporter of the Arian heresy, confiscated a church belonging to the Catholics and gave it to the Arians. Basil went to him and said: 'Lord, it is written that "the king's honour loveth judgement", and also that "the king's judgement is justice". So why have you seen fit to eject the

Catholics from their church and to give it to the Arians?' The emperor replied: 'Are you here again to insult me, Basil? This is no way for a bishop to behave.' 'It is,' Basil retorted. 'And he must even die for justice, if need be.' Then the emperor's major-domo, a man called Demosthenes, who was also an Arian, spoke up in defence of the heretics, but offended Basil with his total ignorance of theology. Basil rounded on him: 'Your job is to think about the emperor's meals, not to make a hash of Christian doctrine!' Demosthenes was covered in embarrassment, and could find nothing more to say.

The emperor then said to the bishop: 'Basil, go and give judgement between them. But do not be influenced by the violent passions of the people.' So Basil went, and met both Catholics and Arians. He told them to shut the doors of the church and seal them, each faction with its own seal, and said that the church would belong to whichever faction could open the doors by their prayers. This was unanimously agreed. The Arians prayed for three days and nights, but when they went to the church the doors were still not open. Then, at the head of a procession, Basil himself went to the church and, after praying, he gave the doors of the church a light blow with his crook and said: 'Lift up your gates, O ye princes;[1] and be ye lift up, everlasting doors, and the king of glory shall come in!' At once the doors swung open, and the people went in and gave thanks to God, and the church was restored to the Catholics.

The emperor, as the *Tripartite History* relates, in an attempt to win Basil over to Arianism promised him great renown. But Basil's response was as follows: 'You might win over a child with such bribes. But men who are fed on the words of God will not suffer even one syllable of the Church's teaching to be changed.' The emperor was indignant at this reply, but, as the same history relates, when he tried to write an order sentencing the bishop to exile, he could not: three times he tried, and three times the pen broke. Then his hand began to tremble so violently that he lost his temper and destroyed the document.

A devout Christian named Heradius had an only daughter whom he intended to consecrate to the Lord, but the Devil, enemy of the human race, got wind of this and caused one of Heradius's slaves to fall madly in love with the girl. Now this youth, realizing that, as a slave, he could never enjoy the favours of a girl so well-born, went off to a sorcerer, promising him a considerable sum of money if he could help him win the girl. 'I cannot do this myself,' the sorcerer said to him, 'but if you wish, I will send you to my master, the Devil, and if you do what he tells you, you will have what you desire.' The youth replied: 'I will do anything you say.' So the sorcerer composed a letter to the Devil and gave it to the youth to deliver. 'Master,' it ran, 'since it is my duty zealously and promptly to entice whomever I can away from the Christian religion and induce them to do your will, so that your kingdom may increase daily, I have sent this youth to you. He is burning with love for a certain young lady, and I beg you to grant him his desires, so that I may win glory thereby, and the power to win over others to your cause.' Giving the youth this letter, he said: 'Go and stand on the tomb of a pagan at dead of night and call on the demons there: hold this letter high in the air and they will be with you in a moment.' The slave went off and called on the demons, and threw the letter in the air. All at once the prince of darkness was with him, thronged by a legion of demons. When he had read the letter, he said to the young slave: 'Do you believe that I can do what you want?' 'Master, I believe,' he replied. 'And do you renounce your Christ?' added the Devil. 'I renounce him,' the slave agreed. 'What treacherous souls you Christians are!' the Devil exclaimed. 'Whenever you need me, you come to me, but when you have got what you want, you immediately deny me and return to your Christ, and he, because he is so forgiving, always welcomes you back! But if you want me to do your will, then give me a statement written in your own hand, saying that you renounce Christ, baptism and the Christian faith, that you are my servant, and ready to be condemned with me on Judgement Day.' The youth wrote all this down immediately, renouncing Christ and binding himself to serve the Devil. At once the Devil summoned the demons whose special province was fornication, and commanded them to go to the girl he named and to set her heart on fire with love for the young slave. This they did, and did so successfully that the girl threw herself on the ground before her father, weeping pitifully. 'Have pity on me, father!' she begged him. 'Have pity on me! I am tormented with love for one of our slaves. Show me a father's love, and let me marry him. I love him so much, and he is causing me such agony. If you do not, I shall soon die, you will see, and you will have to account for that on the Day of Judgement.' Her father was grief-stricken. 'Woe is me!' he cried. 'What has happened to my poor daughter? Who has stolen my treasure? Who has snuffed out the sweet light of my life? I wanted to marry you to the Celestial Bridegroom. I thought to gain my salvation through you, and now you have been driven crazy by some wanton, earthly love. Let me, dearest daughter, let me marry you to the Lord, as I had intended. Do not drive an old man to the grave with a broken heart!' But his daughter cried: 'Father, either grant me my wish, and do it quickly, or soon you will see me dead.' She was sobbing her heart out and almost hysterical with grief, so her father, in utter despair, foolishly listened to the advice of some friends and gave in to her. He married her to the young slave, bequeathed everything he had to her, then bade her a tearful farewell: 'Goodbye,' he said, 'my poor, poor daughter!'

Now when the young couple had been married a while, it emerged that Heradius's son-in-law never went to church, never crossed himself, and never said his prayers. His behaviour was noticed by several of their friends, and they said to his wife: 'Do you know that your husband, the man you chose to wed, is not a Christian, and never enters a church?' When she heard this, she was horrified: she threw herself to the ground, tore her face with her fingernails, and beat her breast and moaned: 'Ah me! Why was I ever born? Why could I not have died that very hour?' But when she told her husband what she had heard, he declared it was a pack of lies, and assured her that the truth was quite different. 'If you want me to believe you,' she told him, 'then let us go to church together tomorrow.' Realizing that he could now keep his secret no longer, he told her the whole story from the beginning. When she heard it, she gave a groan of anguish; then she hurried off to St Basil and gave him a detailed account of all that had happened to her husband and herself. Basil sent for the young man and heard the story from his own lips. 'My son,' he said, 'do you want to return to God?' 'I do, my lord,' he said, 'but I cannot. I have given myself to the Devil and denied Christ. And I wrote a formal statement of my renunciation and gave it to the Devil.' 'Do not worry,' Basil told him. 'The Lord is kind and will receive you if you repent.' Then he took hold of the young man, made the sign of the cross on his forehead and locked him in a cell for three days. At the end of this period he visited him and asked him how he was. 'My lord,' he answered, 'they scream at me; they terrify me; they are destroying me! They have the piece of paper I signed; they wave it at me in accusation. "You came to us," they say, "not we to you."' St Basil said: 'Do not be afraid, my son. Only believe.' And he gave him some food, made the sign of the cross over him again, shut him up in his room and prayed for him. Some days later he went to see him again, and again asked him: 'How are you, my son?' 'Father,' he replied, 'I hear their cries and threats, but I can no longer see them.' Basil again gave him food, and again made the sign of the cross over him, then shut his door and prayed for him. Some days later he returned and asked: 'How are you?' 'I am well, holy father!' replied the young man. 'For today I had a vision: I saw you fighting for me and conquering the Devil!' When Basil heard this, he released him from his confinement, summoned all the clergy, all the religious and all the people to the cathedral, and adjured them to pray for the young man. Then he took him by the hand and led him off to join them. But in an instant the Devil came to him with a host of demons, and, unseen by anyone, seized the young man and tried to wrest him from Basil's grasp. The youth cried out: 'Help me, holy man of God!' But the wicked one attacked him with such violence that, as he pulled him away, he dragged Basil with him, too. 'Arch-fiend!' Basil cried. 'Is your own perdition not enough for you? Must you try to take God's creature to damnation with you?' The Devil replied in a voice so loud that many of those gathered inside the church heard him: 'Basil, you do me wrong!' At that moment all the people sang out: *'Kyrie, eleison!'* ['Lord, have mercy!'], and Basil exclaimed: 'God damn you for this, Satan!' The Devil replied: 'Basil, you do me wrong! I did not seek him out; it was he who came to me. He renounced Christ and bound himself to me. Look! I have what he wrote here in my hand.' Basil replied: 'I shall not cease praying until you give me back that piece of paper.' And as Basil prayed, lifting his hands to heaven, everyone saw a leaf of paper flutter down from above and land in Basil's hands. He caught it and asked the youth: 'Do you recognize this, brother?' 'Yes,' he replied, 'it is written in my own hand.' Basil at once tore the paper in pieces, took the young man into the church, and made certain he was fit to receive the sacrament; he instructed him and gave him a rule of life to adhere to, then delivered him back to his wife.

There was a woman who had committed many sins and had written them all down on a piece of paper, saving the most serious one until last. This list she handed to St Basil, asking him to pray for her and so blot out her sins. Basil duly prayed, then, when the woman unfolded the piece of paper, she discovered that all her sins had been blotted out except the most serious. 'Have pity on me, servant of God,' she said, 'and win me God's pardon for this, as you have for the rest.' 'Away from me, woman!' Basil said to her. 'I am a sinful man, and need forgiveness as much as you do.' But when she insisted, he told her: 'Go to the holy man Ephrem: he will be able to obtain for you what you want.' So the woman went off to the holy man Ephrem and told him why she had been sent to him by St Basil. 'Leave me,' he said, 'for I am a sinful man. Go back to Basil, my daughter. He won pardon for your other sins, and he will be able to do so for this sin, too. But hurry, if you want to find him still alive!' The woman arrived in the city at the moment

Basil was being carried to his tomb. But she followed the procession and began to cry out: 'Let God witness this and judge between the two of us. You yourself could have reconciled me with God, but you sent me away to someone else.' She then threw her list on the bier, and an instant later, when she retrieved it and opened it, she found that the last sin had been completely blotted out. For this mercy she thanked God from the bottom of her heart, and everyone present joined her.

When the saint was near death, and already suffering from his last illness, he sent for a Jew named Joseph, a skilled physician who was very dear to him, because Basil foresaw that he was to convert him to the Christian faith. When Joseph felt Basil's pulse, he realized at once that he was at death's door. He told the bishop's servants: 'Get everything ready for the burial, because he will die at any moment.' Basil heard this and said to him: 'You do not know what you are talking about.' 'Believe me, my lord,' Joseph replied. 'As surely as the sun will go down today, so, too, you will be gone by sunset.' Basil retorted: 'And what if I am not?' 'You cannot possibly live, my lord,' Joseph told him. 'What will you do,' Basil asked him, 'if I live until the sixth hour tomorrow?' 'If you survive until then,' Joseph replied, 'I am ready to die myself!' 'Indeed,' Basil said. 'You will die to sin, but live in Christ!' 'I know what you are suggesting,' Joseph told him. 'If you live until that hour, I will do what you want of me.'

Then St Basil, though according to the laws of nature he should have died at any moment, prayed to the Lord to prolong his life, and lived on until the ninth hour of the next day. When Joseph witnessed this, he was dumbfounded, and believed in Christ. And Basil, finding the strength of spirit to overcome his bodily weakness, got up from his bed, went into church, and baptized Joseph with his own hands. Then he returned to bed and happily rendered up his soul to God. He flourished around AD 370.

32

ST QUIRICUS AND
HIS MOTHER JULITTA

16 June

Quiricus was the son of Julitta, a most noble lady of Iconium. In her efforts to avoid persecution as a Christian, she took her son Quiricus, who was then three years old, to Tarsus in Cilicia. But there, with her child in her arms, she was made to appear before the governor Alexander, and when her two maids saw her arrested, they fled at once and abandoned her. The governor took the child in his arms, and when Julitta refused to offer sacrifice to the gods, he had her flogged with thongs of rawhide. Now when the child saw his mother beaten, he began to weep bitterly and to utter the most pitiful cries. So the governor put his arms round the young Quiricus and held him in his lap, and tried to soothe him with kisses and caresses. But the child, looking back at his mother, shrank from his kisses; he turned his head away in indignation, tore at the governor's face with his nails and uttered cries which seemed to echo his mother's, as if to say: 'I, too, am a Christian!' After struggling for some time he finally bit the governor on the shoulder, and Alexander, furious and smarting with the pain, threw the child violently down the steps of the tribunal, dashing his young brains out all over them. Julitta, when she saw that her son had gone before her to the heavenly kingdom, joyfully gave thanks to God. Then the governor commanded that she be flogged, plunged into boiling pitch and finally beheaded.

In one legend, however, we find that Quiricus, paying as little heed to the tyrant's caresses as to his threats, loudly declared that he was a Christian. (He was, in fact, a tiny child, and as such unable to speak, but the Holy Spirit spoke through him.) When the governor asked him who had taught him to speak, the child said: 'Your stupidity, sir, amazes me! You see how young I am, and you ask me, a child not yet three years old, who gave me this godly wisdom?' As Quiricus was being flogged, he kept crying out: 'I am a Christian!', and each time he uttered the words, he gained new strength to face his ordeal.

The governor had the corpses of both mother and child cut into pieces and gave orders for them to be scattered to the winds, so that they could not be given burial by Christians. But they were gathered by an angel and buried at night by Christians. In the time of Constantine the Great, when peace had been restored to the Church, the location of the bodies of these two martyrs was revealed by one of Julitta's two maids, who still survived, and they were held in great veneration by the whole city. Quiricus and Julitta suffered around the year of our Lord 230, under the governor Alexander.

33

STS GERVASE AND
PROTASE

19 June

Gervase and Protase were twin brothers, the sons of St Vitalis and the blessed Valeria. Having given all their goods away to the poor, they lived with St Nazarius, who was then building an oratory near Embrun with a boy named Celsus, who was helping him by carrying stones. (This mention of St Nazarius having Celsus with him at so early a date is perhaps an anticipation of the facts, since we gather from the life of St Nazarius that he was not brought to him until much later.) But all three of them were brought before the emperor Nero, and the young Celsus followed behind, howling. When one of the soldiers began to cuff the lad, and Nazarius reproached him for this, the rest of the soldiers kicked Nazarius to the ground and trampled him, then shut him up with the others in prison and later threw him into the sea. Gervase and Protase were taken to Milan, where Nazarius, miraculously preserved, was able to join them.

At the same time Count Astasius arrived in Milan on his way to wage war against the Marcomanni. The idol worshippers went out to meet him, and declared that the gods would not deign to speak to them unless Gervase and Protase first offered them sacrifice. So the brothers were at once arrested and invited to sacrifice. But Gervase told Astasius that all their idols were deaf and dumb, and insisted that it was Almighty God whom the count must ask for victory. Astasius, enraged, ordered Gervase to be scourged with leaded thongs until he breathed his last. He then had Protase summoned and said to him: 'You wretch, either choose to live, or die a painful death like your brother!' Protase replied: 'Who is the wretched one – I, who do not fear you, or you, who are clearly afraid of me?' Astasius said to him: 'I, fear you, you wretched man? What do you mean?' Protase replied: 'It is obvious that you fear me and the harm I can do you if I do not sacrifice to your gods. If you were not afraid I would do you some harm, you would not be trying to force me to sacrifice to the idols.' At this the count had him hung upon the rack. Protase told him: 'I am not angry with you, my lord, because I see that your heart is blind. No, I pity you, rather, because you do not know what you are doing. So come, finish what you have begun, so that I may join my brother in the loving embrace of our Saviour!' The count then ordered him to be beheaded. Afterwards a servant of Christ named Philip, with his son's help, stole the bodies and buried them in a stone vault in his own house, and placed at their heads a book which gave an account of their birth, life and martyrdom. They suffered under Nero, whose reign began around AD 57.

The martyrs' bodies remained hidden for ages, but, in the time of St Ambrose, they were discovered in the following manner. Ambrose was at prayer one day in the church of Sts Nabor and Felix, and was neither wide awake nor fast asleep, when two most handsome youths, dressed in tunics and mantles of pure white and wearing short boots on their feet,[1] appeared to him and, with hands outstretched, joined him in prayer. Ambrose prayed that, if this were an illusion, it should not happen again; but that if it were a true vision, it might appear to him a second time. Then, at cockcrow, just as before, the two youths appeared to him again and prayed with him. But on the third night, when he was awake but exhausted with fasting, Ambrose was amazed to see a third figure appear to him, one whom, from the paintings he had seen of him, he recognized as the apostle Paul. The two youths remained silent, but the apostle said to Ambrose: 'These two are youths who, disdaining earthly things, followed my precepts. You will find their bodies exactly where you are standing now. At a depth of twelve feet you will find their tomb covered with earth, and at their head a book containing an account of their lives, from birth to death.'

So Ambrose summoned all his fellow bishops in the neighbourhood. He was himself the first to begin the digging, and he found everything exactly as St Paul had told him. Though three hundred years had passed since their interment, the bodies of the two martyrs were found to be as fresh as if they had been put there that very hour. Moreover, a glorious fragrance of exquisite sweetness emanated from the tomb, and a blind man who touched it recovered his sight. Many other sick people, too, were cured by the merits of these two saints.

It was on the feast-day of Gervase and Protase that peace was re-established between the Lombards and the Roman Empire, and it was to commemorate this occasion that Pope Gregory introduced the custom of chanting the '*Loquetur Dominus pacem in plebem suam etc.*' ['The Lord will speak peace unto his people' (Psalm 85 (86): 8)] at the introit of the mass of their feast-day.

So the office of that day consists of references partly to the saints themselves, and partly to events which occurred on the same date.

In the twentieth book of his treatise *On the City of God*, Augustine relates that, in his own presence and that of the emperor and a great crowd of other people, a blind man recovered his sight at the tomb of the martyrs Gervase and Protase in Milan. (Whether this was the same blind man mentioned above is not known.) Augustine also relates, in the same work, that a youth was bathing his horse in a river near the Villa Victoriana, thirty miles from Hippo, when suddenly a demon attacked him, threw him into the river, and left him for dead. During the singing of vespers that evening in the church of Sts Gervase and Protase, which was near to the river, the youth, seemingly drawn there by the sound of voices, entered the church, yelling and screaming, and held on to the altar so tightly that he simply could not be removed – it was as if he were tied to it. And when the priest adjured the demon to leave the youth, it threatened to tear the youth apart, limb from limb, if it had to go. Then, when finally the demon was made to leave, one of the youth's eyes was left hanging down his cheek, attached only by a thread-like vein. But they put the eye back in its place as best they could, and miraculously, within a few days, through the merits of Sts Gervase and Protase the youth was completely healed . . .

34

ST PETER, APOSTLE

29 June

Peter the apostle stood head and shoulders above all the other apostles for the strength of his religious fervour. It was he who wanted to find out who had betrayed his Lord, because, according to Augustine, if he had known who it was, he would have torn him apart with his teeth; and for this reason the Lord declined to name him. For if he had done so, Chrysostom says, Peter would have leapt up at once and slain him. It was Peter who walked over the waves to the Lord and was chosen to be with the Lord at his transfiguration and the raising of Jairus's daughter; he was the one who found the tribute money in the fish's mouth, received the keys of the kingdom of heaven from the Lord and accepted Christ's command to feed his sheep. He converted three thousand people by his preaching on the day of Pentecost, predicted the deaths of Ananias and Sapphira, cured Aeneas, who was sick of the palsy, baptized Cornelius, raised Tabitha to life again, healed sick people with the mere shadow of his body, was imprisoned by Herod, and set free by an angel.

As to what food he ate and what clothes he wore, we have his own words, as recorded in Clement's *Epistle*. 'I eat nothing but bread and olives,' he said, 'and on occasion some vegetables. What you see me wearing now is all I have for clothes – a tunic and a cloak – and I need nothing else.' It is also said that he always carried with him under his tunic a napkin which he used to wipe away his tears, for he wept frequently; when he recalled the sweet voice and presence of the Lord, the intensity of his love overwhelmed him, and he could not hold back the tears. And when he remembered the sin he had committed in denying the Lord, he would weep profusely. In fact, he used to weep so often that, as Clement puts it, his whole face seemed to be 'wasted' with weeping. Clement also tells us that Peter used to get up to pray at crack of dawn, as soon as he heard the cock crow, and this, too, caused him to burst out weeping. He also tells us, as we find in the *Ecclesiastical History*, that when Peter's wife was being led to her martyrdom, Peter was overcome with joy, called her by name, and cried out to her: 'Dear wife, remember the Lord!'

One day St Peter sent two of his disciples off to preach, and when they had been travelling for twenty days, one of them died. The other returned to Peter and told him what had happened. (The disciple who died is said to have been the blessed Martial; others say it was Maternus. Other accounts say that one of these disciples was the blessed Fronto, and the other, his companion who died, was a priest named George.) Peter handed the disciple his staff and told him to hurry back to his companion and lay the staff upon him. This he did, and his friend, who had already been dead for forty days, at once got up alive.

At that time there was in Jerusalem a sorcerer named Simon, who proclaimed himself the fountain-head of all truth, declared that he could make all who believed in him immortal, and claimed that nothing was impossible to him. On one occasion, as we read in Clement's *Epistle*, he said: 'I shall be worshipped publicly as God; I shall be accorded divine honours; and I shall be able to do whatever I want. Once when my mother Rachel told me to go out into the fields to reap, I saw a sickle lying on the ground and ordered it to do the reaping on its own, and it reaped ten times as much as the other reapers could manage.' According to Jerome, Simon also said: 'I am the Word of God; I am the Comely One; I am the Paraclete, I am the Omnipotent; I am the Soul of God.'[1] He brought bronze serpents to life, made statues of bronze and stone laugh, and dogs sing. Now Simon, as St Linus tells us, wanted to meet Peter in debate, and to prove to him that he was God. So they agreed a day for this confrontation, and Peter went to the meeting place and called to those who were gathered there: 'Peace be with you, my brothers, who are lovers of the truth.' Simon retorted: 'We have no need of your peace. If peace and harmony prevail, we shall never be able to arrive at the truth. Even thieves can be at peace with each other. So do not call for peace, but war! When two men do battle, there is no peace until one of them is vanquished.' Peter replied: 'Why are you afraid of the word "peace"? Wars are born of sin; but where there is no sin, there is peace. Truth manifests itself in debate, just as justice does in good works.' 'Drivel!' Simon snapped. 'I will demonstrate to you the power of my godhead so that you will instantly worship me. I am the source of all power, and I can fly through the air, make new trees spring from the earth, turn stones to bread, and live in fire without being burnt! I can do anything I wish!' Then Peter began to refute him, and to expose all of Simon's magic illusions, whereupon Simon, realizing that he was no match for Peter, threw all his magic books into the sea, fearing that he might be denounced as a sorcerer, and hurried away to Rome, to see if the people there would worship him as a god. As soon as Peter found out about this, he set off for Rome in pursuit of Simon.

Peter reached Rome in the fourth year of the reign of the emperor Claudius, and he remained there for twenty-five years. As John Beleth tells us, he ordained two bishops, Linus and Cletus, as his assistants, one for the area outside the city walls, the other for the city itself. An indefatigable preacher, he converted many to the faith and healed a great number of the sick. In his preaching he always commended and emphasized the importance of chastity, and as a consequence, when he converted the four concubines of the prefect Agrippa, they refused thereafter to go back to the prefect. This enraged Agrippa, and he began to look for an opportunity to do Peter some mischief. But then the Lord appeared to Peter and said: 'Simon and Nero are plotting against you,[2] but do not be afraid, because I am with you to deliver you, and as consolation I shall give you the companionship of my servant Paul, who will arrive in Rome tomorrow.' Peter knew by this, as Linus tells us, that he must soon lay aside his earthly vesture, so at an assembly of the faithful he took the hand of Clement, consecrated him as bishop, and seated him on his own throne of office. After this Paul arrived in Rome, as the Lord had foretold, and with Peter began to preach Christ.

Now Nero held Simon in the highest regard, because he firmly believed him to be the guardian of his own life and well-being, and that of the whole city. One day, according to Pope Leo, as he stood before Nero, Simon suddenly changed his appearance and became by turns an older man and a youth, and when Nero saw this, he began to believe he was in truth the Son of God. So, as the same Leo relates, Simon the Sorcerer said to Nero: 'In order to convince yourself that I am the Son of God, my lord, have me beheaded, and on the third day I shall rise again.' So Nero gave his executioner orders to behead Simon. But, though he thought he was cutting Simon's head off, in fact he beheaded a ram, and Simon, thanks to his magic, was unharmed. He gathered up the remains of the ram and hid them, and for three days went into hiding while the ram's blood dried on the floor where it had dropped. On the third day Simon appeared before Nero and said: 'You can wipe my blood from the floor where it was spilled. Here I am! I was beheaded, but I have risen on the third day, just as I said I would.' When Nero saw him, he was dumbfounded and was finally convinced that

Simon was truly the Son of God. This is Leo's account of what happened. Another time, when Simon was in a room with Nero, a demon in his form was outside, speaking with the people. In the end the Romans held him in such veneration that they set up a statue in his honour with an inscription above it which read: *Simoni Deo Sancto* ['To Simon, the holy God'].

According to Leo, Peter and Paul went to Nero and began to expose all Simon's sham wizardry; and Peter added that just as there are in Christ two substances, namely the divine and the human, so there were two substances in this sorcerer, the human and the diabolical. Simon's reply, as St Marcellus and Leo attest, was: 'I cannot tolerate the slanders of this man any longer. I shall order my angels to avenge me on him.' 'I do not fear your angels,' Peter told him. 'Rather it is they who fear me.' 'Are you unafraid of Simon,' Nero asked, 'even when he performs miracles to prove his divinity?' Peter replied: 'If there is any divinity in him, let him tell me what I am thinking, or what I am doing! But first I will whisper in your ear what I am thinking, so that he dare not lie.' 'Come here, then,' Nero said, 'and tell me what you are thinking.' Peter went over to him and whispered: 'Have someone bring me a barley loaf and give it to me without his knowing.' The loaf arrived, and Peter first blessed it, then hid it in his sleeve. Then he said: 'Let Simon, who claims to be God, say what it is that I have thought, said and done.' 'No!' Simon retorted. 'Let Peter say, rather, what I am thinking.' Peter replied: 'Watch what I do, and I will prove to you that I know what Simon is thinking.' Simon shouted angrily: 'I command great hounds to appear and devour him!' And from nowhere giant hounds appeared and set upon Peter, but he held out the bread he had blessed and at once they turned tail and fled. 'See?' Peter said to Nero. 'I have shown that I knew what Simon was thinking, and not by words, but by action. He promised to send his angels against me, but instead he produced hounds, which proves his angels are more dog-like than god-like!' 'Listen, you two,' Simon said to Peter and Paul, 'I may be powerless to harm you here, but one day, somewhere, it will be my turn to sit in judgement of you. But for the moment I will spare you.'

Then, as Hegesippus and Linus relate, Simon became so puffed up with pride that he boasted he could raise the dead. Now it happened that a young man had died, so Peter and Simon were summoned, and there was unanimous agreement when Simon suggested that whichever one of them could not raise the dead youth should be put to death. First Simon chanted his incantations over the body, and spectators observed the dead youth moving his head. They all began shouting and wanted to stone Peter, but he finally managed to silence them. 'If the dead youth is alive,' he said, 'let him get up and walk and talk. Otherwise I assure you, when the corpse moves its head, it is merely an illusion. Let Simon move away from the bier so that the Devil's trickery can be fully exposed to view.' So Simon was moved from the bier and the youth lay quite motionless. Then Peter, standing at a distance, uttered a prayer, then cried aloud: 'Young man, in the name of Jesus Christ of Nazareth, the crucified, rise up and walk!' And instantly the youth got to his feet and walked about. The people then wanted to stone Simon, but Peter told them: 'He has been punished enough, because he knows that he and his magic tricks have been defeated. And our master has taught us to repay evil with good.' But Simon said: 'I tell you, Peter and Paul, what you desire will never be yours. I will never deign to give you the crown of martyrdom.' Peter replied: 'I pray our desire may be granted. But may nothing good ever come your way, for every word you utter is a lie!'

Then, as St Marcellus tells us, Simon went to the house of Marcellus, a disciple of his, and put an enormous dog on a leash at the door of the house. 'Peter comes to see you often,' he said to Marcellus. 'Let us see if he can get in now.' After a little while Peter arrived and, making the sign of the cross, he untied the dog. The dog was friendly to everyone else, but he chased Simon and caught him, pulled him to the ground, and was about to seize him by the throat when Peter ran up and shouted to him not to bite. The dog did Simon no real harm, but he tore his clothing to shreds and left him lying there naked. Thereupon the crowd of onlookers, and especially the children, chased him away, as did the dog, until they had all run him out of the city as they might a stray wolf.

Unable to bear the shame of this public humiliation, Simon vanished from view for the space of a year, and Marcellus, after witnessing these miracles, became a disciple of St Peter. In time Simon came out of hiding and Nero welcomed him back as his friend. According to Leo, Simon then called the people together and told them that he had been deeply offended by the Galileans; and for that reason he was intending to abandon the city whose protector he had been, and to name the day on which he would ascend to heaven, because he did not deign to live on earth any longer. On the appointed day he climbed to the top of a lofty tower, or, according to Linus, to the top of the Capitol, and, wearing a crown of laurel on his head, leapt off and began to fly. Paul said to Peter: 'Leave me to pray: you take command!' Nero said: 'Simon spoke the truth. You two are charlatans.' Peter said to Paul: 'Look up and see!' Paul looked up and saw Simon flying, and asked Peter: 'What are you waiting for? Finish what you have begun, for the Lord is already calling us!' Then Peter said: 'You angels of Satan, you who keep Simon aloft in the air, I adjure you in the name of our Lord Jesus Christ, carry him no more! Let him fall!' At once Simon was released; he dropped to the ground, his neck was broken and he died. When Nero saw this, he was deeply distressed at the loss of such a man and said to the apostles: 'You have grieved me deeply. I shall have you put to death, and make a terrible example of you!' (This is Leo's account.) Nero then handed them over to a high-ranking official named Paulinus, and Paulinus put them in the Mamertine prison, to be guarded by two soldiers called Processus and Martinianus. But Peter converted them, and they opened the prison door and let the two apostles go free. (After the martyrdom of Peter and Paul, Paulinus summoned Processus and Martinianus to answer for this, and when he discovered that they were Christians, at Nero's command he had them beheaded.) The faithful pressed Peter to leave Rome: this he was reluctant to do, but at last he gave in to their pleas and left. When he came to the gate, as Leo and Linus attest, in the quarter where the church of Santa Maria ad Passus stands today, Peter saw Christ coming towards him and he said: 'Lord, where are you going?' 'I am going to Rome,' Christ answered him, 'to be crucified again.' Peter replied: 'You will be crucified again?' 'Yes,' Christ told him. 'Then I shall go back, Lord,' Peter said, 'to be crucified with you.' After this, as Peter watched and wept, the Lord ascended into heaven. Peter, realizing that what Jesus had said concerned his own martyrdom, went back to the city and told the brethren what had happened.

He was then arrested by Nero's men and brought before the prefect Agrippa, and there, as Linus tells us, his face was radiant as the sun. 'Are you the one,' the prefect asked him, 'who glories in the company of the common people and who keeps all those young women from their husbands' beds?' The apostle told him indignantly that he gloried only in the cross of Christ. Then Peter, as a foreigner, was condemned to be crucified, whereas Paul, because he was a Roman citizen, was condemned to be beheaded. Dionysius, in his letter to Timothy concerning the death of St Paul, says the following about their trial and judgement: 'O my dear brother, if you had witnessed the suffering of their last moments, you would have died of sorrow and grief! Who would not have wept at the moment sentence was pronounced against them, and we heard that Peter was to be crucified and Paul beheaded? Then you would have seen the mob of pagans and Jews striking them and spitting in their faces. And when the terrible moment of their martyrdom came and they were separated from each other, they were bound in chains, those twin pillars of the world, while the faithful groaned and wept. Then Paul said to Peter: "Peace be with you, corner-stone of the Church, shepherd of the sheep and lambs of Christ!" And Peter replied: "Go in peace, preacher of godly living, mediator and guide of the righteous to salvation!" They were then taken away in different directions,' writes Dionysius, 'for they were not executed in the same quarters of the city, and I followed my master.'

Leo and Marcellus say that when Peter came to the cross, he told his executioners: 'Since my Lord came down to earth from heaven, he was raised upon a cross that stood upright. Now he deigns to call me from earth to heaven, my cross should show my head to the earth and point my feet towards heaven. Therefore, since I am not worthy of hanging on the cross as my Lord did, turn my cross round and crucify me upside-down!' The executioners turned the cross and nailed him to it with his feet above and his hands below. When they saw this, the people were enraged; they wanted to kill Nero and the prefect, and set the apostle free, but Peter begged them not to hinder his martyrdom. Hegesippus and Linus state that the Lord opened the eyes of those who were weeping there, and they saw angels with crowns of roses and lilies in their hands and Peter standing with them at the cross, receiving a book from Christ, and reading in the book the words he was speaking. The same Hegesippus says that Peter then began to speak from the cross: 'Lord,' he said, 'I wanted to follow in your footsteps, but I could not presume to be crucified upright. You were always upright, exalted and sublime; but we are children of the first man who bowed his head to the ground, and his fall is mirrored in the way we men are born, for when we come into the world, we seem to be dropped prone upon the earth. Our condition, too, has become so changed that the world thinks what is left is right, and what is right is left! But you, Lord, are everything to me, you are my all in all, and other than you I have nothing. I thank you with all my soul – the soul by which I live, and understand, and cry to you.' (And in these words he touches on two other reasons why he did not want to be crucified in an upright position.)

Peter, knowing finally that the faithful had seen his glory, gave thanks, commended the faithful to God, and gave up the ghost. Marcellus and Apuleius, who were brothers and disciples of Peter, took his body down from the cross, embalmed it in sweet spices and buried it . . .

35

ST PAUL, APOSTLE

30 June

After his conversion the apostle Paul suffered persecution on many occasions, which St Hilary enumerates briefly as follows: 'In Philippi Paul the apostle was beaten with rods and put in gaol with his feet fastened in stocks; in Lystra he was stoned; in Iconium and Thessalonica he was hounded by wicked unbelievers; at Ephesus, thrown to the beasts; at Damascus he had to be let down over the city wall in a basket; in Jerusalem he was arrested, flogged, put in chains and schemed against; in Caesarea, imprisoned and vilified; on his passage to Italy he was exposed to great danger, and when he finally reached Rome he was tried and put to death by Nero.'

Paul was appointed as apostle to the Gentiles. At Lystra he made a lame man get up and walk, and restored to life a young man who had fallen from a window and died. And he performed many other miracles. On the island of Malta he was bitten on the hand by a viper, but it did him no harm, and he shook it off into the fire. It is also said that all those who are descendants of the man who was Paul's host on this occasion are immune from the poison of snake bites. So when a son of that line is born, his father puts snakes in his cradle to prove that the child is really his.

Sometimes we find that Paul is described as inferior to Peter, sometimes as his superior, sometimes as his equal, but the truth of the matter is that he was his inferior in status, but his superior in preaching and his equal in sanctity. Haimo[1] relates that Paul engaged in hard manual labour from cockcrow to the fifth hour, then went about his preaching and most often preached on until nightfall, and found time in the hours that remained for food and sleep and prayer.

When Paul arrived in Rome, Nero had not yet been officially declared emperor, and when he heard that there was a dispute between Paul and the Jews about Jewish law and the Christian faith, he was not greatly concerned. So Paul went about freely wherever he wanted and was at liberty to preach. Jerome, in his work *On Illustrious Men*, remarks that in the twenty-fifth year after the Lord's passion, that is the second year of Nero's principate, Paul was sent to Rome in chains and for the space of two years was kept under house arrest; and during that period he engaged in debates with the Jews. He was then released by Nero and preached the Gospel in the West. In the fourteenth year of Nero's reign, however, in the same year and on the same day that Peter was crucified, he was beheaded.

Paul became widely known and universally admired for his wisdom and piety. He formed friendships with many members of the emperor's household and converted them to the faith of Christ. Some of his writings were in fact read out in Nero's presence and applauded by all present. Even the Senate held him in high regard.

One day towards evening Paul was preaching on a roof-top terrace, and a young man called Patroclus, who was Nero's cupbearer and very dear to his master, because there was a large crowd climbed to a window ledge in order to hear Paul better. In a little while he nodded off, fell from the ledge and was killed. When Nero heard, he was grief-stricken at Patroclus's death, and had at once to appoint another youth to take his place. But Paul learnt of this by divine revelation, and asked some of those present to go and bring him the body of this Patroclus who was so dear to the emperor. They fetched the body, and Paul raised him to life and sent him back with his companions to Nero. So, as Nero was lamenting the loss of his favourite, quite suddenly he was told that Patroclus was alive and at the door. Now when Nero heard that the youth he had a moment ago believed dead was in fact alive, he was shaken, and at first he refused to have him admitted. But at length his courtiers persuaded him to let the boy come in. 'Patroclus!' Nero exclaimed. 'Are you really alive?' 'Yes, Caesar,' he replied, 'I am.' 'Who brought you back to life?' Nero asked. Patroclus replied: 'Jesus Christ, King of all ages.' 'And he will reign for all eternity,' Nero cried angrily, 'and overthrow all the kingdoms on earth?' Patroclus answered: 'Yes, Caesar!' At this Nero slapped him. 'So you are now in that King's service?' he demanded. 'Indeed I am,' Patroclus agreed, 'because he raised me from the dead.' Then five of Nero's courtiers, who were in constant attendance upon him, said to him: 'Why do you strike this youth, Caesar? He is answering you wisely and truthfully. We too are servants of this invincible King!'

Nero at once clapped them in prison, intending, despite his previous affection for them, to have them cruelly tortured. Next he commanded that all Christians be hunted down and punished: they were to be subjected to every kind of torture without even the formality of a hearing. As a result

Paul, among others, was brought before Nero in chains. 'Well, my friend,' Nero said to him, 'you may be a servant of the great King, yet here you are, my prisoner! Why do you lure my soldiers away from me and gather them around yourself?' Paul replied: 'It is not only from your court that I have gathered my soldiers, but from the whole world. And our King will lavish upon them such gifts as will never fail, and he will banish all want for ever. If you will submit to his rule, you, too, will be saved. His power is so great that he will come to judge all men, and will destroy the whole framework of the world by fire.' On hearing Paul say that the framework of the world must be destroyed by fire, Nero flew into a violent rage and gave orders for all Christians to be burnt alive. Paul, however, being judged guilty of treason, was to be beheaded. Subsequently such vast numbers of Christians were executed that the Roman people laid siege to Nero's palace and began to stir up a rebellion against him. 'Stop, Caesar!' they cried. 'Call a halt to the carnage; order them to stop! These people you are killing are our fellow citizens; they are supporters of the Roman Empire!' This frightened Nero, and he changed his edict, forbidding anyone to lay hands on the Christians until the emperor himself had conducted a thorough investigation and reached a decision about them. So Paul was brought back and again put before the emperor. As soon as Nero set eyes on him he screamed: 'Away with this malefactor! Off with the charlatan's head! Don't let the criminal live! Rid me of this seducer of souls, this perverter of minds; wipe him off the face of the earth!' 'Nero,' Paul replied, 'I shall suffer only a short while, but I shall live for ever in the Lord Jesus Christ!' Nero cried: 'Off with his head! He must learn that I am mightier than his king, that I have beaten him once and for all. Then let us see if he manages to live for ever!' 'So that you may know that I am still alive after the death of my body, when my head has been cut off,' Paul told him, 'I will appear to you alive, and then you will know that Christ is the God of life, not of death.' When he had said this, Paul was taken to the place of execution. On his way there the three soldiers who were escorting him asked: 'Tell us, Paul, who is this king of yours, whom you love so much that you would rather die for him than live? What sort of reward will you get for all this?' Paul then preached to them about the kingdom of God and the torments of hell, and so convinced them that he converted them to the faith. But when they told him that he could go free, and go where he wanted, he said: 'God forbid that I should run away, my brothers! I am no deserter, but a true soldier of Christ. I know that I shall pass from this transitory life into life eternal, and soon, when I am beheaded, the faithful will come to take away my body. You must note the spot and come back there tomorrow morning. Beside my grave you will find two men praying, Titus and Luke. Tell them why I sent you to them and they will baptize you, and make you partners and co-heirs in the kingdom of heaven.'

While Paul was speaking, Nero dispatched two soldiers to see if his execution had taken place. Paul tried to convert them, but they said: 'When you are dead and come back to life again, we will believe what you say. In the meantime come and get what you deserve!' At the Ostia Gate, near where Paul was to suffer, he met a disciple of his, a married lady named Plantilla. (According to Dionysius her name was Lemobia, but perhaps she had two names.)[2] In tears Plantilla commended herself to his prayers. 'Farewell,[3] Plantilla,' Paul said, 'daughter of eternal salvation. But loan me that veil you are wearing, and I will use it to cover my eyes. I will return it to you afterwards.' As she handed Paul her veil, the executioners sneered at her and said: 'Why give this impostor, this charlatan, such a costly veil? You will only lose it!'

When Paul finally arrived at the place of execution, he turned to the East, raised his hands to heaven, and with tears in his eyes prayed at length in his own tongue and gave thanks to God. Then he said farewell to his brethren, covered his eyes with the veil Plantilla had given him, knelt on the ground on both knees, offered his neck to the executioner and was beheaded. The moment his head fell from his body, he called out, quite clearly, in Hebrew: 'Jesus Christ!' – the name that had been so sweet to him in life, and which he had uttered so often. (It is said that in his epistles Paul used the name Christ or Jesus, or both, no fewer than five hundred times.) From his wound milk spurted over a soldier's clothing, and then the blood flowed out. A great light filled the sky, and a perfume of wonderful sweetness emanated from his body.

Dionysius, in his letter[4] to Timothy on Paul's death, writes as follows: 'In that saddest of all hours, my beloved brother, when the executioner said to Paul: "Hold out your neck!", the blessed apostle looked up to heaven, made the sign of the cross on his forehead and breast and said: "My Lord Jesus Christ, into your hands I commend my spirit." Then quite cheerfully and willingly he stretched out his neck, the executioner struck and severed his head, and he received the crown of martyrdom. As the sword fell, blessed Paul untied the veil, caught his own blood in it, folded it and handed it back to the woman. When the executioner returned, Lemobia asked him: "Where have you left my master, Paul?" The soldier told her: "He is lying with his friend outside the city in the Valley of the Boxers, and his face is covered with your veil." But she replied: "Look! I have just seen Peter and Paul entering the city dressed in shining robes! They had glittering crowns all radiant with light upon their heads!" Then she held out the blood-stained veil and showed it to everyone, and because of this miracle, many people believed in the Lord and became Christians.' This is the version given by Dionysius.

When Nero heard about this he was terror-stricken, and summoned philosophers and friends to discuss with them all that had happened. While they were in conference, Paul entered the room, though the doors were barred, and, standing before Nero, he said: 'Here I am, Caesar: Paul, soldier of the eternal and unconquered king. Now you can rest assured that I am not dead but alive, and that you, wretch that you are, will die an eternal death for unjustly putting to death the holy ones of God.' With these words he vanished. Nero was so terrified he almost lost his mind. He had no idea what to do. But finally he was persuaded by his friends to release Patroclus and Barnabas along with the other Christians, and he let them go freely wherever they wanted. Next morning the two soldiers, Longinus the captain and Accestus, went to Paul's grave and there saw two men, Titus and Luke, at prayer, with Paul standing between them. When Titus and Luke saw the soldiers, they panicked and took to their heels, and Paul disappeared. But Longinus and Accestus shouted after them: 'We are not here to make trouble, as you think. We want you to baptize us. Paul told us to ask you, and we saw him praying here with you a moment ago.' When they heard this, Titus and Luke came back and baptized them.

Paul's head was thrown into a pit, and, because of all the other people who had been executed and whose heads and limbs had been thrown there, it could never be found . . .

36

ST ALEXIS

17 July

Alexis was the son of Euphemianus, a Roman of the highest nobility and a leading member of the emperor's court. He was waited on by three thousand slaves, all of whom were clad in silk and wore girdles of gold. Euphemianus was a high-ranking magistrate, but a man of great compassion. Every day he had three tables[1] set up in his house for the poor, for orphans and widows and pilgrims, and he served his guests in person, waiting on them hand and foot. He did not take food himself until late, and then did so in the fear of the Lord, in the company of other pious men. His wife, whose name was Aglae, shared his faith and was of the same pious disposition. They were childless until the Lord answered their prayers and gave them a son, and after his birth they resolved to live the rest of their lives in chastity.

Their son was educated in the liberal arts, and excelled in all the branches of philosophy. When he reached adolescence, a young girl of the imperial household was chosen for him and they were joined in marriage. But when the wedding night came and Alexis was alone with his bride in the secrecy of their bedchamber, the pious youth began to instruct his spouse in the fear of God, and to encourage her to preserve her virgin purity. Then he gave her his golden ring and the buckle of the belt he was wearing. 'Take these and keep them,' he told her, 'as long as God pleases, and may the Lord be with us both!' After this he took some of his inheritance and left for the coast; he secretly boarded ship and sailed to Laodicea, and from there went on to Edessa, a city in Syria, where, on a piece of fine linen, an image of our Lord Jesus Christ was preserved, which no human hand had made. On his arrival there he distributed everything he had brought with him to the poor, and put on tattered clothes and began to sit with the other paupers in the porch of the church of Mary Mother of God. Of the alms he received he kept for himself only what was absolutely necessary, and gave away the rest to the other poor people.

Now his father, who was broken-hearted at the departure of his son, sent his servants to comb every corner of the earth looking for him. When some of them arrived in Edessa, Alexis recognized them, but they did not recognize him at all, and they gave him alms as they did to the rest of the paupers. Alexis accepted them and gave thanks to God, saying: 'I thank you, Lord, that you have enabled me to receive alms from my own servants.' When the servants returned home, they reported to their master that they had not been able to find his son anywhere. His mother, from the day of his departure, had spread a sack on the floor of her bedroom, where she spent sleepless nights, sobbing to herself: 'Here I shall stay in perpetual mourning until my son is restored to me!' And Alexis's young wife said to her mother-in-law: 'Until I hear news of my beloved husband, I shall stay here and mourn with you, like a lonely turtle dove.'

When Alexis had passed seventeen years in God's service in the porchway of the church in Edessa, the image of the Blessed Virgin that was kept inside said to the custodian of the church: 'Have the man of God come in, because he is worthy of the kingdom of heaven and the spirit of God rests upon him, for his prayer rises like incense before the sight of God.' But the custodian did not know to whom she was referring, so the Virgin spoke to him again. 'He is the one sitting outside in the porch.' The custodian hurried out and brought Alexis into the church, and, when they learnt what had happened, everyone began to treat him with great reverence. So in order to escape earthly renown, Alexis left Edessa and went back to Laodicea, and there boarded ship with the intention of sailing to Tarsus, in Cilicia. But God planned otherwise, because his ship was blown off course into the port of Rome. When he took stock of what had happened, Alexis said to himself: 'I will go and stay in my father's house: no one will recognize me, and that way I shall not be a burden to anyone else.' So he lay in wait for his father, who was returning home from the palace, surrounded by a crowd of hangers-on, and called after him: 'Servant of God, I am a pilgrim from a foreign land. Take me into your house and let me feed on the crumbs from your table, that God may in turn have mercy on you.' When Euphemianus heard this, thinking with love of his son, he gave orders for the pilgrim to be taken in, gave him a private room in his house, provided him with food from his own table, and assigned to him a servant of his own.

Alexis persevered in prayer and mortified his body with fasting and vigils, and the servants of the household made fun of him at every opportunity, but he bore it all with heroic patience. He lived in his father's house for seventeen years like this without being recognized. Then it was revealed to him that the end of his life was near, and he asked for paper and ink and wrote down a detailed chronological account of his life. One Sunday, after the celebration of mass, a voice from heaven rang out in the sanctuary, saying: 'Come to me, all you who labour and are heavy laden, and I will refresh you.' Everyone fell to the ground in terror, and straight away the voice came a second time: 'Search for the man of God, that he may pray for Rome!' The people looked around but could see no one at all, and the voice called again: 'Look in the house of Euphemianus.' When Euphemianus was questioned, he had no idea what they were talking about. Then the emperors Arcadius and Honorius went with Pope Innocent to Euphemianus's house, and the servant who waited on Alexis came to Euphemianus and said: 'Master, do you think the man they want might be our guest the pilgrim? He is a man of great holiness and forbearance.' Euphemianus immediately ran to the pilgrim's room and found him dead, his face shining like the face of an angel, and he tried to take the piece of paper from his hand, but he could not. So he went and told the emperors and the pope. They went straight to the room where the pilgrim was lying, and the emperors said: 'Sinners though we be, we govern the empire, and his Holiness here has pastoral oversight of the faithful throughout the whole world. So give us the piece of paper you are holding in your hand, and let us see what is written on it.' At once the dead man released it from his grasp, and the pope took it and had it read out before Euphemianus and a great crowd of people who were present. When Euphemianus took in what was being read, he was so overwhelmed with grief that he collapsed in a faint and fell to the ground. Then, when his senses began to return to him, he tore his garments and started to pluck out his grey hair and beard, and to claw at his face. He threw himself upon his son's body and cried: 'Alas, my son! Why have you brought me so much grief, and caused me such pain and misery for so many years? Woe is me! You were the staff of my old age, and now I see you lying dead upon your bier, and you cannot speak a word to me! Ah me, what comfort shall I ever find again?'

Alexis's mother, hearing all this, rushed forward like a lioness breaking the hunter's net. She tore at her clothing, unbound her hair and lifted her eyes to heaven. But finding she could not get to her son's holy body, she cried: 'Let me by, you people, let me see my son, let me see my soul's comfort, the son who suckled at my breasts!' When she reached the body, she fell upon it and cried: 'Alas, my son, light of my eyes, why did you do this? Why have you treated us so cruelly? You saw your poor mother's and father's tears, yet still you would not make yourself known to us. Your own servants insulted you and you did nothing.' Again and again she prostrated herself on his body, now outstretching her arms upon it, now caressing his angelic face with her hands and kissing it. 'Weep with me, all of you!' she cried. 'That I had him in my own house for seventeen years and did not know him! That he should have been my only son! That the servants even insulted him and physically abused him! Ah me! Where shall my eyes find tears enough so that day and night I may pour forth the anguish of my heart?'

Alexis's widow, too, dressed all in mourning, ran up and sobbed: 'Ah me! Today I am all alone, I am a widow, with no one to look to, no one to give me comfort! Now my mirror is broken, my hope is gone! Now begins a grief that has no end!' And her words made the people crowding round weep uncontrollably.

Then the pope and two emperors laid the body on a splendid bier and escorted it to the centre of the city. A proclamation was made to the people that the man of God for whom the whole city had been searching was found, and soon everyone came running to see the saint. Any of them who were sick and touched his most holy body were cured instantly; the blind regained their sight, and people possessed by demons were delivered of them; all the afflicted, no matter what their infirmity, were made well if they but touched his holy body. And when they witnessed these miracles, the emperors themselves helped the pope carry the bier, hoping that they, too, might be sanctified by the holy body. They also gave orders that the streets should be showered with gold and silver coins, so the crowds, with their greed for money, might turn their attentions elsewhere, and allow the saint's body to pass by to the church. But the people forgot their love of money and pressed forward in greater and greater numbers to touch the body of the saint. So it was only with the greatest difficulty that the bier finally got through to the church of St Boniface the Martyr. There they spent a whole week praising God continuously; then they erected a monument, decorated in gold and gems and precious stones, in which, with great reverence, they laid the holy body to rest. From that moment there emanated from this monument a perfume so sweet that everyone thought it must be full of sweet spices. St Alexis died on the 17th of July, around the year of our Lord 398.

37

ST MARGARET

20 July

Margaret was a citizen of Antioch and daughter of Theodosius, patriarch of the pagans. As a child she was entrusted to a nurse, and when she reached the age of reason she was baptized, and so incurred the bitter hatred of her father. One day, when she was fifteen years old, she and some other young girls were looking after her nurse's sheep, and the prefect Olybrius happened to pass by; as soon as he saw how beautiful she was, he fell madly in love with her, and at once sent his men after her. 'Go and seize her,' he told them, 'and if she is freeborn, I shall make her my wife; if she is a slave girl, I shall take her as my concubine.' Margaret was then brought before him, and he asked her about her family and name and religion. She replied that she was of noble birth, her name was Margaret, and she was a Christian. The prefect said: ' "Noble" and "Margaret" suit you perfectly: you are clearly noble, and you are a pearl [Latin: *margarita*] of beauty! But Christianity does not! How can a girl so beautiful and noble worship a God who was crucified?' 'How do you know,' Margaret asked, 'that Christ was crucified?' 'From the Christians' books,' he told her. 'You have read, then, of Christ's suffering and his glory,' she said. 'How can you believe in the one, but deny the other?' Margaret went on to explain to him that Christ had died on the cross willingly for our redemption, but now lived on in eternity. But this angered the prefect, and he had her thrown into gaol.

Next day he summoned her and said: 'You foolish girl, have pity on your beauty! Worship our gods and you have nothing to fear.' Margaret replied: 'I worship him before whom the earth trembles, the sea quakes in fear, and all creatures stand in awe!' 'If you do not obey me,' the prefect told her, 'I will have your body torn in pieces!' Margaret said: 'Christ gave himself up to death for me, so I want nothing more than to die for Christ!'

The prefect had her put on the rack; then she was beaten cruelly with rods, and her flesh was raked with iron combs until the bones were laid bare and the blood gushed from her body as if from the purest spring. All those who were present wept as they watched. 'O Margaret,' they said, 'we pity you, truly! To see your body torn so cruelly! What beauty you have lost because of your unbelief! But there is still time: believe and you will live!' 'You counsellors of evil!' Margaret cried. 'Be off, be gone! This torture of the flesh is the soul's salvation!' And she said to the prefect: 'You shameless dog! Ravening lion! You may have power over the flesh, but my soul is Christ's alone!' The prefect, unable to stand the sight of so much blood, covered his face with his cloak. He then had Margaret taken down and thrown back into her cell, which was at once filled with a miraculous radiance. While she lay there, Margaret prayed the Lord to show her, in visible form, the enemy who was fighting her. A monstrous dragon suddenly appeared before her and sprang at her to devour her, but she made the sign of the cross and it disappeared. According to another account, the dragon got its jaws over Margaret's head and its tongue round her feet and swallowed her; and it was while it was attempting to digest her that she armed herself with the sign of the cross, and this proved too much for the dragon, who burst apart, and the virgin emerged unhurt. But this story of the dragon devouring the virgin, then bursting apart, is considered apocryphal and of no historical value.

The Devil persisted in his attempts to deceive Margaret and changed into the shape of a man. As soon as she saw him she knelt in prayer; then, when she rose again, the Devil went up to her, and took her hand and said: 'Content yourself with what you have done already, and now leave me alone!' But Margaret took hold of his head, threw him to the ground, placed her right foot firmly on his neck and told him: 'Lie there, proud demon, prostrate beneath a woman's foot!' 'O blessed Margaret,' the demon cried, 'I admit defeat! If a young man had beaten me, I would not have minded; but to be beaten by a young girl –! And it hurts me all the more because your father and mother were friends of mine!'

Margaret then made him say why he had come. He told her that it was to get her to obey the prefect's orders. She also made him tell her why he tempted Christians in so many ways, and his answer was that he had an inborn hatred of virtuous men, and though he was often repulsed by them, he was still tormented by a malicious desire to lead them astray. He begrudged man the happiness that he himself had lost, and since he could never regain it himself, he did all he could to take it from others. He also told her that Solomon had shut up a numberless host of demons inside a vase, and after his death the demons had sent flames shooting from the vase, which made people think there was some fabulous treasure inside, so they smashed the vase, and the demons swarmed out and filled the air. But Margaret had heard enough: she lifted her foot and said: 'Be gone, wretch!' And the demon vanished.

Margaret now felt confident that, after having defeated the arch-fiend, she would be able to vanquish his minion. Next day all the people were assembled, and she was brought before the judge. When she again refused to offer sacrifice, she was stripped and her flesh was seared with blazing torches, and everyone was amazed that a girl so young could endure such agony. The judge then had her bound and put in a tank full of water, hoping that, by varying his methods in this way, he would increase the intensity of her suffering. But there was suddenly an earthquake and, as everyone looked on, the young girl emerged unscathed. Instantly five thousand men were converted to the faith, and immediately condemned to die for the name of Christ. The prefect, fearing that others, too, might be converted, swiftly gave the order for blessed Margaret to be beheaded. But first she asked for a while to pray; and she prayed earnestly for herself and her persecutors, and for those who would keep her memory and invoke her name, and asked in addition that any woman who invoked her in the peril of childbirth might be delivered of a healthy child. And a voice came down from heaven, assuring her that her petitions had been granted. She rose from prayer and said to the executioner: 'Brother, lift your sword and strike me!' He struck her head off with one blow, and so Margaret received the crown of martyrdom. According to her Life, she suffered on the twentieth day of July; but other authorities put her death on the thirteenth of that month . . .

38

ST MARY MAGDALENE[1]

22 July

Mary Magdalene is so called because of her connection with the town of Magdalum. She was born of most noble parents who were indeed of royal descent. Her father's name was Syrus, and her mother was called Eucharia. Together with her brother Lazarus and sister Martha she owned Magdalum, a fortified town two miles from Genezareth, Bethany, near Jerusalem, and a large part of Jerusalem itself. But they divided up their inheritance in such a way that Mary kept Magdalum (hence her name Magdalene), Lazarus the family property in Jerusalem, and Martha, Bethany. Mary Magdalene gave herself up entirely to the pleasures of the flesh, while Lazarus devoted much of his time to soldiering, and the prudent Martha was active in managing her sister's and brother's estates, and attending to the needs of her men-at-arms, her servants and the poor. But after Christ's ascension they sold everything they possessed and laid the proceeds at the feet of the apostles.

Since Mary Magdalene was enormously wealthy, and pleasure is the boon companion of affluence, she was as notorious for her abandonment to fleshly pleasures as she was celebrated for her beauty and riches. So much so, in fact, that people soon forgot her real name and referred to her as 'the sinner'. But when Christ was travelling about the country preaching, Mary, inspired by the will of God, hurried to the house of Simon the leper, where she had heard that he was a guest. Being a sinner, she did not dare to be seen among decent people, so she held back and sat at the Lord's feet, washed them with her tears, dried them with her hair, and anointed them with precious ointment (because of the intense heat of the sun the inhabitants of that region often anointed themselves and took baths). And just as Simon the Pharisee was thinking to himself that, if Jesus was a true prophet, he would never allow himself to be touched by a sinful woman, the Lord reproached him for his presumption, and forgave the woman all her sins. It was this Magdalene on whom the Lord conferred such great blessings, and to whom he showed so many signs of his love. For he cast seven demons out of her, set her all on fire with love for him, made her one of his most intimate associates, was a guest at her house, let her provide for him on his travels, and lovingly defended her on many occasions. He took her part against the Pharisee, who said she was unclean; against her sister, who said she was idle; and against Judas, who said she was wasteful. If he saw Mary in tears, he could not hold back his own. Out of love for her he raised her brother to life again, when he had been dead four days; out of love for her he freed her sister Martha from the flux of blood which she had suffered for seven years; and in recognition of her merits he gave Martilla, Martha's maid, the honour of uttering those sweet and glorious words: 'Blessed is the womb that bore you!' For, according to Ambrose, the woman with the flux of blood was indeed Martha, and the woman who uttered these words was her maid. 'It was she [Mary Magdalene], I say, who washed the Lord's feet with her tears, dried them with her hair, and anointed them with ointment. It was she who in the time of grace did solemn penance, who chose the best part, who sat at the Lord's feet and listened to his word, who anointed his head, who stood by the cross at the Lord's passion, who prepared the unguents and anointed his body; she who, when the disciples left the sepulchre, would not go away; and it was she to whom Christ first appeared when he had risen, thus making her an apostle to the apostles.'

Then, fourteen years after the passion and ascension of the Lord, long after the Jews had killed Stephen and expelled the rest of the disciples from Judaean territory, the disciples went off to spread the word of the Lord in the various regions inhabited by the Gentiles. At that time blessed Maximinus, one of the Lord's seventy-two disciples, was with the apostles, and it was to his care that St Peter had entrusted Mary Magdalene. When the disciples went their separate ways, the blessed Maximinus, Mary Magdalene, her brother Lazarus, her sister Martha, Martha's maid Martilla and the blessed Cedonius, who had been blind from his birth but was cured by the Lord, together with many other Christians, were put on board ship by unbelievers and set adrift on the sea without a pilot so that they should all be drowned. But by God's will they reached Marseilles. There they found nobody prepared to take them in, so they sheltered under the portico of a shrine where the people of that region worshipped. When the blessed Mary Magdalene saw the people streaming to the shrine to sacrifice to the idols, she got up, quite calmly, and, with a serene expression on her face and with measured words, began to turn them from their idol worship, and with great single-mindedness to preach the Gospel of Christ. Everyone there admired her for her beauty, for her eloquence, and for her sweet manner of speaking. And it is no wonder that the lips which had pressed kisses so loving and so tender on our Lord's feet should breathe the perfume of the word of God more copiously than others.

Later the prince who ruled that region arrived there with his wife to offer sacrifice to the gods and to pray for a child. Magdalene preached Christ to him and persuaded him not to offer sacrifice. A few days later she appeared to his wife in a vision: 'Why, when you are so very rich,' she asked, 'do you allow God's faithful servants to die of hunger and cold?' She also added the threat that, if she did not persuade her husband to relieve the misery of the faithful, she would incur the wrath of Almighty God. But the lady was frightened to tell her husband about the vision. The following night Magdalene appeared to her again with the same message, but still she said nothing to her husband. The third time, in the silence of the dead of night, Magdalene appeared to both of them, trembling with rage, her face so afire with anger that it seemed that the whole house was ablaze! 'Asleep, tyrant?' she said. 'Are you asleep, you son of Satan, with that viper, your wife, who refused to give you my message? Can you rest, you enemy of the cross of Christ, when your fat belly is stuffed full of all sorts of food, and you let the holy ones of God die of hunger and thirst? Can you lie here in your palace, covered with bedclothes of silk, and see them desolate, without a roof over their heads, and ignore them? No, no! You shall not get away with this, you monster! You know you should help them, and you shall not go unpunished for your procrastination!' With these words she vanished. When the wife awoke she was breathless and trembling; her husband, too, was similarly troubled. 'My lord,' she said, 'have you had the same dream I had?' 'Yes,' he replied. 'I cannot believe it, and it fills me with dread. What are we going to do?' 'It would be better,' his wife said, 'to do as she says, rather than incur the wrath of this God of hers whom she preaches.' So they gave the Christians shelter and looked after their needs.

One day when Mary Magdalene was preaching, the prince asked her: 'Do you think you can defend the faith you preach?' She replied: 'I am more than ready to defend it! My faith is strengthened daily by the miracles and preaching of my master Peter, who governs the Church in Rome.' The prince and his wife then declared to her: 'We are ready to do anything you say if you can get this God whom you preach to grant us a son.' 'He will not deny you this,' Magdalene assured them. Then blessed Mary prayed to the Lord to deign to grant them a son, and the Lord heard her prayers, and the prince's wife conceived. After this the prince was seized with a desire to go to Peter in Rome to see if what Magdalene preached about Christ was the truth. 'What is this?' demanded his wife. 'Are you planning to go without me? Oh no! God forbid! If you go, I go, too: if you come back, I come back with you. Where you stay, I stay!' 'Madam, it cannot be,' her husband told her. 'You are pregnant and the perils of the sea are numberless. You would be running too great a risk. Stay at home and take care of things here.' But she insisted and, using all her feminine guile, she threw herself at his feet in floods of tears, and finally had her way. So Mary made the sign of the cross upon their shoulders to stop the Ancient Enemy harming them on their voyage. Then, loading a ship with a plentiful supply of all the things they needed, they left the rest of their possessions in the safe-keeping of Mary Magdalene and set sail.

They were only a day and a night into their voyage when a gale blew up, the sea began to swell and, as the huge waves pounded them and broke over the ship, everyone on board began to fear for their lives, and especially the prince's pregnant wife, whose health was in a delicate state. Suddenly she was gripped by the pangs of labour; and, racked with pain and in the most pitiful circumstances, she died as she gave birth to a son. The tiny baby felt about him, seeking the comfort of his mother's breasts and uttering the most pathetic cries. Ah! The bitter irony of it! The child is born alive, and in the same moment becomes his mother's murderer, when it is he who should be dead, since he has no one to feed him and keep him alive! What will the pilgrim do, now he sees his wife lying dead and his child whimpering pitifully as he searches for his mother's breast? The prince was beside himself with grief. 'Luckless man!' he cried to himself. 'What will you do now? You longed to have a son, and now you have lost both your son and the mother that bore him!' Meanwhile the sailors were shouting: 'Throw the body overboard before we all go down together. As long as it stays on board, this storm will never let up.' They grabbed the body and were about to throw it into the sea, but the pilgrim pleaded with them. 'No!' he cried. 'Please! If you will not spare me or the mother, at least take pity on the weeping of a poor little child. Wait just a moment. Perhaps she has just fainted with pain – perhaps she may start breathing again.' Then, out of the blue, not far ahead a hilly coastline hove into view, and it occurred to the prince that the best he could do would be to put his dead wife and the baby ashore – anything rather than throw them overboard as food for the monsters of the deep! He offered the sailors bribes, pleaded with them to put in there, and, finally, with great difficulty, got them to agree. Once ashore, however, he was unable to dig a grave, because the ground was too hard, so he picked a sheltered part of the hillside, spread his cloak on the ground, and put the corpse upon it, laying the child at his mother's breast. 'O Mary Magdalene,' he mused tearfully, 'when you landed at Marseilles it was to my utter ruin. Why did I ever take your advice, luckless wretch that I am, and come on this journey? Is this what you prayed for – that my wife might conceive only to die in labour? For conceive she did, and has died in childbirth: my son was conceived only to die, because there is no one to nurse him. Yes, that is all your prayers have brought me! I put my whole life in your hands, and now I put myself in the hands of your God. If he has the power, let him remember the soul of my wife, and, in answer to your prayer, have pity on my son and let him live!' He then wrapped his cloak about his dead wife and the child, and went back on board ship.

When he reached Rome, Peter came to meet him and, seeing the sign of the cross on his shoulder, asked him who he was and where he came from. He told Peter the whole story and Peter replied: 'Peace be with you! You have done well to come here, and the advice you took was good. Do not grieve too much if your wife sleeps and your little child is at rest with her, for the Lord has power to give gifts to whomever he wishes, to take away what he has given, to restore what he has taken away, and to turn your grief to joy.' Peter then took him off to Jerusalem and showed him all the places in which Christ had preached and performed miracles, and also the place where he suffered and the place where he ascended into heaven. For two years Peter instructed him fully in the faith, and then his disciple boarded ship in order to return home again. In the course of his voyage, by God's will, the ship passed close by the same hilly coastline where he had left the body of his wife and his baby son, and, by bribing the crew and pleading with them, he persuaded them to put in there.

Now the little boy had been preserved and kept free from harm by Mary Magdalene, and used often to go down to the seashore and play with the pebbles and shingle there, as children will. As the ship's boat was putting in, the pilgrim saw the small child playing his usual games with the pebbles on the shore and was unable to believe his eyes. He sprang from the boat, but the child, who had never seen anything like a man before, was terrified and ran back to the familiar comfort of his mother's bosom, and hid himself with her under the cloak. The pilgrim followed, determined to discover the truth of the matter, and found the child, a bonny boy, suckling at his mother's breast. He took him in his arms and cried: 'O blessed Mary Magdalene, how happy I would be, how perfectly everything would have turned out for me, if only my wife could come back to life and return home with me! Indeed I know, yes I know and believe without any doubt, that you, who have given me this child and nursed him for two years upon this rock, will be able, by your prayers, to restore his mother to life.' As he finished speaking, his wife began to breathe again. As if waking from sleep, she said: 'Great is your merit, blessed Mary Magdalene, and great the glory you have won! When I suffered the pangs of labour, you served me as midwife, you attended to my every need like a loyal handmaid.' When he heard her speak, the pilgrim exclaimed in astonishment: 'My dearest wife, are you really alive?' 'I am indeed!' she replied. 'I have just come back from the pilgrimage from which you yourself are returning. Just as blessed Peter took you to Jerusalem and showed you all the places in which Christ suffered and died and was buried, and many other places, so I, with blessed Mary Magdalene as my guide and companion, was with you, and I have committed to memory everything I saw.' She then began to describe all the places in which Christ had suffered and all the marvels that she had seen, and her account was accurate in every detail. Overcome with joy at recovering his wife and son, the pilgrim boarded ship again and soon enough they put in at Marseilles. When they entered the city, they found Mary Magdalene among her disciples, preaching. In tears they threw themselves at her feet, told her all that had happened to them, and then received holy baptism at the hands of Maximinus. Subsequently the Christians destroyed all the temples of the idols in the city of Marseilles and built churches to Christ, and they unanimously elected blessed Lazarus as bishop of the city. In due course divine providence took them to the city of Aix, and by many miracles they led the people there to believe in Christ, and blessed Maximinus was ordained bishop of Aix.

In the meantime blessed Mary Magdalene, wishing to devote herself to heavenly contemplation, withdrew to a barren wilderness where she remained in anonymity for thirty years in a place prepared for her by the hands of angels. In this wilderness there was no water, and there were no trees or grass, nor any comforts of any kind, so that it was clear that our Redeemer had meant to feed her not with earthly foods, but with the sweets of heaven alone. Each day at the seven canonical hours she was lifted in the air by angels and actually heard, with her bodily organs of hearing, the glorious harmonies of the celestial chorus. So, filled day by day with this exquisite heavenly fare, when she was brought back to her cave, she had not the slightest need for bodily nourishment.

Now there was a priest who desired to live a solitary life and made himself a cell some twelve furlongs from Mary's cave. One day the Lord opened the eyes of this priest, and he saw quite clearly, with his own eyes, how the angels came down to the place where blessed Mary lived, lifted her in the air, and an hour later returned her to the same place, singing the praises of God. The priest, eager to know if this wonderful vision was a true one, commended himself in prayer to his Creator, and then, with courageous determination, hurried off to Mary's cave. But when he was only a stone's throw away from the place, his legs began to give way, he was gripped with terror, and he started to gasp for breath. If he took a step back, his legs and feet behaved normally; but every time he turned and tried to get closer to the cave, his body was instantly paralysed and his brain benumbed, and he could not move an inch. Then the man of God knew for a certainty that there was some heavenly mystery afoot which was beyond the reach of human experience. So, invoking the name of his Saviour, he cried out: 'I adjure you, in the Lord's name, if you are a human or any rational creature, you who live in that cave, answer me and tell me truly who you are!' When he had repeated this three times, blessed Mary Magdalene answered: 'Come closer, and you will learn the truth about everything your heart desires to know.' The trembling priest had gone half-way towards the cave when she said to him: 'Do you remember the story in the Gospel about Mary, the notorious sinner, who washed the Saviour's feet with her tears, dried them with her hair, and won forgiveness for her sins?' 'I do,' the priest replied. 'And more than thirty years have gone by since Holy Church has believed the story and acknowledged it as fact.' 'I am that woman,' she told him. 'For the space of thirty years I have lived here, unknown to anyone. As you were allowed to see yesterday, each day I am carried aloft by the hands of angels, and seven times every day I have been accorded the privilege of hearing with my own ears the joyous rapture of the heavenly hosts. Now, because it has been revealed to me by the Lord that I am soon to depart from this world, I beg you to go to Maximinus and be sure to give him this message: next year, on the day of the Lord's resurrection, at the hour when he rises to go to matins, he is to go into his church alone, and there he will find me, attended by bands of angels.'

The priest thought he must be hearing the voice of an angel, but he could not see anyone. So he hurried off to Maximinus and told him all that had happened. St Maximinus was overcome with joy and gave heartfelt thanks to the Saviour. On Easter Day, at the appointed hour, he entered his church alone, and saw Mary Magdalene standing in the midst of the choir of angels who had brought her. She was raised several feet above the floor and thronged by angels, with her arms outstretched in prayer to God. Maximinus hesitated to approach her, but she turned to him and said: 'Come closer, father. Do not run from your daughter!' So he went up to her, and, as we read in the writings of Maximinus himself, the saint's visage was so radiant from her continuous daily vision of the angels that one could more easily have looked into the rays of the sun than into her face. Maximinus summoned all the clergy, including the aforementioned priest, and Mary Magdalene wept copiously as she received our Lord's body and blood from the hands of the bishop. Then she prostrated herself before the foot of the altar, and at once her most holy soul passed to the Lord. After her death a perfume of such sweetness flooded the church that for seven days everyone who entered the place was aware of it. Maximinus gave her most holy body honourable burial, embalming it with aromatic spices, and ordered that when he died, he should be buried next to her.

Hegesippus – or according to some sources, Josephus – is in general agreement with this version of the events. He says in one of his treatises that Mary Magdalene, after the Lord's ascension, burnt with such love for Christ, and was so weary of the world, that she wanted never to set eyes on any human being again. Then, after she went to Aix, she withdrew into the desert and lived there for thirty years unknown to anyone. There, as he asserts, she was carried up to heaven by angels every day at the seven canonical hours. But he adds that the priest who visited Mary found her enclosed in her cell. She asked him for something to wear and he gave her a garment, which she put on, and then went with him into the church. There, after receiving communion, she lifted her hands in prayer before the altar and peacefully passed away . . .

39

ST CHRISTOPHER

25 July

Before his baptism Christopher was called Reprobus, but after it Christophorus, 'Christ-bearer'. He bore Christ in four ways: on his shoulders, when he carried him across the river; in his body, through self-mortification; in his mind, through his devotions; and on his lips, by confessing and preaching Christ.

Christopher was by birth a Canaanite, a man of gigantic stature (he was more than twelve feet tall) and of terrifying appearance. As we read in some accounts of his life, it was when he was in the service of a certain Canaanite king that the idea occurred to him of searching out the greatest prince in the world and entering his service. So he went to a very powerful king, who was generally said to be the greatest prince in the world; and when this king saw Christopher, he gave him a cordial welcome and made him a member of his court. One day a minstrel was singing some song in the king's presence in which he made frequent reference to the Devil. Now the king was a Christian, and, whenever he heard the Devil's name uttered, he would make the sign of the cross on his forehead. Christopher observed this and wondered why the king did it, and what such a sign could possibly mean. He asked the king about it, and when he refused to tell him, Christopher declared: 'If you do not tell me, I will not stay with you any longer!' So the king was forced to speak. 'Whenever I hear someone utter the Devil's name,' he told him, 'I use this sign to protect myself in case the Devil gains some power over me and harms me.' Christopher replied: 'If you are afraid of being harmed by the Devil, that must mean that he is greater and mightier than you: otherwise you would not be so frightened of him. So my hopes were in vain. I thought I had found the greatest and most powerful prince in the world. Now farewell! I shall go and seek out the Devil and take him as my master and become his servant!'

So Christopher left him and hurried away in search of the Devil. He was crossing a desert when he saw a vast company of soldiers, and one of them, a fierce warrior of awesome appearance, came up to him and asked him where he was going. Christopher answered him: 'I am looking for my lord the Devil. I want to take him as my master.' The warrior told him: 'I am he. I am the one you are seeking.' Happily Christopher bound himself in perpetual servitude to the Devil, and took him as his master.

They then went on together until they found a cross erected at the side of the highway. As soon as the Devil saw the cross, he fled in terror; he abandoned the highway and took Christopher on a detour through the wildest desert before finally returning him to the road. Christopher, bewildered by his behaviour, asked him why he had been so frightened that he had left the highway and gone on such a lengthy detour over country so rough. But the Devil absolutely refused to tell him, and Christopher said: 'Unless you tell me the truth, I will leave you at once.' So the Devil was forced to speak. 'There was a man called Christ who was crucified,' he said to him. 'And whenever I see the sign of his cross, I am seized with terror; I panic and run away.' Christopher replied: 'Then this Christ is greater and mightier than you, if you are so afraid of his sign. So my efforts have all been in vain. I have still not found the greatest prince in the world! Farewell, then. I am leaving you and going to search for Christ!'

He had been looking for some time for someone who might tell him where to find Christ when at length he came upon a hermit, who preached Christ to him and gave him a thorough instruction in the faith. 'This king you wish to serve,' he told Christopher, 'will require various acts of obedience: one is that you will frequently have to fast.' Christopher replied: 'Let him ask something else of me! Fasting is something I cannot possibly do!' The hermit went on: 'And you will have to pray to him hard and long.' 'I do not know what prayer means,' Christopher told him. 'I cannot serve him in that way either!' Then the hermit asked him: 'Do you know that dangerous river crossing where so many folk have got into difficulties and drowned?' 'I do,' Christopher replied. 'You have the height and you are strong enough,' the hermit said. 'If you were to go and live near that river and carry travellers across, it would be most pleasing to Christ the King whom you wish to serve – and I hope that he may show himself to you there.' 'Yes!' Christopher replied. 'That is the sort of service I can do, and that is the way I pledge myself to serve him.'

So he went to the river and made himself a hut there. In place of a staff he used a long pole to keep himself upright in the water, and, day and night, he carried across the river all travellers who asked his help. After many days of this he was resting in his hut when he heard a child's voice calling to him and saying: 'Christopher, come out and take me across!' He sprang to his feet and went outside, but he could find no one, so he went inside again, but only to hear the same voice calling him again. Again he ran outside and found no one. When it happened a third time and he went out as before, he discovered a child standing at the river bank. The child begged him to take him across, so Christopher lifted him on to his shoulders and, seizing his pole, stepped into the river to make the crossing. But the waters grew gradually rougher and rougher and the child felt as heavy as lead, and the further Christopher went, the higher the waves rose, and the child pressed down on his shoulders more and more until the weight became intolerable. Christopher was in terrible difficulties and feared that he would drown, but after a desperate struggle he finally reached the other side and completed the crossing. Setting the child down on the river bank, he said to him: 'You put me in great danger, my boy! You weighed so much that if I had had the whole world on my back, it could scarcely have felt heavier!' The child replied: 'You should not be surprised, Christopher. You not only had the weight of the whole world on you, you were also carrying him who created the world upon your shoulders! For I am Christ your King, whom you serve in your work here. And so that you may know that I am telling you the truth, when you get back across the river, plant your staff in the earth by your hut, and tomorrow you will see it has sprouted leaves and borne fruit.' And immediately the child disappeared. Christopher duly planted his staff in the ground, and when he got up the next morning he found it had sprouted leaves and dates, like a palm tree.

Later Christopher travelled to Samos, a city in Lycia. Because he did not know the language of the natives, he prayed to the Lord to enable him to understand them. Seeing him rapt in prayer, the local magistrates took him for a madman and left him alone. But when Christopher's prayer was answered, he covered his face and went to the place where the Christians were being martyred, and spoke to those under torture and strengthened them in the Lord. Thereupon one of the magistrates struck him in the face, and Christopher, uncovering his head, said to him: 'If I were not a Christian, I would be quick to avenge that insult!' He then fixed his staff in the ground and prayed to the Lord that it might sprout leaves and convert the people. Instantly it burst into leaf, and eight thousand men were converted to the faith.

Next the king sent two hundred soldiers to bring Christopher to him, but they found him at prayer, and were afraid to tell him of their orders. The king sent another two hundred soldiers and, when they, too, found him praying, they promptly joined him in prayer. Christopher got up and asked them: 'Whom are you looking for?' When they saw his face, they told him: 'The king has sent us to bind you and take you to him.' 'If I choose to resist,' Christopher said, 'you will never take me, bound or unbound!' They replied: 'If you do not want to come with us, then go free, go wherever you want, and we will tell the king we could not find you.' 'No, you must not do that,' he said. 'I will go with you.'

But first Christopher converted the soldiers to the faith; then he made them tie his hands behind his back and take him bound before the king. The king was so terrified at the sight of him that he fell from his throne. When his servants had picked him up again, he asked Christopher his name and where he came from. Christopher told him: 'Before baptism I was called Reprobus, but now my name is Christopher.' 'That was a foolish name to give yourself,' the king said. 'Fancy calling yourself after Christ, who was crucified! He could not help himself any more than he will be able to help you! Now then, you Canaanite good-for-nothing, why will you not sacrifice to our gods?' Christopher said to him: 'Your name Dagnus¹ suits you well, because you are the death of the world, the Devil's accomplice, and your gods are the works of human hands!' The king retorted: 'You must have been reared among wild beasts: you can only utter the wildest things, things unheard of by ordinary men. But if you agree to sacrifice now, I will reward you with the highest honours; if you do not, you will be tortured and put to death.' Christopher refused to sacrifice, so the king imprisoned him, and as for the soldiers he had sent to arrest him, he had them beheaded for confessing the name of Christ. Then he had two beautiful young women, one called Nicaea and the other Aquilina, shut in the same cell as Christopher, promising them handsome rewards if they could entice him into sin with them. At once Christopher immersed himself in prayer. But, distracted finally by the caresses and embraces of these two girls, he got to his feet and asked them: 'What do you want? Why have you been brought in here?' They were terrified by the radiance of his face and said: 'O holy saint of God, have pity on us! Help us to believe in the God whom you preach!' Now the king got to hear of this and he had the two girls brought before him. 'So you, too, have been seduced!' he said. 'I swear by the gods that, unless you offer sacrifice, you will both die, and painfully!' They replied: 'If you want us to sacrifice, have the streets cleared and tell all the people to gather in the temple.' This was done. The two girls went into the temple and, loosing their girdles, they slung them round the necks of the idols, dragged them to the dust beneath, and smashed them in pieces. 'Go and call your doctors,' they cried to the crowd, 'and see if they can heal your gods!' At the king's command, Aquilina was hanged and a great stone was tied to her feet, so that all her limbs were broken. When she had passed to the Lord, her sister Nicaea was thrown into a fire, but when she emerged unharmed, she was at once beheaded.

After this Christopher himself was brought before the king, who ordered him to be beaten with rods of iron; he also had an iron helmet heated in the fire and fixed on his head. Then he had an iron stool made, bound Christopher to it, and a fire was lit beneath it and pitch was thrown on to the flames. But the stool melted away like wax, and Christopher came away unharmed. Next the king had him tied to a stake and ordered four hundred archers to shoot at him. But their arrows all hung in mid-air, and not one of them could find its target. The king, thinking that Christopher had been killed by his archers, began to mock him when suddenly one of the arrows fell from the air, turned round in mid-flight, struck the king in the eye and blinded him. Christopher said to him: 'Tyrant, by tomorrow my life will be at an end. When I am dead, make a paste with my blood, anoint your eye with it, and you will recover your sight.' By order of the king he was led away to the place where he was to be beheaded, and after he had prayed his head was struck from his body. The king took a little of his blood and, laying it on his eye, said: 'In the name of God and St Christopher!' And at once he could see again. This brought about his conversion, and he decreed that anyone blaspheming against God or St Christopher should be summarily executed . . .

40

THE SEVEN SLEEPERS
OF EPHESUS

27 July

The Seven Sleepers were natives of Ephesus. Now when the emperor Decius came to Ephesus to persecute the Christians, he built temples there in the centre of the city so that all the Ephesians could join him in worshipping the idols. And when he gave orders that all Christians should be hunted down, put in chains and forced either to sacrifice or be put to death, everyone was so terrified of what might happen to them that friend betrayed friend, fathers disowned their sons, and sons their fathers.

Now there were seven Christians in that city, Maximianus, Malchus, Marcianus, Dionysius, Johannes, Serapion and Constantinus, who were deeply distressed by what they witnessed. And though they were among the most important officials in the palace, they utterly refused to sacrifice to the idols and hid themselves in their houses, and gave themselves over to fasting and prayer. They were then accused and brought before Decius. That they were Christians was proved beyond doubt, but the emperor was due to leave Ephesus, and he gave them the time until he returned to the city in which to come to their senses. Then he let them go. But while he was away, they shared out all their possessions among the poor, and agreed to steal away together and go into hiding on Mount Celion. There they lay up for some time, and each day one of them would dress up in rags and, pretending to be a beggar, go off to the city to get food.

Now as soon as Decius returned to Ephesus he ordered that they be summoned and made to perform sacrifice. Malchus, whose turn it had been to fetch provisions that day, hurried back to his companions in a panic and told them of the emperor's fury. They, too, were terrified at the news, so Malchus put before them the bread he had brought to give them strength and courage for the trials they were to face. And as they sat down to eat, weeping and sighing as they spoke together, suddenly God willed them to fall asleep.

Next morning, when a search was made and they could not be found,

Decius was enraged that he had let these seven young Christians get away. Then word got about that they had been in hiding on Mount Celion, and that they had given away all their goods to the poor and were determined to adhere to their faith. So Decius had their parents brought before him, and threatened to execute them if they did not tell him everything they knew. The parents repeated the story he had already heard, and complained bitterly of the way their sons had given away their inheritances to the poor. Then Decius, as he wondered what he should do about them, was prompted by God to have the mouth of the cave blocked up with stones so that they should starve to death. These orders his men carried out, and two Christians, Theodorus and Rufinus, wrote an account of their martyrdom and hid it carefully among the stones.

Now three hundred and seventy-two years later, when Decius and all his generation were long dead, in the thirtieth year of the reign of the emperor Theodosius, there was a widespread heresy denying the resurrection of the dead. Theodosius, that most Christian of emperors, was so deeply affected by this, seeing as he did the faith of his people being wickedly undermined, that he put on a hair-shirt, shut himself up in the innermost room of his palace, and spent day after day in abject grief. Seeing this, God in his mercy decided to comfort the afflicted and to strengthen their hopes in the resurrection of the dead; so, opening the vast treasury of his love and compassion, he caused the seven martyrs to wake from their sleep. He prompted a certain citizen of Ephesus to build shelters for his shepherds on Mount Celion. And when the masons were opening up the cave, the saints awoke and greeted each other, thinking that they had been asleep for just one night; then, recalling the gloomy forebodings of the day before, they asked Malchus, who had gone into town for their provisions, what Decius had decided to do about them. Malchus replied: 'As I told you before, people have been out hunting for us, to make us sacrifice to the idols. That is what the emperor wants.' Maximianus replied: 'God knows we will never sacrifice!' And when he had spoken words of encouragement to his companions, he told Malchus to go down to the city and buy bread, to bring back more loaves than the day before, and report exactly what the emperor had commanded.

So Malchus took five *denarii* and, as he left the cave, he wondered at the piles of stones there, but, since his mind was on other things, he thought no more of it. Then, as he warily approached the city gate, he was surprised to see a cross above it. He hurried on from there to the next gate and found another cross above that, and when he found that all the city gates had crosses above them, he was utterly bewildered. Crossing himself, he went back to the first gate, thinking he must be dreaming. Then, plucking up his courage and pulling his cloak over his face, he entered the city and made his way towards the bread shop, and, when he heard people talking openly about Christ, he was dumbfounded. 'How can it be,' he asked himself, 'that yesterday no one dared speak the name of Christ, and today everyone seems to be a Christian? I do believe this is not Ephesus at all. The buildings seem different. It must be some other city, somewhere I have never been before.' So he made inquiries, and when he was assured that it was Ephesus, he thought he must really have lost his mind and decided to go straight back to his companions. But first he went into the bread shop, and when he took out his money to pay, the men there looked at the coins in amazement and whispered to each other that the young fellow must have stumbled on some long-lost treasure. Malchus, seeing them muttering to each other, thought they were going to haul him off to the emperor, and in terror he begged them to keep the loaves and coins and let him go. But they held on to him and asked: 'Where are you from? You must have discovered some treasure from olden times. Let us into the secret, and we will be your partners and we will hide you! You will not be able to keep this quiet otherwise.' Malchus was so scared that he could find nothing to say to them. When they saw that he would say nothing, they put a rope round his neck and dragged him through the streets to the city centre, so that it was soon public knowledge that a young man had found some treasure. All the people of Ephesus crowded round him and eyed him with curiosity, while Malchus tried to convince them that he had found nothing at all. Looking around, however, he could see no one who knew him; and when he searched the faces of the people to see if he could recognize one of his relatives (whom he of course thought to be still alive) and could find none, he stood there dumbly, like an idiot, with the people all milling about him.

Now when St Martin, the bishop, and Antipater, the proconsul (who had recently arrived in Ephesus), heard about this, they ordered the citizens to bring the youth before them, and his coins as well, but to watch out for trouble. When Malchus found himself being pulled towards the church by the people's representatives, he thought he was being taken to appear before the emperor. Then the bishop and the proconsul saw the coins for themselves, and, surprised at their antiquity, asked him where he had found this mysterious treasure. Malchus answered that he had found no such thing; the *denarii*, he told them, had come from his own parents' purse. And when he was asked what city he came from, he replied: 'From here, from this city – if this really is Ephesus.' The proconsul said: 'Then have your parents come here to give evidence on your behalf.' But when he gave their names and no one had heard of them, they accused him of making the story up in order to obtain his release. The proconsul said: 'How can we believe your story about this being your parents' money, when the inscriptions on the coins show they are more than three hundred and seventy-seven years old? They date from the first years of Decius's reign, and are nothing like our coinage today. And how could your parents possibly have been alive so long ago when you are so young? You really expect to fool the councillors and senators of Ephesus with such nonsense? In the circumstances I shall have you handed over to the civil authorities until you tell the truth and say exactly what it is you have found.'

Malchus then fell down before them and said: 'Sirs, in God's name, tell me the answer to my question, and I will tell you all that is in my heart. The emperor Decius, who was in this city – where is he?' The bishop replied: 'My son, there is no emperor on earth called Decius. Long, long ago there was one of that name.' 'This is what so bewilders me, my lord,' Malchus said, 'and no one will believe me. But follow me and I shall show you my companions who are up on Mount Celion, and you can believe them. For this much I do know, that we fled from the persecution of the emperor Decius, and I myself saw Decius yesterday, when he entered this city – if this really is Ephesus!'

After giving the matter deep thought, the bishop said to the proconsul: 'There is some miracle which God wishes to reveal to us through this young man.' So in haste they set out with the youth, and a great crowd of people followed them. Malchus went in to his companions first, and behind him came the bishop, who discovered among the stones the document [which Theodorus and Rufinus had hidden], sealed with two silver seals. Calling the people together, he read out the story of what had happened, and everyone was filled with wonder. Then they saw the saints sitting in the cave, and their faces were as pink as roses in bloom. The people fell to the ground glorifying God, and the bishop and proconsul immediately sent word to the emperor Theodosius, asking him to come quickly and see the miracle God had just worked. At the news Theodosius at once got up from the ground where he was lying, took off the sackcloth he was wearing, and came from Constantinople to Ephesus, glorifying God. Everyone went to meet him, and together they climbed up to the cave. As soon as the saints saw the emperor, their faces shone like the sun; and the emperor went in and fell on his face before them, then rose, embraced them, and wept over each of them in turn. 'Seeing you now,' he said, 'I feel as if I were seeing the Lord raise Lazarus from the dead!' St Maximianus said to him: 'Believe us, it is for your sake that the Lord has raised us to life before the day of the general resurrection, so that you should have absolute faith that there is a resurrection of the dead. For we really have been raised from the dead, we are alive, and just as a baby lives in his mother's womb and comes to no harm, so we have lain here and slept and lived on without feeling a thing.' Then, as everyone watched, they laid their heads on the ground, fell asleep and, obedient to the will of God, gave up the ghost.

The emperor got to his feet and fell upon them, weeping and kissing them, and ordered that golden caskets should be made for their burial. But that very night they appeared to the emperor, saying that, as they had lain until now in the earth, and had risen from the earth, so he should put them back there until the Lord raised them up again. So the emperor commanded that the place should be adorned with gilded stones, and that all bishops who declared their belief in the resurrection should be absolved.

But there are grave doubts about the statement that the saints slept for three hundred and seventy-two years, because they rose from the dead in AD 448, and Decius's reign lasted only a year and three months, ending in AD 252. So in fact they slept for only one hundred and ninety-six years.[1]

41

ST MARTHA

29 July

Martha, who welcomed Christ to her home, was of royal descent.[1] Her father was named Syrus and her mother Eucharia. Her father was governor of Syria and of many coastal territories. Martha inherited through her mother and possessed jointly with her sister three towns: Magdalum and the two Bethanies, and part of the city of Jerusalem. Nowhere do we read that she had a husband or ever lived with a man. This noble hostess attended upon the Lord and wanted her sister to do so, too, because, to her way of thinking, there were not enough people in the entire world to serve so great a guest as he deserved.

After the Lord's ascension, when the disciples went their separate ways, Martha, with her brother Lazarus, her sister Mary Magdalene, blessed Maximinus (who had baptized the two sisters and to whose care the Holy Spirit had entrusted them) and many others were put on boats by the infidels, with no oars, sails, rudders or provisions, and, with the Lord's guidance, landed at Marseilles. From there they made their way to Aix where they converted the people to the faith. St Martha was a gifted speaker and universally popular.

There was at that time in the forest along the banks of the Rhône between Arles and Avignon a dragon, half-beast, half-fish, larger than an ox, longer than a horse, with sword-like teeth as sharp as horns and flanks as impenetrable as twin shields. This monster lurked in the river, killing everyone who tried to pass and sinking their boats. It had come by sea from Galatia in Asia, and was an offspring of Leviathan, an unbelievably savage aquatic serpent, and a beast called Onachus, a native of the region of Galatia, which lets fly its dung like an arrow at anyone who gives chase and can shoot it up to an acre away, scorching whatever it touches as if it were fire. The people begged Martha to help, so she set off with them, and when she found the dragon in the forest, it was in the act of devouring a man. Martha threw some blessed water over it and held up a cross. The beast was at once defeated, and stood there as meek as a lamb while St Martha tied it up with her girdle, and the people pelted it with stones and spears and killed it. The local people called this dragon 'Tarasconus', and that is why, in commemoration of this miracle, the place is still called Tarascon (it had formerly been known as 'Nerluc', i.e. the 'black place', because the forest there was dark and shadowy). With the permission of her teacher Maximinus and her sister, Martha stayed on at this place and devoted herself unremittingly to prayer and fasting. Later she gathered a large community of sisters there, and built a great basilica in honour of Blessed Mary Ever Virgin. She led a life of great austerity, avoiding all meat and fats, eggs, cheese and wine, eating only once a day, and bending her knee in prayer a hundred times each day, and the same number of times each night.

One day Martha was preaching in the region of Avignon, between the city and the river Rhône. A youth standing on the other side of the river wanted to hear what she was saying. Not having a boat to cross in, he stripped off and began to swim across, but the current was too strong, and he was swept downstream and drowned in a moment. It took two days to find his body, which was then laid at St Martha's feet in the hope that she could revive it. She lay on the ground, her arms outstretched in the shape of a cross, and prayed: 'Adonai! Lord Jesus Christ, you who once raised my brother Lazarus, your beloved friend, from the dead! Dear guest, consider the faith of those who are gathered round me and bring this boy back to life!' She took the youth's hand, and in a moment he stood up and received holy baptism.

Eusebius relates in the fifth book of his *Ecclesiastical History* that the woman with a flux of blood, after she had been cured, set up in her courtyard, or her garden, a statue of Christ wearing a robe exactly like the one she had seen him wearing, and treated it with the greatest veneration. Now the grass growing at the foot of this statue, which had had no special properties before, as soon as it touched the hem of Christ's robe became charged with such healing power that many sick people were cured by it. This woman, whom the Lord cured of the flux of blood, is said by Ambrose to have been Martha. St Jerome tells the story, which is also related in the *Tripartite History*, that Julian the Apostate removed this statue of Christ which the woman had set up and placed one of himself there in its place, and it was struck by lightning and smashed in pieces.

The Lord revealed to Martha the date of her death a year before it happened, and for the whole of that year she was stricken with fevers. Then, a week before her passing, she heard the angelic choirs bearing her sister's soul to heaven, and, hastily calling together her community of brothers and sisters, she said: 'My dear companions and disciples, share in my joy, I beseech you! I can see the angelic choirs bearing my sister's soul in triumph to her promised seat in heaven! O my most beautiful and beloved sister! May you live for ever in the blessed abode with the one who was your master, and my guest!' Then St Martha, sensing that her own death was near, asked her friends to light lamps and keep watch around her until she died. But in the middle of the night before the day of her death, those who were keeping vigil at her bedside fell asleep, and a strong wind rushed through the house and blew all the lamps out. Martha, imagining that a host of evil spirits were swarming about her, prayed: 'Father Eloi, dearest guest! My seducers are gathered to devour me! They have lists of all the wrongs I have done. Eloi, do not leave me! Hasten to help me!' Then she saw her sister coming towards her with a torch in her hand, which she used to light the candles and lamps; and as they called out each other's name, all at once Christ was there. 'Come, beloved hostess,' he said, 'and where I am, there you shall be with me. You welcomed me in your house, and I shall welcome you in my heaven, and for love of you I shall grant the prayers of all who invoke your name.'

As the hour of her death drew nearer, she had herself carried outside so that she could see the heavens, and gave the order that she be laid down on a bed of ashes, and that a cross be held before her eyes. She said the following prayer: 'My dear guest, watch over your poor little servant, and, as you deigned to enter my house on earth, so receive me in your heavenly abode!' She then asked for the passion according to St Luke to be read to her, and at the words 'Father, into your hands I commend my spirit', she breathed her last . . .

42

ST GERMAIN,
BISHOP

31 July

Germain was born of noble family in the city of Auxerre. After a thorough schooling in the liberal arts he finally went to Rome to study jurisprudence, and there he won such distinction that the Senate sent him to Gaul to become governor of the whole duchy of Burgundy. In the centre of his native Auxerre, in which as governor he took a special interest, there was a pine tree on whose branches he used proudly to hang the heads of the beasts he had killed to demonstrate his prowess as a huntsman. St Amator, bishop of the city, used often to reproach him for this ostentation, and warned him to have the tree cut down in case some evil befell the Christians because of it, but Germain absolutely refused to listen. One day, however, in Germain's absence, the bishop cut the tree down and burnt it, and when Germain got word of this, forgetting all his Christian principles, he came back to Auxerre at the head of a troop of soldiers and threatened to put the bishop to death. But the bishop learnt by a revelation from God that Germain would be his successor, so he bowed to the governor's fury and withdrew to Autun. Subsequently he returned to Auxerre, cleverly managed to shut Germain up in his church, gave him the tonsure, and predicted that he would succeed him as bishop. And so it came about, for a short while later Amator died a holy death, and the entire populace chose Germain as his successor. Thereupon Germain gave away all his possessions to the poor, and lived with his wife as if she were his sister; and for thirty years he mortified his body, never eating wheaten bread, never touching wine or vegetables, never flavouring his food with salt. Twice a year only he took wine, at Easter and Christmas, but watered it down so much that it tasted of nothing. He was always fasting, and never ate anything until the evening; when he did eat, he would first force himself to swallow ashes, and then make do with a barley loaf. Summer and winter he wore no more than a hair-shirt and a cowl to cover his head, and if he did not give them away, he would wear these garments until they fell apart. He sprinkled ashes on his bed, his only bedclothes were a hair-shirt and a sack, and he had no pillow to lay his head on. He was constantly in tears and wore the relics of saints about his neck, and never took off his clothes, rarely even his shoes or his girdle. Everything he did was superhuman. Indeed, his life was such that, even if there had been no accompanying miracles, it would have seemed unbelievable. And there were so many miracles that, had they not been the clear consequence of his saintly merits, they would have been considered the purest fancy.

Germain was once a guest in a certain household when after supper he was surprised to see the table being laid afresh. He asked for whom they were making these preparations, and was told that they were for the 'good women' who came in the night. That night St Germain decided to keep watch, and he saw a whole crowd of demons coming to the table in the shape of men and women. He ordered them not to leave, then woke the whole household and asked them if they recognized these people. They replied yes, of course, they were all neighbours. Again ordering the demons to stay where they were, Germain sent to each of the neighbours' houses, and they were all discovered to be asleep in their beds. Then, when he adjured the men and women at table to tell the truth, they admitted that they were demons, and confessed that this was the way they fooled humans.

At that time St Lupus was bishop of Troyes. When King Attila laid siege to his city, Lupus positioned himself above the main gate of the city and called out to his enemy, asking him who it was who dared attack them in this manner. 'I am Attila,' came the reply, 'the scourge of God!' God's humble bishop groaned and said: 'And I am Lupus [Latin: 'wolf'], the destroyer of God's flock, alas, and one who needs God's scourge!' He then ordered the gates to be opened. But the enemy troops were blinded by the hand of God, and passed through Troyes, in one gate and out of the other, without either seeing or harming a single person.

Germain later took Bishop Lupus with him to Britain, where the heretics were increasing in number. When they were at sea, a terrible storm blew up, but St Germain had only to utter a prayer and the sea was still again. The natives gave them a respectful welcome, for they had been forewarned of their arrival by the demons St Germain had exorcized from the possessed. The two bishops convinced the heretics of their errors, then returned to their own dioceses.

Once Germain lay ill in bed in a certain place when a fire broke out which set the whole region ablaze. Everyone asked the bishop to let them carry him to safety, but Germain refused: he defied the flames, and, though the fire consumed everything else in a wide radius, it did not touch the house where he was staying.

Later he returned to Britain to refute the heretics a second time. One of his disciples hurried to follow him, but fell ill and died in the town of Tonnerre. On his return blessed Germain had his disciple's tomb opened, and called on him by name, asking him how he was, and if he wanted to continue fighting at his side. At once the dead man sat up and announced that he was completely happy, and had no wish to be called back to life. The saint, with a nod, agreed to let him rest in peace, and he laid back his head and fell asleep again in the Lord.

Once, when Germain was preaching in Britain, the king of Britain refused hospitality to him and his companions. But one of the king's swineherds, after feeding his animals, was on his way back to his cottage with the wages he had received at the palace when he saw blessed Germain and his companions. They were hungry and shivering with cold, so he took them into his cottage and had the only calf he owned killed, in order to provide them with meat. After the meal St Germain had all the calf's bones laid on the hide, uttered a prayer, and at once the calf sprang to life again. The next day Germain hurried off to see the king, and asked him candidly why he had refused to shelter him. Completely taken aback by this, the king was unable to answer him. 'Away with you,' Germain told him, 'and leave your kingdom to a better man!' Then, at God's command, Germain summoned the swineherd and his wife, and, to everyone's astonishment, declared him king. Ever since then the descendants of the swineherd have ruled over the British nation.

The Saxons were once warring against the Britons, and realizing that their numbers were small, they appealed to Germain and Lupus, who happened to be passing by, to help them. The two saints preached the word to them, and soon they were all flocking in droves to receive the grace of baptism. On Easter Day, in the fervour of their faith, they threw down their arms and resolved to rely on courage alone; so, when the Britons got wind of this, they advanced all the more quickly and confidently to meet them. But Germain, who was in the middle of the Saxon host, told them that when he shouted 'Alleluia!', they must all shout 'Alleluia!' in reply. They did as he said, and the charging enemy were suddenly seized with such terror that they threw down their arms and fled in all directions, convinced that not only the mountains, but the heavens themselves were falling upon their heads.

Once, when Germain was passing through Autun, he went to the tomb of the bishop St Cassian, and inquired of the prelate how things were with him. Instantly Cassian replied from his tomb for all to hear: 'I am relishing this sweet repose, and await the coming of my Redeemer.' Germain answered him: 'May your rest in Christ be long! And pray earnestly for us that we may merit the joys of the holy resurrection!'

When Germain visited Ravenna, he was received with great honour by Queen Placidia and her son Valentinian. At supper time the queen sent him a large silver dish loaded with the choicest foods. The saint accepted the gift, but gave the food away to the servants, and kept the silver dish itself for the poor. In return for this gift he sent to the queen a barley loaf on a little wooden dish. This the queen was pleased to receive, and later she had the wooden dish covered with silver. On another occasion the same queen had invited him to dinner, and Germain graciously accepted; but he was so exhausted with fasting and prayer that he had to ride from his house to the palace on a donkey. Then, while the saint was at table, his donkey died. When the queen heard what had happened, she had a horse presented to him, an animal of most placid temperament. But when Germain saw it, he said: 'No, I want my donkey! He brought me here, and he shall take me back.' He then went to where the dead donkey lay and said: 'Up you get, donkey, let us go home again!' At once the animal leapt to his feet, shook himself, and, as if nothing at all had happened, took Germain back to where he was staying. Before he left Ravenna, however, Germain predicted that he had not much longer to live. Shortly afterwards he was stricken with a fever and a week later he died in the Lord. In accordance with his wishes, the queen had his body taken to Gaul. Germain died around AD 430.

St Germain had promised Eusebius, bishop of Vercelli, that on his return he would personally consecrate a church Eusebius had built. But when St Eusebius learnt that Germain had died, he had all the candles lit, intending to consecrate the church himself. But no sooner were they lit than they blew out. Eusebius realized this meant either that the dedication must be done at another time, or that it should be left to another bishop. But when Germain's body arrived in Vercelli and was brought into the church, in a moment, miraculously, the candles burst into flame. St Eusebius then recalled Germain's promise, and knew that what he had promised to do while living, the saint had accomplished after his death. But this story must not be taken as referring to the great Eusebius of Vercelli, or as having happened in his time, because he died in the principate of Valens, and more than fifty years elapsed between his death and that of St Germain. So another, different Eusebius must have been bishop of Vercelli when these events took place.

43

ST DOMINIC

4 August

Dominic, the celebrated founding father of the Order of Preachers, was born in Spain in the village of Calaruega in the diocese of Osma. His father's name was Felix, his mother's Johanna. Before his birth his mother dreamt that she was carrying a little dog in her womb, which held a blazing torch in its mouth, and that when the dog issued from her womb, it set fire to the entire fabric of the world. And when Dominic was baptized, the woman who lifted him from the sacred font saw upon his forehead a brilliant star that lit up the whole universe.

While still a small child and under the care of a nurse, Dominic was often caught leaving his bed at night to sleep on the bare earth. For his education he was sent to Palentia, and such was his passion for learning that for ten years he never tasted wine. When a terrible famine ravaged the city, he sold his furniture and books and gave the proceeds to the poor. His reputation spread, and the bishop of Osma made him a canon regular in his church. Not long after this, since his life was universally judged to be a mirror of perfection, the canons elected him as their sub-prior. Day and night Dominic gave himself up to reading and prayer, begging God unceasingly to deign to give him grace to devote himself entirely to the salvation of his neighbour. He was assiduous in his study of the *Discourses of the Fathers* and soon progressed to a high degree of perfection.

He went with his bishop to Toulouse, but discovered that his host there had been corrupted by the perversion of heresy. Dominic turned him back to the true faith of Christ, and presented him to the Lord as a token of the first-fruits of the harvest to come.

We read in the *Deeds of the Count of Montfort* that one day, after preaching against the heretics, Dominic made a copy of all his most important arguments and gave the document to one of the heretics so that he could ponder his objections at length. That night, when the heretics gathered round a fire, this man brought out and showed them the document he had been given.

His friends said that he should throw it on to the fire; if it burnt, their faith ('heresy', they should have said) would be proved true; if it refused to burn, they would preach the true faith of the Roman Church. So it was thrown on to the fire, and after a short while it suddenly leapt unmarked from the flames. They were all dumbfounded, but one of them, who was more hard-headed than the rest, said: 'Throw it in again. If we try it a second time, we shall be that much more sure of the truth.' In it went a second time, and a second time it leapt out untouched. Again, the sceptic told them: 'Throw it in a third time. Then we shall know for certain: there will be no doubt.' In it went a third time, and again it leapt out untouched, without a mark on it. But still the heretics persisted in their disbelief and bound each other on the strictest of oaths not to reveal what had happened to anyone. But there was a soldier present who had some leanings towards our faith, and he later made the miracle common knowledge. This all happened at Montréal, and something similar is said to have taken place around that time at Fanjeaux, when a solemn disputation with the heretics was in progress.

When the bishop of Osma died, most of St Dominic's companions returned to their homes, but the saint stayed on with a small remnant and resolutely preached the word of God against the heretics. The enemies of the truth mocked him, spitting at him, throwing mud and all sorts of filth at him, and tying wisps of straw on his back to make fun of him. They even threatened to kill him, but he answered them fearlessly: 'I am not worthy of the glory of martyrdom. I have not merited such a death.' Accordingly, when he was passing a place where they lay in wait for him, not only was he unafraid, but he was clearly in the best of spirits, singing to himself as he walked along. Astonished at this, they said to him: 'Have you no fear of death at all?' 'None,' he replied: 'I would have begged you not to kill me quickly, with a few swift blows, but little by little, lopping off my limbs one by one, holding up to my eyes the bits you had cut off, then tearing out my eyes, and leaving my half-dead, mutilated body to wallow in a pool of its own blood – or to kill me in any other way you please.'

He once came across a man who, because of his extreme poverty, had joined the ranks of the heretics. So Dominic resolved to sell himself, so that, with the money he raised, he could relieve the man's distress, and at the same time deliver him from the error into which it had driven him. And he would have gone through with his plan, had not God in his mercy provided otherwise for the pauper.

On another occasion a woman came to him weeping bitterly and told him her brother was a prisoner of the Saracens, and she had no idea how she could secure his freedom. Dominic was moved to deep compassion, and offered to sell himself in order to redeem the prisoner. But God would not permit this, for he foresaw that the saint had a far more important role to play in the redemption of numberless spiritual captives.

When in the neighbourhood of Toulouse, Dominic was a guest in the house of some ladies who had been led into error by the heretics' outward display of piety. So, deciding to use a hair of the dog that bit them,[1] Dominic and his companion fasted the whole of Lent on bread and cold water, keeping vigil during the nights, and, when sleep became a necessity, resting their tired limbs on a bare board. In this way he brought the ladies once again to recognize the truth.

Soon after this he began to think about the establishment of a religious order, whose mission it would be to journey the length and breadth of the world preaching and defending the Catholic faith against the heretics. After he had remained in the region of Toulouse for ten years, that is from the death of the bishop of Osma up to the time of the Lateran Council, he went to Rome with Fulk, bishop of Toulouse, and attended the general council. There he asked the pontiff, Pope Innocent, to recognize for himself and his successors the foundation of an order which would be called, and would in fact be, the Order of Preachers. For some time the pope proved difficult, but then one night he had a dream in which he saw the Lateran Church suddenly threatening to collapse in ruins. But as he looked on in horror, St Dominic came running from the opposite direction, put his shoulders against the building, and kept the whole structure from falling. Upon waking, the pope understood the significance of his vision, and gladly granted the man of God's petition, advising him to return to his brethren and choose one of the already approved Rules, then to come back and receive formal approval. So Dominic rejoined his brethren and told them what the supreme pontiff had said. Now the brethren were sixteen in number, and, after invoking the Holy Spirit, they unanimously chose the Rule of St Augustine, the great doctor and preacher, for preachers they would be called, and preachers they would be. In addition they adopted certain stricter practices which they resolved to observe as constitutions. But meanwhile Pope Innocent had died and Honorius had been raised to the supreme pontificate, so it was from Honorius, in the year of our Lord 1216, that Dominic obtained confirmation of his Order.

Dominic was praying in the church of St Peter in Rome for the increase of his Order, when in a vision he saw those glorious princes of the apostles, Peter and Paul, coming towards him. Peter seemed to hand him a staff and Paul a book, then they said to him: 'Go forth and preach, for that is your God-appointed task.' Then, in an instant, he seemed to see his sons spread throughout the whole world, walking two by two and preaching the word of God to all the people. Accordingly he returned to Toulouse and sent his brethren out, some to Spain, some to Paris, and others to Bologna. He himself went back to Rome.

Before the establishment of the Order of Preachers, a certain monk had an ecstatic vision of the Blessed Virgin: she was kneeling with her hands joined, praying to her son for the human race. Several times Christ refused to listen to his loving mother, then finally, since she persisted, he said: 'Mother, what more can I do, or ought I to do for them? I have sent them patriarchs and prophets, and they did little to better themselves. I went to them myself, then I sent them my apostles, and they killed us all. I sent them my martyrs and confessors and doctors, and they would not listen to them. But since it is not right for me to refuse you anything, I will give them my preachers to enlighten them and purify them. And if they do not mend their ways, I shall visit them myself, in wrath!'

Another monk had a similar vision around the same time; it was when twelve abbots of the Cistercian Order were sent to Toulouse to denounce the heretics. In this vision, when the Son gave the above answer to his mother's prayer, she replied: 'Dear son, you must not deal with them as their evil deserves, but as your grace and compassion require.' Then, won over by her pleading, he replied: 'In answer to your prayers I shall grant them one more mercy: I shall send them my preachers to admonish them and teach them, and if they do not mend their ways, I will spare them no longer.'

A friar minor, who had for a long time been a companion of St Francis, told the following story to several friars of the Order of Preachers: when blessed Dominic was at Rome to persuade the pope to confirm his Order, he had a vision one night in which he saw Christ, upraised in the air, holding in his hand three spears which he brandished menacingly above the world. His mother hurried to his side, and asked what he meant to do. 'The whole world is beset by three vices,' he told her, 'pride, lust and greed. So I will use these three spears to destroy it.' The Virgin fell at his knees and said: 'My dearest son, have pity and temper your justice with mercy!' Christ replied: 'Do you not see what wrongs they do me?' 'Restrain your wrath, my son,' Mary said, 'and wait a while. For I have a faithful servant, a tireless champion who will travel the whole world and conquer it and place it beneath your sway. And I will give him another servant to help him, one who will fight faithfully by his side.' Her son replied: 'Very well. You have appeased me and I grant your request. But I would like to see whom you have chosen for such an important mission.' Thereupon she presented St Dominic to Christ. 'This is a strong and valiant warrior indeed,' he said to her. 'He will be sure to do all you have said.' Then she brought St Francis before him, and Christ commended him as warmly as he had St Dominic. Dominic, during this vision, looked closely at his new ally, and next day, when he came upon him in church, though he had never met him in the flesh, he needed no introduction: he knew him immediately from his vision of the night before. He ran up to him, threw his arms around him, and kissed him affectionately. 'You are my companion,' he cried. 'You will run the same course, side by side with me. Let us stand together and no enemy will prevail against us!' Dominic then told Francis in detail of the vision he had had. From that moment they were one heart and soul in the Lord, and made a rule that their followers should live in the same spirit of friendship for ever.[2]

Dominic had received into his Order a novice from Apulia, but some of this novice's former associates so undermined his resolve that he decided to go back into the world, and absolutely insisted that he be given back his old clothes. On hearing of this, blessed Dominic at once began to pray. Subsequently when the brethren had stripped the youth of his habit and put his shirt on him, he began to shout and scream: 'I am on fire! I am scorching! I am being burnt all over! Take it off, take off this accursed shirt, I am being burnt alive!' And he could get no relief until his shirt was removed, and he was clothed in his novice's habit again and taken back to the cloister.

One night, while Dominic was in Bologna, the other brethren had already retired to bed when a lay brother began to be plagued by the Devil. Friar Reyner, his master, heard what was going on, and hurried to tell blessed Dominic, and the saint had the brother carried into church and put down before the altar. It took ten brothers to restrain him, and when they finally got him there, blessed Dominic said to the demon: 'I charge you, wretch, tell me why you torment one of God's creatures in this way! Tell me why and how you got into him!' The Devil answered: 'I am tormenting him because he deserves it. Yesterday he drank wine in town without the prior's leave, and without making the sign of the cross. So I entered into him in the shape of a gnat – or rather he drank me in with the wine.' The brother's guilt was subsequently established. Meanwhile the first bell for matins sounded, and, as soon as he heard this, the Devil, speaking from inside the brother, cried: 'Enough! I can stay here no longer: the cowled ones are rising.' And so, at blessed Dominic's prayer, the demon was exorcized.

Once, in the region of Toulouse, Dominic had to cross a river with an armful of books; he carried them loose because he had nothing to put them in, and they fell into the water. Three days later a fisherman cast his line into the river and, thinking he had caught a big fish, pulled out the books, which were absolutely unmarked, as perfect as if they had been carefully kept in a chest.

Dominic arrived at a monastery late one night when the brothers had gone to bed. He did not want to disturb them, so he said a prayer, and he and his companions were able to enter the place, though the doors were still barred. The same story is told of Dominic when, with the aid of a Cistercian lay brother, he was engaged in fighting the heretics. Late one evening they came to a church which they found closed. Blessed Dominic uttered a prayer, and suddenly they found themselves inside the church, where they spent the whole night in prayer.

After a long, hard journey, before Dominic entered lodgings, he would satisfy his thirst at a spring, in case when he entered the house he might give offence to his hosts by seeming to drink too much.

A scholar who suffered greatly from temptations of the flesh came one feast-day to the house of the brethren in Bologna to hear mass there. Now that day it happened that blessed Dominic himself was celebrant. When it came to the moment of the offertory, the scholar went up to Dominic and, with great devotion, kissed his hand. And when he kissed it, he smelled an exquisite perfume coming from the saint's hand, a fragrance sweeter than any he had ever known in his life before. From that hour the fever of his lust was miraculously cooled; so much so, in fact, that this scholar who before had been so vain and so lecherous, now became continent and chaste. Ah, how great must the purity, the chastity of the saint's body have been, if the very odour it gave off could so miraculously cleanse a soul of all its impurity!

There was a priest who, observing the great fervour with which Dominic and his friars were preaching, thought he would become one of them, if only he could get hold of a New Testament, which he needed for his preaching. As he was pondering this, a young man appeared who had on him a copy of the New Testament which he wanted to sell. Delighted, the priest bought it at once. But he still had lingering doubts, so he prayed to God, made the sign of the cross on the cover of the book, then opened it; and the first passage his eye fell upon was the chapter in the Acts of the Apostles where St Peter is told: 'Arise and go down, and join them without hesitation, for I have sent them.' So he got up at once and joined the Order.

In Toulouse there was a master of theology who was renowned for his knowledge and academic standing. One morning before daybreak he was preparing his lectures when he felt drowsy, and sank back in his chair and dozed a while; and in a vision he saw seven stars being offered to him. He was still wondering at the novelty of this gift when the stars suddenly grew so greatly in brilliance and number that they lit up the whole world. On waking he was quite perplexed as to the meaning of this vision; but then, when he entered his theology school and began to lecture, St Dominic and six of his friars, all wearing the same habit, came humbly up to the master and told him of their desire to attend his lectures. He then recalled his vision, and was in no doubt that these were the seven stars he had seen.

While Dominic was in Rome, a certain Master Reginald, dean of St Anianus in Orleans, who had taught canon law in Paris for five years, arrived in the city with the bishop of Orleans, intending to board ship there. He had for some time been thinking of forsaking worldly things and devoting himself to preaching, but he was not yet clear as to how he might bring this about. He told a cardinal of his wish, and learnt from him of the establishment of the Order of Preachers. So Reginald summoned Dominic and, as soon as he met him, decided to enter his Order. But suddenly he was stricken with a fever so grave that everyone despaired of his life. St Dominic, however, persevered in prayer and begged the Blessed Virgin, to whom as its special patroness he had entrusted the care of the whole Order, to spare Reginald's life, if only for a short time. All at once, as Reginald lay awake and waiting for death, he saw, quite clearly, the Queen of Mercy coming towards him, accompanied by two most beautiful handmaids. Gently smiling, she said to him: 'Ask of me whatever you wish and I will give it you.' And as Reginald wondered what he should ask, one of the two handmaids suggested to him that he should ask for nothing, but put himself entirely in the hands of the Queen of Mercy. This he did. In answer she stretched forth a virginal hand and anointed his ears and nostrils, his mouth, hands, loins and feet with a healing ointment she had brought with her, uttering, as she anointed each part, the appropriate form of words. At the loins she said: 'May your loins be girt with the girdle of chastity.' At the feet she said: 'I anoint the feet to prepare the way for the Gospel of peace.' She added: 'In three days I shall send you a salve which will restore you to perfect health.' She then showed him a monk's habit. 'Look,' she said. 'This is the habit of your Order.' And Dominic, while at prayer, had exactly the same vision. Next morning St Dominic went to see Reginald and found him well. He heard from his own lips the whole story of his vision, and duly adopted the habit which the Virgin had shown them (for before this the friars had simply worn surplices). On the third day the Mother of God appeared and anointed Reginald's body, and as a consequence not only was the heat of his fever extinguished, but also the fires of passion were quenched in him for ever. As he himself confessed later, he never again felt the slightest stirring of desire. (A monk of the Order of Hospitallers saw this second vision with his own eyes, in the presence of St Dominic, and was utterly dumbfounded.) After this Reginald was sent to Bologna, and there he zealously devoted himself to preaching, and the number of friars began steadily to grow. Then he was sent to Paris, where some days later he died a holy death.

A young man, the nephew of Cardinal Stephen of Fossa Nova, fell headlong with his horse into a ditch, and when he was pulled out was found to be dead. He was taken before Dominic, and at the saint's prayer was restored to life.

An architect hired by the brothers was in the crypt of the church of St Sixtus when the ceiling fell down on him and he was crushed beneath a pile of debris. But St Dominic had his corpse brought up to him from below, and by his intercession at once restored him to life and health.

One day the friars who lived in this same church in Rome, who numbered about forty, found that they had only a little bread left. Blessed Dominic ordered them to put what little was left on the table, and to share it out. They were all gratefully eating their little morsel of bread when two young men entered the refectory; they looked alike and were dressed alike, and the pockets of their cloaks were stuffed with loaves. These they silently laid at the head of the table before Dominic, the servant of God, and then abruptly vanished before anyone could find out where they had come from or where they had gone. St Dominic, with a gesture round the table to his friars, said: 'Now my brothers – eat!'

Once, when Dominic was on a journey and there was a torrential downpour of rain, he made the sign of the cross and kept the rain off himself and his travelling companion as effectively as if the cross had thrown up an awning above them. All around the earth was absolutely awash with the downpour, but not a single drop came within a yard of them.

On another occasion, in the region of Toulouse, he had been taken across a river in a boat and the ferryman demanded a *denarius* for his passage. But the saint promised him instead the kingdom of heaven for the service he had rendered, adding that he was a disciple of Christ and did not carry with him any gold or money. The ferryman pulled at his cloak. 'Either give me your cloak,' he said, 'or pay the money!' The man of God raised his eyes to heaven, prayed silently for a while, and then looked down and saw a *denarius* lying on the ground, provided no doubt by the will of God. 'Look, brother,' he said; 'there is your fare. Take it and let me go my way in peace.'

Once, when the saint was on a journey, it happened that he was joined by another monk, who was well known to Dominic for his holiness of life, but who spoke an incomprehensible foreign tongue. Disappointed that he could not benefit from a mutual exchange of spiritual thoughts, Dominic asked the Lord to enable each of them to speak and to understand the other's language when they conversed. His prayer was granted, and for the three days that they journeyed together they understood each other perfectly.

Another time a man possessed by many demons was brought to Dominic. He took his stole and first placed it around his own neck, then wrapped it round the neck of the possessed man, at the same time commanding the demons not to trouble the man any more. At this the demons, tormented within the possessed man's body, cried out: 'Let us go! Why are you keeping us here and torturing us like this?' 'I will not let you go,' the saint told them, 'until you name someone to stand surety for you that you will never enter this man again.' 'And who,' they said, 'would do that for us?' The saint replied: 'The holy martyrs, whose bodies rest in the church here!' The demons cried: 'We cannot. We have not deserved their help.' 'You had better,' Dominic retorted, 'otherwise I shall never release you from your torment.' In answer the demons said that they would try all they could, and soon after they reported: 'We were successful! Though we did not deserve their help, the holy martyrs have agreed to vouch for us.' When Dominic demanded a sign to verify this, they said: 'Go to the casket in which the martyrs' heads are preserved, and you will find it upside-down.' He did so, and discovered that all they had told him was true.

While Dominic was preaching one day, some women who had been led astray by the heretics threw themselves at his feet and cried: 'Servant of God, help us! If what you have preached today is true, our minds have for a long while now been blinded by the spirit of error.' 'Be strong,' he told them, 'and wait a while, and you will see the sort of master you have been following.' At once they saw a hideous cat leap from their midst – a cat as big as a large dog, with enormous, flaming eyes, a long, broad, bloody tongue that reached down to his navel, and a short tail that stood erect and exposed to view, whichever way he turned, his disgusting hind parts, from which there issued a stench that was unbearable. For a while the monster stalked this way and that around the women, then finally he clawed his way up the bell rope and vanished into the belfry, leaving traces of filth everywhere behind him. Thereupon the women gave thanks to God, and were once again converted to the Catholic faith.

Dominic had convicted a number of heretics at Toulouse once, and they were condemned to be burnt at the stake. But seeing among them a man called Raymond, he told the executioners: 'Save that one: do not burn him along with the rest.' He then turned to Raymond and said to him kindly: 'I know, my son, I know that one day – even if the day is long in coming – you will be a good man, a saint!' So Raymond was released, and for twenty years he persisted in the sin of heresy. But at length he was converted, and was received into the Order of Preachers, where he led an exemplary life as a friar, and died a holy death.

When Dominic was in Spain with some of his friars as companions, a monstrous dragon appeared to him in a vision: its jaws were wide open and it was trying to swallow the brothers who were with him. The man of God realized what this must mean, and urged his brethren to resist with all their might. But later all of them, except Friar Adam and two lay brothers, deserted him. When he asked one of the three left if he, too, wanted to leave, he replied: 'God forbid, father, that I should leave the head to follow the feet!' At these words Dominic began to pray, and in a short time, by the merits of his prayer, he won back nearly all of those who had left him.

Dominic was with his friars at the convent of St Sixtus in Rome when the Holy Spirit came suddenly over him. He summoned the brethren to the chapter house, and publicly announced to them all that four of them would shortly die: two of them a physical, and two a spiritual, death. Soon afterwards two friars did pass to the Lord, and two, in fact, left the Order.

When Dominic was in Bologna, his friars were strongly in favour of admitting to the Order a German who lived there called Master Conrad.

On the vigil of the Assumption of the Blessed Virgin Mary, Dominic was exchanging confidences with the prior of the Cistercian monastery of Casa Mariae, and when the subject came up in the course of their conversation, he told him in confidence: 'Prior, I will tell you something that I have never let out to anyone before – and please do not tell this to anyone as long as I live: I have never in my life asked anything of God that was not granted me, exactly as I wished it.' When the prior observed that he himself might die before Dominic, the saint was inspired to prophesy that the prior would survive him by many years (and events bore out the truth of this prediction). 'Then, father,' the prior said, 'ask God to add Master Conrad to your Order. Your friars seem very eager to admit him.' But Dominic answered: 'Good brother, what you ask is no easy matter!' But after compline, when everyone else had gone to bed, Dominic remained in the church and, as was his custom, spent the whole night in prayer. Next morning, when the brethren assembled for the office of prime and the cantor intoned the hymn '*Iam lucis orto sidere*' ['The star of dawn is risen already'], Master Conrad suddenly appeared, Conrad who was destined to be a new star with a new light. He prostrated himself at blessed Dominic's feet and begged to be clothed in the habit of the Order; and so insistent was he that his wish was granted. Subsequently he became one of the most devout members of the Order, and was an extremely popular teacher. When finally he lay dying and had closed his eyes, and the brethren thought he had passed on, he opened his eyes suddenly, and looked round at his brothers and said: '*Dominus vobiscum*' ['The Lord be with you']. And when they answered: '*Et cum spiritu tuo*' ['And with thy spirit'], he added: '*Fidelium animae per misericordiam Dei requiescant in pace*' ['May the souls of the faithful through the mercy of God rest in peace'], and died peacefully.

Dominic, the servant of God, was possessed of an unruffled spirit, except when he was moved to compassion or pity; and, as a happy heart shows itself in a cheerful face, his inward peace could be seen in the mildness of his outward manner. During the day, among his friars and other companions, while always preserving the rules of propriety, no one was more genial than he; in the hours of night no one was more zealous at prayer or keeping vigil. The day he devoted to his neighbour, the night to God. His eyes were like a well of tears. Often, at mass, at the elevation of the Lord's Body, he was so rapt in ecstasy it was as if he were gazing at Christ himself in the flesh. For this reason he did not generally hear mass with the rest of the community. He would commonly pass the whole night in the church, so that he hardly ever seemed to have a fixed place in which to sleep. And when tiredness overcame him and he had to give in and rest, he laid his head either before the altar, or on some stone, and slept there for a little while. Every night he disciplined himself three times with an iron chain: once for himself, once for sinners still living, and a third time for those suffering purgatory.

He was once elected bishop of Couserans but he flatly refused to accept, declaring that he would rather die than agree to any such appointment.[3] And when he was once asked, when he was spending some time in the diocese of Carcassonne, why he did not prefer to live more in Toulouse, in his own diocese, he replied: 'Because in Toulouse I find too many people who sing my praises. Whereas here in Carcassonne, it is quite the opposite: everyone makes war on me!' When someone asked him which book he had studied the most, his answer was: 'The book of love.'

One night in Bologna, while St Dominic was at prayer in his church, the Devil appeared to him in the guise of a friar. Thinking he was one of the community, St Dominic nodded, motioning to him to go to bed, as the others had done. But the Devil, in mockery, stood there nodding back at him. Then the saint, curious to know who it was who ignored his order, lit a candle from one of the lamps, and looked closely into his face. In an instant he recognized him as the Devil. He roundly rebuked him, but the Devil promptly began to reproach him for breaking the rule of silence. St Dominic however asserted his right to speak, as the head of the community, and then insisted that the Devil tell him how he tempted the friars in choir. He replied: 'I make them arrive late and leave early!' Dominic then took him to the dormitory, and asked him how he tempted the brethren there. He said: 'I make them sleep too long and get up late, so that they are here during the office. And sometimes I make them have impure thoughts.' Next Dominic took him to the refectory, and asked how he tempted the brethren there. In reply the Devil, leaping over the table tops, kept repeating the same words: 'More and less, more and less!', and when St Dominic asked him what he meant by this, he said: 'I tempt some of the brethren to eat more than they should, so that their sin is gluttony. Others I tempt to eat less than they should, so that they are too weak to serve God or to observe the rule of their Order.' Dominic then took him to the parlour, and asked him again how he tempted the brothers there. The Devil in reply rolled his tongue rapidly about in his mouth, producing a strange confusion of sounds. St Dominic asked him what this meant, and he told him: 'This place is wholly mine! When the brothers meet here to talk, I make sure they all talk at the same time. I make them talk a lot of nonsense, and never wait for anyone else to speak.' Finally the saint led the Devil to the chapter house, but when he reached the doorway the Devil would not hear of going in. 'I will never go in here,' he cried, 'because this is an accursed place, it is a hell to me! Here I lose all that I have gained elsewhere. For when I make a brother sin through some negligence, in no time at all he comes to this accursed place and purges himself of his sin by confessing it to everyone. Here they are admonished, here they confess, here they accuse themselves, here they are flogged, here they are absolved. So here I suffer the anguish of losing everything I was so happy to win elsewhere!' With these words, he vanished.

St Dominic was in Bologna when at last he neared the end of his earthly pilgrimage, and there he fell gravely ill. The dissolution of his body was revealed to him in a vision in which he saw a beautiful youth who was calling to him and saying: 'Come, my beloved, come to your joy, come!' So Dominic called together twelve friars from his community at Bologna, and so that he should not leave them like orphans, without a heritage, he gave them his testament. 'There are three commands I bequeath to you, as my sons and heirs, and they are yours to keep in perpetuity: have charity, practise humility, and embrace poverty with open arms!' What he most expressly forbade was that any brother should ever bring temporal possessions into his Order, and he laid his curse and the curse of God Almighty on any man who might presume to defile the Order of Preachers with the dust of worldly riches. As the friars grieved inconsolably at their loss, Dominic gently comforted them: 'My sons,' he said, 'do not be troubled if I leave you in the flesh. I assure you that I shall be more help to you dead than alive!' Then, reaching his final hour, he fell asleep in the Lord in the year 1221 . . .

44

ST LAURENCE,
MARTYR

10 August

St Laurence, deacon and martyr, was a native of Spain, and was brought to
Rome by St Sixtus. According to Master John Beleth, St Sixtus had gone
on a visit to Spain, and there met Laurence and his cousin Vincent, two
young men distinguished for their noble characters and exemplary way of
life. He took them back to Rome, and one of them, Laurence, stayed on
there with him, while Vincent returned home to Spain and there died the
glorious death of a martyr. However, the dates of the martyrdoms of
Laurence and Vincent cast some doubt on the accuracy of Master Beleth's
account. Laurence suffered under Decius, whereas Vincent, still a young
man, suffered under Diocletian and Dacian. But between the reigns of
Decius and Diocletian there was an interval of forty years, in which there
were seven other emperors. So Vincent could not still have been a young
man at the time.

St Sixtus ordained Laurence his archdeacon. At that time the emperor
Philip and his son, also called Philip, had accepted the faith of Christ, and,
having become Christians, did all they could to promote the interests of the
Church. This Philip was the first emperor to accept the Christian faith. It is
said that it was Origen who converted him, though elsewhere we read that
it was St Pontius. Philip reigned in the thousandth year from the foundation
of the City; and so Rome's thousandth year was dedicated to Christ, and
not to pagan gods. The millennium was celebrated by the Romans with a
splendid display of games and spectacles.

Emperor Philip had in his army an officer called Decius, who was renowned
for his military prowess. At the time Gaul was in revolt, so the emperor
sent Decius to quell the rebellion and bring the Gauls under the Roman
yoke once again. Decius was completely successful in his mission, and,
having gained the victory he had wanted, he returned to Rome. The emperor,
hearing Decius was on his way, and intending to reward him with special
honours, left Rome and travelled as far as Verona to meet him. But the

greater the honours accorded to evil men, the more swollen their pride becomes, and Decius, in an excess of arrogance, began to have designs on the empire, and to plot the death of his master. So one day, when the emperor was in his tent resting on his bed, Decius stealthily crept in and cut his throat as he slept. Then, with a mixture of bribery and persuasion, gifts and promises, he succeeded in winning over the army which had accompanied the emperor to Verona, and hurried back at their head to the imperial city.

When the younger Philip got word of this he panicked: as Sicardus relates in his *Chronicle*, he entrusted all his treasures, both his father's and his own, to St Sixtus and St Laurence, so that if he, too, were killed by Decius, they could distribute it among the churches and the poor. (Do not concern yourself that the treasure blessed Laurence distributed is not referred to as the emperor's, but the Church's. It could be that he distributed some of the Church's own wealth alongside that of Emperor Philip, or perhaps they are called the Church's because Philip had left them to the Church to be distributed among the poor. There is serious doubt as to whether Pope Sixtus was even alive at this time.) Philip then fled and went into hiding to avoid falling into the hands of Decius. In due course the Senate went out to meet Decius and confirmed him as emperor. To avoid suspicion of treachery, and to create the impression that he had killed his master out of devotion to the gods of his country, Decius embarked upon a most barbarous persecution of the Christians, ordering that they should be slaughtered without mercy. During the course of this persecution, many thousands of martyrs fell, and among those who won the crown of martyrdom was the younger Philip. Decius then set about trying to discover where Philip's treasure was hidden. Sixtus was brought before him and accused of being a Christian and of having the emperor's treasure in his keeping. Decius promptly had him put in gaol and ordered him to be tortured until he denied Christ and revealed where the treasure was hidden. As he was dragged away, Laurence followed him and cried: 'Where are you going, father, without your son? Where are you going in such haste, holy priest, without your deacon? You never used to offer the holy sacrifice without an assistant! What have I done to offend you, father? Have you found me unworthy of you? Put me to the test, I beg you, see if you have chosen a minister fit for the task you have given him, one worthy of dispensing the Lord's blood!' Sixtus replied: 'I am not abandoning you, my son, nor am I deserting you. You are destined to face greater trials for the faith of Christ! We old men have a lighter course to run: you are young, and you will win a more glorious triumph over the tyrant. In three days you will follow me, a true deacon following his priest!' And Sixtus placed the treasure in Laurence's safe-keeping for distribution among the churches and the poor.

Laurence then went searching night and day for Christians, and helped each of them according to his needs. In his travels he came to the house of a widow who had hidden many Christians in her house. This woman had for a long time suffered migraines, and St Laurence, by laying his hands on her, cured her of her pain. He also washed the feet of the poor, and gave alms to everyone in need. That same night he came to the house of another Christian and found a blind man there, and, by making the sign of the cross over him, succeeded in restoring his sight.

Meanwhile Sixtus had refused to submit to Decius, or sacrifice to his idols, so Decius gave orders that he should be taken off and beheaded. But Laurence ran after him and shouted: 'Do not leave me, holy father! I have already given away the treasure you gave me.' Hearing 'treasure' mentioned, the soldiers seized Laurence and took him to the tribune Parthenius. Parthenius brought him before Decius, and the emperor asked him: 'Where is this treasure of the Church? We know you have it hidden!' When Laurence gave no answer, Decius handed him over to the prefect Valerian and ordered him to make him give up the treasure, and sacrifice to the idols, or to torture him and put him to a painful and lingering death. Valerian in turn put him in the custody of another prefect called Hippolytus, and Hippolytus put him in gaol together with a crowd of other prisoners. Now in this gaol there was a pagan named Lucillus who had wept so much that he had lost his sight. Laurence promised him that, if he would believe in Christ and be baptized, he would restore his sight, and Lucillus begged to be baptized without delay. So Laurence fetched a basin of water and said to him: 'In professing Christ all sins are washed away.' Then, when he had questioned Lucillus carefully about the articles of faith, and Lucillus affirmed that he believed them all, Laurence poured the water over his head and baptized him in the name of Christ. Instantly his blindness went and he could see again. After this miracle, many who were blind came to Laurence and went away with their sight restored.

Hippolytus, observing all this, said to Laurence: 'Tell me where the treasure is.' But Laurence replied: 'Ah, Hippolytus, if you only believe in Jesus Christ, I will show you treasures and I will promise you eternal life.' 'If you do as you say,' Hippolytus told him, 'then I will do all you require of me.' That same hour Hippolytus believed, and he and his whole household received the holy rite of baptism. After his baptism he exclaimed: 'I have seen the souls of the innocent leaping for joy!'

Valerian now ordered Hippolytus to bring Laurence before him. 'Let us walk side by side,' Laurence suggested to Hippolytus, 'for glory awaits both you and me.' They then came before the tribunal and were questioned again about the treasure. Laurence asked for a delay of three days, a request which Valerian granted, leaving him again in the custody of Hippolytus. During these three days Laurence gathered together all the poor, the lame and the blind he came across and took them before Decius in the Sallustian Palace. 'Look!' he said. 'Here you see the eternal treasure, treasure which never diminishes but grows and grows. It is shared among each one of them, and none of them is ever found without his portion. It is their hands that have carried the treasure to heaven.' Valerian, who was with the emperor, said: 'What is the point of all this talk? Have done with your sorcery and sacrifice to our gods!' Laurence retorted: 'Whom should man worship, the one created or his Creator?' Angered at this riposte, Decius had Laurence whipped with leaded scourges and subjected to every kind of torture before his eyes. But when he told him to offer sacrifice if he wanted the tortures to stop, Laurence answered: 'You poor fool, this is the feast I have always longed for!' 'If you call this a feast,' Decius said, 'tell me the names of some other godless creatures like yourself and they can come and share it with you!' Laurence said: 'Their names are already written in heaven: you are not worthy to look upon their faces.'

Decius then had Laurence stripped naked and clubbed, and white hot swords were held against his side. 'Lord Jesus Christ,' Laurence prayed, 'God from God, have mercy on me your servant! When accused, I did not deny your holy name, and when interrogated, I confessed you as my Lord.' Decius said to him: 'It is witchcraft that enables you to defy these tortures, I know it, but you will not defy me much longer. I call all the gods and goddesses to witness: unless you offer sacrifice, you will die the cruellest death imaginable.' He then had Laurence beaten again and again with leaded scourges. The saint prayed: 'Lord Jesus Christ, receive my spirit.' And immediately a voice rang out from heaven, saying: 'You have still many trials to endure.' Decius heard this and, overcome with rage, cried: 'Romans, you have heard demons consoling this wicked blasphemer. He will not worship our gods. He has no fear of pain. He cares nothing for the anger of princes.' He had him lashed again with scorpions, but Laurence, with a smile, thanked him and prayed for all who witnessed his sufferings. Simultaneously a soldier named Romanus was converted and told blessed Laurence: 'I see a beautiful youth standing before you, drying your limbs with a towel. I beg you, in God's name, do not leave me. Baptize me, and make haste.' Decius said to Valerian: 'This is sorcery, surely, that has defeated us.' He then had Laurence untied from the frame he was strapped to and put again in the custody of Hippolytus. Romanus brought a jug of water to Laurence, fell at his feet, and was baptized by him. But Decius found out about this and had Romanus beaten with cudgels; then, when he openly confessed that he was a Christian, he had him beheaded.

The same night Laurence was brought before Decius. Hippolytus was in tears, and longed to shout aloud that he, too, was a Christian, but Laurence told him: 'No, keep Christ hidden in your heart, and when I call to you, hear me and come.' Every possible instrument of torture was now brought before Decius and got ready. Decius gave Laurence an ultimatum: 'You will either sacrifice to the gods or spend the whole night racked with pain.' 'For me the night has no darkness,' Laurence told him. 'Everything is ablaze with light.' Decius snapped: 'Bring in an iron bed, and let this stubborn Laurence rest on that!' The emperor's men stripped Laurence, stretched him on an iron grill, heaped red-hot coals beneath it and bore down upon his body with iron pitchforks. 'Poor wretch,' Laurence said to Valerian, 'can you not see? To me these coals only bring sweet relief! But for you they will be an everlasting torment, because the Lord knows that when accused I did not deny him, and when interrogated I confessed Christ. And now, as I roast on this gridiron, I give him thanks.' Then, with a cheerful smile, he said to Decius: 'Look, fool, you have roasted only one side of me. Turn me over, and then eat.' And then, giving thanks, he said: 'I thank you, Lord, for accounting me worthy to enter your gates.' With these words he gave up the ghost.

Utterly defeated, Decius went back with Valerian to the palace of Tiberius, leaving Laurence's body still over the fire. Next morning Hippolytus removed it, and, with the priest Justin, embalmed it in aromatic spices and buried it in the Campus Veranus. The Christians fasted and kept vigil for three days, mourning and weeping inconsolably . . .

45

ST BERNARD

20 August

Bernard was born in Burgundy at the chateau of Fontaines, of noble and devout parents. His father Tescelin was a gallant knight, active in worldly affairs, but equally zealous in his spiritual life. His mother was named Aleth. She had seven children, six sons and one daughter, all of her sons destined to be monks, and her daughter a nun. As soon as she had given birth to a son, she would offer him to God with her own hands. She would not allow her children to be suckled by anyone but herself: it was as if she hoped with her mother's milk to instil into her children something of her own goodness. As they grew, and as long as they were under her care, she brought them up as if training them for a solitary life rather than a public career, giving them coarse, common food to eat, as if any moment she might be sending them off to a monastery. When she was still pregnant with her third son, Bernard, she had a prophetic dream: what she was carrying in her womb was a little puppy, white all over except for a reddish back, and the puppy was barking. She recounted her dream to a man of God, and he answered with prophetic words: 'You will be the mother of a very fine puppy indeed. He will be the watchdog of the House of God, and will bark loud and long against its foes. He will be a famous preacher, and cure many souls by the virtue of his healing tongue.'

When Bernard was still a child, and suffering from a severe headache, a woman came to his room to soothe his pains with her magic spells, but Bernard pushed her away, screaming with indignation, and threw her out. And God's mercy rewarded the young boy's zeal, because he got up at once from his bed and knew that he was completely better.

On the most holy night of the Lord's nativity, the young Bernard was in church waiting for the morning office when he conceived a desire to learn at what hour of the night Christ was born. Directly the infant Jesus appeared to him, and it was as if he were being born a second time from his mother's womb. Thereafter, as long as he lived, Bernard always regarded that as the exact hour of the Lord's birth, and from that moment on he was endowed with a deeper understanding of this mystery, and a greater eloquence when preaching or writing on the subject of the nativity. Later he produced an excellent little book in praise of the Virgin Mother and her Child: it is among his earliest works, and in it he expounds the text of the Gospel reading that begins: '*Missus est Angelus Gabriel*...' ['The angel Gabriel was sent ...' (Luke 1:26)].

The Ancient Enemy, observing the young man's pious resolution and resentful of his decision to live a life of chastity, laid many traps to lure him into sin. On one occasion Bernard allowed his gaze to rest overlong on a woman, but all of a sudden he blushed at his indiscretion, and punished himself for it most severely: he jumped into a pool of icy water and he remained there until he was frozen almost to death, and by the grace of God all the heat of his carnal desire had cooled. About the same time a girl was prompted by the Devil to slip naked into the bed where Bernard was sleeping. Aware of her presence, Bernard quite calmly and quietly gave up to her the part of the bed where he had been lying, turned to face the other side and went to sleep again. For a while the wretched girl lay waiting expectantly, but then she began to touch him and caress him. Still Bernard did not stir. Finally, brazen though she was by nature, the girl blushed for shame; torn between a feeling of horror at what she had done and admiration for the saint, she got out of bed and fled. Another time Bernard was a guest in the house of a certain married lady who found him so handsome she was inflamed with desire for him. Though Bernard had his bed made up in a separate part of the house, she shamelessly got up in the middle of the night and stole away to find him. As soon as he realized she was there, Bernard cried: 'Thieves! Thieves!' This made the woman run; the whole household got out of bed, lit lamps and began to search for the thief. But when they could find none, they all went back to their beds and fell asleep again. But the guilty woman could get no rest at all. Again she got up and made for Bernard's bed. Again he shouted: 'Thieves! Thieves!' Again a search was made, but the only one who knew the truth did nothing to reveal the thief's identity. The wicked woman made a third attempt, but was thwarted by the same ruse and then, finally, whether through fear of discovery or in despair, gave up. The following day, as Bernard was continuing his journey, his companions twitted him on his behaviour and asked him why he had kept dreaming of thieves. 'I really was attacked by a thief last night,' he told them. 'My hostess tried to rob me of a treasure which, once lost, can never be recovered – my chastity!'

Reflecting therefore on the perils of living with the Serpent, Bernard began to contemplate fleeing from the world, and it was then that he decided to enter the Cistercian Order. When his brothers learnt of this, they tried everything they could to deter him; but the Lord lent him such grace that not only was he undeterred in his resolution, but he also won over all his brothers, and many others besides, to serve the Lord in a life of religion. His brother Gerard, however, who was a hardened soldier, thought his brother's talk idle and utterly ignored his warnings. But Bernard was now aflame with faith and, deeply stirred by his great love for Gerard, said to him: 'I know, dear brother, that suffering alone will make you hear me and understand.' He then laid a finger on his brother's side and said: 'The day will come, and come soon, when a lance will pierce your side, and will open a way to your heart for the advice you now reject.' A few days later Gerard was captured by enemies, wounded by a lance in the very place where his brother had laid his finger, dragged off to prison and kept there in irons. Bernard went to visit him, but was denied permission to speak privately with his brother, so he called out: 'Brother Gerard, I know that very soon we are going to enter the monastery together, you and I!' That very night the fetters fell from his feet, the prison door opened, and Gerard, overjoyed, made his escape and told his brother he had changed his mind: he wanted to become a monk. So in the year of our Lord 1112, Bernard, servant of God, then about twenty-two years old, with more than thirty companions entered the Cistercian Order, some fifteen years after its foundation. As Bernard was leaving his father's house with his brothers, Guido, the eldest, saw Nivard, his youngest brother, who was still a small child, playing in the square with some other boys. 'Hey, Nivard!' he called. 'Now all the lands we stood to inherit are yours, and yours alone.' The young boy gave him an answer that was wise beyond his years. 'So you will all gain heaven,' he said, 'and all you leave to me is earth? That is no fair division!' Nivard lived on with his father for a while, but then followed his brothers into the monastery.

After entering the Order, Bernard, the servant of God, was so totally absorbed in the spiritual life, so wholly occupied in the service of God, that he hardly had any further use for his physical senses. He spent a year in the novices' cell, yet clearly had no idea that its ceiling was vaulted. Despite the countless times he went in and out of the church, he remembered only one window in the apse, whereas in fact there were two.

The abbot of Cîteaux sent some of his monks off to build a house at Clairvaux, and put Bernard in charge of them as abbot. Bernard lived there for a long time in conditions of extreme poverty, often having nothing to eat but beech leaves. The servant of God kept almost constant vigil, pushing his body beyond the limits of human endurance, and used to complain bitterly of all the time he wasted in sleep. He considered that the comparison often made between sleep and death was apt, because, just as the dead seem to men to be merely asleep, so to God men sleeping were as good as dead. So if he heard someone snoring noisily, or saw him sprawling in an unseemly manner, he could hardly bear it, and would say this was because the monk in question was sleeping in a 'sensual' or 'worldly' manner. When he ate, it was rarely with any pleasure, or to satisfy his appetite; it was only through fear of losing all his strength that he took food, and then it was as if he were submitting to torture. After a meal it was his custom to reckon up how much he had eaten, and if ever he found that he had exceeded his normal amount, even slightly, he would not allow himself to go unpunished. He had so mastered the craving for food that to a large extent he actually lost his sense of taste. He once drank some oil that had been put before him in error, and was quite unaware of what he had done until someone remarked in surprise that his lips were greasy. It is also a fact that he was once by mistake given some congealed blood instead of butter, and used it for several days without noticing the difference. He said that water was the only thing he could taste, and that was because, while he was drinking, it cooled his mouth and throat.

He confessed that whatever he had learnt from the Scriptures had come to him while meditating and praying, especially in the woods and fields, and he used to say among his friends that he had never had any teachers except the oaks and beeches. He also admitted that sometimes, when he was meditating or praying, the whole of Holy Scripture had appeared to him like an open book, with everything explained. Once, as he himself relates in his homilies on the Canticle of Canticles, while he was actually preaching, he decided to store in his head some idea the Holy Spirit was suggesting to him (this was not because he did not believe in its authenticity, but he was not entirely certain, and he wanted to have something new to say when he preached on the same subject next time). But a voice came to him, saying: 'While you hold back that thought, you will not receive another.'

As to his clothing, poverty always pleased him, but never uncleanliness. Indeed, he used to say slovenly dress was a sign either of carelessness or an inflated sense of self-importance, or a desire to win the admiration of others. 'Everyone admires the man who does as others do not' was a proverb often on his lips and always dear to his heart. For many years he wore a hair-shirt, so long, in fact, as he could keep it a secret; but as soon as he realized that people knew about it, he abandoned it and dressed like the other monks. When he laughed, he had always to force the laughter out, rather than fight to suppress it: he needed the spur, never the bit.

Bernard used to say that there were three kinds of patience: the first, in bearing insults; the second, in suffering damage to personal property; the third, in sustaining physical injury; and he proved that he possessed all three, as is illustrated by the following examples. He wrote to a certain bishop offering him some friendly words of advice. The bishop was extremely angry, and wrote him a most sarcastic letter, which began: 'I return your greetings, but not in any spirit of disrespect', implying that Bernard's letter to him had been disrespectful. Bernard replied: 'I do not think I am disrespectful, or that I have ever been irreverent to anyone; nor do I ever wish to be, and especially not to a prince of my people.' Again, a certain abbot sent Bernard six hundred silver marks for the building of a monastery, but while the money was on its way, it was stolen by bandits. When Bernard heard the news, all he said was: 'Blessed be God for relieving us of this burden! And we should not be too hard on the men who took the money: it was only human greed that made them do it; and then again, it was a great sum of money, so the temptation must have been correspondingly great.'

Again, a canon regular came to Bernard and insistently asked to be received as a monk. Bernard would not agree to this, and urged him rather to return to his church. 'Why,' demanded the canon, 'have you been at such pains to recommend the way of perfection in your writings, if you then refuse it to one who wants nothing more? If only I had those books of yours with me, I would tear them to pieces!' Bernard replied: 'You have not read in any of my books that you cannot be perfect in your cloister. What I have recommended in all my books is an amendment of life, not a change of scenery.' The canon, in a fury, fell upon Bernard and hit him so hard on the jaw that it became red and swollen. The monks who were nearby rushed to restrain the disrespectful canon, but the servant of God stopped them: he called out and begged them, in Christ's name, not to lay a finger on the man or do him the slightest harm.

To all those who wanted to become novices, Bernard used to say: 'If you are eager to embrace the inward life, then leave outside here the bodies you have brought from the world. Only spirit can enter here: the flesh is of no use whatever.'

Bernard's father, who had stayed on at home alone, now came to the monastery, and there some time later, at a ripe old age, died a peaceful death. Bernard's sister, however, who was married and worldly, and, living as she was in the lap of worldly luxury, exposed to grave spiritual dangers, once went to the monastery to visit her brothers. When she arrived with her entourage, in a great display of finery, Bernard shrank from her as from a net the Devil had cast to catch souls, and refused absolutely to go out and see her. When none of her brothers would come out to meet her, and she even heard one of them, who was acting as janitor, referring to her as a 'dungheap with clothes on', she broke down in floods of tears. 'Though I am a sinner,' she said, 'it was for such as me Christ died. And because I know I am a sinner, I am seeking the counsel and conversation of those who are good. If my brother despises my frail flesh, as God's servant he should not despise my soul. Let him come to me and tell me what to do: whatever he commands, I will do it!' Having received this assurance, Bernard and his brothers went out to her. Because he could not part her from her husband, he forbade her all worldly vanity, and, urging her to follow the good example set by their mother, he sent her back home. On her return she changed so abruptly that, though in the midst of the world, she led the life of an anchorite, and utterly divorced herself from everything worldly. Finally, by dint of persistent pleading, she won her husband over, was released by him from her vows, and entered a nunnery.

Once the man of God fell seriously ill, so ill that he seemed any moment about to breathe his last; in a trance of ecstasy he saw himself being brought before the Judgement Seat of God. Satan, too, stood there, facing him and accusing him of the vilest things. When he had completed the case for the prosecution and it was the man of God's turn to defend himself, Bernard calmly and coolly said: 'I admit that I am unworthy and unable to win the kingdom of heaven trusting in my own merits. But the kingdom is my Lord's, and his right to it is twofold: he won it by inheritance from his father, and by the merit of his passion. Being content with the one, the other he yields to me. And through his gift I have the right to claim my prize, and I shall never be confounded!' At his words the enemy fled in confusion: the meeting was dissolved, and the man of God came to himself again.

The saint so mortified his body with fasting, physical hardships and nightly vigils that he suffered almost permanently from serious ill-health, and could perform his monastic duties only with difficulty. On one occasion he was so gravely ill that the whole community prayed unceasingly for him, and, when he felt a little better, he called his brothers together and said: 'Why do you hold so fast to a wretched creature like me? You are stronger than I, and you have had your way. But now spare me, I beg you, spare me and let me go!'

The saint was elected bishop by many cities, in particular by Genoa and Milan. When they begged him to give his answer, he neither accepted nor bluntly refused them; he said he was not a free agent, but was assigned to the service of others. His brethren, moreover, had foreseen that this might happen, and, acting on Bernard's advice, had secured the authority of the supreme pontiff to prevent anyone robbing them of their beloved abbot.

One day Bernard went off to see his Carthusian brothers, who were all greatly edified by him in every possible way. However, there was one small thing that bothered the prior: it was the saddle Bernard had on his horse, which seemed to him of good quality and not at all indicative of poverty. The prior told one of his monks about this, and the monk mentioned it to the man of God. Bernard was puzzled and asked what saddle he meant. He had ridden all the way from Clairvaux to the Grande Chartreuse, and had not the slightest idea what his saddle looked like. He once journeyed all day long by the side of Lake Geneva and either did not see it, or did not register the fact, because in the evening, when his companions were talking about the lake, they were astonished to hear him ask where this lake was.

Bernard's renown was very great, but his humility was even greater; the whole world could not exalt him so much as he abased himself. Everyone considered him the greatest of men, while he considered himself as the lowliest; everybody regarded him as their superior, while he regarded himself as superior to no one. He would often say that when the people were showering their highest honours and favours on him, it was as if someone else had taken his place, and he was somewhere else, or that it was some sort of dream. But when he was back among the most simple of his brothers, he was always happy, loving as he did their humility, and knowing that he had found himself again. There he was constantly either at prayer or reading, or writing, or meditating, or teaching his brothers.

One day he was preaching to the people, and they were all listening with rapt attention to his every word, when he was tempted by a feeling of complacency. 'Today your preaching is inspired,' he thought. 'Everyone is hanging on your words. They all think you so wise!' But as soon as he felt this mood come over him, the man of God paused a moment, and asked himself if he should go on with his sermon or stop. Then at once, strengthened by God's aid, he silently answered the Tempter: 'You did not help me to begin this, and you will not make me stop,' and confidently went on and finished his sermon.

One of Bernard's monks, who in his previous life had been a lecher and a gambler, was harassed by an evil spirit until he decided to return to the world. Bernard found he could not prevent him from going, so he asked him what he would do for a living. 'I know how to play dice,' the monk replied. 'I shall be able to live off my winnings.' 'If I give you some capital,' Bernard said, 'will you come back each year and share the profit with me?' The monk was delighted at this offer, and gladly agreed. Bernard ordered that he be given twenty shillings, and the monk took them and left. (The saint was doing this in the hope of winning him back, and that, in fact, is what happened.) The monk went off, lost all the money and returned to the monastery door covered in shame. Hearing of his return, the man of God joyfully went out to him and held out the skirt of his habit to receive his share of the winnings. 'I have won nothing, father,' the monk told him. 'I even lost our capital. But if you will, take me back in place of the money.' 'If that is how things are,' Bernard answered him kindly, 'it would be better for me to have you back than to lose both you and the money!'

Once when St Bernard was riding along somewhere, he fell into conversation with a peasant he met, and in the course of it he bemoaned the inconsistency of the heart in the matter of prayer. When the peasant heard him say this, he at once felt superior: when he prayed, he said, his head was steadfast, it was unwavering. But Bernard, wishing to prove him wrong and to curb his foolish complacency, said: 'Step aside for a moment; concentrate as hard as you can, and begin to say the Lord's Prayer. If you can finish it without the slightest inattention or wandering of the mind, I promise you you can have the horse I am riding. But you must promise me that if you think of anything else other than the prayer, you will not dream of hiding it from me.' The peasant was delighted with the challenge, and, considering that the horse was as good as his, he confidently went off and, after a moment's recollection, began to say the Lord's prayer. He was scarcely half-way through it when an irrelevant thought obtruded itself: was he to get the saddle as well as the horse or not? Aware that his concentration had lapsed, he hurried back to Bernard and told him the thought that had nagged him while he was praying, and thereafter he was less inclined to feel so superior.

One of Bernard's monks, Brother Robert, was a blood relative of his; being young, he had listened to the wrong sort of advice, and taken himself off to Cluny. The venerable father for some time disguised his disappointment, but he resolved to try to persuade him in a letter to return. He was outside in the open air as he dictated this letter, and another monk was taking it down, when suddenly, quite unexpectedly, the rain came down in torrents, and his assistant began to fold up his writing paper. 'This is the work of God,' Bernard told him. 'Don't be put off: go ahead and write!' So the monk wrote the letter in the pouring rain. Yet the rain never touched him: though it was raining all around him, the power of charity kept the rain from bothering him.

A monastery the man of God had built was plagued by an unbelievable swarm of flies, which caused intolerable discomfort to the whole community. Bernard simply said: 'I excommunicate them!', and next morning every single fly was found dead.

Bernard had been sent by the supreme pontiff to Milan to reconcile the people there to the Church. On his way back, at Pavia, a man brought his wife to him because she was possessed by a demon. Immediately the Devil began to speak through the poor woman's mouth and hurl insults at Bernard. 'No leek-eating cabbage-guzzler like him,' he said, 'is going to drive me from my little old woman!' The man of God sent the woman to the church of St Syrus, but St Syrus, wishing to defer to his guest, did nothing to cure her and so the woman was brought back to Bernard. The Devil now began to babble through her mouth: 'Silly Syrus will not cast me out,' he said, 'and baby Bernard will not get rid of me either.' The servant of God replied: 'Neither Syrus nor Bernard will do so, but the Lord Jesus Christ.' Then Bernard began to pray, and instantly the evil spirit cried: 'How glad I would be to get out of this old woman! I am in so much pain inside her. How gladly I would leave! But I cannot, because the mighty lord forbids it.' 'Who is this "mighty lord"?' the saint asked him. The Devil replied: 'Jesus of Nazareth!' The man of God said: 'Have you ever seen him?' 'Yes,' the Devil replied. 'Where?' asked the saint. 'In glory,' came the reply. The saint asked: 'And were you, too, in glory?' 'Indeed I was,' the Devil told him. 'What happened that you left?' said Bernard. 'We fell, in our thousands, with Lucifer!' said the Devil. All this he spoke through the old woman's mouth, in a lugubrious voice, for all to hear. The man of God asked him: 'Would you not like to return to that glory?' But the Devil, with a bitter laugh, told him: 'It is too late now!' Then Bernard prayed, and the demon left the woman; but as soon as the man of God left Pavia, the Devil entered into her again, and her husband ran after the saint and told him what had happened. Bernard instructed the man to tie around his wife's neck a piece of paper on which the following words were written: 'In the name of our Lord Jesus Christ, I forbid you, demon, ever to presume to touch this woman again!' This man did, and thereafter the Devil never dared come near his wife.

In Aquitaine there was a poor woman who was tormented by a lustful demon, an incubus. For six years he had abused her and molested her with his insatiable lust. When the man of God arrived in the area, the demon absolutely forbade the woman to go to him; he told her that Bernard could do nothing to help her, and threatened that if she did, when Bernard had gone again, her jilted lover would persecute her most cruelly. None the less she boldly went to see the man of God, and, groaning loudly, she told him all she was suffering. 'Take this staff of mine,' the saint said, 'and put it in your bed. If he can still harm you then, let him try it!' She did as he told her, and, as soon as she was lying in bed, the demon came to her, but he did not dare even go near her bed, let alone get up to his usual mischief. However, he threatened her ominously that, as soon as the saint went away again, he would exact a terrible revenge. When the woman reported this to Bernard, he called all the people together and ordered them to come back with lighted candles in their hands. Then, before the whole assembled company, he banished the demon and forbade him ever to go near this or any other woman again. And so, finally, the woman was completely freed from her possession.

The saint was sent as a legate to this same province, charged with the task of reconciling the duke of Aquitaine to the Church, but the duke refused even to contemplate reconciliation. So, when the man of God went to the altar to celebrate mass, the duke, who had been excommunicated, had to wait for him outside. When Bernard had said the *Pax Domini*, he placed a consecrated host on the paten and carried it outside the church. His face was ablaze, his eyes darted fire, and he addressed the duke with awesome words: 'We have pleaded with you,' he said, 'and you have spurned us. Look: the Son of the Virgin has come to you, the Lord of the Church you are persecuting. Here is your judge, at whose name every knee is bowed. Here is your judge, into whose hands your soul will pass. Will you despise him as you despise his servants? Resist him if you can!' At once the duke's whole body went rigid; then his limbs gave way and he collapsed at the saint's feet.

Nudging him with his foot, Bernard told him to stand up and hear God's sentence. Trembling violently, he got to his feet, and from that moment on did everything the servant of God commanded him.

The servant of God went into the kingdom of Germany to settle a serious dispute that had arisen there, and the archbishop of Mainz sent a venerable cleric to meet him. But when the cleric told Bernard he had been sent by his master to meet him, the man of God replied: 'No: another master has sent you!' The cleric, astonished, assured Bernard that it was indeed the archbishop who had sent him. But the servant of God contradicted him: 'You are mistaken, my son, you are mistaken. It is a greater master who has sent you – Christ himself!' The cleric, realizing what Bernard meant, said: 'You think that I wish to become a monk? Not in the least! I have never thought of such a thing. It has never entered my head.' What happened? While accompanying Bernard on his journey, the cleric bade the world farewell and received the habit from the saint's own hands.

Bernard had received into his Order a knight of very noble family, who followed the man of God for a while but then began to be troubled by the sorest temptation. One of the other monks, seeing how miserable he was, asked him the reason for his unhappiness. 'I know,' came the reply, 'I just know that I shall never be happy again!' The monk reported what he had said to the servant of God, and Bernard prayed especially hard for his recovery. In no time the monk who had been so sorely tempted and so downcast seemed to the rest as merry and jolly as before he had seemed sad. When the monk who had been so concerned for him twitted his friend amiably about his earlier protestations of misery, he answered: 'I did say then that I would never again be happy: but I now say I will never again be sad!'

St Malachy, the bishop of Ireland, an account of whose exemplary life was written by Bernard himself, passed happily to his Lord in Bernard's monastery. The man of God was celebrating his requiem mass when he became aware, by divine revelation, that Malachy was already in glory. So, inspired by God, he changed the form of the post-communion prayer and said in jubilant voice: 'O God, who has made blessed Malachy the equal of your saints in merit, grant, we pray, that we who celebrate the feast of his precious death may also imitate the examples of his life.' When the cantor indicated to Bernard that he had made a mistake, Bernard told him: 'There is no mistake. I know what I am saying.' Then he went and kissed Malachy's sacred remains.

Shortly before Lent Bernard was visited by a large number of students, and he asked them to refrain, at least during the holy season, from their usual frivolities and debauchery. But they would not hear of it, so he gave them some wine and said: 'A toast: to souls!' When they had drunk to this, they suddenly felt different, and when they left the monastery, whereas before they had refused to serve him for a few short weeks, they now gave up the whole of their lives to God.

At length the blessed Bernard, happily nearing his death, said to his monks: 'I leave you three rules of life to observe, rules which, I believe, I have throughout my life observed to the best of my ability: I have never intentionally given offence to any man, and, if I have done so, I have smoothed things over as best I could. I have always trusted less in my own opinion than in that of others; when wronged, I have never sought to avenge myself on the wrongdoer. These, then, are the three things I leave you: charity, humility and patience.'

Finally, after he had performed many miracles, built one hundred and sixty monasteries, and compiled many books and treatises, Bernard fell asleep in the Lord, surrounded by his monks, in AD 1153. He was about sixty-three years of age . . .

46

ST BARTHOLOMEW

24 August

The apostle Bartholomew went to India, which is situated at the end of the earth, entered a temple which housed an idol named Astaroth, and took up his residence there, like a pilgrim. In this idol lived a demon who claimed to heal the sick, but he helped people not by actually curing them, but merely by ceasing to harm them. Now, however, when the temple was crowded with invalids, and daily sacrifices were offered up for the sick, some of whom had been brought even from distant regions, they were unable to obtain any response from the idol. So on they went to another city, where another idol named Berith was worshipped, and asked the idol why Astaroth would not grant them a response. Berith replied: 'Our god is bound by chains of fire, and has not dared to breathe or speak since the hour when the apostle Bartholomew entered his temple.' 'And who is this Bartholomew?' they asked. The demon told them: 'He is a friend of Almighty God, and has come to the province to banish all the gods of India!' 'Tell us what he looks like,' they said, 'so that we shall know him.' The demon told them: 'His hair is black and curly, his complexion fair, his eyes are large, his nose even and straight, his beard is long, with a few grey hairs, his body well-proportioned. He wears a white, sleeveless tunic with a purple border, and over it a white cloak which has purple gemstones at the corners. For twenty-six years now he has worn the same clothes and sandals, and they look neither old nor dirty. He kneels a hundred times daily to pray and a hundred times every night. Angels walk with him and they never let him grow weary or hungry. His expression is always the same, he is unfailingly happy and cheerful. He foresees everything, knows everything, speaks and understands every language on earth; he knows already what I am telling you now, and when you go looking for him he will allow you to see him, if he wishes, but if he does not, you will never be able to find him. But I beg you, if you do find him, ask him not to come here, or his angels may do to me what they have already done to my friend Astaroth!'

So for two whole days they hunted high and low for the apostle, but found no trace of him. Then a man who was possessed by the Devil cried out: 'Bartholomew, apostle of God, your prayers are burning me!' The apostle answered: 'Be silent, and come out of him!' And at once the man was cured. Now Polimius, the king of that region, came to hear about this: he had a lunatic daughter, and so he sent to the apostle and asked him to come and cure her. The apostle duly arrived, and, seeing that the girl was kept in chains because she tried to bite anyone who came near her, he told the king's servants to release her. When none of them dared approach her, he said: 'I already have her demon in my power. He is fast bound. What are you afraid of?' So they unchained her, and found she was cured. Bartholomew then left. The king loaded camels with gold and silver and precious stones and sent men after the apostle, but they could find no trace of him. But next morning, when the king was alone in his bedchamber, the apostle appeared to him and said: 'Why have you been looking for me all day with gold and silver and precious stones? Such gifts are for those who are eager for earthly riches; as for me, I desire nothing earthly or fleshly at all.' Then St Bartholomew began to instruct the king at length about the manner of our redemption; among other things he demonstrated to him that Christ had conquered the Devil in a way that was extraordinarily fitting, and in so doing displayed his power, his justice and his wisdom. It was fitting that the one who had conquered the son of a virgin (that is, Adam, who was born of the earth when it was still virgin) should himself be conquered by the Son of a Virgin. And this victory demonstrated Christ's divine power, since it was this that enabled him to cast the Devil from the kingdom, which he had usurped by engineering the fall of the first man. And just as the man who has vanquished a tyrant sends out his comrades to set up trophies and to overthrow other tyrants, so the victorious Christ sends his messengers everywhere to destroy the worship of the Devil and to establish the worship of Christ. Secondly, it demonstrated Christ's justice, since it was fitting that, since the Devil vanquished man and gained his hold over him by making him eat the apple, he should lose his hold over man to one who vanquished him by fasting. Thirdly, it proved his wisdom, since all the Devil's guile was foiled: his ruse was to snatch Christ up, like a hawk snatching its prey, and carry him into the desert. If he fasted there but did not feel hungry, he would undoubtedly be God; but if he became hungry, he would conquer him, as he had Adam, by making him eat. But he failed, because Christ did become hungry, and so could not be recognized as God; yet he could not be conquered, because he did not yield to the Devil's temptation.

When he had preached the mysteries of the faith to the king, Bartholomew told him that, if he were willing to be baptized, he would show him his god bound in chains. So the following day, when the priests were offering sacrifice to the idol close to the king's palace, the demon began to cry aloud and say: 'Stop sacrificing to me, you poor fools, or you may suffer torture worse than mine! I am bound in chains of fire by an angel of Jesus Christ whom the Jews crucified, thinking that death would subdue him. Instead he took death captive, death who is our queen, and bound our prince, the author of death, in chains of fire!' At once everyone threw ropes about the idol and tried to pull it to the ground, but they were unable to. The apostle, however, ordered the demon to come out of the idol and smash it in pieces. And at once he obeyed, shattering all the idols in the temple as he did so. After this the apostle prayed and all the sick were cured; he then dedicated the temple to God, and commanded the demon to leave and go into the desert.

Next an angel of the Lord appeared to Bartholomew there. Flying around the temple and drawing the sign of the cross with his finger at its four corners, he said: 'Thus says the Lord: "As I have cleansed you all of your infirmities, so this temple shall be cleansed of all its impurity, and of the one who dwelt here, whom my apostle has commanded to leave and go into the desert." But first I will show him to you. Do not be afraid when you see him: make the same sign on your foreheads that I have inscribed upon these stones.' The angel then showed them an Ethiopian, blacker than soot, with a pointed face and a long head with hair reaching down to his feet; his eyes were flaming and shooting sparks like red-hot iron; sulphurous flames blasted from his mouth and eyes; and his hands were tied behind his back in chains of fire. The angel said to him: 'Because you obeyed the apostle's command and left the temple and smashed all the idols, I will release you. But you must go to a place where no human lives, and stay there until the Day of Judgement.' So the Devil was released, and with a deafening shriek he disappeared, while the angel of the Lord, in full view of everyone, flew up to heaven again. After this the king was baptized, together with his wife and children and all his people, and he renounced his kingdom and became a disciple of the apostle. As a result, all the priests of the temples gathered together and went to King Astrages, Polimius's brother, to complain. Angrily they charged the apostle with having destroyed their gods, having desecrated their temple and having used sorcery to dupe their king. Indignantly Astrages sent a thousand armed men to take the apostle prisoner, and when Bartholomew was brought before him, he said to him: 'Are you the one who has perverted my brother?' 'I have not perverted him,' the apostle replied. 'I have converted him.' 'As you made my brother forsake his gods and believe in yours,' the king said, 'so I shall make you forsake your god and sacrifice to mine.' The apostle told him: 'I bound in chains the gods your brother worshipped, and showed them to the people bound, and I made him destroy the idols. If you can do that to my God, you may well make me worship your idols. But if you cannot, I will smash your gods[1] in tiny pieces, and you, for your part, must believe in my God.' While he was still speaking, news reached the king that his god Baldach had fallen to the ground and been shattered. When he heard this, the king tore the purple robe he was wearing, and had the apostle beaten with clubs and then flayed alive. After his death Christians removed Bartholomew's body and gave it honourable burial. As for King Astrages and the pagan priests, they were suddenly possessed by demons and died. King Polimius was ordained bishop, performed his episcopal office in exemplary fashion for twenty years, then, full of virtues, died a peaceful death.

Opinions are divided over the manner of Bartholomew's martyrdom. St Dorotheus, for example, says that he was crucified. He writes as follows: 'Bartholomew preached to the people of India, and also translated the Gospel according to St Matthew into their tongue. He died in Albana, a city in Great Armenia, where he was crucified head downwards.' But St Theodore says that he was flayed. Again, in many books, we read that he was merely beheaded. But these discrepancies can be explained if we assume that he was first crucified, then, before he died, taken down from the cross and flayed, to prolong his suffering, then finally beheaded . . .

We read in a book of the miracles of the saints that there was a Master of Theology[2] who each year celebrated the feast of St Bartholomew with great solemnity. One day, when he was preaching, the Devil appeared to him in the form of a ravishing young girl, and as soon as he set eyes on her, he invited her to dinner. While they were at table, the girl tried every trick she knew to inflame him with desire. Then Bartholomew arrived at the front door in the guise of a pilgrim and asked insistently to be allowed in 'for the love of St Bartholomew'. The girl was against this, however, so a servant took some bread out to him. The pilgrim refused to accept it, and instead asked the master, through his servant, to tell him what characteristic, in his opinion, was peculiar to, and unique in, man? The master thought that it was his ability to laugh, but the girl disagreed: 'No,' she said. "It is sin. Man is conceived in sin, born in sin, and lives in sin.' Bartholomew sent back word that the master's answer was intelligent, but he considered the woman's more profound. He then posed a second question: he asked the master to name the place, no more than a foot in dimension, where God manifested his greatest miracles. 'The place where the cross stood,' the master replied. 'It was there that God worked his greatest marvels.' But the girl said: 'No. It is a man's head, because it contains, as it were, the whole world in miniature.' The apostle expressed his approval of both these answers, then posed a third question: how far was it from the height of heaven down to the lowest depths of hell? The master admitted that he did not know, but the girl cried: 'I see I am vanquished! I know how far it is, because I fell from heaven to hell myself, and now I must show you!' Then with a great shriek the Devil hurled himself into the abyss; and when they looked for the pilgrim, he was nowhere to be found.

A very similar story is told about St Andrew . . .

47

ST GILES

1 September

Giles was born in Athens of royal stock, and instructed in the Holy Scriptures from his earliest years. One day, on his way to church, he met a sick man lying in the street begging alms and he gave him his tunic, and as soon as the sick man put it on, he was well again. After this, when Giles's parents died, he made Christ the sole heir to his patrimony. On another occasion, when he was returning home from church, he met a man who had been bitten by a snake, and with a prayer expelled the poison from his body. Again, when a demoniac turned up among the congregation at church and was disturbing the faithful with his shrieking, Giles drove out his demon and cured him.

But apprehensive of the perils of worldly acclaim, Giles secretly made for the coast. There, looking out to sea, he saw some sailors fighting for their lives in a storm, and by his prayers made the waves calm again. As soon as the sailors reached land, they thanked Giles for what he had done, and, hearing that he was making for Rome, gratefully promised to take him there free of charge.

From there he went on to Arles, where he stayed two years with St Caesarius, the bishop of that city. There he cured a woman who had been fever-stricken for three years. But, craving solitude, Giles secretly left the city and lived for some time with Veredemius, a hermit famed for his holiness. There, by his merits, he was enabled to rid the soil of its barrenness. But the miracles he performed made him famous everywhere: and, fearing again the perils of worldly acclaim, Giles left Veredemius and headed further into the desert, where he found a cave and a tiny spring, and God sent him a doe which came to him at certain hours and supplied him with her milk.

One day some of the king's men came hunting in the locality, and when they saw the doe, they forgot all the other game and chased after her with their hounds. The doe, hotly pursued, fled for refuge to the feet of her foster-son; and Giles, wondering why his doe was making such strange whimpering noises, left the cave to see what was amiss. Hearing the sound of huntsmen, he begged the Lord to spare the nurse he had sent him. Not one of the hounds dared come within a stone's throw of him: instead they all went back to the huntsmen, yelping like things possessed. When night came on, the hunt went home again, and when they came back the next day, they again had to go away empty-handed. Now the king got to hear of this, and, guessing the truth, that God's hand was in this, he hurried to the spot with his bishop and a great crowd of huntsmen. Again the hounds would not approach the doe, again they all came back howling, so the huntsmen encircled the place, which was so thick with thorn bushes that it was virtually inaccessible. Then one of them carelessly let fly an arrow, to flush the doe out, and dealt the man of God a serious wound as he knelt praying for the animal. The soldiers hacked a path through the undergrowth and came out at Giles's cave, and there saw an old man dressed in monk's habit, white-haired and venerable with age, and the doe stretched out at his feet. Ordering the rest of the party to stand back, the bishop and the king dismounted and went up to him. They asked him who he was, where he had come from, why he had buried himself in the depths of such a vast desert, and who had dared to deal him such a cruel wound. When Giles had answered all their questions, they humbly begged his forgiveness and promised to send him physicians to heal his wound. They also offered him many gifts, but Giles refused to have his wound treated, and rejected their gifts out of hand, not even deigning to look at them. Knowing rather that strength is perfected in weakness, he begged the Lord never to restore him to health as long as he lived. But the king came often to visit the hermit, and received from him the food of salvation. He offered him immense riches, but Giles refused to accept them, urging him to use the money to build a monastery where the discipline of monastic life should be rigidly adhered to. This the king did, and Giles, after refusing him many times, finally gave way to the king's tearful entreaties, and agreed to govern the monastery himself.

Now King Charles came to hear of Giles's reputation, and, having persuaded the saint to visit him, gave him a most reverent welcome. During their discussions of spiritual matters, the king asked Giles to pray for him, because he had committed a crime so terrible that he dare not confess it to anyone, even to the saint himself. The following Sunday, as Giles was celebrating mass and praying for the king, an angel of the Lord appeared to him and laid on the altar a piece of paper, which contained details, firstly of the king's sin, and secondly of the pardon he had been granted through Giles's intercession, on condition that he was seriously penitent, confessed his sin, and never committed it again. Finally there was a statement to the effect that anyone who invoked the name of St Giles and asked pardon for his sin, no matter what it was, could be certain that he was pardoned through the saint's merits, provided that he never committed the sin again. Giles gave this document to the king, who duly confessed his sin and humbly begged God's pardon.

Revered by everyone, Giles now left for his monastery. On his way back, at Nîmes, he raised from the dead the son of the ruler there. A short while later he predicted the imminent destruction of his monastery by enemies, and went to Rome, where he obtained from the pope a special privilege for his church and also the gift of two cypress-wood doors, upon which images of the apostles were carved. These he let down into the Tiber, and commended them to God's governance. On his way home he cured a paralytic at Tiberone and enabled him to walk again. Then, when he got back, he found the two cypress-wood doors floating in the harbour there, and, thanking God for having saved them from all the perils of the sea, put them up at the gates of his church, both to beautify the building and to serve as a memorial of his covenant with the See of Rome.

At length the Lord revealed to him that the day of his death was imminent. Giles informed the brothers of this, and, urging them to pray for him, fell happily asleep in the Lord. Many witnesses testified that they heard the voices of angel choirs as they bore his soul to heaven. Giles flourished around AD 700.

48

ST THEODORA

11 September

Theodora, a beautiful woman of noble birth, was married to a rich, God-fearing man and lived in Alexandria in the time of the emperor Zeno. But the Devil, jealous of Theodora's holiness, caused another rich man to lust after her, and he pestered her with a stream of letters and gifts to let him have his way. Theodora rebuffed his messengers and spurned his gifts, but he pestered her so unremittingly that he gave her not a moment's rest, and she began to pine away. Finally he sent a sorceress to her, who urged her unceasingly to take pity on her admirer and yield to his demands. When Theodora replied that she would never commit so grave a sin before the eyes of God who sees everything, the witch added: 'Yes, God knows and sees everything that is done by day, but what people do when evening comes and the sun goes down he cannot see at all.' The young woman asked the witch: 'Is that really true?' 'Indeed it is,' she replied. Deceived by this assurance, the young woman told the witch to have the man come to her at dusk, and said she would do as he wished. When the witch told the man of this, he was jubilant, and at the agreed hour he went to Theodora, lay with her and left. But Theodora soon came to her senses, and began to weep her heart out and beat herself about the face. 'Ah me! Ah me!' she cried. 'I have lost my soul, and destroyed the beauty of my virtue!'

Now when her husband returned home and found her in this wretched and desperate state, not knowing what was wrong, he tried to console her, but she refused to be comforted. Next morning she went to a nunnery and asked the abbess if God could know about a grave sin she had committed at dusk. 'Nothing can be hidden from God,' the abbess told her. 'God knows and sees everything that happens, at whatever hour it is done.' Theodora wept bitterly and said: 'Give me a book of the holy Gospels, and let me find a text for my guidance.' She opened the book and alighted on the words: 'What I have written, I have written.' So she went back home, and one day, when her husband was away, she cut off her hair and put on men's clothing. Then she hurried off to a monastery, which was eight miles away, and asked to be admitted with the other monks, and her request was granted. When asked her name, she told them she was called Theodore. She humbly performed all the duties she was given, and her industry won universal approval.

Then some years later the abbot called 'Brother Theodore' and told him to yoke some oxen[1] and go and fetch some oil from the city. All this time, Theodora's husband had been heartbroken, fearing that she had gone off with another man, until one day an angel of the Lord said to him: 'Get up tomorrow morning and stand in the street called the Martyrdom of Peter and Paul, and the first woman to meet you will be your wife.' Next morning Theodora came along with the oxen, and, seeing and recognizing her husband, she said to herself: 'Ah, my good husband, how hard I am labouring to atone for the sin I committed against you!' When she came up to him, she greeted him, saying: 'God give you joy, sir!' But he did not recognize her at all, so he waited around in the same place all day, before finally giving up and declaring that he had been deceived. Next day, however, he heard a voice saying to him: 'The person who greeted you yesterday was your wife.'

So great was the blessed Theodora's holiness that she performed many miracles. She rescued a man who had been mauled to death by a wild beast, and by her prayers brought him back to life. Then she hunted down the beast and cursed it, and at once it dropped down dead. Now the Devil could not abide her holiness, and he appeared to her and said: 'You arch-whore, you adulteress! You have abandoned your husband to come here and pour scorn on me. I shall use all my awesome powers to war against you, and if I do not make you deny your crucified Lord, then I am not the Devil!' But Theodora crossed herself and the demon at once vanished.

Once she was returning from the city with some camels and put up at an inn; in the night a girl came up to her and said: 'Sleep with me!' Theodora rebuffed her, and the girl went off and slept with another guest, a man who was staying at the same inn. Then her belly began to swell, and when she was asked who the father was, she said: 'That monk Theodore slept with me.' When the child was born they took it to the abbot of the monastery. The abbot reprimanded Theodore, who begged for forgiveness, but he put the boy on her shoulders and expelled her from the monastery. For seven years Theodora lived outside the monastery and nursed the child on the milk of wild animals. The Devil, jealous of her endless patience, took on the appearance of her husband and said to her: 'What are you doing here, wife? Look, I have been dying for want of you, and have never had any consolation! So come, my love, because even if you have been with another man, I forgive you!' Thinking this really was her husband, Theodora told him: 'I will never live with you again, because the son of John the knight slept with me, and I must do penance for the sin I committed against you.' But when she uttered a prayer, suddenly the man vanished, and she knew it had been a demon.

On another occasion the Devil decided to frighten her out of her wits, and demons visited her in the shape of fearsome wild beasts, and a man was goading them on, crying: 'Devour this whore!' But Theodora prayed and they disappeared. Another time a great troop of soldiers came along, with their prince at their head; everyone else was worshipping him, and the soldiers called out to Theodora: 'On your feet, and worship our prince!' But Theodora replied: 'I worship the Lord God!' When her reply was reported to the prince, he had her brought before him and so cruelly beaten that she was thought to be dead, and then the whole company vanished. On yet another occasion she saw a great heap of gold on the ground, but, crossing herself, she fled from it, and commended herself to God. Yet another time she saw a man carrying a basket full of all sorts of food, and he said to her: 'This is from the prince who had you flogged. He says please take it and eat it, because what he did, he did in ignorance.' But Theodora crossed herself and the man disappeared.

When seven years had passed, the abbot, acknowledging Theodora's patience, made his peace with her and took her and the boy back into the monastery. After she had lived an exemplary life there for two years, she took the boy into her cell and closed the door behind her. As soon as the abbot was informed of this he sent certain of his monks to listen carefully to what she said to the boy. Theodora embraced him and covered him with kisses. Then she said: 'My sweetest son, the end of my life is at hand. I leave you to God. Take him for your father and helper. Dearest boy, persevere in fasting and prayer, and serve your brethren with devotion.' With these words she breathed her last, and fell happily asleep in the Lord in about the year AD 470, and the boy wept copiously as he looked on.

That very night the abbot of the monastery had a vision. Preparations were being made for a great wedding, and all the orders of angels and prophets and martyrs and saints were arriving. And there in their midst was a lone woman, in a halo of indescribable glory, and when she reached the place appointed for the wedding, she sat on the bridal couch, and the whole assembled host thronged about her and called her name. Then a voice was heard saying: 'This is the monk Theodore, whom you falsely accused of fathering the child. Seven years have elapsed since that time, and she has been punished enough for sullying her husband's bed.' When the abbot woke he hurried with his monks to Theodora's cell, and discovered that she was already dead. They then went in and uncovered her body, and found she was a woman. The abbot now sent for the father of the girl who had slandered Theodora and told him: 'Your daughter's "husband" is dead!' And the man drew aside her clothing and saw for himself that 'Theodore' was a woman.

All who heard about this discovery were deeply shocked. But an angel of the Lord spoke to the abbot: 'Get up quickly!' he told him. 'Mount your horse and ride into the city, and pick up whomever you meet and bring him back here with you.' Off hurried the abbot, and as he travelled a man came running towards him. He asked the man where he was heading and he said: 'My wife has died, and I am going to see her.' So the abbot helped him up on to his horse, and took him to where Theodora lay. They both wept over her copiously, paid glowing tribute to her virtues, and then gave her burial. Theodora's husband then took over her cell, and remained there until finally he, too, fell asleep in the Lord. The boy followed in the footsteps of his foster-mother, and lived such a virtuous life that when the abbot of the monastery died, he was himself unanimously elected to succeed him.

49

ST EUPHEMIA

16 September

Euphemia was the daughter of a senator. When, during the reign of Diocletian, she saw the terrible ways in which Christians were being tortured and torn apart, she went straight to Priscus, the governor, publicly declared her belief in Christ, and by the example of her steadfast faith strengthened the resolution of all her fellow Christians, even of the men. Now Priscus was putting Christians to death one after another, and he made other Christians stand by and watch their torments, so that, when they saw the terrible butchery of any who refused to yield, they might at least be terrified into offering sacrifice. He barbarously mutilated the saints in front of Euphemia, but, inspired by their steadfast courage, she cried aloud that the governor was wronging her cruelly. This delighted Priscus, who thought she would now agree to offer sacrifice. But when he asked Euphemia what wrong he was doing her, she replied: 'I am a noblewoman: why do you put strangers and nonentities before me? Why do you send them to be with Christ and gain the promised glory ahead of me?' The governor said: 'When I heard you remembering your rank and your sex, I really hoped you might have come to your senses!'

So Euphemia was put in prison, and the next day, with the rest, she was brought before Priscus. While all the other prisoners were in chains, Euphemia was spared this indignity, and again she complained most bitterly, demanding to know why she alone was left unchained, which was contrary to Roman law. For this she was brutally beaten and thrown back in prison. Priscus followed her there and tried to have his way with her, but Euphemia resisted manfully and, by the power of heaven, one of Priscus's hands was suddenly shrivelled. Thinking that he must be under a spell, Priscus sent his chief steward to her to promise her anything she wanted, if only he could persuade her to yield. But the steward could not open the cell door: he used keys, he tried to break his way in with an axe, but he could get nowhere, and, as he struggled, he was suddenly possessed by a demon. He shrieked and tore at his own flesh with his nails, and barely escaped with his life.

Euphemia was then taken from her cell and put on a wheel whose spokes were filled with burning coals. The chief executioner stood below the wheel and had arranged with his men that, as soon as he gave the signal by banging on the floor, they should all turn the wheel together, so that the flames would leap up from the spokes and reduce the girl's body to ashes. But, by the will of God, the executioner dropped the iron pin which held the wheel in place, and when his men heard it hit the floor, they immediately began to pull. The wheel promptly crushed the executioner, but Euphemia, standing upon it, escaped quite unhurt. The executioner's relatives were grief-stricken: they kindled a fire beneath the wheel and tried to burn Euphemia and the wheel together, but, though the wheel did burn, Euphemia was untied by an angel and lifted to a ledge high on the wall, where they saw her standing, out of the reach of the fire.

Appellianus[1] told the governor: 'The strength of these Christians can be broken only by the sword. My advice is that you have her beheaded.' They put ladders against the wall to bring Euphemia down, but when one of the men put out his hand to grab her, he was immediately paralysed from head to foot, and carried down half-dead. Another man, whose name was Sosthenes, managed to climb the ladder, but was instantly converted; he begged Euphemia's pardon, drew his sword, and called to the judge that he would sooner kill himself than lay a finger on a woman whom the angels themselves defended. Euphemia was finally brought down from the ledge, and the governor told his chancellor to get all the young rakes in town together, and let them take their pleasure with her in turn until she died of exhaustion. But when this chancellor entered Euphemia's cell, he found her at prayer, surrounded by a host of shining virgins, and when she urged him to become a Christian, he was instantly converted. Next Priscus hung Euphemia by the hair, but she remained steadfast, and so he had her shut up in prison again without food, and gave orders that after a week she was to be crushed like an olive between four great slabs of stone. But every day she was fed by an angel, and when, on the seventh day, she was placed between the stones, in answer to her prayer they crumbled and turned into a powdery dust. The governor was humiliated at being thwarted like this by a young girl, and ordered her to be thrown into a pit, where three wild beasts were kept, beasts so savage that they devoured anyone who came near them. But they fawned on Euphemia: they ran up to her at once, and linked their tails together to form a seat for her to sit on. When Priscus saw this, he was utterly dumbfounded; indeed, he was close to expiring with anguish when an executioner, stepping forward to avenge this affront to his master, thrust his sword into Euphemia's side and so accomplished her martyrdom. To reward him for this service, Priscus gave him a robe of silk and put a golden girdle about his waist, but, as he came out of the pit, he was attacked by a lion and eaten whole. The governor's men searched for him at length, but found only a few of his bones, the torn robe and the golden girdle. As for the governor Priscus, he wasted away until one day he tried to gnaw his own flesh and was found dead. Euphemia was given honourable burial in Chalcedon, and through her merits all the Jews and Gentiles in Chalcedon believed in Christ. She suffered in about AD 280 . . .

50

ST EUSTACE

20 September

Eustace was first called Placidus, and he was commander-in-chief of the armies of the emperor Trajan. Though he was an idol worshipper, he was constantly engaged in works of charity, as was his wife, who was like him a pagan. She bore him two sons, and Placidus had them brought up with every possible advantage, as befitted a man of high social standing.

As a reward for his tireless devotion to the needs of others, Placidus was, by God's grace, guided towards the way of truth. One day, when he was out hunting, he came upon a herd of deer, and among them he noticed one stag in particular, which was larger and more handsome than the rest, and this stag detached itself from the others and plunged into the thickest part of the forest. While the rest of his men were busy with the other deer, Placidus set off in headlong pursuit after the lone stag, determined to catch it. He gave chase relentlessly, until at last the stag climbed to the top of a rocky outcrop and stopped. Placidus went closer and began to consider how he might capture the beast. Then, as he looked more closely at it, he saw between its antlers the shape of the holy cross. It shone more brightly than the sun, and on the cross was the figure of Jesus Christ, and Christ spoke to him through the mouth of the stag, as once he had done to Balaam through the mouth of his ass. 'Placidus,' Jesus said, 'why do you persecute me? It is for your sake that I have appeared to you in this beast. For I am Christ, whom you worship, though you do not know it. Your alms have risen before me in heaven and so I have come to you, in this deer you were hunting, to hunt you and win you myself.' (Other writers, however, say it was the image of Christ that appeared between the stag's antlers which spoke these words.) When Placidus heard this, he was seized with terror and fell from his horse; after an hour he came to himself again, rose to his feet and said: 'Explain to me what you mean, and I will believe in you.' Jesus said: 'Placidus, I am Christ who created heaven and earth, who caused the light to rise and separated it from the darkness. It was I who appointed the seasons, the days and the years, who formed man from the clay of the earth, who for the salvation of the human race appeared in flesh upon earth, who was crucified and buried, and on the third day rose again.'

Hearing these words, Placidus fell to the ground again. He said: 'Lord, I believe that it is you who have made all things and save those who are lost in error!' The Lord said to him: 'If you believe, go to the bishop of Rome, and have him baptize you.' 'Lord,' Placidus asked, 'do you wish me to tell my wife and sons of this, so that they, too, may believe in you?' The Lord replied: 'Tell them, so that they, too, can be washed clean. Then come back here tomorrow, Placidus, and I shall appear to you again and tell you fully what lies in store for you.'

Placidus went home, and when he and his wife retired to bed, he told her what had happened. 'I, too, saw him last night!' she exclaimed. 'He said to me: "Tomorrow you and your husband and your sons will come to me." And now I know that it was Jesus Christ!' So off they went, in the middle of the night, to find the bishop of Rome, who was overjoyed to baptize them, renaming Placidus Eustace, his wife Theopistis, and his two sons Agapitus and Theopistus.

Next morning Eustace went hunting as he had done the previous day, and when he was in the vicinity of the spot he remembered, he sent his men off in different directions on the pretext that they were to look for fresh tracks. Then, as he stood where he had before, he saw the same vision again, and, falling upon his face, he said: 'Show your servant, Lord, I beseech you, what you promised him.' The Lord replied: 'How blessed you are, Eustace, to have received the cleansing waters of my grace. Now you have overcome the Devil. You have trampled on the one who led you astray. And now your faith will show itself. For because you have abandoned him, the Devil will launch savage attacks upon you. You must suffer much in order to receive the crown of victory; you must endure many hardships in order to be toppled from the lofty vanity of the world and brought low, then exalted again in the glories of the Spirit. So do not lose heart, and do not look back on your past renown, because, through your trials, you are to be revealed as another Job. And when you are humbled, I shall come to you and restore you to your former glory. So tell me: do you wish to accept your trials now, or at your death?' Eustace said to him: 'Lord, if this is how it must be, let the trials come now, but grant us the strength to endure them!' 'Take heart!' the Lord told him. 'My grace shall keep your souls.' With this the Lord ascended to heaven, and Eustace went home and told his wife all that had happened.

After a few days a lethal plague seized his manservants and maids and killed them all. Then, a short while later, all his horses and herds of cattle died suddenly. Then a gang of thieves, seeing all the losses he was suffering, broke into his house at night and stole every single thing they could lay their hands on, robbing him of his gold and silver and everything he possessed. But Eustace gave thanks to God, and, taking his wife and children, and without a possession in the world, fled by night. Because they feared ridicule, they made for Egypt, and all Eustace's property was plundered and reduced to ruins. The emperor and the entire senate were grief-stricken at the loss of such an admirable commander, and could find no trace of him at all.

Meanwhile, as they travelled on, Eustace and his family came to the sea, and, finding a ship there, they boarded it and set sail. Now Eustace's wife was extremely beautiful, and as soon as the ship's captain set eyes on her, he was overcome with lust; so when, at the end of the crossing, he demanded payment from Eustace and discovered that they had no money to pay with, he insisted that the woman be held in lieu of payment, because he wanted her for himself. When Eustace heard this proposal, he absolutely refused to agree, and he stubbornly continued to refuse until the captain, who was determined to have his wife, signalled to his crew to throw him overboard. Realizing what they meant to do, Eustace sadly left his wife on board and disembarked with his two sons. In tears he said to them: 'Ah me! My poor boys! Your mother is given up to a barbarian husband!'

They then came to a river in spate. Eustace, not daring to attempt a crossing with both his sons together, left one on the river bank and took the other across. When he got to the other side he put down the boy he was carrying and hurried back to fetch the other. But when he was in mid-stream, a wolf suddenly bounded up behind him, snatched the child he had just taken across, and ran off into the woods. Giving him up for lost, Eustace pressed on towards the other boy. But, before he could get to him, a lion came along, seized the boy, and made off with him. Eustace had no hope of rescuing his son, since he was still in the middle of the river, and in despair he began to weep and to tear his hair out, and, if divine providence had not restrained him, he would gladly have drowned himself.

Now some shepherds saw the lion with the child wriggling in its jaws and gave chase with their dogs, and, by the will of heaven, the lion left the boy unhurt and disappeared. Elsewhere some farm workers sighted the wolf with the other boy, so they ran after it, making a great hullabaloo, and finally took the child from its jaws. Now both the shepherds and the farm workers happened to be from the same village, and they took the two boys home and looked after them there. But Eustace knew nothing of all this: as he walked along he wept and bemoaned his fate: 'Ah me!' he cried. 'Only yesterday I flourished as the green bay tree, and now I am stripped of everything! Alas! Alas! I used to have troops of soldiers at my command, and now I am on my own, not even allowed the consolation of my sons! I remember, Lord, that you told me I must be tried as Job was tried, but truly I believe my suffering is greater than his. He was stripped of all his possessions, true, but he at least had dung to sit on. I have not even that! Job had friends to share his suffering: all I have had for company is the savage beasts that stole my sons. Job was left his wife: mine has been taken from me. Put an end to my trials, Lord, and set a guard upon my mouth, lest my heart incline to words of malice, and I be banished from your sight!' With these words Eustace tearfully went his way until he came to a village, where for fifteen years he earned a living tending the villagers' lands, while his sons were growing up in the neighbouring village, and did not even know that they were brothers. Meanwhile the Lord took good care of Eustace's wife: the ship's captain never took her to his bed, and in fact he died soon after, and never laid a finger on her.

At this time the emperor and the Roman people were under constant threat from their enemies, and when the emperor remembered Placidus, who had won so many victories against these same enemies, he was plunged into despair at the thought of how his fortunes had declined. So he sent soldiers out to every corner of the world, promising riches and honours to any who could find him. Now two of these men, who had served under Placidus, came to the village in which he was living. Placidus was at work in a field, and when he saw them coming, he recognized them at once from their military bearing. Remembering the high rank he had once held, he became suddenly dejected. 'Lord,' he said, 'these two men served with me once, and I never expected to see them again! So please, grant that I may see my wife again one day! My sons, I know, are lost, because they were eaten by wild beasts.' And a voice came to him saying: 'Have faith, Eustace. Soon you will have all your old honours back, and your sons and wife will be restored to you.'

So Placidus went to meet the two soldiers, who had no idea of his identity. When they greeted him and asked him if he knew a foreigner by the name of Placidus, a man with a wife and two sons, he told them he did not. However, he invited them to stay at his house, and they accepted his invitation. Eustace waited on them hand and foot, but, as he recalled his former station in life, he could not hold back the tears, and had to go outside and wash his face before he could return to wait on them again. But the two soldiers had been thinking, and one of them remarked: 'This fellow is very like the man we are looking for.' 'He certainly is!' the other agreed. 'Let us take a closer look at him. Our general had a scar on his head, a war wound; if this fellow has a scar there, he is our man!' And when they looked, they saw the scar there, and at once knew that this was the man they were looking for. They leapt up and embraced him, and asked after his wife and children. Eustace told them that his sons were dead, and his wife had been taken prisoner. Then, when the news got out, the neighbours all crowded in as if to watch some play upon the stage, and the soldiers regaled them with stories of their general's courage and former glory.

The soldiers then told Eustace of the emperor's orders. They dressed him in the richest clothes, and after a journey of fifteen days they were back in Rome again. When the emperor heard Eustace was on his way, he went out to meet him, and as soon as he saw him he flung himself into his arms. Eustace gave everyone a detailed account of all that had happened to him; then he was hurried off to army headquarters and forced to resume his former command. After counting his forces he discovered that they were far too few to take on such large numbers of the enemy, and gave orders that recruits be levied in every city and village. Now it chanced that the place where his two sons had grown up was obliged to contribute two recruits, and since the locals all thought these two young men would make better soldiers than any of the rest, they sent them off to the commander-in-chief. Eustace was greatly taken with these fine, upstanding young men, and assigned them places of honour in his own mess. Then he went off to war, and, after successfully vanquishing the enemy, he gave his men three days' rest at the very place where, quite by chance, his wife now lived and kept a lowly inn. As God willed it, the two young men were quartered in their mother's inn, though of course they did not know who she was. One midday they were sitting in the sun and swapping stories about their childhood, and their mother, who was seated not far from them, began to listen with great interest to what they were saying. 'All I remember of my childhood,' the elder son told the younger, 'is that my father was commander-in-chief of the armies and my mother was very beautiful. They had two sons, me and my younger brother, and he was very handsome, too. One night they left home with us and boarded a ship for somewhere. When we disembarked, for some reason or other my mother was left behind on the ship. My father was in tears as he carried the two of us along, and then we came to a river: he left me behind on the bank and went across with my younger brother. As he was on his way back to fetch me, a wolf came along and carried off my brother, and before he could reach me, a lion came from behind some trees, grabbed me in its jaws and ran off with me into the forest. But some shepherds rescued me from the lion and took me home, and brought me up there, in the house you yourself know. And I could never find out what happened to my father or my baby brother.' When he heard all this, the younger brother burst out weeping. 'By God!' he said. 'From what you tell me, I am your brother! The people who brought me up used to tell the same story: "We snatched you from the jaws of a wolf!"' At once they fell into each other's arms, kissing and weeping with joy.

Their mother heard all of this, and as she pondered the details of the story, she kept asking herself if they could be her own sons. So the next day she went to the commander and spoke to him. 'Sir,' she said, 'I beg you to have me sent back to my homeland. I am a Roman and a foreigner here.' And as she spoke, she saw the familiar marks about his body, and knew that it was her husband. She could hardly contain herself: she fell at his feet and cried: 'Sir, I implore you, tell me of your former life! Because I think you are Placidus, commander of the emperor's armies, and you are also known as Eustace! This Placidus was converted by the Saviour, and had to endure all kinds of trials. I am his wife! I was taken from him at sea, but was saved from any defilement. We had two sons, Agapitus and Theopistus.' Eustace peered closely at the woman as she spoke and recognized her as his wife. In tears of joy he embraced her, glorifying God, who comforts the afflicted.

Then his wife asked him: 'Sir, where are our sons?' 'They were taken by wild beasts,' he told her; and he explained to her how he had lost them. 'Let us give thanks to God!' she replied. 'He has blessed us two by bringing us back together, and now I think he will give us the joy of discovering our sons again!' 'But I told you,' Eustace said. 'They were taken by wild beasts!' His wife replied: 'Yesterday I was sitting in the garden and I heard two young men exchanging tales about their childhood, and I believe they are our sons! Ask them, and you will hear for yourself!' Eustace summoned them, and as soon as he heard the story of their childhood, knew they must be his sons. He and their mother flung their arms round their necks, weeping copiously and showering kisses on them. The whole army was jubilant, as much for this happy reunion as for their victory over the barbarians.

When Eustace returned to Rome, he found that Trajan had died and been succeeded by Hadrian, whose crimes were even more heinous. But to celebrate the victory Eustace had won, and his reunion with his wife and sons, Hadrian gave them a royal reception and laid on a magnificent banquet. Next day the emperor went to the temple of the idols to offer sacrifice for his victory over the barbarians, and when Eustace refused to offer sacrifice either for his victory or for his reunion with his family, Hadrian urged him to think again. 'Christ is my God,' Eustace told him. 'I sacrifice to him alone!' The emperor was furious at this, and had Eustace set in the arena with his wife and sons, and unleashed a savage lion at them. The lion ran up to them, but then lowered his head, as if in humble adoration, and meekly backed away. Next the emperor had a roaring fire built under a brazen bull, and ordered Eustace and his family to be shut inside and burnt alive. The four saints first prayed and commended themselves to the Lord, then climbed into the bull, and so gave up their souls to the Lord.

Three days later they were removed from the bull in the presence of the emperor. Their bodies were absolutely intact: the heat of the fire had not touched a hair on their heads, nor harmed any part of their bodies. Christians took their bodies away and gave them burial in a hallowed spot, where they subsequently built an oratory. Their martyrdom occurred on 1 November (or according to others, on 20 September) in the reign of Hadrian, which began around AD 120.

51

ST JUSTINA

26 September

The virgin Justina was a native of Antioch, and the daughter of a pagan priest. Every day as she sat at her window she heard the deacon Proclus reading the Gospel, and eventually was converted by him. Her mother told her father of this one night as they lay in bed, and when they had both fallen asleep, Christ appeared to them with his angels and said: 'Come to me and I will give you the kingdom of heaven.' As soon as they woke they had themselves baptized, along with their daughter.

Now the young Justina had been continually pestered by a man called Cyprian (whom she was finally to convert to the faith). This Cyprian had been a sorcerer from his childhood, for when he was seven years old his parents had consecrated him to the Devil. From then on he practised the magic arts, and often he could be seen turning women into beasts of burden, and performing many other amazing illusions. Cyprian fell passionately in love with Justina, and in order to win her (either for himself or, if not, then for a man called Acladius, who also lusted after her), he had recourse to his sorcery. He therefore summoned a demon to his aid, hoping that he would help him to win Justina. The demon duly arrived and asked Cyprian: 'Why have you summoned me?' Cyprian told him: 'I am in love with a girl, one of those Galileans. Can you win her for me, so that I can have my way with her?' The demon replied: 'It was I who cast man out of paradise, I who caused Cain to murder his brother, I who made the Jews kill Christ, and I have caused all mankind untold troubles – you think I could not win over a young girl for you to take your pleasure with? Take this ointment and smear it around the outside of her house, and I will visit her, set her heart on fire with love for you and force her to yield to you!' The following night the demon went to Justina and tried to kindle a sinful passion in her heart. But Justina realized what was happening to her, commended herself reverently to the Lord, and made the sign of the cross over her whole body, to arm herself against evil. At the sign of the holy cross the Devil fled in terror, and went back and stood before Cyprian. 'Why have you not brought me the girl?' Cyprian demanded. The demon replied: 'I saw a sign on her, and I was paralysed, all my strength left me!' So Cyprian dismissed him and summoned a more powerful demon. This demon said to him: 'I heard your command, and witnessed the failure of the last demon you used; but I will put matters to rights, I will accomplish what you desire. I will set upon her and pierce her heart with lustful longings, and you will be able to do whatever you want with her.' So the Devil went to Justina and did all he could to win her over and to set her soul on fire with sinful desire. But once more she piously commended herself to God and, by making the sign of the cross, banished all temptation, and then blew upon the demon and instantly drove him from her. The demon fled in confusion, and did not stop until he stood before Cyprian. 'And where,' Cyprian demanded, 'is the girl I sent you to fetch?' The demon replied: 'I admit I have been beaten, and I am afraid to tell you how! I saw a dreadful sign on her, and instantly I lost all my strength.' Scornfully Cyprian dismissed him and summoned the prince of demons himself. When he came, he said to him: 'This power of yours – is it so ordinary that one young girl can overcome it?' The Devil answered him: 'I will go and plague her with a whole host of fevers, then inflame her soul with white-hot desire, rack every part of her body with raging heats of passion, drive her out of her mind, and parade horrible phantoms before her. And at midnight I will bring her to you.' The Devil then took on the appearance of a young woman, and went to Justina and said: 'I have come to you because I want to live a life of chastity with you. But tell me, please, what is to be the reward for our pains?' The holy virgin replied: 'The reward is great, and the labour light.' The Devil retorted: 'What about God's command, "Increase and multiply and fill the earth"? Dear sister, I fear if we remain virgins we shall be ignoring God's commandment, and we shall risk terrible punishment if we are disobedient and flout his will. We might end up suffering the torments of hell, when we had hoped to win the reward of heaven!' Justina's heart was troubled by these doubts that the Devil had planted in her, and she began to feel the flames of fleshly desire burn so strongly within her that she got up and was on the point of leaving home. But then the holy virgin came to herself again, and, realizing who it was who was talking to her, she armed herself with the sign of the cross and blew upon the Devil, who at once melted away like wax. Simultaneously she felt herself freed from all temptation.

After this the Devil changed himself into a handsome young man and went into Justina's room, where she was lying on her bed. Shamelessly he leapt on to the bed and tried to crush her in a passionate embrace. But Justina, sensing that this was a wicked spirit, quickly crossed herself, and once again he melted away like wax. Then the Devil was permitted by God to plague her with fevers, and he killed many men and their flocks and herds as well, and made those who were possessed prophesy that a great wave of death would sweep through all Antioch if Justina did not agree to be married. So the whole city, laid low as it was by the plague, gathered at the house of Justina's parents and demanded that Justina be given in marriage and the city delivered from this terrible calamity. But Justina would not hear of it, and they all threatened to do away with her; but in the seventh year of the plague, she prayed for them and succeeded in driving the pestilence from the country.

Seeing that he was getting nowhere, the Devil assumed the appearance of Justina herself, hoping that he could somehow sully her reputation, and went to Cyprian, boasting untruthfully that he had brought Justina with him. Then, looking just like Justina, the Devil ran towards Cyprian, and, as if dying with love for him, sought his lips in a kiss. Cyprian, thinking it really was Justina, was overcome with joy. 'Welcome, Justina,' he said, 'loveliest of all women!' But when Cyprian uttered the name of Justina, the Devil was unable to bear it: the instant her name was spoken he vanished like smoke into thin air. Cyprian was annoyed at this deception, and as a result burnt with an even greater lust for Justina. For long hours he kept watch at her door, and by his magic arts changed his appearance, so that sometimes he seemed to be a woman, sometimes a bird; but as soon as she went up to the door, he no longer looked like a woman or a bird, but Cyprian. Acladius, too, turned himself into a sparrow by means of the black arts, in order to fly up to Justina's window. But as soon as she set eyes on him, he no longer appeared as a sparrow, but became himself again; and he began to shake with fear, he was petrified, as he could neither fly away, nor jump to the ground from such a height. But Justina, fearing that he might fall and break every bone in his body, had a ladder brought for him to climb down, and she warned him to put a stop to his mad behaviour, or risk being taken to law and punished for his sorcery. For all these transformations were clearly the work of the Devil.

Thwarted, then, at every turn, the Devil went back to Cyprian and stood shamefaced before him. 'What?' Cyprian said to him. 'You, too, defeated? Is your power so feeble that you cannot overcome one girl and get her in your power? So feeble that, on the contrary, she single-handedly defeats the lot of you and beats you all into pitiful submission? Tell me, pray, where does this extraordinary strength of hers come from?' The Devil answered him: 'If you swear never to abandon me, I will reveal to you the source of the power that brings her victory.' Cyprian asked him: 'What shall I swear by?' 'Swear to me,' said the Devil, 'by my great power, that you will never forsake me.' This oath Cyprian swore. Then the Devil, his mind at rest, told him: 'That girl made the sign of the cross and I was paralysed, I lost all my strength, I melted away like wax before a fire!' Cyprian said to him: 'Then the Crucified is greater than you?' 'Yes,' the demon confessed. 'He is greater than any other power, and he delivers us and all whom we deceive here on earth to be tormented in an everlasting fire!' 'Then I, too, should become a friend of the Crucified,' Cyprian told him, 'in case one day I bring that punishment upon myself.' The Devil retorted: 'You swore to me by the power of my infernal legion, by which none may swear falsely, that you would never forsake me!' 'I despise you and all your murky powers!' Cyprian told him. 'I renounce you and all your devilish minions, and shield myself from harm with the saving sign of the Crucified!' Instantly the Devil fled in confusion.

Next Cyprian went to the bishop. When the bishop saw him, he thought he had come to lead Christians into error, and he said to him: 'Content yourself with those who are outside the Church, Cyprian! For you can do nothing to harm the Church of God. The power of Christ is invincible.' 'I am certain,' Cyprian agreed, 'that Christ's power is invincible.' He then told the bishop all that had happened to him, and had the bishop baptize him. Subsequently Cyprian made such rapid progress, both in his studies and in the spiritual life, that when the bishop died he was himself ordained as his successor. He placed the saintly virgin Justina in a nunnery and made her abbess there over many holy virgins. St Cyprian often sent letters to the martyrs and strengthened them in their trials.

The prefect of that region, hearing of the fame of Cyprian and Justina, had them brought before him and asked them if they were willing to sacrifice to his gods. But they stood firm in the faith of Christ, so he had them plunged into a cauldron of boiling wax, pitch and fat, but miraculously this seemed merely to refresh them, and caused them not the slightest pain. One of the pagan priests said to the prefect: 'Let me stand by the cauldron and I will soon master them, however strong their powers!' He moved to the side of the cauldron and cried: 'Great is your godhead, Hercules, and yours,

Jupiter, father of the gods!' Instantly fire spouted from the cauldron and burnt the priest to a cinder. After this Cyprian and Justina were pulled from the cauldron, sentence was passed on them, and they were both beheaded. Their bodies were thrown to the dogs and left exposed for seven days, then they were transported to Rome (though now, it is said, they repose at Piacenza). They suffered in the reign of Diocletian, around AD 280.

52

STS COSMAS AND
DAMIAN

27 September

Cosmas and Damian were brothers, born of a devout mother called Theodoche, in the city of Egea. They were skilled in the art of medicine, and received such grace from the Holy Spirit that they could cure every kind of sickness, not only in humans but also in animals, and this they did without ever asking payment.

A lady named Palladia, who had spent everything she had on doctors, went finally to the two saints, and they restored her to perfect health. So she offered St Damian a little gift, and, when he refused to take it, she begged him to, swearing oaths so solemn that he finally accepted it: not because he really wanted the lady's gift, but to acknowledge the sincerity of her gratitude, and to avoid seeming to show disrespect for the Lord's name, which the lady had used in her appeals to him. When St Cosmas found out about this, he gave instructions that his brother's body should not be buried with his. But the following night the Lord appeared to Cosmas and exonerated Damian of all blame for accepting the gift.

Hearing of the brothers' fame, the proconsul Lysias had them summoned and asked them their names, their country of origin and their circumstances. The holy martyrs replied: 'Our names are Cosmas and Damian; we have three other brothers, Antinous, Leontius and Euprepius. Our homeland is Arabia; and, so far as possessions are concerned, Christians know nothing of them.' The proconsul ordered them to go and fetch their brothers and to sacrifice with them to the idols. But they all absolutely refused to offer sacrifice, so Lysias had them tortured, concentrating on their hands and feet. They merely laughed at the pain, and he ordered them to be bound in chains and thrown into the sea, but immediately they were rescued by an angel and set before the proconsul again. 'By the great gods!' he cried, when he realized what had happened. 'This is sorcery! How otherwise could you make light of such tortures and calm the sea like that? Teach me this magic craft of yours, then, and in the name of the god Adrian I will follow you.'

No sooner had he spoken these words than two demons appeared and struck him terrible blows about the face. 'Good sirs,' he cried aloud, 'I beg you, pray for me to your Lord!' They did so, and at once the demons vanished.

But then the proconsul said: 'You see how angry the gods are with me because I thought of abandoning them! So I will no longer allow you to blaspheme them.' He ordered the saints to be cast into a roaring fire, but they were not harmed in the least; on the contrary the flames suddenly darted out and consumed many who were standing by. So they were stretched on the rack; but an angel kept watch over them, and, when their torturers became exhausted with beating them, set them before the proconsul again, unharmed. Lysias then had the three other brothers shut up in prison, and ordered Cosmas and Damian to be crucified and stoned by the people. But the stones rebounded on those who threw them and a large number of people were wounded. The proconsul was now in a terrible rage, and had the three other brothers brought out of prison and made them stand by the cross while four of his soldiers shot arrows at Cosmas and Damian. But the arrows doubled back and wounded many in the crowd, while the holy martyrs were not even touched. Thwarted at every turn, Lysias was at his wit's end, and next morning had all five brothers beheaded. The Christians, mindful of what St Cosmas had said about not being buried with Damian, were wondering how and where the martyrs should be buried when suddenly a camel came along and told them, in a human voice, that the saints should be buried together in a single tomb. Cosmas and Damian suffered under Diocletian, whose reign began around AD 287 . . .

53

ST JEROME

30 September

Jerome was the son of a nobleman called Eusebius, and began life in the town of Stridon, on the boundaries of Dalmatia and Pannonia. While still a young man he went to Rome and there received a thorough education in Latin, Greek and Hebrew. In grammar his teacher was Donatus, in rhetoric the orator Victorinus. Day and night he devoted himself to the study of the Holy Scriptures; he drank deeply from them, and later poured forth his knowledge in profusion.

At one time, as he relates in a letter to Eustochius, he avidly read Cicero by day and Plato by night, because he found the unpolished language of the prophetic books displeasing. Then, about half-way through Lent, he was stricken with a fever so sudden and so violent that his whole body went cold, and the warmth of life could be felt only in the throbbing of his chest. Preparations were therefore already being made for his funeral when he was suddenly hauled off before the judge's tribunal and asked what sort of man he professed to be. Jerome unhesitatingly declared that he was a Christian. 'You lie,' the judge told him. 'You are a follower of Cicero, not Christ. For where your treasure is, there is your heart also!' Jerome had no answer, and the judge without further ado ordered him to be soundly flogged, whereupon Jerome cried out: 'Have mercy on me, Lord, have mercy on me!' All those present begged the judge to pardon the young man, and Jerome swore to him an oath: 'Lord, if ever I possess or read profane works again, then truly I shall have forsaken you!' As soon as he uttered these words, the judge dismissed him, and he suddenly revived and found himself drenched in tears, and all over his shoulders he discovered terrible bruises from the flogging he had received before the tribunal. After this he was as zealous in his study of spiritual works as he had ever been in his reading of pagan literature.

When he was thirty-nine years old, Jerome was ordained a cardinal priest in the church of Rome, and when Pope Libanius died, he was universally acclaimed as worthy of the supreme pontificate. But there were certain clerics and monks whom Jerome had censured for their wanton behaviour, and they were so furious with him that they began to plot his downfall. On one occasion, according to John Beleth, they smuggled some women's clothing into his room in an attempt to involve him in a scandal. When Jerome got up, as usual, to go to matins next day, he put on the women's clothes which his enemies had put by his bedside, thinking they were his own, and went off to church in them. His enemies clearly intended that people should think he had a woman in his bedroom. Realizing to what lengths these people would go in their mad recklessness, Jerome gave way to them and went to stay with Gregory of Nazianzus, the bishop of the city of Constantinople. After being instructed by Gregory in the Holy Scriptures, he set out at once to live in the desert. An account of all he endured there for Christ's sake is given in a letter he wrote to Eustochius: 'How often, living in that desert, in that vast, sun-scorched wilderness which makes such a terrifying abode for the monks that inhabit it, how often I dreamt I was in Rome surrounded by every luxury! My limbs, all raw, twitched beneath the sackcloth. My skin was filthy and burnt black, like the flesh of an Ethiopian. All day I wept, all day I groaned, and if ever sleep overcame me, resist it as I might, my bones, with scarcely any flesh to hold them together, grated on the bare ground. Of my food and drink I say nothing: even those that are sick there drink only cold water, and to eat anything cooked would be thought a sinful indulgence. My only companions were scorpions and wild beasts, yet often I seemed to be surrounded by bevies of young girls, and, though my body was frozen and my flesh shrivelled, the fires of lust raged within me! So I wept continually, and struggled to subdue my rebellious flesh with week-long fasts. Often days and nights were all one to me, and I would beat my breast without pause until the Lord brought me peace again. I even dreaded my own cell, because it shared so many of my guilty thoughts. Furious with myself, and determined to suffer all alone, I plunged still further into the wilderness, and, as the Lord is my witness, after long weeping, I seemed, at times, to be surrounded by bands of angels.'

Then, after four years of this penitential existence in the desert, Jerome returned to the town of Bethlehem, to which he devoted the rest of his life, remaining like a domesticated animal at the manger of his Lord. He re-read his library of books, which he had kept carefully hidden away, and other books as well; he fasted every day until evening, and gathered around him many disciples who followed his holy way of life. He laboured for forty-five years and six months over his translation of the Scriptures. To the end of his life he remained a virgin – or so at least this legend states; but in a letter to Pammachius, he says of himself: 'I laud virginity to the skies – not that I myself possess it.'

In the end Jerome became so enfeebled and exhausted that he lay on his bed, and had to haul himself upright by a rope which hung from a beam above him, in order to carry out what he could of his monastic duties.

One day, as evening came on, Jerome was sitting with the community to hear the sacred lessons read when suddenly a lion came limping into the monastery.[1] The other monks at once fled, but Jerome greeted the lion as if he were a guest. The lion showed him his hurt foot, and Jerome called back the brethren and told them to wash the beast's foot and to find out exactly where the wound was. When they did so, they discovered that his pad was full of thorns; so, with great care, they removed them, and the lion recovered and became so tame that he lived among the brethren like a household pet. But then, realizing that the Lord had not sent them the lion so that he could have his wound treated, but so that he could do them some service, Jerome acted on the advice of the community and gave the lion a special duty to perform. The monks kept an ass which carried their firewood in from the forest, and the lion was to lead this ass out to pasture and watch over it while it grazed. And so he did. As soon as the lion was entrusted with the protection of the ass, he was its constant companion, accompanying it to pasture like a conscientious shepherd, and making sure to keep careful watch over it as it grazed. However, in order to feed himself, and so that the ass could perform its daily work, he would always bring it back home at exactly the same hour. Then one day, when the ass was at pasture, the lion fell deeply asleep, and some merchants who were passing by with a train of camels saw the ass on its own, and smartly made off with it. When the lion woke and could not find his companion, he ran this way and that, roaring his head off; but he could not find the ass, and finally he returned sadly to the gates of the monastery. He was so ashamed of himself, however, that he dared not go in, as he always did. The brothers noticed that he had come back later than usual and without the ass, and, supposing that he had been driven by hunger to eat the animal, they refused to give him his usual rations. 'Go and eat what is left of that dear little ass,' they told him. 'Eat until your greedy belly is full!' But they were not entirely convinced that the lion could have done such a wicked thing, so they went out into the pastures to see if they could find any clue as to what had happened. They discovered nothing, so they reported the matter to Jerome. Acting on his advice, they made the lion do the ass's work, and loaded all the firewood they cut on to his back. The lion bore all this patiently until one day, when his work was done, he went out into the fields, and ran in every direction in his eagerness to find out what had happened to his companion. Then suddenly, in the distance, he saw the traders with their loaded camels and, leading the caravan, the ass. (In that region of the world it is usual, when taking camels long distances, to have an ass lead the way with a rope round its neck, so that they keep moving in the right direction.) The lion recognized the ass immediately, and with a deafening roar he rushed upon the merchants and put them to flight. Then, roaring horribly all the while, and thumping the earth mightily with his tail, he drove the terrified camels, laden as they were, all the way back to the monastery. When the monks saw them arriving, they told Jerome, who said: 'Wash the feet of our guests, dearest brothers. Offer them food, then await the will of the Lord.' The lion now began to run about the monastery as he had done before, stretching himself out on the ground before each of the brothers in turn and wagging his tail, as if to beg pardon for the crime he had never committed. Jerome, foreseeing what was going to happen, said to the brethren: 'Go, brothers, and get ready to provide our guests with all they need.' While he was still speaking, a messenger came to tell him that guests were at the door, and they wanted to see the abbot. Jerome went to meet them; they were the merchants, and, as soon as he appeared, they threw themselves at his feet, begging his pardon for the theft they had committed. Jerome kindly made them get up, and advised them in future to take only what was theirs, and not to steal what belonged to others. They begged Jerome to accept half of their consignment of oil in return for his blessing, and finally, after much persuasion, he agreed to this. They also promised to donate the same amount of oil to the monks on an annual basis, and to instruct their heirs to do the same.

Now in early times there was no set liturgy, and each individual chanted in church whatever he chose. So the emperor Theodosius, as John Beleth relates, asked Pope Damasus to appoint some learned man to regularize the liturgy of the Church. Damasus knew that Jerome had a complete mastery of Latin, Greek and Hebrew, and was an expert in all branches of knowledge, so he entrusted the task to him. Jerome divided the psalter into daily portions, assigned to each day its proper nocturn, and, according to Sigbert, ordained that a *Gloria Patri* [Glory (be) to the Father] should be sung at the end of every psalm. Then he appointed the epistle and Gospel readings to be sung through the whole cycle of the year, and put everything else pertaining to the liturgy, excepting the chant, into a proper logical order. All this he sent from Bethlehem to the supreme pontiff, who, with his cardinals, gave it his wholehearted approval and sanctioned its use in the Church for all time. After this Jerome built himself a tomb at the mouth of the cave where his Lord had lain, and there, at the age of ninety-eight years and six months, he was finally buried . . .

54

ST REMY

1 October

Remy it was who is said to have converted King Clovis and the Frankish nation to Christ. The king's wife was a deeply Christian lady named Clothilda, and she tried hard to convert her husband to the faith, but was unable to do so. When she gave birth to a son, she wanted to have him baptized, but the king absolutely forbade it. But Clothilda could not rest until she gained the king's consent and had her son baptized. Then, almost immediately afterwards, the baby died. 'It is now clear,' the king told his wife, 'that Christ is a pretty worthless God, if he could not keep alive a child who might have won great glory for his faith!' She replied: 'On the contrary this makes me realize God's great love for me, because I know he has taken to himself the first-fruits of my womb, and given my son an everlasting kingdom – one far better than your own.' Then the queen conceived again and gave birth to another son, and as soon as she could persuade the king to consent, she had him baptized, as she had her firstborn. But at once he fell gravely ill and everyone despaired of his life. The king told his wife: 'Truly, this God of yours is a feeble God, if he cannot keep alive those who are baptized in his name. If you bore a thousand sons and had every one of them baptized, they would all die!' But the boy got better and recovered his health, and eventually succeeded to the throne after his father died. The faithful Clothilda kept trying to convert her husband to the faith, but he resisted her at every turn . . . [1] When King Clovis finally did become a Christian, he decided to endow the church of Rheims, and he told St Remy that he was willing to give him as much land as he could walk round while he himself was enjoying his midday sleep. Remy agreed to this and set off. But there was a man who had a mill on part of the land Remy circled, and, as he passed by, this miller indignantly chased him off. 'My friend,' Remy said to him, 'don't take it so hard. We can share this mill, you and I.' But the miller repulsed him, and at once the mill-wheel began to turn in the opposite direction. He called after St Remy: 'Servant of God, come back and we can have equal shares in the mill.' But Remy said: 'No, it shall be neither mine nor yours!' And instantly the earth yawned open and swallowed every trace of the mill.

Foreseeing that a famine was coming, Remy amassed large quantities of corn in a granary, but some drunken countryfolk, scornful of the old man's caution, set fire to the granary. When Remy heard of this, he went to the scene; he was now advanced in years, and, feeling the chill of evening, he began to warm himself at the fire. Quite unperturbed, he remarked: 'A fire is always good. But those who started this, and their descendants after them, will be punished. The men will suffer from ruptures, and the women from goitres.' And his curse was fulfilled until the people who inherited it were finally dispersed by Charlemagne.

It should be noted that the feast of St Remy which occurs in January celebrates the day of his happy death; whereas this feast-day marks the translation of his sacred body. After his death his body was being taken on a bier to the church of Sts Timothy and Apollinaris, but when it drew alongside the church of St Christopher, it suddenly began to weigh so much that it could not be moved any further. The bearers finally turned to prayer, and begged the Lord to let them know if it was here, by any chance, in the church of St Christopher, where a thousand holy relics already reposed, that he wanted the saint's body to be buried. Instantly they were able to lift the body with the greatest of ease, and they laid the saint to rest in the church with all due honours. Subsequently many miracles occurred there, and the church was enlarged and a crypt built behind the altar to house the saint's relics. But when the body was disinterred, and they tried to remove it to its new resting-place, they were unable to move it an inch. The clergy began a vigil of prayer, but around midnight they all fell asleep; then next morning, on the first day of October, they found that the coffin containing St Remy's body had been carried by angels to the crypt. Many years later, however, on the anniversary of this miracle, the relics were transferred, in a silver casket, to a more beautiful crypt. Remy flourished around AD 490.

55

ST FRANCIS

4 October

Francis, servant and friend of the Most High, was born in the town of Assisi, and became a merchant. Until he was about twenty years of age, he lived a futile existence. The Lord then chastized him with the scourge of ill-health, and very soon made a new man of him, and from that moment on Francis was endowed with prophetic powers. One day he and a number of his friends were captured by their Perugian enemies, and clapped in a fearsome dungeon. There, while everyone else bemoaned their fate, Francis seemed positively jubilant, and when his fellow prisoners took this amiss, he replied: 'I tell you, I have reason to be happy: before I die, I shall be worshipped as a saint throughout the whole world.'

On another occasion he made a pilgrimage to Rome, and there he took off the clothes he was wearing and put on a beggar's rags, then took his place among the other beggars in front of St Peter's and greedily devoured any scrap he got, like all the rest. And he would have done this sort of thing more often if people who knew him had not stopped him because they were embarrassed.

The Ancient Enemy tried to seduce him from his holy purpose, and, projecting into his mind the image of a hunch-backed woman who was a fellow citizen of Assisi, he threatened to deform Francis in the same way if he did not give up this foolish way of life. But he was strengthened by the Lord, and heard him saying: 'Francis, choose the bitter instead of the sweet, and despise yourself if you really want to know me.' Then one day he came across a leper, and, though he normally recoiled in horror from such people, Francis remembered his Lord's words, and ran up to the man and kissed him. Immediately the leper vanished. So Francis hurried to the quarter of Assisi where the lepers lived, and lovingly kissed their hands and gave them alms.

One day he went into the church of St Damian to pray, and an image of Christ miraculously spoke to him: 'Francis,' Christ said, 'go and repair my house, which, as you see, is all falling in ruins.' From that hour Francis's soul melted, and his heart was pierced with compassion for the crucified Christ. Tirelessly he set about rebuilding the church: he sold everything he possessed and tried to give the proceeds to a priest, but the priest refused to take the money for fear of what Francis's parents might do. So Francis flung the money on the ground at his feet, to show it meant no more to him than dust. His father responded by having him seized and tied up. But Francis returned the money to his father, and handed him back even the clothes he had on him; then he fled naked into the arms of the Lord, and put on a hair-shirt. The servant of God also enlisted the aid of a simple individual whom he took as his adopted father, and asked him, whenever his real father heaped curses on him, to counteract this by blessing him.

One winter's day, Francis's brother caught him at his prayers: Francis was wearing only the flimsiest of rags and shivering with the cold, and his brother said to a friend: 'Tell Francis to sell you a penn'orth of his sweat!' Francis heard this remark and promptly rejoined: 'Indeed I shall sell it, but to my Lord.'

Then one day he heard the words Jesus spoke to his disciples when he sent them out to preach, and at once resolved to carry out every one of his commandments to the last letter. He took off his shoes, wore a single, cheap tunic, and, instead of a leather belt, used a piece of rope. Then one snowy winter's day, while he was walking through a wood, he fell into the clutches of some robbers; when they asked him who he was, he told them he was 'God's herald'. So they grabbed him, and threw him into the snow, with the taunt: 'Lie there, then, herald of God, you bumpkin!'

Many men, high-born and low-born, both clergy and lay, rejected all worldly pomp and followed in Francis's footsteps, and the saint taught them how to practise the life of perfection advocated in the Gospels, to embrace poverty, and to tread the path of holy simplicity. He also composed a Rule based on the Gospels for his own observation and that of all his disciples, present and future, and this was approved by Pope Innocent. Thereafter Francis began to sow the seeds of God's word with even greater zeal, going about the cities and towns with a fervour that was remarkable.

There was one friar who seemed, outwardly at least, a man of extraordinary holiness, but who was extremely eccentric in his behaviour. He observed the rule of silence so strictly that he refused to speak when he made his confession, and merely nodded and shook his head. His fellow friars all sang his praises and called him a saint, but the man of God confronted them and said: 'Stop this, brothers! Do not let me hear you praise his devilish pretence! Challenge him to confess once or twice a week, and if he does not, this is the Devil's work – a snare, a deception, a sham!' So the brothers challenged him to do this, but he pressed his finger to his lips, shook his head, and gestured to them that he would in no circumstances agree to make his confession. Shortly afterwards he returned to the world, like a dog to its vomit, and ended his days in a life of crime.

Once when on a journey, and too tired to proceed on foot, the servant of God was riding on an ass. His companion, Friar Leonard of Assisi, who was as tired as Francis, began to think to himself: 'This man's parents were not the social equals of mine.' At once the man of God got down from the ass and said to the friar: 'It is not right that I should ride while you go on foot. You are of better family than I.' Abashed, Leonard fell at Francis's feet and begged his pardon.

As he was going along the road one day a noblewoman came running up to him, and, wondering why she was so weary and out of breath, Francis asked her what she wanted. 'Pray for me, father,' she said. 'I made a vow to lead a life of holiness, but my husband is keeping me from fulfilling it. He does all he can to stop me serving Christ.' 'Go home, my daughter,' Francis told her, 'and you will shortly be comforted by him; and tell your husband in the name of Almighty God and in my name that now is the time to win his salvation: the reward will come later.' The woman relayed this message to her husband, and suddenly he underwent a change, and promised thereafter to live in chastity.

Coming across a peasant who was fainting from thirst in the desert, Francis by his prayers caused a spring of water to flow from the earth.

Prompted by the Holy Spirit, Francis once confided the following secret to a friar who was his close companion: 'There is on earth today a servant of God for whose sake, as long as he lives, the Lord will not allow famine to rage among mankind.' And sure enough, his prediction came true. But when Francis departed from the scene, everything changed completely: after his blessed death he appeared to the same friar and told him: 'Now it is on its way – the famine which the Lord would not allow on earth while I was alive.'

On Easter Day the friars of the monastery at Greccio had laid the table more elaborately than usual, with white cloths and glasses. When the man of God saw this, he turned and left the refectory, and, finding the hat of a pauper who was staying at the monastery, he put it on his head, and with a stick in his hand went outside and waited at the door. Then, as soon as the friars started their meal, he began to call to them from the doorway, begging them for the love of God to give alms to a poor, sick pilgrim. The beggar was invited inside. In he went, and, lying on the ground on his own, he put his dish in the ashes of the fire. The friars were bewildered when they saw him do this, but he told them: 'I saw the table laid and all those decorations, and I knew it could not be for the poor folk who go begging from door to door.'

Francis loved poverty, both in himself and in others, so much that he always referred to his 'Lady Poverty'. But whenever he saw someone poorer than himself, he was envious of him, and afraid that he was being outdone. One day he saw a poor little man coming his way and remarked to his companion: 'This man's need puts us to shame: it is a scathing criticism of our own poverty. Instead of my riches I chose my Lady Poverty. But look – she shines more gloriously in him!'

Once a poor man went by him, and Francis was moved to deep compassion. But his companion remarked: 'He may be poor now, but there is probably not a man in the land as rich as he would like to be.' The man of God said to him: 'Quick, off with your cloak and give it to him, and fall down at his feet and acknowledge your guilt.' And the friar at once obeyed him.

One day he met three women, all exactly similar in looks and dress, who greeted him with the words: 'Welcome to Lady Poverty!' Then they disappeared in a flash and were no more to be seen.

Once the man of God went to Arezzo, where a civil war had broken out, and as he reached the outskirts of the city, he saw demons dancing in glee over the place. He called his companion, whose name was Silvester, and told him: 'Go to the city gate, and order the demons, in the name of Almighty God, to leave the city.' Silvester hurried to the gate and there shouted at the top of his voice: 'In the name of God, and by order of our father Francis, leave here, all you demons!' And in a short time the Aretines were at peace again with one another.

While this Silvester was still a secular priest, he had a dream in which he saw a golden cross coming from Francis's mouth: its tip reached up to heaven, and its outspread arms enclosed the whole world in their embrace, from pole to pole. Stricken with remorse, Silvester abandoned the world and faithfully modelled his life on that of the man of God.

Francis was deep in prayer one day when, three times, the Devil called him by name. When the saint answered, the Devil told him: 'There is not a sinner in the world whom the Lord would not pardon, if he repented; but if a man kills himself with the severity of his penances, he will never find mercy.' By a revelation the servant of God knew at once that this was the Enemy trying to deceive him, and to dampen his ardour. Aware that he had not succeeded in his purpose, the Ancient Enemy suddenly caused Francis to experience a fierce temptation of the flesh. But as the feeling came over him, the man of God took off his clothing and scourged himself with a knotted rope, muttering as did so: 'Now then, brother ass! This will teach you! A beating is what you need!' But the temptation would not go away, so Francis went out and threw himself naked into the snow. Then he made seven snowballs, put them on the ground in front of him and said to his body: 'Look: this big one is your wife, these four are your two sons and two daughters, and the other two are your manservant and maidservant. Hurry up and put some clothes on them, they are dying of cold. But if you find it too much to care for so many, then serve one Lord and him alone!' At once the Devil fled in confusion, and the saint returned to his cell glorifying God.

Once Francis had been invited to stay as the guest of Leo, cardinal of Santa Croce, and he spent some days at his house. But one night demons visited him and gave him a fearful beating. Francis called his companion, told him what had happened and explained: 'These demons are the agents of our Lord, sent by him to punish our transgressions. Now I cannot recall any offence that I have not washed clean through God's mercy and by doing penance; but perhaps he has permitted his agents to assault me because I am a guest in the courts of the mighty, and this could arouse nasty suspicions in my poor little brothers who may think I am living in the lap of luxury!' So, as soon as it was light, he got up and left the place.

Once while he was at prayer he heard whole troops of demons running over the roof of the monastery and making a terrible din. He got up and went outside, and, crossing himself, he said: 'In the name of Almighty God, you demons, do all that is within your power to my body, do your worst. I will willingly endure it all, because I have no greater enemy than my body, and when you vent your fury on it, you will be doing me a service and avenging me on my adversary.' At this the demons disappeared in confusion.

A friar who was a close companion of the saint was rapt in ecstasy and saw, among the thrones in heaven, one which was pre-eminent in honour, and more radiant with glory than any other. As he wondered for whom this splendid throne might be reserved, he heard a voice saying: 'That throne

belonged to one of the fallen princes, and now awaits the humble Francis.'
When he had finished praying, the friar questioned the man of God. 'Father,'
he asked, 'what is your honest opinion of yourself?' Francis replied: 'I
consider myself to be the greatest of sinners.' Instantly the Spirit spoke in
the friar's heart: 'See how truthful your vision was. Humility will raise the
humblest soul to the throne that was lost through pride.'

In a vision the servant of God once saw above him a crucified seraph,
who imprinted the marks of his crucifixion on Francis so clearly that he,
too, seemed to have been crucified. His hands and feet and side were marked
with the prints of the cross, but Francis took great pains to hide these
stigmata from everyone else. There were a few who saw these marks while
he was still alive, though nothing to compare with the large numbers who
saw them after his death.

That these marks were really the stigmata was proved by many miracles:
suffice it to mention here just two of them, which happened after Francis's
death. In Apulia a man named Roger was standing before a painting of
St Francis when he began to wonder whether it could really be true that
Francis had been blessed by this miracle, or whether it had merely been a
pious illusion, or a deliberate fraud on the part of his friars. As he pondered
these thoughts, he heard a sudden sound, like a bolt shot from a crossbow,
and felt a stinging wound in his left hand, though he could see no hole in
his glove. But when he removed the glove he discovered on the palm of his
hand a deep wound such as an arrow might make; it seemed to be on fire,
and burnt him so cruelly that he all but fainted with the pain. Immediately
he regretted his doubts, and declared that he believed absolutely in St Francis's
stigmata; and two days later, after imploring the saint's aid 'by his stigmata',
his wound was instantly healed.

The second miracle happened in the kingdom of Castile. A man who was
devoted to St Francis was hurrying off to compline one evening when he
was set upon by an assassin who had mistaken him for someone else. He
was mortally wounded and left half-dead. As he lay there the brutal murderer
drove his sword so far into his throat that he was unable to pull it out again,
and had to leave it and go. People came running from every direction, and
there was a great hue and cry, everyone weeping and wailing as if the man
were dead. But at midnight, when the monastery bell sounded for matins,
the man's wife called out: 'Up you get, sir, off to matins, the bell is calling
you!' At once the man raised his hand as if he were gesturing to someone
to pull the sword from his throat, and as people looked on in amazement,

the sword came out, and flew through the air into the distance as if flung by the hand of some prize fighter. Immediately the man was perfectly well again, and he got to his feet and said: 'Blessed Francis came to me and held his stigmata to my wounds, and their sweetness soothed all the pain away, and my wounds closed miraculously at their touch! He was on the point of going, but I gestured to him to draw out the sword, because otherwise I could not speak. He grasped it, gave a mighty pull and set it flying away; then he gently brushed the wounds on my throat with his holy stigmata and at once they were completely healed.'

In the city of Rome those two great luminaries of the world, Sts Dominic and Francis, were once in the company of the bishop of Ostia, who was later to become supreme pontiff. The bishop asked them: 'Why do we not make some of your friars bishops and prelates? They surpass all the rest by their teaching and example.' There followed a long argument between the two saints as to who should reply. In the end Francis's humility prevented him from taking the lead, and Dominic in turn yielded to him and answered. 'My lord,' he said, 'my friars, if only they realized it, have already been raised to an exalted status; for my own part I could not permit them to attain to any higher dignity.' Then Francis gave his reply: 'My lord, my friars are called "minor" to guard them from ever aspiring to become greater.'

Blessed Francis was full of dove-like simplicity and exhorted all creatures to love their Creator; he preached to the birds and they listened to him; they allowed him to touch them and never left him until he gave them his permission. Once when he was preaching, some swallows were twittering, and at his command they instantly fell silent. At the Portiuncula a cicada used to perch on a fig tree by his cell and sing incessantly, so the man of God held out his hand and called to her: 'Sister cicada, come here to me.' At once the cicada obediently hopped on to his hand. 'Sing, sister cicada,' Francis said, 'and give praise to your Lord!' And the cicada immediately began to sing and flew off only when Francis gave her leave.

Francis was reluctant to touch lanterns or lamps or candlesticks in case he spoiled their lustre by handling them. He walked over stones with special reverence, in deference to Peter, whose name means 'stone'. He would pick tiny worms up off the road in case they were squashed under the feet of passers-by; and in winter he had honey and fine wines put out for the bees in case they died of starvation in the cold. He called all living creatures his 'brothers'. Whenever he looked at the sun, the moon and the stars, he was filled with an extraordinary, inexpressible joy at the Creator's love, and he would call on them all to love their Creator. He refused to be tonsured with the large crown because, as he explained: 'I want my brother fleas to have their share in my head.'

A very worldly layman once came upon the servant of God preaching in the church of St Severinus, and by divine revelation saw St Francis transfixed by two gleaming swords in the shape of a cross, one passing vertically from his head to his feet, and the other horizontally through his breast from the tip of one hand to the other. Though he had never seen Francis before, he recognized him immediately by this sign, and, overcome with remorse, he entered the Order and there finally ended his days in holiness.

Francis's eyesight became weaker and weaker through his continual weeping, but when people urged him to desist, he replied: 'One must never reject a vision of everlasting light out of love for a light we share even with flies.' But his friars kept pressing him to have an operation to improve his eyesight, and when the surgeon was ready, with his instrument red-hot in his hand, the man of God said: 'Brother fire, be kind to me now, be courteous! I pray the Lord, who created you, to temper your heat for me.' With these words he made the sign of the cross over the iron, and, though it was pressed deep into his tender flesh, searing him from ear to eyebrow, he said himself that he could feel no pain.

The servant of God was at the hermitage of St Urban one day when he was taken seriously ill, and, feeling his whole strength failing, he asked for a cup of wine. But there was no wine to give him, and a cup of water was brought to him instead. This he blessed with the sign of the cross, and immediately it turned into choice wine. What the poverty of that remote place could not supply was obtained by the purity of a saintly man; and no sooner had he tasted the wine than he was well again.

Francis preferred to hear himself abused rather than praised. So when people sang his praises as a great saint, he ordered one of his friars to bludgeon his ears with abuse; and when this friar, much against his will, called him a bumpkin, a moneygrubber, a simpleton and a useless fool, Francis was delighted. 'The Lord bless you!' he said. 'What you say is absolutely true, and it is just what I ought to hear said of me.'

The servant of God preferred to obey, rather than to command, to accept, rather than give, orders. For that reason he gave up his position as general of the Order, and asked for a guardian to whose will he would be subject in all things. He used also to promise his obedience to the friar who accompanied him on his travels, and this was a promise he unfailingly kept.

One of his friars had committed an act of disobedience, but subsequently showed signs of repentance. However, in order to instil fear into the others, the man of God had this friar's cowl thrown on to the fire; then, after it had been in the fire for an hour, he ordered it to be removed and returned to its owner. And when the cowl was retrieved from the flames, it showed not the slightest trace of burning.

Once, when Francis was walking through the Venetian marshes, he came upon a great gathering of birds singing there, and said to his companions: 'My sisters the birds are praising their Creator. Let us go and stand in their midst and sing the canonical hours to the Lord!' And the birds did not fly away when they joined them, but their twittering was so loud that Francis and his companions could not hear each other. 'Sister birds,' Francis called, 'stop your singing until we have paid our debt of praise to the Lord.' At once they fell silent; then, when the friars had finished lauds, Francis gave them permission to continue, and they started to sing again as they had before.

A knight kindly invited Francis to be his guest at supper one day, and Francis told him: 'Brother host, take my advice: confess your sins, because soon you will be eating elsewhere.' The knight at once obeyed, made all the necessary provisions for his household, and received the sacrament of penance. No sooner had they gone in to sit at table than the host breathed his last.

Once Francis came upon a great flock of birds and greeted them as if they were endowed with reason. 'My brother birds,' he said, 'you really ought to sing the praises of your Creator, who has clothed you with feathers, given you wings to fly with, granted you the clean, fresh air, and directs your lives so that you have no care at all.' The birds began to stretch their necks towards him, to spread their wings, open their beaks, and look at him intently. Francis walked through their midst and, as he did so, brushed them with his cloak, yet not a single one of them moved until he gave his permission, and then they all flew away together.

He was preaching once at the castle of Alvianum, and he could not be heard for the twittering of the swallows who were building their nests. 'Sister swallows,' he said to them, 'it is my turn to speak. You have said enough. Be quiet, now, until I have finished preaching the word of the Lord!' They obeyed him at once and fell silent.

One day the man of God was passing through Apulia when he found a large purse, positively bursting with money, lying on the road. When his companion saw it he wanted to take it and give the money to the poor, but Francis would not hear of it. 'My son,' he said, 'it is not right to take what belongs to someone else.' But his companion was absolutely insistent; so after a moment's prayer Francis told him to pick up the purse, which now contained, instead of the money, a snake. The friar saw it and was frightened, but, wishing to obey and do as he was told, he took the purse in his hands, and immediately a great serpent slid out. St Francis said: 'To the servants of God money is the very Devil, a snake with a deadly bite.'

A friar who was sorely tempted to sin conceived the idea that if he possessed something written in the father's own hand, he would be rid of the temptation at once. But he could not bring himself to mention this to Francis. Then one day the man of God sent for this friar and said: 'Bring me paper and ink, my son. I want to compose something in praise of God.' When he had finished, he gave what he had written to the friar and said: 'Take this, and keep it carefully until the day of your death.' At once all temptation left him. Later, when the saint lay ill in bed, this same friar began to think: 'Our father is approaching death. What a comfort it would be to me if I could have his cloak after he dies!' A short while later St Francis called him and told him: 'I am bequeathing you this cloak of mine: after my death it will be legally yours.'

Francis was once staying at Alessandria in Lombardy, and his worthy host asked him to obey the command of the Gospel and eat everything put before him. Moved by this show of devotion, the saint agreed, and his host rushed off and prepared a prize capon for dinner. While they were at table, an unbeliever came begging for alms 'for the love of God'. Hearing the blessed name of God, his saint sent a leg of the bird out to the fellow. But the wretched man kept it and next day, while the saint was preaching, he showed it to everyone he met. 'Look!' he said: 'Look what sort of fare that friar eats – yes, the one you honour as a saint! He gave me this last night.' But what everyone saw was not a leg of capon but a fish, so they all scoffed at him, thinking the man must be crazy. When the beggar realized what had happened, he felt ashamed of himself and begged everyone's pardon; and the instant he came to his senses, the meat became a leg of capon again.

Once, when Francis was sitting at table and listening to a reading about the poverty of the Blessed Virgin and her Son, he got up suddenly from his seat and began sobbing uncontrollably; then he lay down, in floods of tears, and ate the rest of his bread on the bare ground.

Francis always believed that the greatest reverence should be shown to the hands of priests, since they were authorized to consecrate the sacrament of the Lord's Body. Hence he often said: 'If I were to meet a saint coming down from heaven and at the same time a poor little priest, I would run first to the priest to kiss his hands and tell the saint: "Wait for me, St Laurence! This man's hands touch the Word of Life: they have a power that is more than human."'

In his own lifetime Francis performed many famous miracles. Bread brought to him to be blessed healed many sick people. He turned water into wine, and a sick man who tasted it was instantly restored to health. And he performed many other miracles besides.

As he neared the end of his life, though enfeebled by long illness, Francis had himself placed naked on the bare earth, called all his community to him, and laid his hands on each of them in turn; he blessed all those present, and gave each a piece of bread as our Lord did at the Last Supper. He invited all living creatures to praise God, as was his wont: even death itself he urged to sing God's praises, death that is so feared and hated by all men! He went to meet death happily, and, greeting her like a long-awaited guest, he said: 'Welcome, my sister Death!' Then, his last hour having come, he fell asleep in the Lord . . .

56

ST PELAGIA

8 October

Pelagia was the most celebrated lady of Antioch. She had boundless possessions and wealth, and was endowed with extraordinary beauty; but she was also conceited in manner, ostentatious and fickle, and shameless in thought and deed. One day she was parading through the city decked out in all her finery: everything she wore seemed to be gold and silver and precious stones, and wherever she went she filled the air with a confusion of delicious scents. Before her and behind her went a troop of young men and maidens, all dressed in the richest garments. As she passed by she was seen by a holy father, Nonnus, bishop of Heliopolis (now known as Damietta), and, shamed by the thought that she took more time and trouble to please the world than he did to please God, he began to weep bitterly; he fell to the pavement, beat his head upon the ground, and drenched the earth with his tears. 'O God most high,' he said, 'forgive me, sinner that I am! The trouble this harlot has taken over her appearance today is more than I have taken in a whole lifetime. Lord, let not a harlot's finery put me to shame in the sight of your dreadful majesty! She has spared no effort to beautify herself for her earthly lovers, and I, who meant to please you, my immortal Lord, have failed to do so through my negligence.' He said to his companions: 'I tell you, truly, God will bring this woman forward against us at the Last Judgement. Think of the care she lavishes on her appearance to please her earthly lovers, while we care so little about pleasing the heavenly Bridegroom!'

While he was saying this and other things in the same vein, he suddenly fell asleep and in a vision saw a black, foul-smelling dove flying about him as he celebrated mass. When he sent away those who were unbaptized, the dove disappeared. Then after mass it came back again, whereupon the bishop plunged it into a vessel of water and it came out clean and white, and flew away so high that it passed out of sight. At this point Nonnus woke up.

One day, when Nonnus went to church and preached, Pelagia was present, and she was so overcome with remorse that she sent a letter to him, which ran as follows: 'To the holy bishop, disciple of Christ, from Pelagia, disciple of the Devil: if you wish to prove that you are truly a disciple of Christ, who, I have heard, came down from heaven to save sinners, then receive me. I am a sinner, but penitent.' Nonnus replied: 'Please, do not tempt my humility, because I am a sinful man. But if you really wish to be saved, you may see me – but not alone. I shall be among others of the faith.' So Pelagia went to see Nonnus and found him among many of his followers. She clasped his feet, wept bitterly and said: 'I am Pelagia, a sea [Greek *pelagos* = sea] of evil tossed by waves of sin. I am an abyss of perdition, a sink of iniquity, a snarer of men's souls. I have deceived so many, ruined so many, and now I shudder to remember it all.' 'What is your name?' the bishop asked her. 'The name I was given at birth was Pelagia,' she told him, 'but people call me Margaret [Latin *margarita* = pearl] because of all the finery I wear.' The bishop then welcomed her kindly, made her do proper penance for her soul's salvation, carefully instructed her in the fear of God, and gave her new life with the sacrament of holy baptism.

The Devil was watching this, and he cried aloud: 'Oh, the violence I suffer at the hands of this doddering old man! The outrage! You hateful old wretch! Cursed be the day you were born to fight me! You have robbed me of my fondest hope!' But then one night, when Pelagia was asleep, the Devil went to her and woke her, and said: 'My lady, what wrong have I ever done you? Have I not given you all the wealth you could wish for, and fame? Just tell me, please, how I have hurt you, and I will make amends at once. Only, I beg you, do not abandon me, or the Christians will laugh me to scorn.' But Pelagia crossed herself and blew at the Devil, and he immediately vanished. Three days later she got together all her possessions and distributed them among the poor. Then, a few days after that, without telling anyone, she slipped away in the night and went to the Mount of Olives, where she adopted the dress of a hermit, installed herself in a tiny cell, and served God, practising the strictest abstinence. She was revered by everyone, and came to be known as Brother Pelagius.

Some time later one of Bishop Nonnus's deacons arrived in Jerusalem to visit the holy places. His bishop had told him that after he had seen all the holy places he should make enquiries about a certain monk called Pelagius and visit him, since he was a true servant of God. The deacon did so, and was immediately recognized by Pelagia, though he had no idea who she was, because she had grown so thin. 'Do you have a bishop?' Pelagia asked him. 'Indeed I do, sir,' he replied. 'Ask him to pray for me,' she told him, 'because he is truly an apostle of Christ.' Three days later the deacon went back to Pelagia's cell, but when he knocked on the door and no one came, he forced open a window and discovered that she was dead. He hurried off to tell his bishop this news, and the bishop and his clergy and all the monks assembled to give a fitting burial to the holy hermit. Then, when they took the corpse out of the cell, they discovered it was that of a woman, and in great astonishment they gave thanks to God and gave the holy body honourable burial. Pelagia died on 8 October around AD 290.

57

ST THAIS, COURTESAN

8 October

Thais the courtesan, as we read in the *Lives of the Fathers*, was so beautiful that many men sold all they had to possess her and reduced themselves to penury, and her young lovers were so jealous of each other that they frequently fought duels outside her house and stained the threshold with their blood.

Now a monk named Paphnutius came to hear of this, so he put on layman's clothes, took a single gold piece and set out to the city in Egypt where Thais lived. When he found her, he gave her the gold piece as if in payment for the sin they were to commit. She took the money and asked him inside to her room. But when he went in and she invited him to climb on to the bed, which was spread with sumptuous coverlets, he said to her: 'If there is somewhere more private, let us go there.' She led him through several rooms, but each time he kept saying that he was afraid of being seen. So finally she told him: 'There is a room where no one ever goes: but if it is God you fear, there is no place hidden from his eyes.' When the old monk heard this, he said: 'Then you know there is a God?' Thais answered that she did, and she knew of the world to come, and also of the punishment of sinners. 'Then if you know all this,' he demanded, 'why have you led so many souls astray? You will have to account not only for your own soul, but for all those others you have corrupted as well, and you will be damned.' When Thais heard these words, she fell at Paphnutius's feet and tearfully begged him to help her. 'I know, father, that a sinner may repent, and I am sure that I can obtain forgiveness if you pray for me. Give me three hours, that is all I ask. Then I will go wherever you tell me and do whatever you command me.'

The monk named the place she must go to, and Thais got together all the things she had earned from her career in sin, carried them into the city centre, and, as all the people watched, set fire to them. 'Here,' she cried, 'all of you who have sinned with me! Come and see me burn everything you have given me!' And what she disposed of was worth four hundred pounds of gold.

When everything was burnt, she hurried to the place the holy man had decided upon. Paphnutius had found a monastery of virgins, and there he shut her in a tiny cell and sealed the door of the cell with lead, leaving her only a tiny window through which her scanty meals could be passed. He gave orders that the others were to bring her no more than a morsel of bread and a little water each day. As the old man was leaving, Thais said to him: 'Father, where am I to pass water, when nature calls?' 'In your cell,' he told her, 'as you deserve. You are not worthy to utter the name of God, or to have the name of the Trinity on your lips, or to lift your hands to heaven in prayer. Your lips are full of iniquity, and your hands are stained with sin. Just kneel and face the east and repeat this prayer, over and over again: "You who have formed me, have mercy on me!"'

When Thais had been shut away for three years, Paphnutius took pity on her and visited Abbot Anthony to ask him if God had forgiven her her sins. When Anthony heard the facts of the case, he called his disciples together and told them to spend the whole night in prayer, each one on his own, in the hope that God would give one of them the answer to Paphnutius's question. They all prayed earnestly until suddenly Father Paul, Anthony's leading disciple, saw a bed in heaven: it was decked out with costly coverlets and guarded by three virgins with shining faces. These three virgins were Fear of Future Punishment, for it was this that had rescued Thais from evil; Shame for Past Sin, which had won her a pardon; and Love of Righteousness, which was what had converted her to the things of heaven. When Paul remarked to the virgins that such great honour could be reserved only for Abbot Anthony, a voice from heaven replied: 'This is not for your Father Anthony, but Thais the courtesan.' Paul told Paphnutius of his vision next morning, and, understanding at last the will of God, Paphnutius joyfully took his leave. He went back to the monastery, but when he unsealed the door of Thais's cell, she asked him to allow her to remain in seclusion. 'Come out,' he told her. 'God has forgiven you your sins.' She replied: 'As God is my witness, the day I entered this place I tied all my sins up into a bundle and placed it before my eyes. And just as the breath has yet to leave my nostrils, so the sight of my sins has never left my eyes. I have wept all this time, as I thought of them.' Paphnutius told her: 'It is not because of your penance that God has forgiven you your sins, but because, in your heart, you always feared him.'

When finally he took Thais from her cell, she lived a further fifteen days, then died a peaceful death . . .

58

STS DIONYSIUS,[1] RUSTICUS
AND ELEUTHERIUS

9 October

Dionysius the Areopagite was converted to the faith of Christ by the blessed apostle Paul, and it is said that he was called 'the Areopagite' after the quarter of Athens in which he lived. (The Areopagus was the quarter of Mars, because it was where the temple of Mars stood. The Athenians called the various quarters of the city by the names of the gods worshipped locally, so they called the area in which Mars was worshipped the Areopagus, Ares being the Greek name for Mars. The quarter in which Pan was worshipped was called Panopagus, and so on.) Now the Areopagus was a celebrated part of the city because it was the haunt of the nobility, and it contained the schools of the liberal arts. This, then, was the home of Dionysius, an eminent philosopher, who, because of his immense knowledge of theology, was also known as 'Theosophus', i.e. 'God's sage'. With him lived Apollophanes, a fellow philosopher. This same quarter was also the home of the Epicureans, who held that man's happiness consisted solely in bodily pleasure; and the Stoics, who maintained that it could be achieved only through the practice of virtue.

On the day of the Lord's passion, when darkness covered the whole earth, the philosophers in Athens could find no natural cause to account for what had happened. It was not a natural eclipse of the sun because the moon was not in the vicinity of the sun, and an eclipse happens only when the sun and moon are in conjunction. And the moon, at that time, was fifteen days old, and so at its greatest distance from the sun. What is more, no eclipse robs the whole earth of its light, nor can it last three hours. But it is clear that this eclipse did plunge the whole earth into darkness: firstly, because Luke the Evangelist says so; secondly, because the Lord of all creation was suffering; and thirdly, because it was reported in Heliopolis in Egypt, and in Rome and Greece and Asia Minor. That the eclipse was observed in Rome is attested by Orosius. 'When the Lord was nailed to the cross,' he writes, 'a mighty earthquake shook the world; whole rock faces were split apart in the mountains, and many parts of great cities were levelled. This was no ordinary earth tremor. That same day, from the sixth hour onwards, the sun was totally blotted out and a pitch-black night covered the earth, and in that terrifying darkness people could see all the stars of heaven, though it was still the middle of the day.'

The same phenomenon occurred in Egypt, as Dionysius recalls in a letter to Apollophanes: 'The earth was uniformly covered in a dense fog of darkness, until, as it gradually melted, the sun reappeared, its orb clear again. We applied the law of Philip Arrhidaeus, and established what we all knew perfectly well already, that the sun was not due for an eclipse. I remarked to you: "Revered Apollophanes, repository of knowledge, as yet we do not know the reason for this mystery: tell me, mirror of learning, to what do you ascribe these mysterious events?" And you answered me with the voice of a god, and a wisdom greater than human: "My dear Dionysius, there is some turmoil in the affairs of heaven." I made a careful note of the day and year of this event, and later, when I realized that all the signs corresponded with what Paul had repeatedly told us, as we hung upon his lips, then I surrendered to the truth, and was finally freed from the toils of delusion.' Dionysius also records the eclipse in a letter to Polycarp in which he writes of himself and Apollophanes: 'We were both in Heliopolis at the time and standing together when, to our amazement, we saw the moon pass in front of the sun, though it was not the time for an eclipse. Then again, from the ninth hour until evening, we saw the moon, in quite extraordinary fashion, restored to its earlier position opposite the sun. We watched the eclipse beginning in the east and advancing to the western limit of the sun's course, then returning again; we observed the waning and waxing of the light, not from the same side of the sun, but from the side diametrically opposite.' At the time in question Dionysius had gone with Apollophanes to Heliopolis in Egypt in order to study astrology; and from there he subsequently returned to Athens.

That the eclipse took place in Asia, too, is attested by Eusebius. He states in his *Chronicle* that he had read among the writings of the pagans that there was at the same time a mighty earthquake in Bithynia, a province of Asia Minor, and the greatest eclipse of the sun in recorded history; and that at the sixth hour the day turned to night, a night so black that stars were seen in the sky, and at Nicaea, a city in Bithynia, the earthquake flattened all the buildings. Finally, as we read in the *Scholastic History*, these disasters led philosophers to conclude that the God of nature was suffering. Elsewhere we read that they said: 'Either the order of nature is being overturned, or the elements are deceiving us, or the God of nature is suffering and the elements are suffering with him.' Yet another source has Dionysius say: 'This strange night, which causes us so much wonder, heralds the advent of the whole world's true light.'

The Athenians then erected an altar to this new deity which bore the inscription: 'TO THE UNKNOWN GOD'. (Every altar had its own inscription, giving the name of the god to which it was dedicated.) And when people wanted to make burnt offerings and sacrifices to this deity, the philosophers told them: 'It is not our gifts that this god needs. Kneel before his altar and pray to him. He does not want the slaughter of animals, but the heart's devotion.'

When Paul arrived in Athens, the Epicureans and Stoics challenged him in debate. 'What does he mean,' some of them asked, 'this chatterbox?' Others said: 'He seems to be a preacher of new gods.' So they took Paul off to the philosophers' quarter to put his new teaching to the test. 'You are telling us things we have never heard before,' they said, 'so we want to know what they mean.' (The Athenians liked nothing better than to propound or hear about some new theory.) Paul then walked past the altars of the gods and said to the philosophers: 'This "unknown god" you worship, he is the God I preach to you, the true God who made heaven and earth.' Then he said to Dionysius, who he realized was more learned in theology than the others: 'This "unknown god", Dionysius, who is he?' Dionysius replied: 'He is the true God, who has never revealed himself like the other gods. So he is unknown to us, unknowable, but in time to come he will appear and he will reign for ever.' Paul asked: 'Is he a man or only a spirit?' Dionysius answered: 'He is both God and man, but he is unknown because he lives in heaven.' 'He is the God I preach,' Paul said. 'He came down from heaven, took flesh, suffered death, and on the third day rose again.'

Dionysius was continuing the debate with Paul when a blind man chanced to cross the street in front of them, and Dionysius said to Paul: 'If you say to this blind man "In the name of my God, see!" and he sees, I will believe. But do not use magic words, because it may be that you know words which have this power. I will dictate to you what you must say. You must use the following words: "In the name of Jesus Christ, who was born of a virgin, was crucified and died, and rose again and ascended into heaven, see!" ' But to avoid any suspicion of trickery Paul told Dionysius to speak the words himself. So Dionysius repeated them to the blind man, word for word, and at once he recovered his sight. Thereupon Dionysius, his wife Damaris and his whole household were baptized. After he had been accepted into the faith, Dionysius was instructed for three years by Paul, and then ordained bishop of Athens, where his dedicated preaching converted the city itself, and most of the area around it, to the faith of Christ.

It is said that Paul revealed to Dionysius what he had seen when he was transported to the third heaven, as Dionysius himself seems to hint in several places. This would explain why he has written of the hierarchies of the angels, their orders, ranks and functions, with such brilliant clarity that one would not think he had learnt it from someone else, but had himself been transported to the third heaven, and there seen everything he describes.

Dionysius was richly endowed with the gift of prophecy, as is clear from the letter he wrote to John the Evangelist, who had been sent into exile on the island of Patmos. In it he prophesies John's return: 'Rejoice, my beloved friend,' he writes, 'my dearest John, so sorely missed, so worthy of my love, so well beloved!' And further on: 'You will be released from your confinement on Patmos and return to the land of Asia, and there, living a life in imitation of God's goodness, hand down an example to all who come after you.' Dionysius was present at the dormition[2] of the Blessed Mary, as he seems to imply in his book *On the Divine Names*.

When he heard that Peter and Paul had been imprisoned by Nero in Rome, Dionysius appointed someone else as bishop in his place and went to visit them. Then, when the two apostles had both been martyred, Clement became pope, and after a while Clement dispatched him to France, with Rusticus and Eleutherius as his associates. Dionysius proceeded to Paris, where he converted many to the faith, built a great number of churches, and appointed clerics of appropriate rank for each. God's grace shone so radiantly in him that time and again the pagan priests stirred up the people against him, and they came in an armed mob to kill him, but as soon as they saw Dionysius, they forgot all thoughts of violence, and fell fawning at his feet, or else they were seized with panic and fled from his presence. But the Devil, jealously observing that his own worship was daily diminishing, while the faithful were multiplying and the Church was prevailing against him, aroused in the emperor Domitian such a savage hatred that he issued a decree that anyone discovering a Christian must either force him to sacrifice to the idols, or put him to every kind of torture. The prefect Fescenninus was accordingly sent from Rome to Paris to persecute the Christians, and there he found blessed Dionysius preaching to the people. He at once had him arrested and beaten, spat upon and mocked; then he ordered him to be bound tightly in cords of toughest hide and brought before him, together with his associates Rusticus and Eleutherius. Then, as the three saints faced him and steadfastly asserted their faith in God, a noblewoman appeared and declared that her husband Lubius had been led astray by the charlatans in the most shameful way. So her husband was sent for at once, and when he, too, stood firm and acknowledged his faith in God, he was cruelly executed. A dozen soldiers then flogged the saints, loaded them with chains of iron, and threw them into prison.

The following day Dionysius was stretched naked upon an iron grill over a roaring fire, but as he lay there he sang to the Lord: 'Thy word is pure, tested by fire, and thy servant holds it dear' [Psalm 118 (119):140]. Then he was lifted off and thrown to wild beasts that were ravenous with hunger. But as they rushed savagely at him, Dionysius made the sign of the cross and they became gentle as lambs. He was next thrown into a great furnace, but the fire went out, and he was unharmed. Then he was nailed to a cross, and left hanging there for hours in agony before they took him down and cast him into prison again with his two associates and many other Christians. There Dionysius celebrated mass and, as he gave communion to his fellow prisoners, the Lord Jesus appeared to him in a great blaze of light. He took bread and said to Dionysius: 'Take this, my beloved, for your reward with me is very great!'

Soon after all three were again brought before the prefect and subjected to further tortures. Then, finally, as they steadfastly proclaimed their faith in the Holy Trinity, their heads were cut off with axes before the statue of Mercury. Instantly St Dionysius stood up, took his head in his arms, and, with an angel leading the way, and a heavenly light going before him, he walked two miles, from the place called Martyr's Hill [Montmartre] to the spot where, by his own choice and by God's providence, he now lies at rest . . .

59

THE ELEVEN THOUSAND
VIRGINS

21 October

The following is an account of the glorious martyrdom of the eleven thousand virgins. In Britain lived a most Christian king named Nothus (or Maurus) who had a daughter called Ursula.[1] Ursula was exceptionally virtuous, wise and beautiful, and her fame swiftly spread far and wide. The king of Anglia, whose power was immense, and who had subjected many nations and brought them beneath his sway, came to hear of Ursula's renown, and declared that his happiness would be complete if she were married to his only son. The young man himself also passionately desired this union. So they dispatched an official embassy to the girl's father, and the ambassadors made him generous promises and paid him elaborate compliments, but also added the direst threats about what might happen if they returned empty-handed to their master. Now King Nothus was in a terrible dilemma, firstly because he thought it would be improper of him to hand over a girl who was such a devout Christian to a worshipper of idols; secondly because he knew that she would never agree to such a marriage; and thirdly because he was absolutely terrified of the savage reprisals the pagan king might exact. Ursula, however, inspired by God, persuaded her father to agree to the king's proposal, but only on the following conditions: that the king and her father were to grant her ten, carefully selected, virgins as companions, and then assign to her and each of her ten virgin companions one thousand other virgins; that a fleet of triremes should be assembled for her use; that she should be allowed a space of three years in which to fulfil her vow of virginity; and that her betrothed should be baptized and, during the three years, instructed in the faith. Ursula was acting shrewdly in all this: she hoped that, since her conditions were so difficult to meet, her suitor might have second thoughts about the marriage; or else that she might be presented with an opportunity to dedicate all the virgins, as well as herself, to God. But the young man accepted the conditions willingly, and compelled his father to agree. He was baptized forthwith, and ordered that everything

Ursula had demanded be done with all possible speed. Ursula's father also gave orders that his daughter, whom he loved dearly, should take with her as many soldiers as she and her company needed for their assistance and protection.

Then the virgins flooded in from all sides, and people came running from far and wide to witness this great spectacle. Many bishops came to join the virgins on their pilgrimage, among them Pantalus, bishop of Basle, who led them to Rome, came back with them, and with them suffered martyrdom. St Gerasina, the queen of Sicily, came, too. (She had married a cruel beast of a man, but had made him as gentle as a lamb.) Gerasina was the sister of Bishop Maurisius and of Daria, St Ursula's mother. Ursula's father had written a letter to his sister-in-law telling her of Ursula's secret plan, and, inspired by God, she at once left her kingdom in the hands of one of her sons and set sail for Britain with her four daughters, Babilla, Juliana, Victoria and Aurea, and her little son Adrian, who, because of his love for his sisters, had insisted on joining the pilgrimage. At the invitation of Queen Gerasina virgins gathered there from many different lands, and she remained their leader until finally sharing in their martyrdom. When Ursula's demands had been met, and the virgins were finally assembled and the ships and provisions were ready, the queen revealed the secret to her comrades, who unanimously swore loyalty to this unique crusade. Then, running to and fro busily, they began their preparations. Sometimes, as if they were already at war, they staged a simulated flight; they practised all kinds of ploys, trying out every manoeuvre they could think of, and leaving nothing to chance. Sometimes they came back from their exercises at midday, sometimes only just before darkness fell. Princes and noblemen streamed to see the great spectacle and were all filled with admiration and joy.

Finally, after Ursula had converted all the virgins to the faith, they set sail, and in the space of one day, sped by a favourable wind, they reached the Gallic port of Tyella, and from there went on to Cologne. In that city an angel of the Lord appeared to Ursula and told her that they would all return to Cologne, every one of them, and there receive the crown of martyrdom. Then, acting at the angel's behest, they set off for Rome and put in at the city of Basle, where they left the fleet and went on to Rome on foot. Pope Cyriacus was delighted at their arrival (he was himself of British origin, and found many blood relatives among the virgins), and so he and his entire clergy welcomed them with every possible honour. That same night it was divinely revealed to the pope that he would win the palm of martyrdom at their side. But he kept this to himself, and meanwhile baptized many of the virgins who had not yet received the sacrament.

Cyriacus, the nineteenth pope after Peter, had ruled the Church now for one year and eleven weeks, and, seeing that the time was ripe, he summoned his court and informed them of his intention; then, in the presence of them all, he resigned his office and all its privileges.[2] Everyone protested at this, especially the cardinals, who thought he was mad to relinquish the glory of the pontificate in order to chase off after some silly women. But he absolutely refused to listen, and appointed a holy man named Ametos as pope in his place. And it was because he resigned from the apostolic see against the wishes of his clergy that the said clergy removed his name from the register of popes, and, from that time on, the sacred band of virgins lost all the support they had enjoyed within the Roman curia.

Now there were in the Roman army two villainous commanders named Maximus and Africanus, who, seeing this vast gathering of virgins and the great numbers of men and women that flocked to join them, were afraid that because of them the Christian religion might become too widespread. So they investigated the route the virgins were taking, and sent messengers to their kinsman Julius, who was a chief of the Hunnish people, asking him to lead his army against them, since they were Christians, and to massacre them when they reached Cologne. Cyriacus duly left Rome with this noble company of virgins. He was followed by Vincent, a cardinal priest, and James, who had left his native Britain for Antioch, where he had held the office of archbishop for seven years. James had been on a visit to the pope, and had already left Rome when he heard of the arrival of the virgins, so he hurried back to share in their crusade and in their martyrdom. Maurisius, bishop of the city of Levicana, who was the uncle of Babilla and Juliana, and Follarius, bishop of Lucca, and Sulpicius, bishop of Ravenna, were all in Rome at the time and they, too, joined the virgins on their march.

Ethereus, Ursula's betrothed, had remained in Britain, and subsequently, through the message of an angel, was commanded by the Lord to urge his mother to become a Christian. (Ethereus's father had been converted, but had died in the same year, and his son had succeeded to the kingdom.) Now when the holy virgins were returning from Rome with the above-mentioned bishops, Ethereus was prompted by the Lord to go and meet his bride-to-be, and to win the palm of martyrdom with her at Cologne. In obedience to God's commands he had his mother baptized, then, taking her, his little sister Florence (who was already a Christian) and Bishop Clement, he went off to meet the virgins and to share their martyrdom. Marculus, bishop of Greece, and his niece Constantia, the daughter of Dorotheus, king of Constantinople, also went. (Constantia had been pledged in marriage to the young son of a king, but, when he died before their wedding, she had vowed her virginity to the Lord.) They had been urged by a vision to go to Rome, and there they, too, joined the army of virgins to share their martyrdom.

So all the virgins, together with the bishops already mentioned, travelled back to Cologne, where they found the city under siege by the Huns. As soon as the barbarians saw them they rushed at them with terrifying yells, and, like wolves savaging a flock of sheep, put all of them to the sword. They slaughtered every one of them, until at last they came to blessed Ursula. But their chief was so captivated by her extraordinary beauty that he tried to console her for the death of her virgin band, and promised to make her his wife. Ursula contemptuously spurned his offer, and the Hun, realizing that she despised him, let fly an arrow at her, transfixed her and so accomplished her martyrdom.

One of the virgins, a girl named Cordula, had hidden herself on board ship that night in terror, but next day she gave herself up of her own volition to be killed, and so she, too, won her crown of martyrdom. But because she had not suffered with the rest, her feast was never celebrated, until, long afterwards, she appeared to an anchorite and instructed her to see that her own feast should be remembered on the day following that of the other virgins. The martyrdom of these virgins took place in AD 238 . . .

60

STS CHRYSANTHUS
AND DARIA

25 October

Chrysanthus was the son of Polimius, a nobleman of the highest rank. He was a Christian and had been fully instructed in the faith, and his father, unable to win him back to the worship of idols, had him locked up in a room, and sent five young girls in to him hoping that they would use their charms to seduce him. But Chrysanthus prayed, asking God not to let him be overcome by that raging beast, lust, and instantly the five girls became so drowsy they could neither eat nor drink. Yet the moment they were taken out of the room they regained their normal appetites.

Then Daria, a virgin dedicated to the goddess Vesta and an astute young lady, was asked to go in to Chrysanthus and reconcile him to the gods and his father. As soon as she entered the room, Chrysanthus reproached her for the extravagance of her dress. Daria replied that she was dressed as she was not for ostentation's sake, but in order to win him back to the gods and to his father. Chrysanthus attacked her again, asking her how she could worship as gods and goddesses creatures whom pagan authors and artists portrayed as dissolute and promiscuous. Daria answered that the philosophers had merely given human names to the elements of nature they worshipped. Chrysanthus countered this by saying: 'If one man worships the earth as a goddess and another, a countryman, ploughs it, clearly the earth gives more by way of reward to the countryman than to the worshipper. And the same is true of the sea and the other elements.'

Finally Daria was converted, and Chrysanthus and she were united in the bond of the Holy Spirit, though they pretended to be married in the flesh. Subsequently they converted a great number of people to Christianity, among them the tribune Claudius, who had earlier put Chrysanthus to the torture, together with his wife and children and many of his fellow soldiers. As a result, by order of the emperor Numerianus, Chrysanthus was shut up in a stinking dungeon, but the stench was changed into a heavenly fragrance. Daria was turned over to a brothel, but a lion which had escaped from the amphitheatre posted itself as a guard at the brothel entrance. When a man was sent to take Daria's virginity, the lion seized him and then seemed to be waiting for Daria to tell it what to do with its captive. Daria told it not to harm the man, but to let him go; and the man was at once converted and ran through the city shouting out that Daria was a goddess. Huntsmen were dispatched to capture the lion, but instead they were all seized by the beast, and laid at the girl's feet and converted by her. The prefect then had a great fire built at the doorway to Daria's room, hoping that she and the lion would both be burnt to death. And when the lion saw what was happening, it panicked and began to roar, so Daria told it it could go wherever it wanted so long as it harmed no one. Though the prefect inflicted all kinds of torture upon Chrysanthus and Daria, nothing he did hurt them in the slightest. Finally the chaste couple were thrown into a pit and buried under a hail of earth and stones, and so were consecrated as martyrs to Christ . . .

61

STS SIMON AND JUDE, APOSTLES

28 October

Simon of Cana and Jude, also called Thaddaeus, were brothers of James the Less and sons of Mary of Cleophas, who was married to Alphaeus.[1] After the Lord's ascension Jude was sent by Thomas to Abgar, king of Edessa. This King Abgar, as we read in the *Ecclesiastical History*, sent a letter to our Lord Jesus Christ which ran as follows: 'King Abgar, son of Eucharias, sends greetings to Jesus, the good Saviour, who has appeared in the region of Jerusalem. I have heard about you and the miracles of healing you perform, that you do this without drugs or herbs, and that, with a mere word, you make the blind see, the lame walk, cure lepers and bring the dead back to life. Having heard all this, I have come to the conclusion that you must be one of two things: either you are God and have come down from heaven to do these things, or else you do them because you are the Son of God. So I am writing to ask you to have the goodness to visit me and to cure me of the sickness from which I have suffered so long. I have also discovered that the Jews are murmuring against you, and plotting to take your life. So come and visit me: my city is small, but decent enough, and it has sufficient to supply both our needs.'

The Lord Jesus answered him as follows: 'Blessed are you, who have believed in me, though you have not seen me! It has been written of me that those who do not see me will believe, and those who do see me will not. I thank you for inviting me to visit you, but I must finish all the things I was sent here to do, and after that go back to the One who sent me. So when I am taken up to heaven, I will send one of my disciples to you to cure you and give you new life.'

When Abgar learnt that he would not be able to see Christ in the flesh, according to a story found in an ancient history attested to by John Damascene in Book Four, he sent a painter to Jesus to paint his portrait, so that even if he could not see him face to face, he might at least see his likeness in the portrait. But when this painter arrived, he found Jesus's face gave off a radiance so brilliant that he could not see it clearly, or look closely at it, and consequently he was unable to execute his commission. Realizing this, the Lord took a piece of clothing of the painter's and, laying it on his face, left an impression of his features on the linen, then sent it to King Abgar. According to John Damascene, the same ancient history gives a description of this image: the Lord had fine eyes, handsome eyebrows and a long face, and he stooped, which is a sign of maturity. The letter our Lord Jesus Christ wrote to Abgar is said to have possessed such power that no heretic or pagan could live in the city of Edessa, and no tyrant ever dared harm it. If any nation took up arms and moved against Edessa, it was said, a child would climb above the city gate and read the letter aloud, and the enemy either fled in terror or made peace the very same day. (And this actually happened in early times, or so the story goes.) But later Edessa lost this special privilege and was eventually captured and profaned by the Saracens because of the great tide of wickedness that swept throughout the East.

After the Lord's ascension, as we read in the *Ecclesiastical History*, the apostle Thomas sent Thaddaeus (or Jude) to King Abgar in fulfilment of God's promise. When he reached the king and told him he was the promised disciple of Jesus, Abgar saw in his face a marvellous and godlike splendour. Astonished and frightened at the sight, he glorified the Lord. 'Truly,' he said, 'you are a disciple of Jesus, the Son of God! For he told me: "I will send you one of my disciples to cure you and give you life."' Thaddaeus replied: 'If you believe in the Son of God, you will obtain all your heart's desires.' 'Indeed I do believe,' Abgar told him, 'and I would willingly kill the Jews who crucified him if I had the chance, and the Roman authorities would not try to stop me.' Now Abgar was a leper, according to some accounts; so Thaddaeus took the Saviour's letter and rubbed his face with it, and instantly he was completely well again.

Jude preached first in Mesopotamia and Pontus, and Simon in Egypt. Then they both went to Persia and there came up against two magicians, Zaroes and Arphaxat, whom Matthew had banished from Egypt. At this time Baradach, the commander of the king of Babylon's army, was about to lead a campaign against the Indians, but when he consulted the gods, he could get no response. His representatives duly went to the temple in a neighbouring city and there were answered that it was because of the arrival of the apostles that the gods could give no response. So Baradach sent men in search of them, and when they were found, he asked them who they were and what their business was. 'If it is our nationality you wish to know,' they answered, 'we are Hebrews. If our beliefs, we confess we are servants of Christ; if our purpose in coming here, it is for your salvation.' The commander replied: 'When I return in triumph, I will hear you.' 'It would be more fitting,' the apostles told him, 'if you learnt about the One whose help will enable you to win that triumph, or at least to find the rebels ready to make peace.' The commander said: 'I can see you are more powerful than our gods! So tell us how this war is going to end.' The apostles replied: 'To convince you that your gods are liars, we order them to answer your questions, and when their answers show they know nothing, we shall have proved that everything they have said was a pack of lies.' The priests of the idols duly gave their answer: there would be a great war and many people on both sides would perish in the fighting. The apostles began to laugh. 'How can you laugh,' the commander asked them, 'when I am so afraid?' 'You have nothing to fear,' the apostles told him, 'because you are going to have peace. Tomorrow, at the third hour of the day, an Indian embassy will arrive here and surrender to you and sue for peace.' The priests of the idols hooted in derision at this. 'They only want to lull you into a false sense of security,' they told the commander, 'so that the enemy can catch you off your guard and defeat you.' 'We have not asked you to wait a month,' the apostle retorted. 'One day is all we ask. Tomorrow you will triumph, and there will be peace.' So the commander put the two apostles under guard, intending to await the outcome: then, if they had told him the truth, to pay them the honour they deserved; or else, if they were lying, to punish them for their crime.

The next day things turned out exactly as the apostles predicted, and the commander would have had the priests burnt alive, but the apostles stopped him, because they had been sent not to kill the living, but to restore the dead to life. The commander was astonished that they would not allow their rivals to be put to death and refused to take a share of their possessions, so he took them before the king and told him: 'Sire, these two men are gods masquerading as men!' Then, in the presence of the two magicians, Zaroes and Arphaxat, he told the king the whole story. The two magicians were mad with envy and declared that the apostles were possessed of evil powers, and craftily plotting against his kingdom. 'Pit yourselves against them,' the commander said, 'if you dare!' The magicians replied: 'If you want to see men struck dumb in our presence, bring us the most eloquent speakers you can find, and if they can stand before us and speak, then you will have your proof that we have no powers at all.' A large number of lawyers were brought before the magicians, and instantly they were struck dumb, so paralysed, in fact, that they could not even indicate what they meant by nodding their heads. And the magicians said to the king: 'To prove that we are gods, we will allow them to speak, but not to walk; then we will let them walk again, but stop them seeing, even with their eyes wide open.' They did exactly as they had promised: the lawyers were embarrassed and bewildered, and the commander took them off to show the apostles. But when the lawyers saw the rags Simon and Jude were wearing, they thought the apostles beneath their contempt. 'It often happens,' Simon told them, 'that golden, gem-encrusted caskets contain objects of no worth, while precious, jewelled necklaces are kept in the cheapest wooden boxes. The man who wants to possess a treasure pays less attention to the container than to what is contained inside. So promise to abandon your idol worship and to adore the One, invisible God, and we will make the sign of the cross on your foreheads, and you will be able to prove that the magicians are frauds.' The lawyers duly renounced the idols and received the sign on their foreheads. Then they rejoined the king and faced the two magicians; and so far from falling under their influence again, they treated them with contempt in front of everyone. Furious at this, the magicians conjured up a great slithering swarm of serpents. At the king's call the apostles came in at once, filled their cloaks with the snakes, and threw them down in front of the magicians. 'In the name of the Lord, you shall not die,' they told them, 'but the serpents will mangle and tear your flesh until you shriek in agony.' In a flash the snakes began to eat them alive, and the magicians howled like wolves. The king and his attendants begged the apostles to let the snakes finish them off, but the apostles answered: 'We were sent to bring the dead back to life, not to cause death to the living.' Then, after praying, they ordered the serpents to take back all the poison they had discharged, and after that to go back where they had come from. And as the serpents drew out the poison again, the magicians felt pain more agonizing than they had before when they were being bitten. The apostles told them: 'You will feel pain for three days; but on the third day you will be well again – and perhaps then you may turn from your evil ways.' For three days the magicians were in such terrible pain they could neither eat nor drink nor sleep. Then the apostles visited them and said: 'Our Lord will not accept service that is forced. So get up now, you are well again. Off you go: you are free to do exactly as you wish.' But the magicians were as bitterly hostile as ever. They gave the apostles a wide berth and began to stir up practically the whole of Babylonia against them.

Some time after this, the unmarried daughter of a certain duke became pregnant, and when she gave birth to a son, she accused a saintly deacon of having raped her and claimed that he was the father. Her parents had decided to put this deacon to death, but then the apostles came on the scene, and asked them when the child had been born. 'Today,' they told them, 'at daybreak.' 'Bring the infant here,' the apostles said, 'and bring the deacon you are accusing here as well.' This they did, and the apostles said to the child: 'Tell us, child, in the Lord's name, if the deacon really did what they say.' The child replied: 'The deacon is a chaste and saintly man and has never defiled his flesh.' The girl's parents were now insistent that the apostles should ask him who was really guilty of the crime, but the apostles replied: 'Our duty is to absolve the innocent, not to damn the guilty.'

About the same time two savage tigresses that had been kept in separate cages escaped and devoured everyone that crossed their path. But the apostles went up to them, appealed to them in the name of the Lord, and made them as gentle as lambs.

The apostles then planned to leave the area, but yielded to the entreaties of the people and stayed on for a further year and three months. During that time, more than sixty thousand people, not counting children, were baptized, together with the king and the princes.

The two magicians already mentioned went to a city called Siani, where there were seventy priests of the idols. They poisoned these priests' minds against the apostles, inciting them to seize both of them as soon as they set foot in the place, and either to force them to sacrifice to the idols, or kill them on the spot. The apostles, having passed through every other part of the province, finally arrived in Siani, and immediately the priests and all the people seized them and carried them off to the temple of the Sun. And through the mouths of the possessed the demons began to cry out: 'What do you want with us, apostles of the living God? As soon as you come near, we are scorched to death!' Then an angel of the Lord appeared to Simon and Jude and said: 'You must make your choice: either all these people must die in an instant, or you must be martyred.' The apostles answered him: 'We must beg God in his mercy to convert these people, and to lead us to the palm of martyrdom.' The apostles called for silence, then announced: 'To prove to you that these idols are inhabited by demons, look: we order each of them to come out and to smash his own image!' Instantly, as everyone stared in amazement, two Ethiopians, black and naked, came out of the idols, smashed them and disappeared, shrieking horribly. When they saw this, the priests rushed at the apostles and cut them to pieces. At the same moment, though the weather was fine and the sky clear, there were suddenly such violent flashes of lightning that the temple was split asunder in three different places, and the two magicians were burnt to cinders. The king had the apostles' bodies brought to his city, where in their honour he built a church of great magnificence . . .

ST QUENTIN

31 October

Quentin, who was of noble birth and a Roman citizen, went to the city of Amiens and there performed many miracles. At the order of Maximian, he was arrested by the prefect of the city, then beaten so long that his assailants fainted with exhaustion. After this he was thrown in prison, but an angel freed him, and Quentin made his way to the centre of the city and there preached to the people. He was arrested again, and stretched on the rack until his veins burst; then he was whipped with thongs of rawhide, and had boiling oil, pitch and fat poured all over him. But he not only endured all this, he actually mocked the judge, who was so enraged he forced lime, vinegar and mustard into Quentin's mouth. But when Quentin still remained impassive, he was taken off to Vermand, where the judge hammered two skewers down the length of his body, from his head to his knees, and drove ten iron spikes under his fingernails, before finally having him beheaded.

His corpse was thrown into the river, and remained there unknown to anyone for fifty-five years until it was discovered by a Roman noblewoman, who was blind. This lady was deep in prayer one night when an angel prompted her to make haste and go to the town of Vermand, where, in such and such a place, she was to search for the body of St Quentin and give it honourable burial. So, taking a sizeable escort, she went to the spot the angel had described, and, as she knelt there in prayer, St Quentin's body, incorrupt and fragrant, floated to the surface of the river. As a reward for her kindness in burying the body, her eyesight was restored; and before returning home she built a church at Vermand in the saint's honour.

THE FOUR CROWNED
MARTYRS

8 November

The four crowned martyrs, who were beaten to death with leaded scourges by order of Diocletian, were named Severus, Severianus, Carpophorus and Victorinus. At first their names were not known, but after many years they were made known by divine revelation, and it was decided that their memory should be honoured under the names of five other martyrs, Claudius, Castorius, Simphorianus, Nicostratus and Simplicius, whose martyrdom had occurred two years after theirs. These last were master sculptors who refused to carve an idol for Diocletian and would not offer sacrifice on any terms; so, by order of the emperor, in about AD 287, they were placed alive in lead coffins and thrown into the sea. Pope Melchiades decreed that the four earlier martyrs should be honoured under the names of these later five and they should be called the 'Four Crowned Martyrs' until such time as their names became known. But the custom persisted even after their names were discovered, and they have always been known by this title.

ST MARTIN, BISHOP

11 November

Martin was a native of Sabaria in Pannonia, but grew up in Italy, at Pavia, and served in the army with his father, who was a military tribune, under the emperors Constantine and Julian. But he did so against his will, for from his earliest years he had enjoyed God's favour, and when he was twelve, against his parents' wishes, he ran off to a church and asked to be received as a catechumen. He would then have gone off to live the life of a hermit, had he not been prevented from doing so by the weakness of his constitution. Then the emperor decreed that the sons of veterans should serve in their fathers' place in the army, and Martin, at the age of fifteen, was forced to become a soldier. He made do with only one serving man, and Martin more often than not served him, and regularly took off his boots and cleaned them for him.

One winter's day Martin was passing through the gateway at Amiens when he came across a poor beggar who had scarcely a rag to cover him and had received no alms all day. Martin, realizing that the privilege of helping this beggar had been reserved for him, drew his sword and cut the cloak he was wearing in two, then gave one half to the beggar and covered himself with the other. The next night, in a vision, he saw Christ wearing the half of his cloak with which he had covered the beggar, and heard him saying to the angels: 'Martin, who is still a catechumen, gave me this cloak to cover me.' The saintly Martin did not allow this to make him conceited; instead, seeing it as proof of God's goodness, he had himself baptized at the age of eighteen. But he served a further two years in the army, yielding to the insistence of his commanding officer, who promised him that, when his own term as tribune was over, he, too, would renounce the world.

At this time the barbarians were making incursions into Gaul, and the emperor Julian, who was setting out to fight them, had made generous donations to his troops in an attempt to win their allegiance. But Martin had no intention of continuing as a soldier. He refused the money he was offered and told the emperor: 'I am a soldier of Christ, I am not permitted to fight.' Julian indignantly retorted that Martin was refusing to fight, not for religious reasons, but because he was frightened at the impending war. Fearlessly Martin replied: 'If you impute my decision to cowardice and refuse to believe it is dictated by my faith, tomorrow I will stand unarmed at the head of the army, and in the name of Christ, without shield or helmet, but with the sign of the cross to protect me, I shall pass through the lines of the enemy untouched!' So he was ordered to be kept under guard, to make sure that he faced the enemy unarmed, as he had promised. But next day the enemy sent an embassy offering to surrender themselves and all their possessions, and there can be no doubt that it was by the merits of this holy man that the victory was won without bloodshed.

After this Martin gave up soldiering and went to join Hilary, bishop of Poitiers, who made him an acolyte. But in a dream the Lord commanded Martin to visit his parents, who were still pagans, and warned him that he would suffer many hardships on the way. And indeed, as he was crossing the Alps, he fell into the hands of robbers, and one of them aimed a blow at his head with an axe, but another managed to grab the man's hand and restrain him. Finally his hands were tied behind his back, and he was handed over to another of the robbers to be kept under guard. When the robber asked Martin if he was afraid, Martin answered that he had never felt so safe, because he knew that it was especially in times of danger that God's mercy was close to hand. He then began to preach to the man and converted him to the faith of Christ. So the robber sent Martin on his way again and thereafter lived an exemplary life.

As Martin left Milan behind him, the Devil met him in human form and asked him where he was heading. Martin replied that he was going where the Lord called him. The Devil retorted: 'Wherever you go, the Devil will fight you tooth and nail!' Martin told him: 'The Lord is my helper, I will not fear what men can do to me.' The Devil at once vanished.

Martin subsequently converted his mother, though his father persisted in his unbelief. When the Arian heresy spread throughout Christendom, Martin was almost alone in resisting it, and for this he was given a public beating and thrown out of the city. So he went back to Milan and built a monastery there, but he was evicted from it by the Arians, and, with a single priest for company, he went to live on the island of Gallinaria. There one day he ate a salad in which he had inadvertently put some hellebore, a deadly poison, and soon felt near to death; but he saved himself and banished all his pain by the power of prayer.

When he heard that blessed Hilary was returning from exile, he went to meet him, and took this opportunity to build a monastery in the neighbourhood of Poitiers. One day, upon returning to this monastery after a short absence, Martin found that one of his catechumens had died before baptism. He took the body to his cell, then, stretching himself upon it, he prayed and brought the catechumen back to life again. This same catechumen used to relate that, when his sentence had been pronounced, he was condemned to a region of darkness, but two angels reminded the judge that he was the man for whom Martin was praying, and the judge then ordered the two angels to take him back again and return him to Martin alive. Martin also brought back to life a man who had hanged himself.

When the people of Tours found themselves without a bishop, they begged Martin to accept the office, but he vigorously resisted them. Some of the other bishops who had assembled there in synod were against Martin's appointment, because of his ugly face and his generally unprepossessing appearance. Their ringleader was a bishop named Defensor [Latin: 'defender']. Now it happened that no lector was present, so one of them took the Psalter and read the first Psalm he came upon. It was the one with the verse: 'Out of the mouth of babes and sucklings hast thou perfected praise, to destroy the enemy and his defender' [Psalm 8:2]. So Bishop Defensor was defeated, and his objections were unanimously overruled. Martin was duly ordained bishop, but because he could not stand the noise of the city, he founded a monastery some two miles outside Tours, where he lived, in great austerity, with eighty disciples. No one drank wine there, except when forced by ill-health to do so; and wearing comfortable clothes was looked upon as a crime. Many cities chose their bishops from the members of this community.

Now a cult was growing up around an unknown man who was supposed to be a martyr. But Martin could discover nothing about his life or his merits, so he stood one day on his tomb and prayed the Lord to reveal to him who the dead man was, and what were his merits. Then, when he turned to his left, he saw a ghost standing there, as black as black can be. He commanded him to speak, and the ghost confessed that he had been a robber and had been executed for his crimes. So Martin at once had his altar demolished.

In the *Dialogue* of Severus and Gallus, the disciples of St Martin (a work which supplies many of the details omitted by Severus in his Life of Martin), we read that Martin had one day to go to the emperor Valentinian to ask him for some favour. But the emperor, knowing that what Martin was about to ask him for was something he did not want to give, had the doors of the palace barred against him. After twice being refused entrance, Martin dressed in sackcloth, sprinkled himself with ashes, and for a whole week mortified himself by abstaining from food and drink. After this he was told by an angel to go to the palace, and this time he made his way, without any hindrance, into the presence of the emperor. When Valentinian saw Martin coming, he was angry that he had been let in and refused to rise to greet him, until suddenly the throne he was seated on caught fire and the flames scorched his imperial behind. Then, angry as he was, he had to rise to meet St Martin and, as he did so, he admitted that he had felt the power of God. He embraced the saint affectionately and, before he could even ask his favour, granted him everything he wanted. He also offered him numerous gifts, but Martin would not accept them.

In the same *Dialogue* we read how he raised a third person from the dead. A young man had died and his mother pleaded tearfully with Martin to bring him back to life. The saint knelt in prayer in the middle of a field before a vast crowd of pagans, and, as everyone watched, the dead youth got to his feet. As a result the pagans were all converted to the faith.

Even inanimate and vegetable objects and irrational creatures obeyed the saint. Inanimate things, such as fire and water, obeyed his will. Once Martin set fire to a pagan shrine, and the wind caught the flames and spread them to the house next door. He climbed on to the roof of the house and plunged into the midst of the advancing flames. At once the flames turned back into the teeth of the wind, so that the two elements seemed to be locked in conflict, each of them struggling for mastery. We read in the same *Dialogue* that when his ship was in danger of sinking, a merchant who was not yet a Christian cried out: 'God of Martin, save us!' And immediately the sea became quite calm.

The vegetable kingdom also obeyed him. He once demolished a very ancient pagan temple, and was about to cut down a pine tree dedicated to the Devil, when the countryfolk and the pagans tried to stop him. One of them said: 'If you have such faith in your God, let us cut this tree down, and you let it fall on you. If your God is with you, as you say, you will not come to any harm.' Martin agreed. The tree was cut through, and, as it swayed threateningly towards the spot where they had tied him, he made the sign of the cross at it and it fell in the opposite direction! It all but crushed the countryfolk, who thought they were standing out of harm's reach; and when they saw this miracle, they were all converted to the faith.

Examples of irrational creatures doing Martin's bidding occur frequently in the *Dialogue*. Once, when he saw some dogs chasing a baby hare, he commanded them to stop: they immediately did so and stood stock still, as if they were rooted to the spot. And, seeing a snake coming towards him once when he was swimming across a river, Martin said to it: 'In the name of the Lord, go back!' As the saint spoke, the snake turned about and crossed to the far bank. With a groan Martin remarked: 'Snakes listen to me, but men will not!' Similarly when a dog kept barking at one of Martin's disciples, the disciple said to the dog: 'In Martin's name, be silent!' And the dog at once fell silent, as if his tongue had been cut out.

Blessed Martin was a man of great humility. Once in Paris he came across a leper from whom everyone was recoiling in horror and he kissed him and gave him his blessing, and the man was immediately healed. When he was in the sanctuary of his cathedral, he never sat on his bishop's throne: no one ever saw him sit down in church. And all he had in his cell was a little three-legged stool, the sort country people use.

But he was also a man of great authority, because he was regarded as an equal of the apostles, and this was because of the grace of the Holy Spirit, which descended upon him in the form of fire to strengthen him, as had happened to the apostles. And the apostles visited him frequently, as if they regarded him as one of their number, because we read in the same *Dialogue* that one day, as Martin was sitting alone in his cell, and his disciples Severus and Gallus were waiting outside, they were suddenly amazed to hear several different voices speaking together inside. When later they asked Martin about this, he said: 'I will tell you, but please, you must tell nobody else. Agnes, Thecla and Mary came to me.' And that was not the only time it happened. Martin admitted they often came to visit him, and the apostles Peter and Paul also regularly appeared to him.

He also had a strict sense of propriety. On one occasion, when he was a guest of the emperor Maximus at dinner, the cup was offered to Bishop Martin first, and everyone expected that he would give it next to the emperor. But instead he handed it to the priest who had accompanied him, considering that no one present was more worthy to drink after himself, and judging it improper to put a king or his courtiers before a priest.

His patience was endless, and never failed him. Bishop though he was, his clerics often treated him disrespectfully without censure, but their behaviour never affected his goodwill towards them. No one ever saw him angry or sad or laughing: all that was ever heard from his lips was Christ, and all he ever had in his heart was love, peace and compassion.

There is a story in the same *Dialogue* that once Martin was riding along on a little donkey; his tunic was made of coarse material, and he was wrapped in a long, trailing black cloak. A company of mounted soldiers was coming towards him, and their mounts took fright at this apparition, and began to prance and rear. The soldiers leapt down, grabbed Martin and gave him a vicious beating. He said not a word, but, as the blows rained down, he turned and offered them his back, which incensed them all the more, because they thought he was trying to insult them by pretending he felt no pain. But when they remounted, their horses stood rooted to the ground; they were immovable, like so many blocks of stone, however hard they were whipped. Finally the soldiers went back to Martin and apologized for the wrong they had unwittingly done him; and when he gave them leave to go, their horses went off at a canter.

He was assiduous in prayer. As we read in his legend, not an hour, not a single moment passed when he was not engaged in either prayer or study. Whether reading or working with his hands, Martin never ceased from mental prayer. Just as blacksmiths, hammering away at the iron, keep tapping the anvil between blows to lighten their labour, so Martin, whatever he happened to be doing, would be constantly at prayer.

He subjected himself to great austerities. In a letter to Eusebius Severus relates that Martin once visited a village in his diocese, and the priests there made up a bed for him, with a deep, luxurious layer of straw. When he retired, Martin was horrified at the unfamiliar softness of his bed, since he was used to sleeping on the bare ground with a single haircloth to cover him. Regarding this as a disgrace, he got up, threw all the straw in a corner, and lay down on the ground. In the middle of the night the straw caught fire. Martin awoke, but when he tried to get out of the room he could not, and the flames enveloped him and set his clothes on fire. But he took refuge, as always, in prayer, and, making the sign of the cross, remained unharmed as the flames leapt around him; and whereas before he had been scorched by their heat, they now seemed just like a refreshing shower of dew. The monks woke up and came running, expecting to find Martin dead, but when they pulled him from the fire he was quite unharmed.

He had a deep compassion for sinners and welcomed with open arms anyone who was willing to repent. Indeed, the Devil once took Martin to task for giving a second chance to sinners and allowing them to do penance. But Martin replied: 'If even a pitiful wretch like you would stop plaguing mankind and repent your misdeeds, I could promise you Christ's mercy, so great is my trust in the Lord!'

His pity for the poor was boundless. We read in the *Dialogue* that one feast-day, when Martin was on his way to church, a naked beggar followed him. Martin asked his archdeacon to give the poor man some clothes, but when the archdeacon made it clear that he was in no haste to do so, Martin went into the sacristy, gave his own tunic to the beggar, and sent him on his way again. The archdeacon then reminded Martin that it was time for him to celebrate mass, but Martin told him that he could not do so until the poor man (by which he meant himself) had something to put on. The archdeacon did not understand this, for since the bishop was wearing a cope, he had no means of knowing Martin had nothing on underneath it, and he explained that there was no poor man there to clothe. 'Bring me a tunic,' Martin told him, 'and the poor man will have all the clothing he needs.' So the archdeacon had to go off to the market place, and for five pieces of silver he hurriedly bought a cheap, short tunic – the sort called a *paenula*, because there is 'almost nothing of it' [Latin *paene nulla* = 'almost nothing'] – and took it back and crossly threw it at Martin's feet. Martin went into a corner and put it on. The sleeves came down only as far as his elbows and the hem to his knees, but none the less he went out to celebrate mass. While mass was in progress, a globe of fire appeared above his head which was seen by many people present, and it was for this reason that Martin was accorded the same status as the apostles. After recounting this miracle Master John Beleth adds that when Martin raised his hands to God, as the celebrant does during the mass, the linen sleeves of his tunic fell back (his arms were thin, without much flesh on them, and the tunic reached only to his elbows) and his arms were left bare. But then, miraculously, angels descended with bracelets of gold studded with precious stones and made sure that his arms were decently covered.

Once Martin happened to catch sight of a sheep that had been shorn and remarked: 'That sheep has fulfilled the Gospel commandment. She had two coats, and she gave one to someone who had none. You should follow her example!'

The saint was a powerful exorcist of demons and often drove evil spirits from people who were possessed. We read in the *Dialogue* that there was a cow that was tormented by a demon, and she ran amok and gored one person after another. Then, in a mad rage, she charged at Martin and his companions as they walked along. He raised his hand and told the cow to halt. She halted, stood stock still and Martin saw a demon sitting on her back. 'Get off, you fiend,' he shouted contemptuously, 'and stop tormenting this harmless beast.' At once the demon was gone, and the cow lay down humbly at Martin's feet; then, when he gave the word, she went back to her herd as meekly as could be.

The saint had great cunning when it came to recognizing demons. Indeed, they were so obvious to him that, whatever form they assumed, he could see through their disguise without difficulty. At times they appeared to him in the person of Jupiter, most often as Mercury, occasionally as Venus or Minerva. Whatever their disguise he would call them all by their proper names and fiercely denounce them. Mercury he found the most troublesome; Jupiter he said was dumb and slow-witted. Once the Devil appeared to him in his cell disguised as a king; dressed in purple, he wore a crown and golden shoes, and his expression was serene and happy. There was a lengthy silence which the Devil finally broke: 'Martin,' he said, 'do you not recognize the one you worship? I am Christ. I have come down to visit the earth, but I wanted to show myself to you first.' Martin was astonished at this, but still he said nothing, so the Devil spoke again: 'Martin, why do you doubt the evidence of your own eyes? I am Christ!' Then, guided by the Holy Spirit, the saint replied: 'The Lord Jesus Christ did not predict that he would come down dressed in purple and with a shining crown upon his head. I shall not believe that Christ has come unless he looks as he did when he suffered and bears the marks of the cross on his body.' At these words the Devil disappeared and left Martin's cell full of a noisome stench.

Martin knew the time of his death long before it occurred, and shared this knowledge with his brothers. Meanwhile he went to visit the parish of Candes to settle some dispute, and on his way he saw some ducks on a river diving and catching fish. 'Just like demons!' he remarked. 'They lie in wait for the unwary, they catch them before they even know it, when they have caught them they devour them, and once they start they are never satisfied.' So he ordered the birds to leave the river and go off into the desert somewhere, and instantaneously they all flocked together and flew away towards the mountains and the forests.

When he had stayed some while in Candes, his strength began to fail, and he told his disciples that his end was near. 'Why are you leaving us, father?' they all asked him, in floods of tears. 'Whom shall we turn to, if you abandon us? Ravening wolves will prey upon your flock!' Martin was so moved by their tearful entreaties that he wept, too, and he prayed: 'Lord, if I am still necessary to your people, I will not shirk the task. Your will be done!' Martin was torn: he wanted neither to leave his brothers, nor to stay separated from Christ any longer. For some time he was in the grip of a raging fever and in great discomfort, as he lay on his bed of sackcloth and ashes; but when his disciples asked him to let them put some straw down for him, he said: 'My sons, a bed of sackcloth and ashes is the only bed for a Christian to lie on. If I leave you any other example, then I have sinned.' He kept his eyes and hands constantly lifted towards heaven, and gave his indomitable spirit not a moment's respite from prayer. He lay all the time on his back, and when his priests asked if they could turn him on his side and make his poor body more comfortable, he replied: 'Let me be, brothers. Let me gaze towards heaven, rather than the earth, so that my spirit may rise direct to God.' As he spoke he saw the Devil standing near him. 'What are you here for,' he cried, 'bloodthirsty beast? There is no corruption in me. Abraham is waiting to receive me in his bosom.' And with these words, in the reign of Arcadius and Honorius, which began around AD 390, and in his eighty-first year, Martin surrendered his soul to God. His face was as radiant as if he were already in glory, and many people heard choirs of angels singing round his bed . . .

65

ST BRICE

13 November

Brice, one of St Martin's deacons, was extremely jealous of him and never lost an opportunity for abusing the saint. Once, when a pauper was trying to find Martin, Brice told him: 'If it is that madman you want, you will have to look higher! He is the one who is always gazing up to heaven like a lunatic.' Then, when the pauper had got what he wanted from Martin, the saint called Brice and said to him: 'Do I seem like a madman to you, Brice?' Brice, covered in shame, denied that he had said any such thing, but Martin retorted: 'You think my ears were not at your mouth because you spoke at a distance? Let me tell you something: the Lord has granted my request that you should succeed me as bishop; but you must know that you will suffer many trials.' Brice laughed when he heard this and said to everyone: 'Was I not telling the truth when I said he was mad?'

After Martin's death Brice was elected bishop, and from that moment, though still given to arrogance, he devoted himself to prayer and a life of chastity. In the thirtieth year of his episcopate, a woman who wore a nun's habit and did his washing for him conceived and gave birth to a son. At this the entire population of the city gathered at Brice's door with stones in their hands and shouted: 'For too long, out of respect for St Martin, we have turned a blind eye to your immorality, but we can no longer kiss hands that are so black with sin.' Brice stoutly denied their accusation. 'Bring me the child!' he demanded. The child, now thirty days old, was fetched and Brice said to him: 'I command you, in the name of God's son, to declare in front of everyone here whether I am your father.' The child replied: 'No, you are not my father.' The people now pressed Brice to ask the child who his father was, but Brice told them: 'That is not my business. I have done all I had to do.' The people then attributed all of this to magic. 'You have no right to call yourself our shepherd,' they said, 'and you are not going to lord it over us any longer!' So Brice, in order to prove his innocence, carried burning coals in the skirts of his cloak all the way to St Martin's tomb, while everybody watched. He then shook out the coals, and his cloak had not a mark on it. 'Just as my cloak was untouched by the coals,' he told them, 'so my body is as innocent of all contact with a woman.' But the people were still unconvinced, and they hurled insults and abuse at him, and removed him from office. So St Martin's prophecy was fulfilled.

In great distress Brice went to see the pope and stayed in Rome with him for seven years, and, by doing penance, atoned for all the wrongs he had done to St Martin. Back in Tours the people made Justinian their bishop, and sent him to Rome to confront Brice and defend his own right to the episcopate against him. But he died on his way there, at Vercelli, and so the people of Tours elected Armenius in his place. Then, when the seven years were up, Brice returned to Tours with the pope's full backing. He put up for the night six miles from the city, and that same night Armenius breathed his last. Brice learnt of his death by revelation, and he told his party to get up at once and go with him to the funeral of the bishop of Tours. But as Brice was entering the city by one gate, the dead Armenius was being carried out by another. After the burial St Brice became bishop again, and continued in office for another seven years. Having led a praiseworthy life, he finally died a peaceful death in the forty-eighth year of his episcopate.[1]

66

ST ELIZABETH

19 November

Elizabeth was the illustrious daughter of the king of Hungary. Her birth therefore was noble, but she made it still nobler by her faith and Christian devotion. She ennobled a lineage already noble by her example, added lustre to its name by her miracles, and enriched it by the grace of her sanctity. The Author of Nature, as it were, raised her above nature. For while still a child, though reared as a princess in the lap of luxury, she either utterly rejected the pleasures of childhood, or else turned them into ways of serving God. What is abundantly clear from her earliest years is her remarkable sincerity, and the strength and tenderness of her devotion. Throughout her childhood she accustomed herself to the practice of good works, spurning idle games, fleeing from worldly prosperity, and growing always in her reverence for God. When she was only five years old, she spent so long in church praying that her friends and maids had difficulty tearing her away; and her servants and young playmates noticed that, during their games, if any of them made off in the direction of the chapel, Elizabeth would always follow them, just to have a chance of going inside. When she went in, she would either kneel or prostrate herself completely on the floor; and though she had not yet learnt to read, she would often put an open Psalter in front of her in church to give the impression that she was reading and so discourage people from disturbing her. She would also make a game of lying on the ground and measuring herself against the other girls, but it was only ever to show her reverence for God. When she was playing the game of rings, or any other game, she put all her hope in God. And out of her winnings, and whatever happened to come her way from other sources, the little Elizabeth gave a tithe to the poor girls of her own age, encouraging them to be regular in reciting the Lord's Prayer and the Hail Mary.

As Elizabeth grew in years she grew even more in the strength of her religious devotion. She chose the Blessed Virgin, Mother of God, as her patroness and advocate, and St John the Evangelist as guardian of her chastity. Once, when slips of paper with the names of different apostles written on them were placed on the altar and the girls each picked one at random, Elizabeth's prayer was answered, and three times she got the one with St John's name on it. Indeed, her devotion to St John was so great that she could refuse nothing that was asked in his name. To guard against the seductions of worldly success, she made a practice each day of denying herself some part of her good fortune. If, for example, she was winning in some game, she would stop it and say: 'I do not want to go on. I give up the rest for God.' And when her girlfriends asked her to dance with them, she would dance just one set, then say: 'Let once be enough: let us forgo the rest for God.' So, in this way, she would keep them from idle, worldly pursuits. Elizabeth always loathed immodesty in dress and herself loved clothes that were restrained and simple.

She disciplined herself to say a fixed number of prayers each day, and if she was so busy that she could not say them all and her maids made her go to bed, she would keep vigil with her heavenly spouse until she had fulfilled her vow. And she kept feast-days with such intense devotion that, no matter what the pretext, she would not allow her sleeves to be laced on[1] until after mass was over. Also she would not allow herself to wear gloves before midday on Sundays; this she did both to show respect for the Lord's Day and to satisfy her own religious zeal. She also made a practice of binding herself by a vow to keep these observances, so that no one could ever dissuade her from fulfilling her intention. She followed the divine office with such reverence that at the reading of the Gospel, or at the consecration of the host, she would remove her sleeves (if by chance they had already been laced on), take off her necklaces and any other ornament she was wearing on her head, and lay them on the floor.

After Elizabeth had passed her maidenhood in prudence and innocence, she was compelled to marry. She did so in obedience to her father's command, but, as a result, she was to reap a great Christian harvest, a reward for keeping her faith in the Trinity and observing the Ten Commandments. Though against her will, she consented to marital intercourse, not to satisfy any physical desire, but out of deference to her father's will, and in order to bear children whom she could raise for the service of God.[2] So, although she was bound by the law of the marriage bed, she was never a slave to its pleasures. This she proved when she made a solemn vow in the hands of her confessor, Master Conrad, that if she outlived her husband, she would live the rest of her life in continence.

Elizabeth was married, then, to the landgrave[3] of Thuringia, a match befitting her royal birth, and one ordained by divine providence so that she could bring countless souls to the love of God and enlighten the ignorant. And though her outward circumstances had changed, her spiritual aspirations remained the same. Her intense devotion and humility towards God, her extreme austerity and self-denial, and her boundless generosity and compassion towards the poor, are all clearly illustrated in the examples that follow.

Elizabeth was so ardently devoted to prayer that she often hurried off to church and arrived before her maids did, as if, by her secret prayers, she hoped to win some special grace from God. Often, too, she got up in the night to pray, though her husband begged her to spare herself and allow her body some rest. She had told one of her maids, who was closer to her than the rest, that if her mistress overslept, she should wake her by tugging at her foot. And on one occasion, feeling for her mistress's foot, the maid mistakenly knocked against the landgrave's foot. He woke with a jump, but when he found out what was going on, he took it all in good part and tactfully pretended nothing had happened. Often, in order to make her prayers a richer sacrifice to God, Elizabeth would wet them with a copious flood of tears – but these were tears she usually shed happily, without any unbecoming change of expression: she wept for sorrow, yet the sorrow brought her joy, and this joy lent her face an added beauty.

So great was her humility that, for the love of God, she never refused any task, however mean and lowly, but performed it with the utmost zeal. On one occasion she came across a sick man who was horribly deformed and whose head was so dirty it stank, but she clasped him to her bosom, cut off his filthy hair, and then washed his face, while her maids watched her and laughed. On Rogation Days she always followed the procession barefoot, wearing a simple woollen shift, and at the station churches she sat to hear the sermon among the poor women, as if she were poor and low-born like them. When she went to be churched after giving birth, she never wore gold-embroidered dresses or jewellery as the other wives did, but, following the example of the Virgin Mary, she carried her child in her arms and humbly offered it at the altar, with a lamb and a candle, to show her contempt for worldly pomp, and her wish to model her life in every way upon that of the spotless Mary. Then, when she returned home, she would give some poor woman the clothes she had worn to church. Another illustration of her humility is the fact that though her privileges were almost limitless and her station exalted, she submitted herself in obedience to a poor priest called Master Conrad. He was a pauper, but celebrated for his learning and religious zeal; and while she continued to honour the obligations of marriage, and with her husband's consent, Elizabeth schooled herself to such unquestioning obedience that she did whatever Conrad told her with reverence and joy: her aim thereby was to win the merit of obedience, and to follow the example of her Lord and Saviour, who 'became obedient even unto death'. Once she was summoned by Master Conrad to hear a sermon he was to preach, but the margravine[4] of Meissen called unexpectedly, and prevented her from attending. Conrad saw this as flagrant disobedience and angrily refused to forgive her until he had her stripped to her shift and soundly whipped, together with some of her maids who had also misbehaved themselves.

Elizabeth subjected herself to an asceticism so rigorous that, with her vigils and disciplines and fasting, her body wasted almost to nothing. Often she kept from her husband's bed and went all night without sleep in order to devote herself to prayer and to commune with her heavenly father in secret; and when she was forced to stop and sleep, she slept on mats on the floor. When her husband was away, she passed whole nights in prayer with her heavenly spouse. She also regularly had her maids come to her bedroom and flog her, to repay her Saviour for the scourging he had received and to suppress any temptations of the flesh.

So far as food and drink were concerned, Elizabeth showed such moderation that, though dishes of every kind were set before her on her husband's table, she sometimes contented herself with nothing more than a piece of bread. Master Conrad forbade her to touch any food her husband offered her about which she had the slightest reservations, and she observed this rule with such scrupulousness that, while others ate their fill of all sorts of delicious foods, she and her maids would take only coarser fare. Often she would sit at table and simply play with her food, carefully cutting it in pieces so that she might appear to be eating, and not be thought of as a fanatic, while courteously ensuring that her guests were enjoying themselves. On one occasion, when she was tired out after a long journey and she and her husband were offered foods which seemed unlikely to have been honestly acquired, she would not touch them: instead she joined her maids and quietly ate some hard black bread dipped in warm water. For this reason her husband assigned to her certain of his revenues, and these provided her, and those of her maids who wished to follow the same way of life, with enough to live on. Elizabeth often sent back the luxurious fare she was served and asked instead for plain food, the kind of food ordinary people ate. All this her husband bore without complaint, and declared that he, too, would gladly do the same if he were not worried about the trouble he would cause his entire household.

Though Elizabeth was of the highest nobility, she yearned for nothing more than poverty, so that she might make amends to Christ, who had been poor, and prevent the world from claiming any part of her. So from time to time, when she was alone with her maids, she would put on shabby clothes and cover her head with an old, tattered veil and say to them: 'This is how I shall go about when I have become truly poor.' Though she was strict in curbing her own appetite, she was so lavish in her generosity to the poor that she could never let a single one go hungry. She ministered to all of them with such liberality that the people called her 'the Mother of the Poor'.

She was tireless in performing the seven works of mercy, intent as she was on winning the eternal kingdom and reigning there for ever, and on receiving the Father's blessing along with the chosen at his right hand. She covered the naked by providing clothes for the poor, by supplying the linen necessary for the burial of pilgrims and the destitute, and for the robes children wore at their baptism. She would often lift such children from the font herself, and sew them clothes with her own hands, because, as their godmother, she would be able to help them more. It happened one day that she gave a rather smart dress to a poor woman, who was so overcome with joy when she saw this magnificent gift that she collapsed and was thought to be dead. Elizabeth was deeply distressed at the thought that her gift had proved too much for her and been the cause of her death, but she prayed for her and the woman got to her feet again, fully recovered. Often Elizabeth sat with her maids and spun wool herself and had clothing made from it, wishing not only to reap the fruits of her honest labours, but also to set an example of true humility and to have something to offer up to God that she herself had toiled over.

She also fed the hungry, and was always giving provisions to the poor. Once, when her husband the landgrave had gone off to the court of Emperor Frederick, which was then at Cremona, she amassed the whole year's harvest from his granaries, gathered together the poor from far and wide, and supplied them each with their daily needs, because there was a dearth throughout the land and a severe famine threatened. And, however little she was able to give these people, miraculously it proved enough for the day. Often, when she ran short of money, she sold her jewellery in order to relieve the poor; and she was always stinting herself or getting her maids to go without something and putting it by for the poor.

She also gave drink to the thirsty. On one occasion she was serving beer to the poor, and when she had given plenty to everyone, it was discovered that her jug was still as full as it had been at the start.

She also sheltered pilgrims and beggars, and for this she had a large house built at the foot of the hill beneath the castle, where she cared for large numbers of sick people and visited them daily, despite the hardship involved in climbing up and down the hillside. She provided them with all the necessities of life, and, offering them words of encouragement, taught them patience in their suffering. Though she had always found evil smells difficult to endure and it was high summer, for the love of God she insisted on seeing every one of the sick, no matter how foul and rank their sores, and applied salves to their wounds, wiping them with the veil from her own head, and nursing them with her own hands, though her maids could scarcely bear even to watch. In the same house Elizabeth fed the children of poor women and saw that they were shown every care, and she was always so sweet and kind to them that they all called her 'mother', and whenever she came into the house, they all followed her about as if they really were her own children, and clustered eagerly in front of her vying for her attention. She once bought some little pots and rings and other toys made of glass for the children to play with, and, holding them in a fold of her cloak, she was riding up the hill to the castle when they all spilled out and fell over a precipice on to the rocks below. But not a single one was broken.

She also visited the sick. Her heart was so ruled by her compassion for their miseries that she regularly went looking for them, trying to find where they lived, and made sure to visit them. No road was too difficult, no journey too long, and she would enter their poor little rooms as if she were some old and faithful friend, supplying them with all they needed as well as offering them words of consolation. So she was rewarded for five distinct merits: for her goodness in visiting the sick; for the long journeys it involved; for the abundance of her compassion; for her words of comfort; and for her generosity in almsgiving.

She often assisted with the burial of poor folk, attending devoutly to their funerals and dressing their bodies in clothes she had made herself, once even tearing up the large linen veil she was wearing to make a winding-sheet for a pauper's corpse. She laid out their bodies with her own hands, and dutifully stayed at the grave for the funeral rites.

In all this the devotion of her husband was beyond praise. Though preoccupied with a great number of other affairs, he was devoted to the service of God, and since he was unable to attend to such things himself, he gave his wife complete freedom to do anything that might bring glory to God and win the salvation of his soul. But Elizabeth longed to see her husband use his great military prowess in the defence of the faith, and, urging the righteousness of the cause, she persuaded him to go to the Holy Land. It was while he was there that the landgrave, that faithful prince and sincere Christian, a man renowned for his unwavering faith and wholehearted devotion, gave up his soul to God and received a glorious reward for his good works.

Elizabeth now embraced the state of widowhood with characteristic zeal, determined not to be deprived of the reward of a widow's continence, and to reap a great Christian harvest by observing the Ten Commandments and practising the seven works of mercy. But no sooner had news of her husband's death spread throughout Thuringia than some of her late husband's vassals accused her of being a wastrel and a spendthrift and shamefully hounded her out of the country. But as a result her remarkable patience was fully revealed, and she achieved at last the poverty she had so long desired.

Night was falling as she arrived at the house of an innkeeper, and, giving grateful thanks to God, she retired to lie down in a corner where pigs had been kept. Next morning she went on to the house of the Friars Minor and asked them to sing a *Te Deum* in thanksgiving for the trials she was enduring. The following day she was ordered to take her children and go to live in the house of a couple who had always been her enemies. There she was given the tiniest room to sleep in, and treated so unkindly by the man and his wife that she finally had to leave. She could bring herself to bid farewell only to the walls: 'I would gladly say goodbye to the owners,' she said, 'if they had been kind to me.' So she was forced to go back to her pigsty at the inn and to send her children away to various other places to be looked after. As she was walking along a narrow pathway, using stepping stones to avoid a sea of mud, she saw coming towards her an old woman to whom she had done many kindnesses. She, too, was stepping from stone to stone, but she refused to let her benefactress pass, and Elizabeth fell right in where the mud was thickest. But she got up with a smile on her face, and laughed as she wiped the mud from her clothes.

Her aunt, who was an abbess, soon took pity on Elizabeth's extreme poverty and took her to the bishop of Bamberg, who was her uncle. He received Elizabeth with all due courtesy and craftily insisted that she stayed on as a guest in his house, with the intention of marrying her off a second time. When Elizabeth's maids, who, like their mistress, had made a vow of continence, learnt of his plan, they were heartbroken, and in floods of tears they told blessed Elizabeth. But she consoled them. 'I trust in the Lord,' she said, 'for love of whom I have vowed perpetual continence. He will strengthen me in my resolution. He will check all violence, and baffle all the intrigues of men. If by chance my uncle intends to marry me to another man, I shall oppose him heart and soul, I shall contradict his every word. And if no other way of escape is left me, I will cut off my nose so that no man could bear even to look at me!' Then at the bishop's order Elizabeth was taken away to a castle, where she was to be kept until she was given to someone in marriage. There, as she tearfully commended her chastity to the Lord, heaven willed it that her husband's bones were brought back from overseas, and the bishop had her released so that she could go to receive her husband's remains and show them proper respect. The bishop went in solemn procession to meet the landgrave's bones, and Elizabeth, with deepest devotion, and weeping copiously, received them. Raising her eyes to heaven, she said: 'I thank you, Lord, for deigning to console me in my wretchedness by allowing me to receive the bones of my husband, who was so dear to you. You know, Lord, that I loved him dearly, as he loved you; yet for love of you I denied myself his company and persuaded him to go to the relief of your Holy Land. And however much I wish I were living with him still, even if we were paupers and I had to travel the whole world begging, you know I would not give a single hair of my head to have him back again, or beg for his life to be restored, against your will. So I commend him and myself to your gracious keeping.' Then, so as not to lose the abundant rewards which are given to those who live lives of evangelical perfection and are transferred from the left hand of misery to the right hand of glory, Elizabeth adopted the plain, coarse, grey habit of a nun.

After her husband's death she lived in perpetual continence, practised unquestioning obedience, and embraced voluntary poverty. She wished also to go begging from door to door, but this Master Conrad would not permit. The clothes she wore were shabby and threadbare: her grey cloak had been lengthened, and the sleeves of her tunic were patched with cloth of a completely different colour. When her father, the king of Hungary, heard of the terrible life his daughter was leading, he sent one of his counts to persuade her to come back and live with him. When this count saw Elizabeth in her threadbare habit, humbly sitting and spinning, he was both bewildered and shocked, and he exclaimed: 'Never has a king's daughter appeared in such shabby clothes, or been seen spinning wool!' He insisted that she return with him, but Elizabeth would not hear of it, preferring to live in poverty with the poor rather than in the lap of luxury with the rich. And so that her heart might be completely at one with God, and nothing stand in the way of her deep devotion, she asked the Lord to inspire her with contempt for all worldly things, to tear from her heart her love for her children, and to enable her resolutely to disregard all insults. In answer to her prayer she heard the Lord reply: 'Your prayer is granted.' Then she told her maids: 'The Lord has heard my voice, because I regard all earthly things as dross. I care no more for my own children than for any of my neighbours, and I pay no heed to insults and abuse. It seems I no longer love anything but God.'

Master Conrad for his part would often make her do things that were disagreeable and vexatious, and he would deprive her of the company of anybody to whom he thought her attached. He even dismissed two of her most loyal maids, both favourites of Elizabeth, who had grown up with her and known her since childhood, and this separation caused great heartache on both sides. But the holy man did this in order to break her will, so that she could offer up all her love to God, and also so that none of her maids should remind her of her former celebrity. In all these matters Elizabeth showed unhesitating obedience and unfailing patience, in order that through patience she might win her soul, and through obedience the glorious meed of victory. She also used to say: 'If for God's sake I hold a mortal man in such awe, how great must be my awe of the heavenly Judge! I therefore chose to give my obedience to a poor and needy man, Master Conrad, rather than to some bishop, so that I could deny myself every possibility of earthly consolation.'

Once, at the pressing invitation of some nuns, Elizabeth went to visit their convent, but she had not obtained the consent of her master, and he had her whipped so severely that three weeks later the marks of the lashes could still be seen. But she said to her maids, as much to console them as herself: 'When a river is in spate, the grass on its banks is flattened, and when the water subsides, it springs up straight again. So, when trouble comes our way, we should bow in humility before it; and when it is past, we should lift ourselves to God again in spiritual joy.'

So deep was her humility that she would not permit her maids to address her as 'my lady': she insisted that they use the more familiar singular (that is, the form used when addressing inferiors).[5] She washed the dishes and other cooking utensils, and, in case her maids should try to stop her, she would send them off on errands elsewhere. She also used to say: 'If I could have found a life more lowly, I would have chosen it.'

In order, with Mary, to possess 'the better part' [Luke 10:42] Elizabeth was assiduous in the practice of mental prayer, and during this prayer she was granted special graces: to weep copiously, to have frequent visions of heaven, and to kindle the love of God in others. When she seemed particularly happy, she would shed tears of rapturous devotion, and tears of joy ran down her cheeks like the waters of some crystal fountain. It was as if she were sorrowful and exultant all at once, but this weeping never marred or lined her face. She said of those who screw up their faces when they weep: 'You would think they want to frighten the Lord away! They should give God what they have to give him joyfully, and with a smile on their face.'

While engaged in her prayers and contemplations, Elizabeth often had heavenly visions. One day in the holy season of Lent she sat in church with her eyes fixed intently on the altar, as if she were gazing in wonder at the presence of God himself. She stayed there for some time, consoled and refreshed by this divine revelation. Then, when she returned home, she felt so weak that she had to sit and rest on the lap of one of her maids, and, as she gazed through the window with her eyes fixed on the heavens, her face was irradiated with such joy that she suddenly, unexpectedly, burst out laughing. Then, after a while, when the bliss of this joyous vision passed, she suddenly began to weep. Then, as she opened her eyes again, she recaptured her earlier happiness, and when she closed them, she was in floods of tears again. And so, until the hour of compline, her divine consolations continued. For a long time Elizabeth did not utter a single word; then finally she broke her silence and said: 'Yes, Lord, you wish to be with me and I with you, and I want never to be separated from you!' Later her maids asked her, for the honour of God and their own edification, to tell them what she had seen in her vision, and Elizabeth, yielding to their insistent pleas, said: 'I saw the heavens opened, and Jesus bending down to me with great kindness, showing me the brightness of his face. A feeling of indescribable joy flooded over me as I saw him, and when he went away I was left with a terrible sense of loss. Then he took pity on me and renewed my joy by showing me his face again and said: "If you wish to be with me, I will be with you." What I said in reply, you heard.' When she was pressed to describe the vision she had seen at the altar, too, she answered: 'I may not say what I saw there. But I was filled with joy, and I saw all the wonders of God.'

Often, when she was at prayer, her face took on a wonderful radiance and her eyes pierced like the rays of the sun. Often, too, her prayer was so fervent that it kindled the love of God in others. She once saw a fashionably dressed young man and called him over to her and said: 'You seem to lead a very dissolute existence. What you should really be doing is serving your Creator. Do you want me to pray to God for you?' 'I do,' he replied. 'Yes, I beg you to, with all my heart.' So she began to pray for him, and told him to pray, too, but very soon the young man cried out: 'Enough. My lady, stop, please!' But Elizabeth prayed even harder, and the youth's cries became even more desperate. 'Stop!' he shouted. 'I feel faint. I am on fire!' He had in fact become so hot that he was positively streaming with sweat, his body was convulsed, and he flung his arms about like a madman. Some passers-by tried to restrain him, and found his clothing was absolutely drenched in sweat and his body too hot to touch, and all the time he was screaming: 'I am all on fire! It is devouring me!' But as soon as Elizabeth finished her prayer, the burning sensation was instantly gone; the youth came to himself again, and subsequently, guided by God's grace, he entered the Order of Friars Minor. This raging heat he had experienced was a demonstration of the extreme ardour of Elizabeth's prayers, ardour of such intensity that it could kindle fire in the heart of even a lukewarm youth. But the youth, accustomed as he was to the pleasures of the flesh and not yet ready for those of the spirit, had no idea what had happened.

Elizabeth had now reached the very summit of perfection, but she never let her longing for the quiet contemplation enjoyed by Mary cause her to forget the onerous duties performed by Martha. Her devotion to the seven works of mercy has already been illustrated, and, after she took the veil, she was as assiduous in her good works as before. For her dowry she had received two thousand marks. Part of this she distributed among the poor, and with the rest she built a large hospital at Marburg. As a result everyone regarded her as a spendthrift and a wastrel, and people called her mad; and because she could accept all these insults with a smile, they remarked caustically that she had been too quick to banish her husband's memory from her heart, and condemned her for being so cheerful. After the hospital was finished, Elizabeth gave herself up to the service of the poor, like some common serving woman, and lovingly looked after their every need, bathing them, putting them to bed and tucking them under the covers, and commenting happily to her maids: 'How lucky we are to bath and shelter the Lord as we do!' And while attending to the sick she humbled herself to such a degree that, when nursing a young child who had only one eye and was covered in scabs, she carried him in her arms to the privy seven times in one night, and happily washed the sheets he had soiled. There was also a woman who was hideously disfigured with leprosy whom she often washed and put to bed, giving her her medicines, paring her nails, and crouching at her feet to untie the laces of her shoes. She persuaded the sick to make their confession and receive communion, and, in the case of one old woman who adamantly refused, had her whipped before she got her to relent.

When she was not looking after the poor, Elizabeth used to spin wool that was sent her from a monastery, and whatever she was paid for the work she divided among the poor. After many long years of poverty, when she received five hundred marks from her dowry, she distributed the money among the poor. She arranged them all in a row, then tucked up her skirts and went along handing them their share, having first made a rule that if any of them took someone else's place in order to receive alms a second time, he would have his hair cut off. Now a girl called Radegund, whose hair was her crowning glory, happened to be passing and called at the hospital, not to receive alms, but to visit her sister who was sick. She was brought before blessed Elizabeth as if she were a criminal, and, though she wept and struggled, Elizabeth ordered that her hair should be cut off at once. When some of the inmates protested her innocence, Elizabeth replied: 'At least in future if she goes to dances, she will not be able to show off her hair, or be so keen to indulge in other frivolities!' Blessed Elizabeth then asked the girl if she had ever thought of leading the religious life, and she replied that she would have done so long ago, had she not been so inordinately proud of her hair. Elizabeth told her: 'Then I am happier that you have lost your hair than if my own son had been made emperor.' Without further delay Radegund took the veil, stayed at the hospital with Elizabeth, and lived an exemplary life.

Once, when a poor woman gave birth to a baby girl, St Elizabeth lifted her from the sacred font and gave her her own name, Elizabeth. She supplied all the mother's needs, even cutting the sleeves from her maid's coat for the woman to wrap her baby in and giving her her own shoes. Three weeks later the woman abandoned her child and quietly disappeared with her husband. When Elizabeth got to hear of this, she at once began to pray, and the man and his wife were unable to travel a step further; they were compelled to come back to her and beg her forgiveness. Elizabeth soundly reprimanded them for their ingratitude, as was proper, then handed them back their baby to look after, and made sure they had everything they needed.

As the time approached when the Lord had determined to call his beloved Elizabeth from the prison of this world and reward her for spurning the kingdom of mortals by granting her a place in the kingdom of angels, Christ appeared to her and said: 'Come, my beloved, come to the eternal home I have prepared for you!' She was then stricken with a fever, and, as she lay with her face turned to the wall, those who stood round her heard her singing the sweetest melody. One of her maids asked her what it was and Elizabeth told her: 'A little bird sat between me and the wall, and sang so prettily that it made me sing, too.' Elizabeth was unfailingly cheerful throughout her illness, and was continually at prayer. The day before she died she said to her maids: 'What would you do if the Devil came to you?' A moment later she cried aloud, three times: 'Be gone!', as if she were driving the Devil away. Then she said: 'It is nearly midnight, the hour when Christ chose to be born, the hour he lay in his manger.' And, as the hour of her passing drew near, she said: 'Now it comes – the moment when God Almighty calls his friends to the celestial wedding feast!' A short while later, her life drew peacefully to its close. She died in the year of our Lord 1231 . . .

67

ST CECILIA

22 November

Cecilia, the celebrated virgin, was of noble Roman birth and raised in the faith of Christ from her very cradle. Hidden in her heart she always carried the Gospel of Christ; night and day her converse with God and her prayers were unceasing, and her constant plea was that the Lord should preserve her virginity. She was betrothed to a youth named Valerian, and the date of her wedding had already been decided. But when the day came, under her gold-embroidered garments she wore a hair-shirt next to her flesh; and as the organ music swelled, Cecilia sang in her heart to the Lord alone. 'Lord,' she sang, 'keep my heart and my body undefiled, so that I may not be shamed.' She fasted for two or three days at a time, and in prayer commended her fears to the Lord. When the wedding night came and she and her spouse were finally alone together in the privacy of the bridal chamber, she said to him: 'My dearest, most loving young friend, there is a secret I have to confess to you, but only if you solemnly swear you will keep it in strictest confidence.' Valerian swore that he would never disclose it, no matter what the circumstances, and that nothing could ever make him betray it. Then she told him: 'I have as my lover an angel of God, who watches over my body with unceasing vigilance. If he sees you so much as touch me with impure thoughts in your heart, he will strike you down at once, and you will lose the most precious bloom of your youth. But if he knows that your love for me is pure, he will love you as he loves me, and show you his glory.' Directed by the will of God, Valerian replied: 'If you want me to believe you, show me this angel, and if I am satisfied that he is really an angel, I will do whatever you tell me. But if I find you love another man, I shall draw my sword and kill you both!' Cecilia said: 'If you believe in the true God and promise to be baptized, you will be able to see my angel. Go to the third milestone out of the city on the Appian Way and say to the poor folk you find there: "Cecilia has sent me to you so that you can take me to Urban, the old holy man. I have a secret message for him." When you see him, tell him everything

I have said to you, and when you have been purified by him, you must come back here, and then you will see the angel.'

Valerian set out at once, and, following the directions he was given, found St Urban, who was hiding among the tombs of the martyrs. When he told him everything Cecilia had said, Urban lifted his hands to heaven. 'Lord Jesus Christ,' he said, his eyes full of tears, 'author of all chaste counsel, reap now the fruit of the seeds you have sown in Cecilia's heart! Lord Jesus Christ, good shepherd, your handmaid Cecilia has served you like a busy bee! The spouse she received as a raging lion she has sent to you as the meekest lamb.' Then suddenly there appeared an old man dressed in snow-white garments, holding a book written in letters of gold. When Valerian saw him, he was so frightened he fell to the ground in a faint, but the old man helped him to his feet, and read from the book as follows: 'One God, one faith, one baptism; one God and Father of all, who is above all, in everything, and in all of us.' When he had read these words, the old man asked Valerian: 'Do you believe this, or do you still doubt?' Valerian cried: 'There is no greater truth under heaven!' At once the old man disappeared. Valerian was then baptized by St Urban and when he returned home he found Cecilia in her room talking to an angel. The angel held two crowns of roses and lilies in his hand, and gave one to Cecilia and the other to Valerian and said: 'Guard these crowns with spotless hearts and pure bodies, because I have brought them to you from God's paradise, and they will never fade or lose their fragrance, nor ever be seen by any except those who love chastity. As for you, Valerian, since you had faith in the good counsel you were given, ask whatever you wish, and it shall be granted.' Valerian replied: 'Nothing is dearer to me in this life than the love of my only brother. My wish therefore is that he may know the truth as I do.' The angel said: 'The Lord will grant your petition, and you will both come to him with the palm of martyrdom.'

At this point Tiburtius, Valerian's brother, entered the room, and, smelling the heady fragrance, he said: 'I wonder where the scent of roses and lilies can be coming from at this time of the year. If I were holding bunches of them in my hands, they would not give off such a heavenly fragrance! I tell you, I feel invigorated; I feel suddenly as if I were a different person!' 'We have crowns which your eyes cannot see,' Valerian told him, 'crowns bright as the gayest flowers and white as snow. Because I prayed for you, you were able to smell their fragrance; and now, if you believe, you will be able to see them, too.' Tiburtius said: 'Am I hearing all this in some dream, or are you telling me the truth, Valerian?' 'Until now,' Valerian replied, 'we have been living in a dream. But now we hold fast to the truth!' 'How have you come to know of this?' Tiburtius asked. 'An angel of the Lord taught me,' Valerian told him, 'and you will be able to see him, once you are purified and have renounced the worship of idols.' . . . Cecilia then demonstrated to him that idols were devoid of both feeling and speech, and did so with such clarity that when Tiburtius replied, he said: 'No one but an ass could refuse to believe you!' Cecilia kissed him upon the breast and said: 'Today I acknowledge you as my brother. God's love has made your brother my husband, and now your renunciation of the idols will make you my brother. So go with Valerian to be purified, and then you will see the faces of the angels.' 'Tell me, brother, I beg you,' Tiburtius asked Valerian, 'where are you taking me?' Valerian replied: 'To Urban the bishop.' Tiburtius said: 'Do you mean the Urban who has been repeatedly condemned to death and is living in hiding? If he is found, he will be burnt alive, and we shall go up in flames with him! While we are searching for a god hidden in heaven, we shall be consumed in a furious inferno on earth!' 'If this life were the only life,' Cecilia told him, 'we would be justified in fearing to lose it. But there is another, better life, which is never lost, of which the Son of God has told us. Everything in creation was fashioned by the Son born of the Father, and into everything he created, the Holy Spirit, who proceeds from the Father, breathed life. And this Son of God came into the world and showed us, by his words and by his miracles, that there is another life.' 'You state categorically that there is only one God,' Tiburtius objected. 'How, then, can you now declare that there are three?' Cecilia replied: 'In human knowledge three distinct faculties are involved: reason, memory and understanding. Similarly in the one divine being there can be three persons.' She then proceeded to tell him of the coming of the Son of God and of his passion, and to explain the many ways in which his suffering was apt. 'The Son of God was chained so that humanity could be freed from the chains of sin. Our blessed Saviour was cursed so that accursed man might be blessed. He allowed himself to be mocked so that man might be freed from the mockery of demons. He let a crown of thorns be put on his head to save us from the damnation that was to fall upon ours. He drank the bitter gall to cure in man his sweet indulgence. He was stripped in order to cover the nakedness of our first parents. He was hung upon a tree to wipe out man's sin, which began at the tree.' After hearing this Tiburtius said to his brother: 'Have pity on me! Take me to the man of God so that I may receive purification.' So he was taken to Urban and purified, and subsequently he often saw the angels of God, and instantly obtained whatever he asked for in his prayers.

Valerian and Tiburtius devoted themselves to works of charity, and saw to it that the saints put to death by the prefect Almachius received proper burial. Almachius summoned the brothers and demanded to know why they were burying condemned criminals. Tiburtius answered him: 'Would that we were the slaves of these men you call "condemned"! They spurned what seems to be, and is not, and found what cannot be seen to be, but is.' 'And what,' the prefect asked, 'is that?' 'What seems to be real and is not,' Tiburtius replied, 'is everything in this world, which is what leads man to extinction. What cannot be seen, but is, is the life of the righteous and the punishment of the wicked.' 'In my opinion,' the prefect said, 'you are out of your mind!' He then had Valerian brought forward and said to him: 'Since your brother is not sane, perhaps you will give me a sensible answer. You are obviously utterly deluded: you renounce all pleasures and strive after everything that is the enemy of pleasure.' Valerian answered this by saying that in wintertime he had seen idle bystanders laugh at farm workers and ridicule them, but in summer, when the time came to harvest the glorious fruits of their labours, those who had been thought stupid were celebrating, and those who had seemed so smart began to feel sorry for themselves. 'In the same way,' he continued, 'we, too, suffer shame and hardship now, but in the future we shall receive glory and our eternal reward. Whereas you who take your fleeting pleasures now, in future will find only eternal grief.' The prefect retorted: 'You mean that we, who are all-powerful princes, face eternal grief, and you, the lowest of the low, will have joy without end?' Valerian answered: 'You are no princes, you are insignificant little men, born in our time and soon to die, and then you will have more to account for before God than all the rest of us put together.' The prefect exclaimed: 'Why do we waste time bandying words? Offer libations to the gods and you can leave here unharmed!' The saints answered: 'We offer sacrifice every day to the true God.' 'What is his name?' demanded the prefect. 'You could never discover his name,' Valerian told him, 'if you had wings and could fly!' 'So Jupiter is not the name of this god?' asked the prefect. 'Jupiter,' Valerian retorted, 'is the name of a murderer and adulterer.' 'So the whole world is in error,' Almachius sneered, 'and you and your brother alone know the true God!' Valerian replied: 'We are not alone. Countless numbers have accepted this holy doctrine.' The saints were now handed over to the custody of Maximus, who made the following appeal to them: 'Noble flower of Roman youth!

Most loving brothers! How can you hasten to your deaths like this as if to some banquet?' 'If you promise to believe,' Valerian told him, 'you will see our souls in glory after we die.' 'If that should happen,' Maximus said, 'may I be blasted by a thunderbolt if I do not believe in this one and only God you adore!' What followed was that Maximus and his entire household and all the executioners were converted and baptized by Urban, who visited them in secret.

As night ended and the new day dawned, Cecilia came to Maximus's house and cried aloud: 'Up, soldiers of Christ! Cast off the works of darkness and put on the armour of light!' The brothers were then led to the fourth milestone from the city and ordered to sacrifice before the statue of Jupiter, and when they refused, they were both beheaded. Maximus swore that at the hour of their martyrdom he saw shining angels and the brothers' souls going from them like virgins from a nuptial chamber, and the angels carrying them in their bosoms to heaven.

When Almachius heard that Maximus had become a Christian, he had him scourged to death with leaded thongs. St Cecilia buried his body alongside those of Valerian and Tiburtius. Almachius now started proceedings to sequestrate the property of the two brothers. He had Cecilia, as Valerian's wife, brought before him, and ordered her either to sacrifice to the idols or to be sentenced to death. The men who had arrested her urged her to sacrifice, and wept bitterly at the thought of such a lovely and well-born young girl going willingly to her death. But she said to them: 'Gentlemen, I am not losing my youth, but exchanging it, giving clay for gold, a hovel for a mansion, a dingy back street for a resplendent courtyard! If someone offered you gold for a copper, would you not quickly accept it? And whatever a man gives him, God repays a hundredfold! Do you believe what I am telling you?' They replied: 'We believe that Christ must be the true God, if he has a handmaid such as you.' So Cecilia summoned Bishop Urban and more than four hundred people were baptized.

Almachius now had Cecilia brought before him a second time and asked her: 'What is the truth about you?' 'I am free-born,' she replied, 'and of noble family.' 'I am asking about your religion,' Almachius said. 'Then you have begun badly,' Cecilia told him. 'Your question was ambiguous.' 'What prompts you to give such a brazen answer?' Almachius demanded. 'A clear conscience and a sincere faith,' came the reply. 'Do you not understand,' Almachius asked her, 'how powerful I am?' Cecilia retorted: 'Your power is a balloon full of air. Prick it and it crumples, the whole thing collapses and comes to nothing.' 'You began by insulting me,' Almachius stormed, 'and you continue to insult me!' 'No,' Cecilia objected. 'You cannot complain of insults when what is said is the truth. Either tell me what I have said that is untrue, or else admit that you are in the wrong. We who know the holy name of God can never deny it, and it is better to die happy than to live on in unhappiness.' 'Why do you speak with such arrogance?' Almachius asked. 'It is not arrogance you hear,' Cecilia told him, 'but my unshakeable resolve.' 'You poor girl,' he said, 'do you not know that I have absolute power, the power to give life or to take it?' Cecilia replied: 'Now I have proof that you are a liar: it is public knowledge that you can take life from the living, but you cannot give life to the dead. You are therefore a minister of death, not of life.' 'Give up this silliness,' Almachius insisted, 'and sacrifice to the gods!' 'Something must be wrong with your eyes,' Cecilia retorted. 'What you call gods, all the rest of us can see are no more than blocks of stone. Just reach out and touch them, and let your hand teach you what your eyes cannot see!'

Exasperated, Almachius had Cecilia taken back to her house, and there ordered her to be plunged in a boiling bath and kept there all night and all day. But Cecilia lay back in the bath as if cooling herself on a hot day, and did not even perspire. When Almachius was informed of this, he gave the order for her to be beheaded in her bath. Her executioner struck her on the neck three times without being able to cut off her head, and, since there was a law saying that the victim should not receive more than three blows, he went off covered in blood and left her only half-dead. Cecilia survived three days, during which she gave all her possessions to the poor and commended all those she had converted to Bishop Urban. 'I prayed for a delay of three days,' she told him, 'so that I could commend these souls to your holiness, and ask you to consecrate my house as a church.'

St Urban laid her body to rest in a place where bishops were buried, then consecrated her house as a church, as she had requested. Cecilia suffered around AD 223, in the time of Emperor Alexander, though elsewhere we read that she suffered in the reign of Marcus Aurelius, who was emperor in about AD 220.

68

ST CLEMENT

23 November

Clement, the bishop, came of noble Roman stock. His father's name was Faustinianus, his mother's Macidiana, and he had two brothers, Faustinus and Faustus. Now his mother Macidiana was a woman of outstanding beauty, and her husband's brother burnt with desire for her. Every day he forced his attentions on her, and while she gave him not the slightest encouragement, she was afraid to tell her husband about it, in case it started a feud between the two brothers. So she had the idea of going abroad for a while, to give her brother-in-law time to forget his unlawful passion, which her presence merely inflamed. In order to obtain her husband's consent she cleverly pretended that she had had a dream, which she described to her husband as follows: 'In this dream a man came to me and told me to take the twins, Faustinus and Faustus, and leave the city at once, and to stay away until he ordered me to return. And if I did not do this, I would die, and my children with me.'

When her husband heard this he was deeply disturbed, so he packed his wife and the twin boys off to Athens with a large retinue of servants, intending that she should live and have his sons educated there. (Clement, however, his youngest son, who was only five years old, he kept with him for company.) So Macidiana and her two sons set sail, but one night their ship was wrecked, and she was separated from her children and cast ashore on a rocky island. Convinced that her two sons had been drowned, she was so crazed with grief that she would have thrown herself into the sea, had she not nursed the hope that she might at least recover their bodies. But when she finally realized she was not going to find them either dead or alive, she began to scream and howl, she tore her hands with her teeth, and refused to let anyone comfort her. Many of the local women came and told her of their own misfortunes, but nothing they said could console her. Then one of them told her that her husband had been a sailor and had been lost at sea while still only a youth, and that because of her love for him she had refused to marry again. Macidiana drew some comfort from this, and went to live with the woman, earning her living day by day with her handiwork. But she had inflicted such serious damage on her hands with her teeth that soon they lost all feeling and movement and she was no longer able to work with them. Then the woman who had taken her in became paralysed and bedridden, and Macidiana was compelled to beg, and she and her friend had to live off whatever she could manage to find.

When a year had passed since his wife and two sons had left home, Faustinianus sent messengers to Athens to find where they lived and to let him know how they were. But these messengers never returned. So he sent more messengers, and when they came back and reported that they had not been able to find any trace of his family, he finally left his son Clement in the care of tutors and boarded ship to look for his wife and children himself. But he, too, never came back.

So Clement was left an orphan, and for twenty years he was unable to unearth a single clue as to the disappearance of his father or mother or brothers. Clement devoted himself to the liberal arts and became a highly accomplished philosopher. But what he most fervently desired and most assiduously sought to discover was a way of proving the immortality of the soul. To this end he constantly attended the schools of the philosophers, and there he was cheered when he seemed to find proof that the soul was immortal and saddened whenever the conclusion was that it was mortal. Finally St Barnabas came to Rome and preached the faith of Christ. The philosophers treated him as a madman and an idiot and mocked him. Then one of their number (according to some authorities, this was none other than Clement), who had at first laughed at him like the rest and poured scorn on his preaching, tried to make a fool of Barnabas by asking him the following questions: 'The gnat is a tiny creature: how is it that it has six feet and six wings, while the elephant, which is an enormous animal, has no wings and only four feet?' 'You fool!' Barnabas replied. 'I could easily answer your question, and would, if you were asking it in order to learn the truth. But it would be absurd to talk to people like you about creatures, when you know nothing about the One who created them. You do not know the Creator, so inevitably you are in error about his creatures.' This remark went straight to the heart of the philosopher Clement; so much so that, after learning about the Christian faith from Barnabas, he hurried off to Judaea to see St Peter. Peter instructed him fully in the faith of Christ and gave him conclusive proof of the soul's immortality.

It was at this time that Aquila and Nicetas, the disciples of Simon the Magician, finally saw through the deceptions he practised, abandoned him and took refuge with St Peter and became his disciples.

Peter questioned Clement about his family and Clement told him all he knew about his mother and brothers and his father, adding that he believed his mother and brothers had been lost at sea and that his father had died, either of grief or, like the others, in a shipwreck. When he heard Clement's tale, Peter could not refrain from weeping.

Then one day Peter went with his disciples to Antandros, and from there happened to put in at the island, six miles off, where Macidiana, Clement's mother, was now living. Now on this island stood some gigantic, shimmering columns, and Peter and his companions were admiring them when a beggar-woman came by, and Peter remonstrated with her for not preferring to earn a living with her hands. 'They only look like hands, sir,' she explained. 'But I have bitten them so badly that there is no feeling left in them at all. I wish to heaven I had thrown myself into the sea and put an end to my miserable existence!' 'What are you saying?' Peter demanded. 'Do you not know that the souls of those who take their own lives are severely punished?' She replied: 'Oh, if only I could be sure that souls live on after death! I would gladly kill myself just to see my dead children again, if it were only for an hour!' Peter asked her why she was so unhappy and she told him the whole story. 'We have a young man with us,' he told her, 'named Clement, and he says that everything you have told me happened to his own mother and brothers.' This news was too much for Macidiana, who fainted with the shock and fell to the ground. When she came to herself again, she told Peter tearfully: 'I am the young man's mother!' She threw herself at Peter's feet and begged him to let her see her son as soon as possible. 'When you see him,' Peter cautioned her, 'do not give yourself away at once: wait until we have set sail and our ship is clear of the island.' She promised to do as he said, and Peter took her hand and led her to the ship where Clement was waiting. When Clement saw Peter holding a woman by the hand, he began to laugh. But as soon as Macidiana came face to face with her son, she could contain herself no longer and threw herself at once into his arms, and began to shower kisses on him. Thinking the woman must be insane, Clement indignantly pushed her away and indicated to Peter his intense annoyance. But Peter said: 'What are you doing, Clement, my son? Do not reject your own mother!' At these words, Clement burst into tears and fell to the ground beside the woman, and slowly recognized her as his mother. Then, at Peter's command, they fetched the woman who had taken in Macidiana, and he cured her paralysis instantly. Next, Macidiana asked Clement about his father. 'He went off to look for you,' he replied, 'and never came back.' Hearing this, she merely sighed, the great joy she felt at finding her son again more than compensating for her other sorrows.

While all this was going on, Nicetas and Aquila had not been present; but now they came back and, seeing a woman with Peter, they asked who she was. 'It is my mother!' Clement told them. 'God has given her back to me, with the help of Peter, my master.' Peter then told them the whole story, and when Nicetas and Aquila heard it, they jumped suddenly to their feet in utter amazement. 'Great God in heaven!' they cried. 'Is what we have just heard true or is it all a dream?' 'My sons,' Peter assured them, 'we are all quite sane. It is the truth.' Rubbing their eyes in disbelief, the two young men exclaimed: 'We are Faustinus and Faustus! Our mother thought we were drowned at sea!' And they rushed into their mother's arms and covered her with kisses. 'What can this mean?' she asked. 'They are your sons Faustinus and Faustus,' Peter repeated, 'the sons you thought were lost at sea.' When Macidiana took this in she was delirious with joy and swooned. Then, when she came to, she said: 'My dearest sons, please tell me how you escaped.' 'When our ship broke apart,' they told her, 'we held on to a piece of wood until some pirates came upon us and took us on board their ship. They gave us different names and then sold us to a respectable widow whose name was Justina. She treated us as her own sons and made sure we had a proper education in the liberal arts. Finally we studied philosophy and became the disciples of a man called Simon Magus, who had been educated with us. But eventually we realized he was a charlatan and left him once and for all, and, through the mediation of Zacheus, became Peter's disciples.'

Next day Peter took the three brothers, Clement, Aquila and Nicetas, and retired to a secluded spot to pray. But an old man accosted them; though shabbily dressed, his bearing was dignified and he said: 'I pity you, brothers. In my opinion, however pious your intentions, you are making a grave mistake. There is no God, this worship of yours is meaningless, and there is no such thing as providence. Everything is governed by chance and the planets that influence your birth. I have proved all this for myself beyond doubt, for my knowledge of astrology is unsurpassed. So do not deceive yourselves: whether you pray or not, your destiny is predetermined by the stars.'

While the old man was speaking, Clement considered him closely and was suddenly struck by the thought that he had seen him somewhere before. At Peter's command the three brothers engaged in lengthy argument with him, and by clear reasoning succeeded in proving the existence of providence. In the course of the argument they addressed the old man, out of respect, as 'father', until Aquila suddenly objected: 'Why must we call him "father",' he asked, 'when one of our commandments is that we call no one on earth by that name?' He then turned to the old man and said: 'Do not be offended, father, if I take exception to my brothers calling you "father", for we have a commandment not to call anyone by that name.' When Aquila said this, everyone present burst out laughing, including the old man and Peter, and when Aquila asked them why, Clement told him: 'Because you are doing just what you criticized the rest of us for doing – you called him "father"!' But Aquila disputed the matter: 'Honestly,' he said, 'if I did, I was not aware of it.' Finally, when the debate about providence came to an end, the old man commented: 'I would indeed believe in a providence, but my conscience forbids me to subscribe to such a belief. I know my own horoscope and that of my wife, and I know that everything the stars foretold for each of us came true. If I tell you the aspects of the planets at my wife's birth, you will see with what accuracy they determined her future life. The day she was born, Mars and Venus were over the centre, the moon in descent in the house of Mars and on the boundaries of Saturn. Now this configuration makes women adulteresses, makes them fall in love with servants, travel to foreign parts, and die a watery death. And that is just what happened. She fell in love with one of her servants, but, fearing the disgrace that would ensue if she were found out, she ran away with him and was lost at sea. In fact, as my own brother told me, she first fell in love with him, but when he would have none of it, she turned to her slave to satisfy her lust. But she cannot be blamed for her behaviour: it was the stars that made her do what she did.' He then told them of the dream she had made up, and how she and her children had perished in a shipwreck on their way to Athens. His sons longed to throw themselves into his arms and tell him everything, but Peter held them back. 'Keep quiet,' he told them, 'until I say otherwise.' Then he said to the old man: 'If today I restore your wife to you, as chaste as the day you married her, and your three sons with her, will you believe that astrology is nonsense?' 'You cannot possibly do as you say,' the old man replied. 'Nothing can happen unless it is in the stars.' 'Well,' Peter answered, 'this is your son Clement, and here are your twin sons Faustinus and Faustus.' The old man's limbs gave way: he collapsed in a faint and his sons rushed to clasp him to them, fearful that his breathing had stopped. But at length he came to and heard their account of all that had happened. Then suddenly his wife appeared and cried tearfully: 'Where is my husband and lord?' And she kept repeating this as if she had lost her mind, until the old man ran to her, weeping uncontrollably, and crushed her in his arms.

Then, as they all stood there together, a man came up with news that Apio and Ambio, two great friends of Faustinianus, were staying as guests of Simon Magus. Faustinianus was overjoyed to hear of their arrival and went off to visit them. No sooner had he gone than a second messenger came with news that one of Caesar's agents had arrived in Antioch with orders to hunt down all sorcerers and put them to death. So Simon Magus, out of hatred for Faustinianus's two sons, who had turned their backs on him, imposed his own likeness on their father's face, so that everyone would think he was not Faustinianus, but Simon Magus, and this way he, and not Simon, would be arrested and executed by Caesar's men. Simon himself then left the area. When Faustinianus returned to Peter and his sons, the latter were horrified to hear someone with Simon's face speaking with their father's voice. Peter alone was able to see his real face, and when his sons and wife ran from him and hurled abuse at him, he called out: 'Why are you abusing your own father? Why are you running from him?' They told him it was because he had the face of Simon the Sorcerer. (Simon had in fact concocted an unguent, which he had smeared on Faustinianus's face and magically impressed his own features on him.) Faustinianus was distraught. 'How wretched can a man be?' he moaned. 'In one day I am reunited with my wife and sons, yet I cannot celebrate my happiness with them!' His wife tore her hair, and his sons wept bitterly.

Now while Simon Magus was in Antioch, he had slandered Peter unceasingly, calling him a fiendish sorcerer and a murderer, and in the end he had roused the people to such a pitch of animosity against him that they would have torn him apart with their teeth. So Peter said to Faustinianus: 'Since you look like Simon, go to Antioch and defend me in front of the people there: pretend you are Simon and retract everything Simon has said about me. Then I shall come to Antioch myself and remove this strange mask you are wearing, and give you back your own face for everyone to see.' (But the idea that blessed Peter ordered Faustinianus to lie is simply inconceivable: God does not need humans to lie. So Clement's *Itinerarium*, where this story is found, must be apocryphal, and, whatever some may think, is not to be trusted in points of detail. On the other hand, if one considers Peter's words carefully, it can be argued that he did not tell Faustinianus to say that he was Simon Magus, but to let the people see his counterfeit face and, speaking as if he were Simon, to praise Peter and retract the slanderous things Simon had been saying about him. And when Faustinianus said he was Simon, he did not mean that he was really Simon, but outwardly Simon. So when he said: 'I, Simon, etc.' (see below), it should be taken to mean: 'I who seem to all appearances to be Simon.' He was Simon only in the sense that everyone thought he was Simon.) So Faustinianus, Clement's father, went off to Antioch, called the people together and told them: 'I, Simon, have an announcement to make: I confess to you that everything I said about Peter was untrue. Not only is he not a liar or a sorcerer, but he was sent for the salvation of the world. So if I ever say anything else against him, banish me as a liar and a sorcerer myself! I am now doing penance because I admit that I have slandered him. I warn you, therefore, to believe Peter: if you do not, you and your city are doomed.'

When Faustinianus had carried out all Peter's commands and won the people over to his side again, Peter joined him, said a prayer over him, and removed from him every trace of resemblance to Simon. The people of Antioch welcomed the apostle warmly and with great respect, and enthroned him as their bishop. When news of this reached Simon, he hurried back to Antioch and summoned a meeting of the people. 'I am amazed,' he told them, 'that after I had given you all the rules of life you needed, and warned you against Peter and his lies, you have not only listened to him, but actually elected him as your bishop.' At this they all rounded on him in fury. 'We think you are an absolute monster!' they cried. 'A couple of days ago you were saying how sorry you were to have wronged Peter. Now you seem bent on ruining us all – yourself and us with you!' And they all fell on him, and without further ado threw him ignominiously out of the city. This episode is included by Clement in his autobiography.

After all this Peter went on to Rome and, knowing that he would soon be martyred, he ordained Clement to be bishop after him. But when the prince of the apostles died, Clement showed great foresight. Anticipating the possibility that some later pope might adopt Peter's precedent and seek to appoint his own successor in the Church, thereby turning the sanctuary of God into an hereditary possession, he let first Linus, and then Cletus, succeed to the papacy before him. After them Clement was elected and made to govern the Church, and he proved such a paragon of virtue that he was as popular with Jews and Gentiles as he was with the whole of

Christendom. He had a list of the names of all poor people in each of the provinces, and would not permit any he had cleansed in the waters of holy baptism to be reduced to begging in public.

It was from Clement's own hands that the virgin Domitilla, a niece of the emperor Domitian, took the sacred veil. He also converted Theodora, the wife of the emperor's friend Sisinnius. Theodora promised to live in chastity for the rest of her life, and her husband, in a fit of jealousy, followed his wife into the church one day without her knowing, to find out why she went there so often. Inside, St Clement was uttering a prayer, and as the people responded 'Amen' Sisinnius was instantly struck blind and deaf. 'Quick! Get me out of here!' he told his servants. 'Take me outside!' But his servants took him on a complete circuit of the church without managing to find any doors. Theodora noticed them wandering about, but at first she held back from them, thinking her husband would recognize her. Then, after a time, she asked them what was going on and they told her: 'Our master wanted to see and hear what was not permitted, and he has been struck blind and deaf.' Theodora immediately prayed, asking God to let her husband find his way outside, then said to the servants: 'Go now, and take your master home.' When they had gone, she told St Clement what had happened. At her request St Clement at once went to her husband and found him with his eyes wide open, but seeing and hearing absolutely nothing. So Clement said a prayer for him, and his sight and hearing were restored. But when Sisinnius made out Clement standing next to his wife, he was beside himself with rage, suspecting that he was the victim of some sorcery or other, and ordered his servants to seize Clement. 'He used magic to blind me,' he said, 'so that he could come visiting my wife!' He told them to tie Clement up and then drag him away. But though they thought, as did Sisinnius himself, that they were tying up Clement and his clerics and dragging them about, in fact, all they did was to pass their ropes round some pillars and blocks of stone. Clement said to Sisinnius: 'If you can honour blocks of stone as gods, you deserve no better than to drag them about after you.' Sisinnius still thought he had Clement tied up and told him: 'I shall have you killed!' But Clement left, asking Theodora to keep praying until the Lord visited her husband. While she prayed, the apostle Peter appeared to her and said: 'Through you, your husband shall be saved, in accordance with the teaching of my brother Paul, who said that "the unbelieving husband shall be saved by his wife's faith"' [1 Cor. 7:14]. With these words Peter disappeared. That moment Sisinnius called his wife and begged her to pray for him and to ask Clement to return. Clement duly arrived, instructed Sisinnius in the faith and baptized him together with three hundred and thirteen of his household.

Through this Sisinnius many noblemen and friends of the emperor Nerva came to believe in the Lord. As a result, the official who controlled the temple funds bribed a large number of people to stir the mob to violence against St Clement. But Mamertinus, the urban prefect, could not tolerate such a disturbance, and had Clement brought before him. He cautioned him and tried to get him to see his point of view, but Clement replied: 'I wish you would listen to reason. If a pack of dogs attacks us, snarling and threatening to tear us to pieces, they cannot alter the fact that we are rational beings and they are irrational dogs. A riot started by ignorant men has nothing sound or true about it.'

Mamertinus wrote to the emperor Trajan about Clement, and in reply received the order that Clement must either offer sacrifice or be sent into exile across the Black Sea to the desert that lay in the vicinity of the city of Chersonesus. The prefect wept as he said to Clement: 'May this God of yours whom you worship with such purity of heart grant you his aid!' Mamertinus then gave him a ship and provided him with everything he needed, and many clerics and lay people followed Clement into exile.

During the voyage, Clement landed on an island where he found more than two thousand Christians who had been condemned to quarry marble there, and the moment they saw St Clement, they wept their hearts out. Clement consoled them, telling them: 'Through no merits of my own, the Lord has sent me to you to share in your crown of martyrdom.' When they told him that they had to carry water on their backs from a place six miles away, he said: 'Let us all pray to our Lord Jesus Christ and ask him to reveal to his followers a spring and streams of water here, in this very spot; that he who, when the rock was struck in the desert of Sinai, made water flow from it in abundance, may grant us a spring of water here and give us cause to be grateful for his goodness.' After he had prayed, he looked around him this way and that, until he saw a lamb with its right foot raised, as if it were indicating a certain spot on the ground. Clement, realizing that this was the Lord Jesus Christ, and that he alone could see him, hurried towards the spot. 'Here!' he cried to his companions. 'In the name of the Father and of the Son and of the Holy Spirit, dig here!' But because they could not see the lamb and did not know where to dig, Clement seized a stick and aimed a light blow at the earth beneath the lamb's upraised foot. At once a stream of water gushed out in such floods that it soon swelled to the size of a river. Then, amid universal jubilation, St Clement cried: 'The stream of the river makes glad the city of God! [Psalm 45(46):4].' When news of this miracle spread, people crowded to the spot and on one day more than five hundred received baptism at Clement's hands. The Christians then tore down all the pagan temples through the region and in the space of a single year built seventy-five churches.

Three years later the emperor Trajan, whose reign began in AD 106, was informed about all this and dispatched one of his generals to restore order. But the general, finding that all the Christians there were ready to die for their faith, backed down before their vast numbers, and punished their leader alone. He threw Clement into the sea with an anchor tied to his neck, saying as he did so: 'Now the Christians will not be able to worship him as a God!' Afterwards a vast crowd of the faithful gathered on the seashore and Cornelius and Phoebus, who were disciples of Clement, told them all to pray that the Lord would reveal to them the body of his martyr. Instantly the sea drew back three miles, and everyone walked out over the dry sands until they found a miniature temple, all of marble, which God had made ready, and inside, in a coffin, the body of St Clement with the anchor by his side . . .

69

ST CATHERINE

25 November

Catherine, the daughter of King Costus, had a thorough education in all the liberal arts. Now when Emperor Maxentius issued a decree that everyone, rich and poor alike, should come to Alexandria to offer sacrifice to the idols and was putting to death any Christians who refused to do so, Catherine was eighteen years old. One day she happened to be alone in her father's palace, surrounded by all her riches and servants, when she heard the cries of animals and singing and cheering, and she quickly sent a servant to investigate. When she learnt what was going on, she took some of her servants with her and, arming herself with the sign of the cross, went to witness the spectacle. There she saw many Christians giving way to their fear of death and offering sacrifice. This pierced her to the quick, and she boldly confronted the emperor. 'Caesar,' she said, 'your high rank demands, and reason dictates, that I pay my respects to you, and so I would if you would only acknowledge the Creator of the heavens and renounce the worship of idols.' Then, standing at the door of the temple, she reasoned at length with the emperor, using every sort of argument, syllogistic, allegorical, metaphorical, logical and transcendental. Then, reverting to everyday language, she said: 'I have put all these arguments to you with care, as to a man of intelligence; but tell me, why have you wasted your time gathering all these people together to worship these stupid idols? You admire this temple, which was built by the hands of workmen; you admire precious ornaments that in time will be blown like dust before the wind. You ought rather to wonder at the heavens and the earth, the sea and all that is in them; wonder at the ornaments of heaven, the sun, the moon and the stars, wonder at their constant labour on our behalf; how, since the beginning of the world, they have run both night and day to the west and then returned to the east, yet are never wearied, nor will be till its end. Consider all this, then ask yourself who is mightier than they. And when he grants you that knowledge and you know him, and you can find no one that is his equal,

worship him, glorify him, for he is the God of Gods and Lord of Lords!'
Catherine then spoke at length and with such great wisdom on the incarnation
of the Son of God that the emperor was dumbfounded and unable to reply
to her. He finally recovered his composure and said: 'Young lady, let me
please finish this sacrifice, and then I shall give you my reply.' He then had
her taken to his palace and kept under close guard. He was struck not only
by the depth of her learning, but also by her beauty; for Catherine was
exquisitely lovely, a girl of truly exceptional beauty, and loved and admired
by everyone.

When he returned to the palace, the emperor said to Catherine: 'I have
heard your eloquence and admired your learning, but I was too busy
sacrificing to the gods to understand all you said fully. So now let us begin
again. First, tell me about your family.' Catherine replied: 'Scripture says:
"Speak not of yourself, either in praise or dispraise: for only fools do so,
driven by thoughts of empty glory." But I will tell you of my parentage, not
out of pride, but in all humility. I am Catherine, only daughter of King
Costus, and though I was born in the purple and received a good education
in the liberal arts, I have renounced everything and taken refuge in the Lord
Jesus Christ. The gods you worship can help neither you nor anyone else.
How I pity the poor wretches who worship idols! When they call on them
in time of need, they are not there; in tribulation they cannot succour them;
in times of danger they cannot defend them.' 'If it really is as you say,' the
emperor replied, 'then the whole world is in error, and you alone are speaking
the truth! But nothing you have said is corroborated by more than two or
three witnesses, so even if you were an angel or some heavenly power, no
one would be inclined to believe you – and still less so since clearly you are
just an insignificant young girl.' Catherine replied: 'I beg you, Caesar, do not
allow your anger to get the better of you. There is no room for destructive
passion in a wise man's soul. As the poet says: "Let your mind govern you,
and you will be a king; but let your body, and you will be a slave."' 'I see
you are out to entangle me in a web of damnable sophistry,' the emperor
said, 'and meanwhile you are trying to draw out the argument by quoting
the philosophers.' Then, realizing that he was unable to match Catherine's
wisdom, he secretly wrote to all the most celebrated scholars and orators,
ordering them to come immediately to the governor's residence in Alexandria,
and promising them lavish rewards if they could defeat this disputatious
young lady with their arguments. At his command fifty orators converged
on Alexandria from the various provinces, men unsurpassed in every branch

of human knowledge, and when they asked why they had been summoned from such remote parts of the empire, Maxentius told them: 'There is a girl here whose reasoning and intelligence are beyond compare. She refutes all the wise men, and declares that all our gods are demons! If you triumph over her, you can go back home with any honour you care to name.' This provoked one of the orators to reply indignantly: 'How very sensible of the emperor to summon all his greatest scholars from the furthest end of the earth because of some trivial disagreement with a young girl, when the least of our pupils could have refuted her without the slightest trouble!' The emperor answered: 'I could, of course, have used force to make her offer sacrifice, or tortured her to death, but I thought it would be better if you refuted her with your arguments.' 'Have the girl brought before us,' they replied. 'When she is forced to see how rash she has been, she will realize that she has never met men of real learning before.'

When Catherine was told about the ordeal which faced her, she put herself wholly in God's hands, and suddenly an angel of the Lord appeared at her side and exhorted her to be steadfast, telling her not only that she could never be vanquished by her adversaries, but also that she would convert them and set them on the path to martyrdom. Then she was taken before the orators. 'What sort of justice is this?' she asked the emperor. 'You match fifty orators against one girl, and while you promise them lavish rewards if they defeat me, you force me to fight without offering me any hope of reward. No matter: my reward will be the Lord Jesus Christ, who is the hope and crown of those who fight for him.'

The orators began by denying that God could become man or suffer, but Catherine showed that this had been predicted even by the pagans. For Plato describes God as a 'mutilated sphere'.[1] The Sibyl, too, says: 'Happy the god who hangs from a high tree!' The young girl debated with the orators in the most learned fashion and refuted them with the clearest of proofs, until they were quite dumbfounded: they could find nothing to say, and they stood there speechless. Their defeat absolutely infuriated the emperor, and he began to hurl abuse at them and ask how they could all let themselves be put to shame so ignominiously by one young girl. Then one of them, their appointed spokesman, answered him as follows: 'Caesar, no one has ever before been able to face us in argument without being defeated instantly. But the spirit of God is speaking in this girl, and her words have made such an impression on us that we have no idea what to say against Christ; either that or we are too frightened to speak at all! Consequently, Caesar, we solemnly declare that, unless you can produce stronger arguments in support of the gods we have worshipped hitherto, we are all converted to Christ.' At this the emperor flew into a wild rage and ordered them all to be burnt in the centre of the city; but Catherine gave them words of encouragement, inspired them to face their martyrdom with resolution, and carefully instructed them in the faith. When they bemoaned the fact that they were going to their deaths without baptism, she replied: 'You need have no fear. The shedding of your blood will count as your baptism, as it will be your crown.' The orators then armed themselves with the sign of the cross and were thrown into the flames, and so rendered up their souls to the Lord. But neither their hair nor their clothing was so much as touched by the fire. Their bodies were duly buried by the Christians.

After this the tyrant spoke to Catherine again: 'O noble Catherine, have regard for your youth! You shall live in my palace and be second only to my queen! I will set up your statue in the centre of the city and the whole world shall worship you as a goddess!' Catherine retorted: 'Stop saying such things. It is wicked even to think them. I have given myself as a bride to Christ. He is my glory; he is my love; he is my delight and joy. Neither flattery nor torture can turn me from his love.' This made the emperor fly into another rage: he ordered her to be stripped, scourged with scorpions, thrown into a pitch-black dungeon, and left there with nothing to eat for a period of twelve days. For certain pressing reasons the emperor now had to leave Alexandria, and during his absence the queen, smitten with love for the young Catherine, hurried to her cell under cover of darkness with the captain of the imperial guard, a man called Porphyrius. When she went in, the room was flooded with indescribable brilliance and she saw angels soothing the young girl's wounds with unguents. Catherine began at once to preach to her of the joys of eternity and, when she had converted her to the faith, she predicted that she would win the crown of martyrdom. So they continued talking until deep in the night. Porphyrius, after hearing all that had transpired, fell at Catherine's feet and, along with two hundred of his men, received the faith of Christ. And throughout the whole twelve-day period during which the tyrant had decreed that Catherine should be starved, Christ sent a white dove down from heaven to refresh her with celestial food. Then the Lord appeared to her amid a throng of angels and virgins and said: 'My daughter, you see before you your Maker, for whose name you have undergone this painful trial. Be steadfast, for I am with you.'

As soon as the emperor returned, he had Catherine brought before him again. He expected her to be in great distress after such a long fast, but when he found her even more radiant than before, he could only think that someone must have been feeding her during her imprisonment. Incensed, he ordered her guards to be put to the torture. But Catherine told him: 'I received the food from no man. It was Christ who fed me through an angel.' 'Please take to heart what I am going to say,' the emperor told her, 'and do not fob me off with any more ambiguous answers. I do not wish to have you as my servant: you will reign as a queen in my realm, a powerful, highly honoured and glorious queen.' 'Now will you please hear me?' Catherine replied. 'Pay careful attention to what I am asking you and give me your honest opinion. Whom should I choose: a king who is powerful, immortal, glorious and magnificent; or one who is weak, mortal, ignoble and repellent?' Indignantly the emperor replied: 'Make your choice: either sacrifice and live or submit to excruciating torture and die!' 'Put me to whatever torments you can devise!' Catherine told him. 'Why waste time? I long only to offer my flesh and blood to Christ, as he offered himself for me. He is my God, my lover, my shepherd and my only spouse.'

Now one of the emperor's captains suggested the following plan to his furious master: in two or three days he could have four wheels made – wheels with iron saws and razor-sharp nails projecting from their rims – and he could tear the girl into shreds with this ghastly device, and, by making an example of her, put fear into the hearts of all the other Christians. It was decided that two of these wheels should turn in one direction and the other two in the opposite direction, so that their combined action, as they drove down on her from above and came up at her from below, would first mangle her flesh and then tear it in shreds. But on the day appointed for her execution, the holy virgin prayed to the Lord to destroy the machine, both for the glory of his name and for the conversion of all the people who were present. At once an angel of the Lord struck the device and smashed it with such violent force that four thousand pagans were killed.

At this point the queen, who had been watching everything from a concealed position above, suddenly came down and bitterly condemned the emperor for his barbarous cruelty. This enraged him, and when she refused to offer sacrifice, he ordered that she should have her breasts torn off and then be beheaded. As she was led away to her martyrdom, she asked Catherine to pray for her. Catherine answered: 'Do not be afraid, my lady, so beloved of God! Today you will exchange a transitory kingdom for one that is everlasting, and a mortal spouse for one who is immortal.' This inspired the queen with such courage that she actually urged the executioners not to delay in carrying out their orders. They then led her outside the city, tore off her breasts with iron lances, and then cut off her head. Porphyrius removed her body and gave it burial.

Next day, when a search was made for the queen's body, it was nowhere to be found. The tyrant had a succession of innocent people dragged off to their deaths until Porphyrius thrust himself forward and cried: 'I am the one who buried the handmaid of Christ, and I, too, have received the Christian faith!' Maxentius nearly went out of his mind. With a roar of rage he exclaimed: 'Woe is me! Who is more wretched than I? Now Porphyrius, my closest, dearest friend, my comfort in every trial and tribulation – even Porphyrius has been led astray!' When he broke the news to the imperial guard, they answered without hesitation: 'We, too, are Christians, and we are ready to die for our faith!' The emperor was now delirious with rage. He ordered them all to be decapitated, Porphyrius as well, and their bodies to be thrown to the dogs. Then he summoned Catherine and told her: 'Although you used witchcraft to cause the queen's death, no matter – you can still be the foremost lady in my palace if only you come to your senses. Today, then, you must either offer sacrifice to the gods or lose your head.' She replied: 'Do whatever you wish. You will find me ready to endure whatever I must.' So he passed sentence on her and condemned her to death by beheading.

When she was taken to the place of her execution, Catherine raised her eyes to heaven and prayed: 'O hope and salvation of the faithful, O honour and glory of virgins, Jesus, good king, I beseech you that whoever keeps the memory of my passion or invokes me at the moment of his death, or in any time of need, may be heard in mercy and his prayer granted.' And a voice was heard saying: 'Come, my beloved, my bride! See, heaven's gate is opened to you! And to all who celebrate your martyrdom with devotion, I promise heaven's protection in answer to your prayer.'

When Catherine was beheaded, milk flowed from her body instead of blood, and angels took up her body and carried it from that place to Mount Sinai, a journey of more than twenty days, and there gave it honourable burial. Her bones still give off a constant stream of oil, which heals all bodily infirmities. Catherine suffered under the tyrant Maxentius, or Maximinus, whose reign began around AD 310 . . .

70

ST JAMES THE MUTILATED

27 November

The martyr James, called 'The Mutilated', was of noble birth, but nobler still for his faith. He came from Elape in Persia. James was born of most Christian parents, and his wife, too, was a devout Christian. He was well known to the king of the Persians and was foremost among the nobles of Persia, and in due course he let himself be swayed by the king and his great affection for him and was persuaded to worship the idols. When his mother and wife heard about this, they at once wrote to him, saying: 'In order to gratify a mortal man, you have deserted the one who is the fount of life; to please one who will soon be foul with the stench of decay, you have forsaken the eternal fragrance! You have exchanged truth for falsehood and, by bending to a mortal's will, you have abandoned the judge of the quick and the dead. You must understand therefore that from now on we shall be strangers to you, and shall not live in the same house as you a moment longer.' James wept bitterly when he read the letter. 'If I have estranged my own mother, who gave me birth, and my wife,' he mused to himself, 'how much more must I have estranged my God!' And he plunged into an orgy of self-recrimination for the wrong he had done. Then someone went to the king and told him that James was a Christian. The prince summoned him and said: 'Tell me, are you a Nazarene?' 'Yes,' James answered, 'I am.' 'Then you are a sorcerer,' the prince said. James replied: 'God forbid that I should be any such thing!' The prince threatened James with all kinds of torture, but James told him: 'Your threats do not trouble me; your rage is like the wind blowing over a stone: it quickly passes, I hardly hear it.' 'Do not be foolish,' the prince warned him, 'or you will die a painful death.' 'You ought not to call it "death",' James replied. 'A better name would be "sleep", since after a short while we are permitted to rise again.' 'You should not let the Nazarenes fool you when they tell you death is a sleep,' the prince said, 'because even the mightiest emperors fear it.' James replied: 'We do not fear death because we hope to pass from death to life.'

Then, on the advice of his friends, the king sentenced James to death, and, to strike terror into the hearts of other Christians, it was to be death by dismemberment. Some who heard this wept out of compassion for him, but James told them: 'Do not weep for me. Mourn for yourselves, because I am passing to eternal life, but you are doomed to eternal torments!'

Thereupon the torturers cut off the thumb of his right hand and James cried out: 'Jesus of Nazareth, my deliverer! Accept this branch of the tree of your mercy. Does not the vine-dresser prune away the smaller branches so the vine can grow stronger and be crowned with more abundant fruit?' One of them said to him: 'If you agree to sacrifice, I will spare you and bring you ointment to heal your wound.' 'Have you never looked at a vine stock?' James said. 'The little tendrils are cut away, and when the earth warms up in due course, each of the knots that is left by the pruning knife puts forth a new shoot. So, if a vine needs pruning to increase its yield later in the season, how much greater is the need of the Christian, who is grafted on to Christ, the true vine!' The torturer then stepped forward and cut off his right forefinger. Blessed James said: 'Accept these two branches, O Lord, that your right hand has planted.' Then a third finger was cut off. James said: 'I will bless the Father and the Son and the Holy Spirit. I am now freed from a threefold temptation, and with the three youths rescued from the fiery furnace, I will praise you, O Lord, and, in company with the choir of martyrs, I will sing hymns to your holy name, O Christ!' A fourth finger was cut off. 'Protector of the sons of Israel,' James said, 'you whose greatness was foretold in Jacob's fourth blessing, accept from your servant the offering of his fourth finger, blessed as in Juda.' When the fifth finger was cut off, he cried: 'My joy is complete!' The torturers urged him to relent. 'Spare yourself now,' they said, 'or you may soon be dead. And do not worry that you have lost a hand: there are many one-handed men who have all the riches and honours that they could wish.' Blessed James answered them: 'When shepherds shear their sheep, do they take the wool only from the right side and forget the left? And if a dumb animal like a sheep is ready to lose his whole fleece, how could a rational being, such as I, object to losing his life for God?' So the cruel butchers set to and cut off the little finger of his left hand. James said: 'Though you were great, Lord, for our sake you chose to become little and lowly. Therefore I give you back the body and soul which you created and redeemed with your own blood.' A seventh finger was cut off and James said: 'Seven times a day I have praised the Lord' [Psalm 118 (119):164]. The eighth was cut off and James said: 'On the eighth day Jesus was circumcised, and on the eighth day every Hebrew male is circumcised, so that he may be admitted to the ceremonies of the Law. So, Lord, let the mind of your servant be circumcised, so that it may pass beyond these pagans with their unclean foreskins, and I may come and gaze upon your face.' The ninth finger came off and he said: 'At the ninth hour Christ gave up the ghost upon the cross, and so, Lord, as I smart with the loss of this ninth finger, I confess your name and give you thanks.' The tenth finger was cut off and he said: 'Ten is the number of the Commandments, and Iota is the first letter of Jesus's name.'[1]

At this point some of the bystanders said: 'James, you were once our dearest friend. All you have to do is to acknowledge our gods before the consul, and you will win a reprieve. You may have lost your hands, but there are physicians with the skill to relieve your suffering.' 'God forbid that I should practise such a wicked deception!' James answered them. 'No one who puts his hand to the plough and then looks back is fitted for the kingdom of God' [Luke 9:62]. Angrily the men came back and cut off the big toe of his right foot and James said: 'Christ's foot was pierced and blood flowed from it.' A second toe was removed and he said: 'This day is greater than any other that I have known: today, reborn, I shall be with Almighty God.' They now cut off a third toe and threw it in front of him. James smiled and said: 'Go and join your friends, third toe. As the grain of wheat produces abundant fruit, so you, on the last day, shall find rest with your companions.' A fourth came off and he said: 'Why are you sad, my soul, and why so disquieted within me? Hope in God, for I will praise him still, the salvation of my countenance, and my God' [Psalm 42 (43):5]. When the fifth was cut off he said: 'Now I can begin to say to the Lord that he has made me a fitting companion of his servants.'

They then proceeded to cut off the little toe of his left foot and James said: 'Be of good cheer, little toe! The resurrection is for great and small alike. If not a single hair of the head shall perish, how could you ever be separated from your fellows?' Off came the second toe. 'Pull down the old house,' cried James. 'One more beautiful awaits me.' After the third was removed James said: 'The anvil is hardened by hammering.' The fourth went and he said: 'Comfort me, God of truth, for my soul trusts in you and my hope shall be in the shadow of your wings until this iniquity is past' [Psalm 56 (57):1]. The fifth came off and he said: 'There, Lord: my twentieth sacrifice to you.'

The men then cut off his right foot. 'Now I have a gift to offer to the

King of heaven,' James said, 'for love of whom I endure all this.' They cut off the left foot and he cried: 'You are the worker of miracles. Hear me, Lord, and save me!' They then cut off his right hand and he said: 'May your mercies help me, Lord!' And when the left one fell, he said: 'You are the God who works miracles.' Now they cut off his right arm and he said: 'Praise the Lord, O my soul! I will praise the Lord while I live, I will sing to my God, as long as I have any being' [Psalm 144 (145):1]. Now they cut off his left arm and he said: 'The sorrows of death have surrounded me, but in the name of the Lord I will be avenged.' Next they cut off his right leg, severing it at the thigh. James was now in unspeakable agony and he cried out: 'Lord Jesus Christ, help me! The anguish of death has closed about me!' And he told his executioners: 'The Lord will clothe me in new flesh, which the marks of your wounds will not defile.'

By this time the men were exhausted, since they had been hard at work dismembering James from dawn until the ninth hour of day. But still they continued, and they next cut off his left leg at the thigh. James cried out: 'Lord Almighty, hear me, half-dead as I am, you who are Lord of the living and the dead! I have no fingers, Lord, to stretch out to you; no hands to extend to you in prayer. My feet are cut off. I have no knees and cannot kneel to you. I am like a house which has lost the columns that support it and is on the verge of collapse. Hear me, Lord Jesus Christ, and deliver my soul from its bondage!'

After he spoke these words, one of the executioners stepped forward and decapitated him. Later Christians came and stole his body away, and gave it honourable burial. James suffered martyrdom on the twenty-seventh day of November.

71

STS BARLAAM AND JOSAPHAT[1]

27 November

Barlaam, whose biography was painstakingly compiled by St John of Damascus, was enabled by God's grace to convert King Josaphat to the faith. This was at a time when all India was full of Christians and monks, and a mighty king named Avennir came to power and cruelly persecuted all the Christians, and especially the monks. Now it happened that a friend of the king, indeed the leading noble of his court, was prompted by divine grace to leave the palace and enter a monastic order. When the king learnt of this, he was absolutely enraged: he ordered his men to comb every desert in the land, and when the man was finally found, he had him brought before him. Previously this nobleman had always worn the richest clothes and lived in great affluence, and, seeing him now covered in a shabby tunic and emaciated with hunger, he said to him: 'You fool, you must be out of your mind! How could you give up all the honours you enjoyed to humiliate yourself like this? Why, you have made yourself the laughing stock of all the children!' 'If you want to hear why I have done this,' the man replied, 'then banish your enemies, drive them far away from you!' When the king asked him who these enemies were, he told him: 'Anger and greed. It is they that keep you from seeing the truth. If you want to hear what I have to say, you will need prudence and justice as your allies.' 'Very well,' said the king. 'So be it.'

'They are fools,' he began, 'who despise the things which really are, as if they were illusory, and strive to grasp things that are illusory, as if they existed. No one who has not tasted the sweetness of the things that really are will learn the truth about the things that are not.' He then spoke at length about the mystery of the incarnation and about the faith, until the king finally told him: 'If I had not promised you at the start that I would banish all anger from this discussion, I assure you, by now I should be having you burnt alive. So go, get out of my sight! If I set eyes on you again, you will die a painful death!' Miserably the man of God left him, disappointed that he had not suffered martyrdom.

King Avennir had been childless, but now a beautiful boy was born to him, whom he called Josaphat. He assembled a vast crowd of people to offer sacrifice to the gods in thanksgiving for the birth of his son and summoned sixty astrologers, whom he anxiously questioned about his child's future. Their reply was almost unanimous: he would be both powerful and affluent. But one of them, one wiser than the rest, said: 'This child born to you, O King, will not rule in your kingdom, but in another, one incomparably better. I predict that he will be a follower of the Christian religion, which you are persecuting.' (The words were not his own: he spoke by divine inspiration.) This horrified the king, and he had a luxurious palace built in a separate quarter of his city for his son to live in. There he installed a group of handsome youths as his companions and instructed them never to mention death or old age, or illness, or poverty, or anything which could possibly make the prince sad. They were to confine their talk to pleasant things, so that Josaphat might be preoccupied with happy thoughts and prevented from thinking about the future. If any of his attendants fell sick, the king gave instructions that he should be removed from his service at once, and someone in perfect health made to take his place. In addition he forbade anyone ever to say anything to his son about Christ.

Now at this time there was another man in the king's entourage who was secretly a most devout Christian, and he was the most important of the king's ministers. One day, when he went off hunting with the king, he came upon a poor man lying on the ground nursing one of his feet, which had been savaged by a wild beast. The poor man asked him if he would take him and look after him, and suggested that in return he might possibly be able to do him some service. 'I will gladly give you shelter,' the nobleman told him, 'but I do not see how you could be of use to me.' 'I am a word-doctor,' the man told him. 'If someone is wounded by something said about him, I know the right remedy to apply.' The nobleman thought he was talking nonsense, but for God's sake he took the man in and had him looked after.

Now this nobleman had enemies at court. They were jealous and malicious men, and, seeing in what great favour he was with the king, they laid charges against him: not only had he turned to the Christian faith, they told the king, but he was also agitating the common people and currying favour with them in an attempt to seize the throne for himself. 'But if you want proof of this, your majesty,' they said, 'summon him in secret, speak to him about the brevity of human life, and tell him that you have decided to abandon the glories of kingship and put on the habit of the monks whom, in your ignorance, you have been persecuting. Then see what his answer is.' The king did exactly as they suggested, and the nobleman, unaware of the deception, burst into tears and applauded the king's decision. Then, reminding him of the vanity of the world, he advised him to act on it as quickly as possible. The king was now sure that everything he had been told was true and he was furious, but he made no reply, and the nobleman, taken aback by the gravity of the king's expression as he listened, worriedly took his leave. Then he remembered that he had a word-doctor at home, and he told him the whole story. 'Take it from me,' the man told him, 'the king suspects you. He thinks you spoke as you did because you have designs upon his throne. So go and shave your head, take off those clothes and put on a hair-shirt, and at crack of dawn go to the king. When he asks you what all this means, say: "Here I am, my lord, all ready to follow you! For, though the path you wish to tread is a hard one, if I am with you, I shall find it easy. I have been your companion in prosperity, and now I shall be the same in adversity. Here I am, then, at your service. What are you waiting for?"' The nobleman did exactly as he was told. Dumbfounded, the king denounced the nobles who had lied about his friend and showered even greater honours upon him than before.

Meanwhile the king's son, who lived in the palace his father had built for him, had come of age and received a thorough education in every branch of learning. He wondered why his father had shut him away as he had, and one day he took one of his most trusted servants aside and asked him about this. He said that not being allowed to set foot outside the palace made him extremely miserable, so much so, in fact, that he had lost all taste for food and drink. When word of this reached his father, he was deeply upset, so he had some fine horses made ready and sent troops of young people to go ahead of the prince, cheering wherever he went, trying hard to ensure that he should be spared the sight of anything unpleasant. Now one day, as the young prince was riding along with his retinue, he was confronted by a leper and a blind man. He was astonished at what he saw, and asked his servants who these men were and what was wrong with them. 'These are infirmities men suffer from,' they told him. 'Do they happen to everyone?' the prince asked. When they told him they did not, he asked: 'Do we know who are fated to suffer these infirmities, or do they happen to people simply at random?' They replied: 'Who can see into the future?' This was a new experience for Josaphat, and it disturbed him deeply.

On another occasion the prince came across a very old man with a wrinkled face and a bent back; he had lost all of his teeth, and when he tried to speak he could only mumble and drivel. Josaphat was bewildered at this extraordinary sight and asked his companions to explain what had happened to the man. When he learnt that it was because of his extreme old age that the man was in this state, he asked: 'And what will be his end?' 'Death,' they told him. 'Does death happen to all men,' he asked, 'or only to some?' 'Everyone must die,' they told him. He then asked: 'After how many years does this occur?' 'Old age sets in at eighty or a hundred,' they said, 'and then death follows.' The young prince brooded over this endlessly, and became deeply dejected. In his father's presence he put on a cheerful face, but secretly he longed for guidance and instruction in these matters.

At that time there was a monk of spotless life and reputation who lived in the desert in the land of Sennaar. His name was Barlaam. Now Barlaam learnt by revelation all that was happening to the king's son; he dressed himself up as a merchant and went to the capital, found the prince's tutor and said to him: 'I am a merchant and I have a precious stone to sell which gives sight to the blind, restores hearing to the deaf, enables the dumb to speak, and instils wisdom into the foolish. Take me to the king's son and I will offer it to him.' The man replied: 'You seem like a man of good sense, but your words make very little sense! However, I know something about stones, so show me this stone of yours, and if it proves to be what you claim it is, the king's son will make you rich and famous.' Barlaam told him: 'My stone also has another virtue: if someone with poor eyesight, whose life is not perfectly chaste, should set eyes on it, he loses his sight completely. Now I know something of medicine and I can see your eyes are not good. But I have heard that the king's son leads a chaste life and has fine, healthy eyes.' 'If what you say is true,' the tutor replied, 'do not show me the stone. My eyes are not good and I revel in all the blackest vices!' He therefore apprised the king's son of what had happened and took Barlaam in to him without delay.

Prince Josaphat received him with great respect, and Barlaam said to him: 'Your majesty, you have done well to disregard my humble appearance. There was once a great king who was riding along in his gilded chariot and came upon some paupers dressed in tatters and emaciated with hunger. He leapt straight down from his chariot, threw himself at their feet and worshipped them, then he rose to his feet and covered them with kisses. The nobles who were in his retinue were scandalized by his behaviour, but, not daring to criticize the king to his face, they told his brother that the king had conducted himself in a manner unbefitting his royal dignity, and the king's brother taxed him with the matter.

'Now it was this king's custom, whenever one of his subjects was to be executed, to send a herald to the door of the condemned man's house to proclaim his fate by sounding a special ceremonial trumpet. As evening fell that day, he had a herald sound the trumpet at the door of his brother's house. When his brother heard it, he despaired of his life; he could not get a moment's sleep that night and he made his will. Next morning, dressed in black, he went in mourning with his wife and children to the doors of the palace. The king had him brought in and said to him: "Fool! If you can be so frightened by your own brother's herald, when you know you have done him no wrong, how frightened do you think I must be of the heralds of my Lord, against whom I have sinned so greatly, heralds who proclaim my death with a blast louder than any trumpet's and announce to me the awful arrival of the Judge?"

'He then had four caskets made, two of them completely covered on the outside with gold and filled with the rotting bones of corpses, and the other two painted with pitch on the outside, but filled with precious stones and pearls. Then he called the noblemen who he knew had complained about him to his brother, placed the four caskets before them and asked them which two were the more precious. The nobles judged that the gilded caskets were the precious ones, and the others of little value. Then the king had the two gilded caskets opened, and immediately an intolerable stench was given off. The king told them: "These caskets are like men who wrap themselves in the most gorgeous robes, but inwardly are riddled with every filthy vice." Then he had the other two opened, and a marvellous fragrance wafted from them. "These are like those paupers whom I treated with such reverence," he said. "The clothes that cover them may be poor, but inwardly they breathe the fragrance of every virtue. You pay heed only to what is on the outside: you do not think of what is inside." So,' Barlaam told the prince, 'in giving me such a welcome, you have acted exactly as the king did.'

After this Barlaam began to deliver a long discourse on the creation of the world and man's disobedience, and the incarnation and passion and resurrection of the Son of God, dwelling at length on the Day of Judgement and the reward of good and evil. He also fiercely condemned idol worshippers, and to illustrate their stupidity he told the following story: 'An archer once caught a small bird called a nightingale, and he was on the point of killing it when the nightingale spoke to him and said: "What good will it do you to kill me? You will not be able to fill your belly with a bird like me. But if you let me go, I will give you three pieces of advice, which, if you follow them carefully, will prove very useful to you." Dumbfounded at hearing the bird speak, the man agreed to let it go, if it gave him the advice it promised. The bird said: "Never strive after anything that is unattainable; never grieve over anything that is lost irretrievably; and never believe anything that is unbelievable. Follow these three precepts and you will prosper." So the man let the nightingale go, as he had promised, and as it flew about, it said to him: "Hard luck! You were a fool to trust me. You have lost a priceless treasure today, because I have inside me a pearl bigger than an ostrich egg!" When he heard this, the man bitterly regretted letting the bird go and kept trying to catch her again. "Come into my house," he called. "I will show you every courtesy, and promise faithfully to let you go." The nightingale replied: "Now I know for a certainty that you are a fool. You have not profited from any one of the rules I gave you. You have lost me for ever, yet you are still miserable. You are still trying to catch me, even though you cannot fly after me. And you believed I had a pearl inside me bigger than an ostrich egg, when the whole of my body is not that big!" So people who put their trust in idols are fools,' Barlaam told the prince, 'because they worship what they have made with their own hands, and the things they call their "guardians" they have to guard themselves.'

Next Barlaam embarked on a lengthy discussion of the false pleasures and vanities of the world, supporting his argument with many illustrations. 'Those who hanker after bodily pleasures and allow their souls to perish of hunger,' he said, 'are like the man who, while fleeing headlong from a unicorn to avoid being devoured, fell into a deep pit. As he fell, he caught hold of a bush, and managed to set his feet on a slippery and precarious ledge. Then, when he looked up, he saw two mice, one white and one black, busily nibbling away at the roots of the bush he had grabbed, which they had nearly eaten through. At the bottom of the pit he saw a fearsome, fire-breathing dragon, with its jaws wide open ready to devour him. And on the ledge supporting his feet, he saw the darting heads of four asps. Then, as he looked up again, he noticed a tiny trickle of honey dropping from the branches of the bush, and, forgetting the dangers which beset him on every side, he gave himself up entirely to the pleasure of tasting that tiny, sweet drop of honey. Now the unicorn stands for death, which continually pursues man and tries to seize hold of him; and the pit is the world, with all its evils. The bush is life, which every hour of every day and night is being eaten away, as it were by white and black mice, and coming closer to its final ruin. The ledge with the four asps is the human body composed of its four elements, elements which, if disordered, bring about the body's dissolution. The fearsome dragon bent on devouring mankind is the mouth of hell; and the sweetness on the branches of the bush represents the false pleasures of the world by which man is seduced, so that he pays little heed to the peril he is in.'

Barlaam gave Josaphat another illustration: 'Lovers of this world are like the man who had three friends, of whom he loved one more than himself, the second as himself, and the third less than himself – in fact, hardly at all. Now this man got himself into serious trouble and had been summoned by the king, so he hurried off to the first friend and asked him for help, reminding him how much he had always loved him. "I do not even know who you are!" the friend told him. "I have to be with some other friends today, and they are friends I shall have for ever. But I can give you a couple of scraps of haircloth: you could use those to wrap yourself in." In great distress he went on to the second friend and made the same request for help. "I have no time to fight your fights for you," he said. "I am beset by enough troubles of my own. But I will go with you as far as the palace gates, then come straight back home to look after my own affairs." Dejected and desperate, the man finally went to the third friend and, with a downcast expression, he said: "I hardly know what to say to you, because I have not loved you as I ought. But I am in terrible trouble, without a friend in the world, and I am begging you to forgive me and help me." With a cheerful smile, the third friend replied: "Truly I consider you a very dear friend, and I have not forgotten your kindnesses to me, however trifling they may have been. I shall go on ahead of you and intercede for you with the king, and plead with him not to hand you over to your enemies." Now the first friend stands for the possession of riches, for which a man will undergo so many perils, but then, when finally death comes, he has nothing to show for it all but a few poor rags in which to be buried. The second friend represents a man's wife, children and parents, who accompany him only as far as his grave, then go straight back home and attend to their own affairs. The third friend is faith, hope, charity, almsgiving and the other good works which, when we leave our bodies, can go on ahead and intercede for us with God and deliver us from our enemies, the demons.'

Barlaam told him yet another story: 'There was a great city once where it was the custom each year to elect an unknown foreigner as prince. He was given absolute power and allowed to do whatever he wanted, and he ruled the land without any constraints. So this prince would live in the lap of luxury and fondly imagine that this was the way things would remain, but each year the citizens would rise in rebellion against him, haul him naked the length and breadth of the city, and pack him off to exile on a remote island where he found neither food nor clothing, and suffered cruelly from hunger and cold. Then one year a foreigner was elected as prince who knew exactly how these people carried on, so he sent vast convoys of treasure on ahead to the island, and when his year came to an end and he was sent into exile, he was able to enjoy untold pleasures there, whereas his predecessors had all starved to death. Now that city stands for the world; its citizens are the princes of darkness, who use the world's false pleasures to entice us; and then, when we expect it least, death comes upon us, and we are plunged into the place of darkness. But the riches we send ahead of us to eternity are those that pass through the hands of the poor.'

Barlaam had now given the king's son a thorough grounding in the faith, and the prince wanted to leave his father and become his disciple. But Barlaam said: 'If you do that, you will be like the young man who ran away from home because he refused to marry a noblewoman. As he journeyed he came to a place where he found a young woman at work: she was the daughter of a poor old man, and as she toiled she was cheerfully sounding the praises of God. "What are you doing, woman?" he asked her. "You are so poor, yet you thank God as if you had received the richest gifts from him." She replied: "A little medicine often cures a serious illness, and in the same way giving thanks for little gifts can bring us greater gifts. In any case these outer things are not ours, only the inward things are, and there God has given me gifts in plenty. He has made me in his own image; he has given me understanding; he has called me to share his glory, and already opened the gateway of his kingdom to me. And for gifts so many and so rich, it is right that I should praise him." The young man was deeply impressed by what the girl said and asked her father for her hand in marriage. "You cannot have my daughter," the old man told him, "because you are the son of rich and noble parents, and I am a pauper." When the youth insisted, the old man said: "I cannot give you my daughter and let you take her off to your father's house. She is my only child." "Then I will stay with you," the young man said, "and live exactly as you do." He took off his finery, put on some of the old man's clothes, and stayed there with him and married his daughter. Then, after some time, when the old man was quite sure of his son-in-law's worthiness, he took him into his bedroom and showed him an enormous pile of treasure, more wealth than he had ever seen before, and gave him every penny.'

'That is my situation exactly,' Josaphat exclaimed. 'I think that story was all about me! But tell me, father, how old are you and where do you live, because I never want to leave your side.' 'I am forty-five years of age,' Barlaam told him, 'and live in the desert in the land of Sennaar.' Josaphat said: 'I would have put you upwards of seventy, father.' Barlaam replied: 'If you are counting every year since my birth, then that is a good estimate. But I do not count all the years I spent in the pursuit of worldly vanities. For then, in my inward life, I was dead, and I refuse to count years of death as years of life.'

Josaphat would have followed Barlaam into the desert, but Barlaam told him: 'If you do this, I will only be deprived of your company and cause my brother monks to be persecuted. Wait for the opportune moment, then you shall join me.' Barlaam then baptized the king's son, instructed him fully in the faith, kissed him goodbye, and went back to his cell in the desert.

When the king heard that his son had become a Christian, he was heartbroken. Then one of his friends, a man called Arachis, in an attempt to console him, said: 'Your majesty, I know an old hermit who is of our religion. He is the spitting image of Barlaam. Let him pretend to be Barlaam! He will begin by defending the Christian faith, then let himself be won over, then renounce everything he ever taught, and so the prince will come back to us.' This Arachis then assembled a large army and let it be known that he was going in search of Barlaam. In fact, it was Nachor, his hermit friend, he found, but when he returned he pretended that he had arrested Barlaam. When Josaphat heard the news that his master had been seized, he wept bitterly, but it was later revealed to him that the hermit was not, in fact, Barlaam.

Now his father the king came to see him and said: 'My son, you have caused me such sadness! You have dishonoured my old age and robbed me of the light of my eyes! Why have you done this, my son, why have you abandoned the worship of my gods?' His son replied: 'I have fled the darkness, father, and run to the light. I have forsaken the error of my ways and recognized the truth. So do not waste your time: you will never get me to turn from Christ, any more than you could touch the vault of heaven or drain the deepest sea! I tell you, it is impossible.' The king replied: 'And who is it that brought all this misery upon me, but myself, I who have been more generous to you than ever father was to son before? As a result of which, you are so headstrong and self-willed and so uncontrollably stubborn that you act like a madman in defiance of your own father. The astrologers were right when they declared at your birth that you would be arrogant and disobedient to your parents. But now, unless you agree to do as I say, I will cease to regard you as my son. I shall be your father no longer, but your enemy, and I will do to you such things as I have never done before, even to my enemies!' Josaphat answered: 'Why are you so sad, sir, when I stand to gain so much? What father was ever sad at his son's good fortune? Very well, I shall no longer call you father, and if you attack me, I shall flee from you as I would from a serpent!' The king angrily left him and told his friend Arachis of his son's obstinacy. Arachis advised him not to use any harsh words to his son; the young prince, he said, would be more easily won over by persuasive and quiet talk. So the following day the king went to his son again and embraced him and kissed him. 'My dearest son,' he said, 'honour your father's old age! Respect him as you ought! Surely you know that it is right to obey a father and make him happy, and wrong to do the opposite and make him angry? Sons who go against their fathers always come to grief.' Josaphat told him: 'There is a time for loving and a time for hating, a time for peace and a time for war. We must never obey anyone who tries to turn us from serving God, even if they are our mother or father.' Seeing how stubborn his son was, the king said: 'I can see your mind is made up and you are determined not to obey me. Come now, let us at least both believe in the truth together! That Barlaam, who led you astray, is a prisoner of mine. Let representatives of my religion and yours meet this Barlaam, and I will send out a herald to assure the Galileans that they can come here without fear. Let them engage in debate: if your friend Barlaam wins, we will embrace your faith; but if our side wins, you must accept ours.' The king's son agreed to this. The king and his friends then told the counterfeit Barlaam what he must do: first he was to pretend that he was defending the Christian faith, and then allow himself to be defeated.

The two sides duly met, and Josaphat turned to the counterfeit Barlaam and said: 'You know how you taught me, Barlaam. If you defend the faith you have taught me, I will abide by your teaching until the day I die. But if you are defeated, I shall avenge myself on you instantly for the wrong you have done me. I shall tear out your heart and your tongue with my own hands and feed them to the dogs, so that others in future may think twice before presuming to deceive the son of a king!' What Josaphat said made Nachor sick at heart and filled him with foreboding: he saw that he had fallen into a trap of his own setting, and that he was inescapably caught. So, after taking stock, he decided that his best chance of staying alive was to side with the king's son, for the king had told him in front of everyone to defend his son's faith fearlessly. Then one of the king's spokesmen got up and said: 'Are you Barlaam, who led the king's son astray?' Nachor replied: 'I am Barlaam. But I did not lead the king's son into error, I saved him from error.' 'Many great and famous men have worshipped our gods,' the man retorted. 'How is it that you dare rebel against them?' Nachor answered: 'The Chaldaeans, Greeks and Egyptians were all mistaken in calling creatures "gods". The Chaldaeans thought the elements were gods, when in reality they were created to be of service to them and subservient to them, and are corrupted by many passions. The Greeks think that wicked men are gods, like Saturn, for example, who they say ate his own sons and cut off his genitals and threw them into the sea, and from them Venus was born; and Saturn was also bound by his son Jupiter and thrown into Tartarus. Jupiter is also described as king of the gods, yet they say he often transformed himself into the likeness of animals in order to commit adultery. The goddess Venus, too, was an adulteress, they say, for she at various times had Mars and Adonis as her lovers. The Egyptians worshipped animals such as the sheep, the calf and the pig. But Christians worship the Son of the Most High, who came down from heaven and became a man.' Nachor presented a lucid defence of the Christian faith, which he corroborated with such cogent, solid arguments that the king's spokesmen were tongue-tied and did not know how to answer him. Josaphat was overjoyed that the Lord had defended the truth through one who was an enemy of the truth. But the king was enraged and he ordered the meeting adjourned, as if he intended to continue the debate on the following day. Josaphat said to his father: 'Either let my master stay with me tonight, so that we can agree on the answers we must make tomorrow, and you take your people off with you and confer with them, or else leave your men with me and take my master with you. Otherwise it would be unfair, and you would be abusing your power like a tyrant.' So the king let Nachor stay with his son, still hoping that he might persuade him to relent.

When Josaphat got back home with Nachor, he said to him: 'Do not think I do not know who you are. I know you are not Barlaam, but Nachor the astrologer.' He then began to preach the way of salvation to Nachor, converted him to the faith, and next morning sent him off to the desert, where he received baptism and led the life of a hermit.

Now a sorcerer by the name of Theodas came to hear about all this, and he went to the king and promised him that he would get his son to embrace the beliefs of his father again. 'If you can,' the king assured him, 'I will set up a statue of gold in your honour, and offer sacrifice to you as to the gods!' Theodas said: 'Remove all your son's attendants from the palace and have beautiful, elegant women take their place. Tell them to be constantly in his company, waiting on him and chatting to him, and never leaving his side for a moment, and I will send one of my spirits to him to set him on fire with lust. Nothing is more certain to lead young men astray than the sight of beautiful women.' He then told the king the following story: 'There was a king who had just been presented with a son, and his most renowned physicians told him that if, in the first ten years of his life, he set eyes on the sun or moon, he would lose his eyesight. So the king had a cave dug out of solid rock and made his son live there until his tenth birthday. When the ten years had passed, the king ordered that all sorts of objects should be brought before his child so that he could learn their names and functions. So his servants showed the young prince gold and silver, precious stones, sumptuous garments, horses from the king's stables – in fact, every kind of object – and when he asked what each of the things was called, the servants told him its name. Now when the prince first set eyes on a woman and asked, with some enthusiasm, what he should call them, the king's sword-bearer in jest told him they were "demon temptresses". And when the king asked his son what he had liked most of all the things he had seen, he told him: "Those demon temptresses, of course. Nothing set my heart on fire as they did!" Take my word for it, your majesty,' Theodas concluded. 'This is the only way you will get the better of your son.'

So the king had all his son's attendants thrown out, and sent in a bevy of beautiful girls to keep him company. They flirted with him constantly and never stopped trying to seduce him, and Josaphat had no one else to turn to, no one to talk to or to share his meals with, and the evil spirit sent by the sorcerer entered into the young man and lit a raging fire in his vitals. So, while the evil spirit was deep inside him inflaming his passion, the girls were all around him, rousing his ardour to fever pitch. Josaphat was in absolute torment, and deeply troubled by what was happening; but he commended himself wholly to God and instantly he received Heaven's comfort, and all temptation left him.

Next the king sent in to Josaphat the orphan daughter of a king, a girl of extraordinary beauty. The saintly prince at once attempted to convert her, but she told him: 'If you want to stop me worshipping the idols, you must be joined to me in marriage. Christians do not disapprove of marriage, they are in favour of it. Their patriarchs and prophets and the apostle Peter all had wives.' Josaphat answered her: 'Your arguments are wasted on me. Christians are indeed allowed to have wives, but not those who have vowed their virginity to Christ.' 'If that is your decision,' she said, 'then so be it. But if you want to save my soul, grant me one little request: sleep with me tonight, just once is all I ask, and I promise you I will become a Christian first thing tomorrow morning. For if, as you say, there is joy in heaven among the angels when a sinner repents, surely the one responsible for the conversion must be owed a very special reward. Just do as I ask this once and you will win my salvation.' With these words she began to shake the fortress of Josaphat's soul to its foundations. The demon saw what was happening and said to his fellows: 'You see how that girl has shaken him, and we could not shake him in the slightest. Come on, let us strike now, and strike him hard: the right moment has come!' The saintly young man felt himself in a terrible dilemma, troubled by his feelings of lust and at the same time (at the Devil's prompting) by a sincere concern for the girl's salvation. In a flood of tears he began to pray, and, as he prayed, he fell asleep and saw himself being taken into a lovely, flowery meadow, where the leaves of the trees, rustling in a pleasant breeze, whispered gently and gave off a wonderful fragrance; the trees were laden with brightly coloured, delicious fruits; and there were thrones of gold, inlaid with precious stones, and couches embellished with the most sumptuous coverings, and streams of clearest water flowing by. Then he was taken into a city whose walls were of pure gold and shone with a dazzling brilliance, where ethereal hosts sang a song that no mortal ear had ever heard. And a voice said to him: 'This is the place of the blessed.' When his guides began to lead him away, Josaphat asked them to let him stay there, but they told him: 'You must endure more hardship and inflict suffering upon yourself if you are to return here.' They then took him to the foulest place imaginable, a region where all was filth and decay, and told him: 'This is the place of the wicked.' Then Josaphat woke up, and the beauty of the young princess and the other girls seemed to stink worse than dung.

So the evil spirits went back to Theodas, and when he heaped abuse on them for their incompetence, they said: 'Before he made the sign of the cross, we made a savage attack on him, we had him in terrible trouble. But once he armed himself with the sign of the cross, it was he who launched a furious assault on us!' Then Theodas went with the king to see Josaphat, hoping that he himself could win him over. But the sorcerer was won by the very person he wanted to win. He was converted by Josaphat, received baptism, and thereafter lived an exemplary life.

In desperation the king acted on his friends' advice and made over half his kingdom to his son. Now Josaphat longed with all his heart to live in the desert, but in order to spread the faith, he undertook to rule the kingdom for a time, and built churches and set up crosses in his cities, and converted all his subjects to Christianity. Finally the king, too, yielded to his son's arguments and persuasion, accepted the faith of Christ and was baptized. He left his entire kingdom to Josaphat, then devoted himself to works of charity and lived in piety for the rest of his days.

In due course Josaphat named Barachias as king in his place and several times tried to flee, but his people always caught him and brought him back. Finally, however, he did manage to escape, and, as he made his way through the desert, he gave a poor man the royal robes he had on, and thereafter wore only the poorest clothing. The Devil set many traps for him. Sometimes he would rush at him with a drawn sword and threaten to run him through unless he gave up his life of holiness; at other times he appeared to him in the form of a wild beast, gnashing his teeth and making fearsome, bellowing noises. But Josaphat calmly told him: 'The Lord is my helper, I shall not fear what any man can do to me.'

For two years he wandered the desert, looking for Barlaam without any success, until at last he came upon a hermit's cave and, standing at the entrance, called out: 'Bless me, father, bless me!' Hearing his voice, Barlaam hurried out, and they fell eagerly into each other's arms and clung to each other so tightly that it seemed neither would ever let the other go. Josaphat told Barlaam everything that had happened to him, and Barlaam thanked God from the bottom of his heart. Josaphat remained with him there for many years, and lived a life of extreme austerity and virtue. Barlaam finally ended his days in peace in about AD 380. Josaphat, who had renounced his kingdom at the age of twenty-five, lived the life of a hermit for thirty-five years, until, renowned for his many virtues, he died a peaceful death and was buried alongside Barlaam. When King Barachias heard the news, he went there with a large army, reverently took up the two bodies, and transported them to his city, where many miracles have taken place at their tomb.

EXPLANATORY NOTES

1. ST ANDREW *(30 November)*

1. *Murgundia*: Murgundia or Margundia in the MSS. There is no place-name which credibly fits this. Morgentum in Sicily is the nearest, but there is no reason to think Matthew or Andrew was ever there. Some other unsubstantiated accounts suggest Matthew died in Persia. This is a good example of the geographical confusion and uncertainty regarding these early and largely fictitious accounts.

2. ST NICHOLAS *(6 December)*

1. *Council of Nicaea*: The First Council of Nicaea was held in 325 and was important especially for the adoption of the Nicene Creed to defend the faith against the Arians. There is no reliable evidence that Nicholas attended, though a bishop of Myra very likely would.

2. *magic oil*: Translation of the Latin *oleum Mydyaton*. The second word is probably a corruption of some word meaning 'Median, of the Medes'. 'Median oil' was a term used for Greek fire, whose main ingredient, naphtha, came from that area, modern northern Iran (R. F. Seybolt, 'A Troublesome Medieval Greek Word', *Speculum* 21 (1946), 38–41). 'Greek fire' was an inflammable material used for setting fire to enemy ships or military installations, first recorded as used by Greeks of Constantinople.

3. ST AMBROSE *(7 December)*

1. *son of Ambrose the prefect of Rome*: Ambrose's father was Aurelius Ambrosius, praetorian prefect of Gaul.

6. ST ANASTASIA *(25 December)*

1. *Palmaria*: In fact, Anastasia died at Simium, now Sremska Mitrovica. This whole account is a fiction designed to explain a church apparently named after her in Rome, and it typifies the biographical unreliability of many of these Lives.

7. ST JOHN, APOSTLE AND EVANGELIST *(27 December)*

1. *St John, Apostle and Evangelist*: Whether the apostle and the evangelist were in fact the same person has generally been doubted, but it is still considered not impossible. Clearly they were thought to be one in medieval times.

2. *Helinandus*: A Cistercian monk of Perseigne in Sarthe, of the latter part of the twelfth century, who wrote biblical commentaries.

8. ST THOMAS OF CANTERBURY *(29 December)*

1. *the year of our Lord 1174*: Thomas Beckett was in fact martyred in 1170. This is typical of the inaccuracy of dating often to be found in these Lives, whether from errors in Jacobus's sources or carelessness by early copyists. In the Notes which follow, attention has not been drawn to many less striking examples.

10. ST ANTHONY, ABBOT *(17 January)*

1. *Abbot*: Anthony was not an abbot in the sense 'head of monastery'. The word derives from the Syriac *abba*, 'father', and was often applied in the East to hermits, especially those who attracted a following of disciples. His sojourn in the desert and his temptations were so well known that Voragine felt no need to specify his surroundings at the beginning of the Life, as he implies by starting the fourth paragraph 'When he went into another part of the desert'.

15. ST IGNATIUS *(1 February)*

1. *'amor'* ['love'] . . . *'dilectio'* ['charity'] : The Greek word *agape* was adopted in order to avoid the sensual connotations of the word *eros*, and similarly the Latin *amor* was usually replaced by *caritas* or, as here, *dilectio*.

20. ST MATTHIAS, APOSTLE *(24 February)*

1. *legend . . . preserved at Trier*: It is not clear what this means. Presumably Voragine had no direct knowledge of any tradition or written account at Trier and was relying on a report in some intermediate source.

21. ST GREGORY *(12 March)*

1. *do not call me 'Naomi'*: The Latin text of Graesse reads 'Noemi'.

2. *Why do you ask . . . wonder*: This translation of *quod est mirabile* is taken from the Jerusalem Bible (Judges 13:18). The Authorized Version reads 'seeing it is secret'.

3. *Trajan was restored . . . irrevocable sentence*: This story of the rescue of Trajan's soul was widely current in the Middle Ages, and raised issues of much interest concerning the virtuous pagans and the efficacy of prayer for souls of the dead. It was therefore discussed by serious theologians, such as Thomas Aquinas, and is referred to twice by Dante (*Purgatorio* X. 73–96 and *Paradiso* XX. 43–8 and 109–11), and in Langland's *Piers Plowman* (B-text XI. 141ff). Just after this (in l. 160) Langland also refers to *The Golden Legend* when Trajan says: 'The *Legenda sanctorum* yow lereth more largere than I yow telle.'

4. *the book which the Greeks call Lymon*: The Greek *Leimon*, 'meadow', was the name given to a book of stories and anecdotes about monastic life by John Moschus (d. 619). It was known in Latin as *Pratum Spirituale*.

25. ST GEORGE *(23 April)*

1. *Close by this city . . . lair*: Farmer (*Oxford Dictionary of Saints*) says that the Dragon story was widely disseminated from *The Golden Legend*, which may be true, but it certainly did not originate there, since Jacobus's practice was to compile from existing sources, not to invent new material of this kind. However, it is absent from many earlier versions, such as that of Ælfric. For a suggestion on the origins of dragon stories, see Mâle, who proposes that the dragon represents paganism or idolatry, and in this case the young lady stands for the province of Cappadocia (*L'Art religieux du XIIIe siècle en France*, trans. Marthiel Mathews as *Religious Art in France: The Thirteenth Century*, p. 288).

28. ST JAMES THE LESS, APOSTLE *(1 May)*

1. *Alphaeus means . . . 'thousandth'*: The etymologies with which Jacobus begins many of the Lives (see Introduction) have almost all been left out of this translation, but this one is retained as an example. It is fairly typical, except that it is shorter and less complicated than many.

2. *Cleophas*: According to John 19:25, Clopas was the husband of Mary, the sister of the mother of Jesus, and according to Mark 15:40, this Mary was the mother of James the Less. Some early authorities, trying to reconcile these two statements, argued that the Greek form 'Clopas' was equivalent to the Aramaic 'Alphaeus'. There seems to be even less reason to think that Joseph was his brother, and it is interesting to see in this passage such writers as Beleth and Jacobus puzzled by these inconsistent traditions and trying to make sense of them. (See F. L. Cross and E. A. Livingstone, *The Oxford Dictionary of the Christian Church*, 2nd edition, 1974.)

3. *ecclesiastical histories*: The Latin has this in the plural, but it is no doubt meant to be the *Historia ecclesiastica* by Eusebius, from which, in fact, much of our information about Hegesippus comes.

29. ST PETRONILLA *(31 May)*

1. *St Petronilla*: Almost nothing is known about Petronilla, except that she was an early Roman martyr. But she was *not* the daughter of Peter, and this whole account is fictitious. Despite this, she has had a considerable following in Rome, France and England.

30. ST BARNABAS, APOSTLE *(11 June)*

1. *Firstly, he was orderly . . . the name of our Lord Jesus Christ*: This passage exemplifies a certain type of medieval writing in which paragraphs are carefully structured in numbered subdivisions, sometimes, as in this case, several successive paragraphs being patterned in the same way. This can lead to various types of confusion when scribes muddle the numbers of main paragraphs with those of sub-paragraphs, or when errors affect the numbers themselves, or when, as in this case, the first of the sub-paragraphs is in each case not numbered. For the sake of clarity the missing numbers have here been inserted. Examples of this sort of writing are to be found in Chaucer's *Parson's Tale*, which was based ultimately on such works as the *Summa casuum poenitentiae* of Raymund of Pennaforte and the *Tractatus de viciis* of William Peraldus, both of the thirteenth century.

31. ST BASIL, BISHOP *(14 June)*

1. *Lift up your gates, O ye princes*: This is what the Latin text says. The Psalm, of course, reads: 'Lift up your heads, O ye gates' (Psalms 24(25):7).

33. STS GERVASE AND PROTASE *(19 June)*

1. *youths dressed in tunics . . . on their feet*: The precise details, including the short boots, suggest that whoever was ultimately responsible for this passage had a painting in mind; it is also said shortly afterwards that Ambrose knew paintings of Paul and was confident that he could recognize him from them.

34. ST PETER, APOSTLE *(29 June)*

1. *I am the Omnipotent; I am the Soul of God*: Graesse has the cryptic *ego omnia dei*, while Benz cites the variant *ego omnipotens, ego omnia dei facio*. A more feasible version: *ego omnipotens, ego anima Dei*, is suggested by Vignay's fourteenth-century French translation, which may represent the correct reading from a manuscript in this instance more accurate than the sources used by Graesse and Benz, and is here adopted.
2. *Simon and Nero are plotting against you*: This apparent *non sequitur*, since one would expect Agrippa to be involved, is probably the result of conflation of earlier versions.

Agrippa doubtless incited Nero against Peter, and indeed reappears later in this Life acting against him on Nero's behalf.

35. ST PAUL, APOSTLE (30 June)

1. *Haimo*: Haimo, bishop of Halberstadt (d. 853), wrote a *Historiae sacrae epitome*.
2. *Plantilla . . . two names*: One might think it more likely that one of the sources was wrong than that the lady had two names.
3. *Farewell*: The injunction *Vade*, 'Go', which appears in the Latin, seems peremptory; the emended reading *Vale*, 'Farewell', has therefore been adopted.
4. *his letter*: No copy of this letter is known to survive.

36. ST ALEXIS (17 July)

1. *he had three tables*: Supplying three tables for four categories of the poor seems odd, but that is what the text apparently says. Probably the number was originally *.iiij.* and this was misread, such numerical errors being common; or it may be that the poor are divided into these three categories, which would seem rather incomplete.

38. ST MARY MAGDALENE (22 July)

1. *St Mary Magdalene*: Much of this account is now regarded as apocryphal. Mary Magdalene (Luke 8:2) was identified with the sister of Martha and Lazarus (John 12:3) and also with the sinner at the house of Simon (Luke 7:37) from an early period, but neither these identifications nor her part in the evangelization of Provence are generally accepted, though the story as here given was long regarded as correct. One notes, however, that Jacobus was aware of differing versions (p. 166), and also that he discussed the uncertainty about who said: 'Blessed is the womb that bore you.'

39. ST CHRISTOPHER (25 July)

1. *Dagnus*: I have been unable to discover what verbal play on this name is intended.

40. THE SEVEN SLEEPERS OF EPHESUS (27 July)

1. *But there are grave doubts . . . ninety-six years*: Here Jacobus correctly points out that the account he is using cannot be right. The additional discrepancy between the figure of three hundred and seventy-two years given at this point and the earlier reference by the proconsul to a date five years earlier for the coins may mean that they are imaginatively described as not new when the Sleepers acquired them, but it is more likely that at some stage a scribe got the first figure wrong by inserting a *v*.

41. ST MARTHA *(29 July)*

1. *Martha ... royal descent*: Martha was the sister of Lazarus and Mary, often thought to have been Mary Magdalene. From none of the three mentions of Martha in the New Testament is there any ground for believing that her family owned extensive property; and there is no reason to suppose that she was involved in the conversion of Provence. Her Life is an extreme example of how elaborate legends could develop from small beginnings.

43. ST DOMINIC *(4 August)*

1. *to use a hair of the dog that bit them*: Latin *ut sic clavum clavo retunderet*, literally 'to drive out one nail with another'.

2. *their followers ... friendship for ever*: It is interesting to note the even-handedness with which the Dominican writer Jacobus treats Dominic and Francis, albeit in a story told by a Franciscan. Relations between the two Orders were generally, and certainly officially, good.

3. *He was once elected ... such appointment*: Dominic in fact twice refused bishoprics. So did Jacobus the first time he was asked, and it is perhaps ironic that he accepted in due course, though his reluctance was doubtless unfeigned.

46. ST BARTHOLOMEW *(24 August)*

1. *As you made my brother ... I will smash your gods*: The apparent inconsistency between singular and plural is probably because a single god for each king is first referred to, and then Bartholomew thinks in terms of destroying all the various gods of the region.

2. *Master of Theology*: This story about the temptation of the Master of Theology is much the same as one about a bishop in 'St Andrew', so the latter has not been included in this volume. Jacobus notes this similarity himself with an implication of scepticism: 'A very similar story is told about St Andrew.'

48. ST THEODORA *(11 September)*

1. *some oxen*: In the Latin text 'Theodore' sets off with oxen (*boves*) and apparently passes her husband 'with camels' (*cum camelis*), which is corrected in this translation. It seems surprising that such an error, whether resulting from a conflation of sources or scribal carelessness, should have been repeated in many copies.

49. ST EUPHEMIA *(16 September)*

1. *Appellianus*: Appellianus appears out of the blue and is presumably the residue of some earlier version which has been abbreviated.

53. ST JEROME *(30 September)*

1. *a lion came limping ... monastery*: As a result of the following story, the lion is Jerome's emblem. Both story and lion really belong, however, to St Gerasimus, and became attributed to Jerome because of the relative similarity of their names.

54. ST REMY *(1 October)*

1. *at every turn ... :* The sentence here omitted states that an account of Clovis's conversion is given under Remy's other feast-day, which occurs after Epiphany and is not included in this selection.

58. STS DIONYSIUS, RUSTICUS AND ELEUTHERIUS *(9 October)*

1. *Dionysius*: Dionysius, as he appears in this tradition, is a conflation of three people: Dionysius the Areopagite; a mystical philosopher of the fifth century whose works were attributed to the latter; and Denys, the missionary who was sent into Gaul.

2. *dormition*: A technical term used in the Eastern Church, the 'falling asleep' of the BVM; in the West this is known as the 'assumption'. After her earthly life had ended, the Virgin Mary did not die but was taken up body and soul into heaven.

59. THE ELEVEN THOUSAND VIRGINS *(21 October)*

1. *Ursula*: Ursula's Life is said by Farmer (*Oxford Dictionary of Saints*) to have reached its final form in *The Golden Legend*, but is more likely to have done so in Jacobus's source, since he was not given to modifying his material (see Introduction). This substantially fictitious tale has been highly productive artistically, perhaps the two most famous paintings of the story being the series by Memling in Bruges and that by Carpaccio in Venice. It may be that Ursula and some companions were martyred at Cologne in about 400. It has been suggested that an incorrect expansion of 'M' as *milia*, 'thousands', instead of 'martyrs', led to 'eleven virgin martyrs' becoming 'eleven thousand virgins', and that the misinterpretation was supported by the discovery of a previously unknown burial ground.

2. *Cyriacus, the nineteenth pope ... privileges*: This story of Cyriacus is, of course, as fictitious as the rest of the Life. The only pope who ever resigned was Celestine V in 1294, and most commentators believe that he is the sinner referred to by Dante

(*Inferno* 3.58–60) as *colui che fece per viltate il gran rifiuto*, 'the one who made through cowardice the great refusal', and consigned to the vestibule of hell.

61. STS SIMON AND JUDE, APOSTLES *(28 October)*

1. *sons of Mary of Cleopas . . . Alphaeus*: For Mary, daughter of Cleopas, see the text in 'St James the Less, Apostles', p. 125, and note 2 on p. 361. Jude may have been James's brother, but there is no reason to suppose that Simon was.

65. ST BRICE *(13 November)*

1. *Having led . . . episcopate*: Given the account of his Life as here related, it seems surprising that Brice had sufficient status to merit a place in the Church liturgical calendar. But there he was, and he is included in this selection as a contrast to many others. In 1002 King Ethelred the Unready ordered a notorious massacre of Danes which took place on St Brice's day.

66. ST ELIZABETH *(19 November)*

1. *she would not allow her sleeves to be laced on*: This translates *ut etiam manicas sibi consui nulla ratione pateretur*; and 'she would remove her sleeves if by any chance they had already been laced on,' translates *manicas, si forte consutae essent, solveret*. It is not clear whether the meaning should be 'laced on' or 'laced up', or whether to translate *solveret* as 'loosen' instead of 'remove'. Miss Linda Woolley of the Textiles and Dress Department of the Victoria & Albert Museum has kindly informed me that, while there are some references to detachable sleeves in the fourteenth century, little relevant documentary evidence exists for the thirteenth, so the matter must remain uncertain. If sleeves were regarded as an adornment, removal seems more likely than that they should hang loose.

2. *in order to bear children . . . God*: Her resignation to the bearing of children for the service of God may seem a sensible acceptance of the impossibility of being allowed to remain 'chaste' in her case, but it is notably at variance with the reactions of the many virgin martyrs.

3. *landgrave*: A rank more or less equivalent to count.

4. *margravine*: Wife of a margrave, a rank more or less equivalent to marquis.

5. *She insisted that they use . . . inferiors*: It is interesting that Jacobus thinks it necessary to explain this usage. Osbern Bokenham, several of whose *Legendys of Hooly Wummen* (ed. Mary S. Serjeantson, EETS OS 206) are taken from *The Golden Legend*, translates this passage:

> . . . Nere in the plurere noumbyr speken hyr to,
> But oonly in the syngulere, she hem dede deuyse,
> As souereyens to subiectys be won to do. [ll.10350–52]

69. ST CATHERINE *(25 November)*

1. *Plato describes . . . sphere*: Translates Latin *nam Plato adstruit Deum circumrotundum et decurtatum.* A perhaps more literal translation would be: 'For Plato describes a god perfectly spherical and truncated.' The text must surely be corrupt.

70. ST JAMES THE MUTILATED *(27 November)*

1. *Iota . . . Jesus's name*: Iota is the *ninth* letter of the Greek alphabet, but Yod, its equivalent, is tenth in the Hebrew alphabet.

71. STS BARLAAM AND JOSAPHAT *(27 November)*

1. *Sts Barlaam and Josaphat*: This fictitious tale is ultimately derived from an Indian account of Buddha. It is not certain that John of Damascus was involved in its creation or transmission.

TEXTUAL VARIANTS

Listed below are my deviations from Graesse's text. Unless otherwise indicated, they are readings recorded in Benz. **Z** refers to the variants listed by Zuidweg and **P** to those listed by Plezia. **CS** indicates the translator's own emendations.

Reference to Graesse is to his page and line-number. Where one saint's Life ends and another begins on the same page, the number given refers to lines of Latin text, excluding titles and chapter-numbers.

This translation	*Graesse*	

ST ANDREW

Murgundiam	13:17	Margundiam
Antiochiam	13:31	Achayam
aquam sparsit	14:3	sparsit
in uno momento	14:9	in monumento
domus tota: CS	15:21	domus tua
Audire autem te volo	17:1	Audire a te volo
Egeas eum iterum	17:23	iterum
milibus	18:10	millia
lascivum	18:25	laetum
dulcissimae	18:26–7	dilectissimae
recipiat	18:32	recipias

ST NICHOLAS

earum: P	23:3	eorum
suscipienda	23:33	suscipiendo
mydiacon	24:29	Mydiaton
contra naturam		in naturam
portui Andriacatico	25:8–9	portui Adriatico
imperio	25:25	impios

ST AMBROSE

Probus praefectus	251:14 probus praefectus
[]	252:28–36 Cum viri Thessalonicae civitatis ... non negavit
sermo esset in ore eius	253:33 sermo esset, more eius
bonus esset episcopus	254:37 bonus esset
orationis	255:9 oris

ST THOMAS, APOSTLE

praeter	33:6 pater
hebraia fistulam	33:17 Hebraeam fistulam
suadebat	33:22–3 satagebat
detur	33:26 tradatur
pretio	36:18 <precibus sive> pretio
potioni	37:25 passioni
tu putas, quod, sicut dicit Carisius, Deus meus mihi irascetur	38:28–9 tu putas quod sicut Carisius Deus mihi irascetur
comminuet	38:30 comminuet adoratu
Deum tuum Deus meus	38:31 Deum tuum Deus

ST ANASTASIA

filia Praetextati (*Acta* of St Anastasia)	47:30 filia praetaxati
Fausta	48:1 Fantasta
Agape ... Chionia ... Irene	48:11–12 Agapete ... Thionia ... Yrenia
percutiebant, alii in faciem eius expuebant	48:22 percutiebant

ST JOHN, APOSTLE AND EVANGELIST

et in perpetuum permansura	59:1 permansura
ignis: CS	59:3 ignis
apostoli: Z	59:5–6 apostolorum
intulerit	59:25 videro
et eis coram omnibus: Z	59:29 et coram iis omnibus
suscitaveris: Z	59:34 suscitaverit
erant: P	61:23 erunt

ST THOMAS OF CANTERBURY

ad	67:5 <ad>
ne horum cuiquam clericorum	68:25 ne horum cuiquam

ST HILARY

interea: CS	99:18 intera

ST SEBASTIAN

[ ]	110:9 igitur dum ... 110:14 mecum eris
habitare: P	112:1 habere
Lucinae	112:22 Luciae
CCLXXXVII: P	112:26 CLXXXVII

ST VINCENT

vergis	118:19 verbis
patibulum	118:34 craticulum
flamma sanguine respergitur	119:1 flamma respergitur
vincimur	119:8 vincimini
in terra	120:1 terra

ST JOHN THE ALMSGIVER

ut Eleymon	126:25 ut eleymor
ferentem, et habentem	127:32 ferentem et habentem,
aperiebat	128:19 ei aperiebat
et non imputaretur: CS	129:15 ut non imputaretur

ST IGNATIUS

fuisti ei	155:8 fuisti
tollite, vinculis ferreis alligate in cippo: CS	157:3 tollite vinculis ferreis, alligate in cippo

ST BLAISE

ferae	167:11	fere
adoremus cum reverentia, mitte eos	168:21	adoremus, cum reverentia mitte eos
dixerant: CS	168:23	dixerat
illae		illi
fluebat: P	168:39	fluebant
vel nunc adoras deos vel non?	169:15	vel nunc adora Deos vel non.

ST AGATHA, VIRGIN

sub Decio	173:4	sub Daciano

ST AMAND

in trajectensem	175:20−21	in terra jacentem

ST MATTHIAS, APOSTLE

pythonico … pythonicus: Z	184:10 and 12	phitonico … phitonicus
in marinis fluctibus: Z	185:6	his marinis fluctibus
accusaretur in multis, respondit	187:30−31	accusaretur, in multis respondit

ST GREGORY

189 (page number)	198	
tutius: P	189:7−8	ut tutius
multa: CS	189:9	multra
angustiis: CS	189:27	augustiis
quaedam: P	189:29	quodam
dimisisti: P	190:21	demisisti
cognoscitis	191:26−7	cognoscitur
magni	191:33	magis
dixit	192:11	dicit
ora pro nobis Deum, rogamus	192:12	ora pro nobis, Deum rogamus
fui,: CS	192:24	fui;
quae non sunt	192:25	quia non sunt

quia dixistis	192:26 quae dixistis
omne quod petieris, per me: CS	194:38 omne, quod petieris per me,
nolebat. (new para.) Cum Mauritius ... persequeretur, inter caetera	195:29–31 nolebat, cum Mauritius ... persequeretur. Inter caetera
lascive: CS	198:4 lasciva
suspicientes: CS	198:14 suscipientes
iura	199:16 vira
DCIV: CS	199:20 DCVI

ST BENEDICT

Enfide	204:20 Aeside
sub eo	205:29 cum eo
et se dolerent	205:30 et grave esse sedule
lacum: P	206:27 locum
eumque vexare: P	208:36 eumque is vexare
praeposuerat: P	210:31 proposuerat
quibus: P	210:35 cui
defluere	212:3 affluere
episcopi Capuani	212:24 episcopi capitalis

ST GEORGE

domum tuam: Z	260:26–7 domum tuum
Georgius: Z	261:14–15 Gregorius
[ ]	261:16 sed te ipsum salvare festines
ad viscera	262:23 viscerum
promissione: Z	263:11–12 permissione
quae sunt maleficia	263:30 quae malitia
saepius, ne: Z	264:1 ne saepius

ST MARK, EVANGELIST

ei deus	266:5 eidem
non modo	266:8 mox modo
dei	266:17 Petri

ST MARCELLINUS, POPE

infirmato capite	271:18–19 in capite infirmato
ipse autem iam poenitens	271:24 ipse autem poenitens

ST JAMES THE LESS, APOSTLE

licet enim Jacobo Zebedei natu sit prior	296:9 licet enim Jacobus Zebedaei prior natus sit
religionibus	296:10–11 regionibus
prior	296:11 posterior
posterior	296:12 prior
vos: CS	297:16 nos

ST PETRONILLA

respondit: Ad puellam inermem cum militibus armatis venisti? Si uxorem me desideras, fac matronas et virgines honestas ad me post tres dies venire et cum ipsis veniam ad domum tuam.	343:13–15 respondit: Si me in uxorem desideras, iubes ad me virgines venire, quae me usque ad domum tuam debeant sociare.
Nicomedes	343:22 and 23 Nicodemus
a Justo eius clerico	343:24–5 a Justo clerico

ST BARNABAS, APOSTLE

septuaginta duobus	346:23 LXII
bonitati: CS	347:29 bonitate
in fronte aciei tepidus	348:28 in frontis facie trepidus
Johanni: CS	348:33 Johanne
quidam fratres . . . praestolantur	349:3–4 quidam frater . . . praestolatur

ST BASIL, BISHOP

ignis	121:7 ingens
eam: P	122:31 eum
minas	124:22 misericordias

| post aliquos dies | 124:24 XL die |
| plasma | 124:34 palmam |

STS GERVASE AND PROTASE

requirere debere	354:28 habere
caligulis: CS	355:18 caliculis
manibus extensis	manibus extensi
jejuniis	355:22 vigiliis
perspexerat	355:24 prospexerat
Gervasii: CS	336:9 Gregorii
cantarentur: CS	336:10 cantaretur
relocaverunt	336:16 revocaverunt

ST PETER, APOSTLE

ego omnipotens, ego anima Dei	370:27–8 ego omnia dei
Nazareni crucifixi	373:6 Nazareni
Videns hoc: CS	374:22 Audiens hoc
Timothee: Z	374:27 Timotheus
crucem meam: Z	375:8 crucem meum
totum quod es, tu mihi totum: CS	375:23–4 totum, quod es tu mihi totum,

ST PAUL, APOSTLE

| prudenter: CS | 382:10 prudentem |
| vale: CS | 383:23 vade |

ST ALEXIS

magnae vere patientiae (Gr. 'Alii')	405:16 magnae vitae et patientiae
pontifici	405:20 pontificibus
daemoniaci curabantur et omnes infirmi a quacumque infirmitate detenti tacto corpore sancto curabantur.	406:23 daemoniaci curabantur.

ST MARY MAGDALENE

relevaret	410:3	revelaret
patris tui: P	410:8	patris tuae
peregrinus	411:12	and 19 Peregrinus
si potens est, memor sit	411:34	si potens es, memor sis
relocata: CS	413:20	revocata
descendebant: CS	413:25	discedebant
relocabant	413:27	revocabant
angelis	415:9	angelo

ST CHRISTOPHER

venit in mentem: Z	430:21	venit in mente
quandocumque: P	430:28	and 34 quemcumque
persensissem: Z	432:23–4:	praesensissem
protulisse: Z	432:32	pertulisse
qui torquebantur: Z	432:37	et qui torquebantur
in domino confortabat	432:38	in domino, confortabat
introductae: Z	433:33	interductae
terram: Z	434:2	tetram

THE SEVEN SLEEPERS

latentibus: Z	435:16	latentes
respondit: 'Sicut dixi . . .': Z	436:15	respondit sicut dixit . . .
Malchus: Z	436:20	Marcus
superpositum: Z	436:23	suppositum
credemus: Z	437:24	credimus
viventes	438:21	videntes
jacuerant	438:27	jacuerunt
confitentes	438:30	confidentes
surrexerunt: Z	438:32	surrexerant

ST MARTHA

locus	444:31	lacus
solo	445:13	sola

ST GERMAIN, BISHOP

suspendebat: CS	448:16 suspendebant
Trecasinae	449:23 Trahasmae
Ternodorum	450:5 Cordomarum
infirmatus	450:5–6 infirmitatus
Placidia	450:39–451:1 Placida

ST DOMINIC

fabricam	466:24 machinam
subprior	467:2 supprior
horrore	468:3 honore
dilatatione	469:12 delatione
binos et binos et verbum domini populis praedicantes,	469:18 binos et binos,
vel	469:24 ve
gratiam et misericordiam	469:34 misericordiam
quem: CS	470:17 quos
officium	judicium
lubricum: P	471:28 lubricus
Aniani	472:22 Amiani
extunc	472:29 tunc
nares, os, manus, renes et pedes	473:4 nares, manus eius et pedes
ecclesia apud Romam	473:32 ecclesia
dubium	474:17 dubio
fratres	475:32 fratres patres
materia	476:10 inter alia
a Deo	476:12 adeo
lector	476:25 lector in ordine
misericordiam . . . requiescant: P	476:29 memoriam . . . requiescunt
Conseranensem	477:11–12 Cotoronensem, aliis Citaviensem
ex fratribus	478:23 fratribus

ST LAURENCE, MARTYR

baptizavit. Statimque qui caecus fuerat lumen recepit	491:7 baptizavit

clamare vellet	492:21	clamaret
afferuntur coram Decio	492:23	afferuntur

ST BERNARD

Decelinus (= Tescelin)	528:6	Coelestinus
Aleth	528:7	Aaleth
[]	528:10	promiserat
invidit	529:1	incidit
non infideli, minus tamen fidenti	531:17	non fideli nimis, tamen fidenti
indices	531:20	judices
parcendum	532:3	ferendum
ab ipso	533:1	ab episcopo
inattentione: CS	534:37	intentione
de se ut prius sentire temere	535:7	de se postea temere
scribere ne: P	535:14	scribere me
sedavi	538:5	celavi

ST BARTHOLOMEW

Astaroth	540:29	Ascaroth
vester	541:5	noster
Polimius	541:29	Polemius
jussionem	543:8	visionem

ST GILES

quandam	582:39	quendam
Veredemio	583:2	Veredonio
divinitus praeparatam	583:6	praeparatam
rem esse a Deo, ut erat, suspicatus	583:17	rem ut erat suspicatus
postulavit.	584:14	postulavit,

ST THEODORA

speciosa	397:1	sponsa
Petri et Pauli	398:6	Petri apostoli
bobus: CS	398:7	camelis

ST EUPHEMIA

| zonaque | 622:3 | et torque |

ST EUSTACE

ut per hunc: Z	713:3	et per hunc
imago Christi	713:5	imago
Theopistem: CS	713:26	Theospitem
Agapitum	713:27	Agapetum
Theopistum: Z		Theospitum
posset: Z	714:25	possent
nutu: P	716:28	nutu tamen
in navi: Z	716:37	in mari
eos	718:8	eos sanctos

ST JUSTINA

| plures homines | 634:27 | plures |
| [] | 636:22-3 | VI cal. Octobres |

STS COSMAS AND DAMIAN

| quomodo vel ubi | 638:14 | quomodo |

ST JEROME

triginta novem	654:26	XXIX
pedem: CS	655:36	pedes
lingua latina, graeca	657:16-17	lingua graeca
eorum	660:9	eius
deferretur, secus ecclesiam	660:16	deferretur secus ecclesiam sancti
Sancti Christophori coepit		Christophori, coepit

ST FRANCIS

miratus	664:37	miseratus
consolationem	665:4	sonsolationem
[]	665:25	unicum
in latum	666:13	latus
monere	666:24	manere
castaldi	666:36	Castaldi

castaldos	666:39	Castaldus
inedia	669:3	media
pulices	669:8	simplices
chirurgus	669:20	chirurgicum
parere	669:37–8	peragere
horam	670:4	moram
Alvianum	670:27	Almarium
nudum poni se	672:1	poni se

ST PELAGIA

Nonnus	674:16	Veronus
Damietta		Damieta
[]	675:6	per nuntium
congregavit	675:31	praeparavit et congregavit

ST THAIS, COURTESAN

Paphnutius	677:29ff.	Pafuntius
peccastis mecum	678:20	peccastis, mecum
futurae, qui: Z	679:8	futurae, quae
commissae, qui: Z	679:9	commissae, quae

STS DIONYSIUS, RUSTICUS AND ELEUTHERIUS

numinum	681:13	nominum
nescimus	682:4	nescias
doctrinae, Apollophanes: CS	682:5	doctrinae Apollophani,
genuflexiones: Z	682:37	genuflectationes
ad fidem: Z	683:32	ab fidem

THE ELEVEN THOUSAND VIRGINS

Maurisii	702:19	Macrisii

STS CHRYSANTHUS AND DARIA

sensisse	700:22	sanxisse

STS SIMON AND JUDE, APOSTLES

vero primo	708:1	autem postea

pax huc vobiscum intrabit	708:22–3	pax huc nobiscum intravit
Siani (CS. cf. Benz: Suanir)	710:21	Samir

ST QUENTIN

Ambienensem	711:26	Ambianum
praeses tandem	712:6	tandem

ST MARTIN, BISHOP

saepius detrahebat	741:28	detrahebat
profectum igitur	742:25	profectus igitur
apostolis. Unde et apostoli frequenter eum tamquam comparem visitabant.	745:13	apostolis.
Ovem etiam tonsam	747:14	Qui etiam tonsam
CCCXC	748:32	CCCXCV

ST BRICE

aemulus	751:1	exemplum
prunas ardentes in byrro	751:26	prunas ardentes

ST ELIZABETH

sancti Johannis nomen	753:31	nomen sancti Petri
a puellis	753:37	cum puellis
nobis	754:1	vobis
statum: CS	754:31	statum mentis
mendici	755:28	medici
imminebat, et quantumcumque alicui parum daret, divina tamen virtute illa die sibi sufficiebat.	757:20	imminebat
sibi deficiebat		iis deficeret
etiam	757:21	enim
exhortatoriis	757:30	excitatoriis
curabat: CS	758:14	currebat ad
donec alicui in conjugium traderetur	759:26	donec in conjugium tenderetur
si propter Deum	761:1	propter Deum

volui	761:4	voluit
abdicarem	761:5	adbicaret
tanta humilitate se	761:12	tantae se humilitati
amorem dei	761:21	amorem
consistens	761:30	exsistens
ipsarum	762:6	ipsorum
serenissimum	762:8	sincerissimum
tam sollicita	763:11	sollicita
MCCXXXI: CS	764:34	MCCXXVI

ST CECILIA

homunciones	775:10	homuntiones
hos	777:7	nos

ST CLEMENT

callide	778:4	valde
nisi quia saltem	778:16	nisi quia
ob sui amorem: CS	778:23	ob hoc sui amorem
[]	784:14–17:	Nonnulli ... annumerari.
eam: CS	784:32	eum
[]	785:7	jacentes
participem: P	786:2	principem
pede dextro erecto	786:8–9	pede erecto

ST CATHERINE

te si animo rexeris: CS	791:15	tu si animo rexeris

ST JAMES THE MUTILATED

oves	801:3	pecora
profitere	801:21	profitere Deum
spera: CS	801:34	spero

STS BARLAAM AND JOSAPHAT

cadentibus	813:32	candentibus
et illi: Z	813:37	et ille
coepit ei: Z	815:20	coepit et
cum dilexerit semper,: Z	816:38	cum dilexerit, semper

rex, senem quendam	818:38	rex senex, quendam
a praedicto principe	819:3	praedicto principe
tempus odiendi (Aldus, *Vitae Patrum*)	819:32–3:	tempus obediendi
se permettere: Z	820:4	se promittere
vestimentis	822:28	ornamentis

READ MORE IN PENGUIN

In every corner of the world, on every subject under the sun, Penguin represents quality and variety – the very best in publishing today.

For complete information about books available from Penguin – including Puffins, Penguin Classics and Arkana – and how to order them, write to us at the appropriate address below. Please note that for copyright reasons the selection of books varies from country to country.

In the United Kingdom: Please write to *Dept. EP, Penguin Books Ltd, Bath Road, Harmondsworth, West Drayton, Middlesex UB7 0DA*

In the United States: Please write to *Consumer Sales, Penguin Putnam Inc., P.O. Box 12289 Dept. B, Newark, New Jersey 07101-5289*. VISA and MasterCard holders call 1-800-788-6262 to order Penguin titles

In Canada: Please write to *Penguin Books Canada Ltd, 10 Alcorn Avenue, Suite 300, Toronto, Ontario M4V 3B2*

In Australia: Please write to *Penguin Books Australia Ltd, P.O. Box 257, Ringwood, Victoria 3134*

In New Zealand: Please write to *Penguin Books (NZ) Ltd, Private Bag 102902, North Shore Mail Centre, Auckland 10*

In India: Please write to *Penguin Books India Pvt Ltd, 11 Community Centre, Panchsheel Park, New Delhi 110017*

In the Netherlands: Please write to *Penguin Books Netherlands bv, Postbus 3507, NL-1001 AH Amsterdam*

In Germany: Please write to *Penguin Books Deutschland GmbH, Metzlerstrasse 26, 60594 Frankfurt am Main*

In Spain: Please write to *Penguin Books S. A., Bravo Murillo 19, 1° B, 28015 Madrid*

In Italy: Please write to *Penguin Italia s.r.l., Via Benedetto Croce 2, 20094 Corsico, Milano*

In France: Please write to *Penguin France, Le Carré Wilson, 62 rue Benjamin Baillaud, 31500 Toulouse*

In Japan: Please write to *Penguin Books Japan Ltd, Kaneko Building, 2-3-25 Koraku, Bunkyo-Ku, Tokyo 112*

In South Africa: Please write to *Penguin Books South Africa (Pty) Ltd, Private Bag X14, Parkview, 2122 Johannesburg*

A CHOICE OF CLASSICS

Aeschylus	**The Oresteian Trilogy**
	Prometheus Bound/The Suppliants/Seven against Thebes/The Persians
Aesop	**Fables**
Ammianus Marcellinus	**The Later Roman Empire (AD 354–378)**
Apollonius of Rhodes	**The Voyage of Argo**
Apuleius	**The Golden Ass**
Aristophanes	**The Knights/Peace/The Birds/The Assemblywomen/Wealth**
	Lysistrata/The Acharnians/The Clouds
	The Wasps/The Poet and the Women/ The Frogs
Aristotle	**The Art of Rhetoric**
	The Athenian Constitution
	De Anima
	Ethics
	Poetics
Arrian	**The Campaigns of Alexander**
Marcus Aurelius	**Meditations**
Boethius	**The Consolation of Philosophy**
Caesar	**The Civil War**
	The Conquest of Gaul
Catullus	**Poems**
Cicero	**Murder Trials**
	The Nature of the Gods
	On the Good Life
	Selected Letters
	Selected Political Speeches
	Selected Works
Euripides	**Alcestis/Iphigenia in Tauris/Hippolytus**
	The Bacchae/Ion/The Women of Troy/ Helen
	Medea/Hecabe/Electra/Heracles
	Orestes and Other Plays

READ MORE IN PENGUIN

A CHOICE OF CLASSICS

READ MORE IN PENGUIN

A CHOICE OF CLASSICS

Plautus	**The Pot of Gold and Other Plays**
	The Rope and Other Plays
Pliny	**The Letters of the Younger Pliny**
Pliny the Elder	**Natural History**
Plotinus	**The Enneads**
Plutarch	**The Age of Alexander** (Nine Greek Lives)
	The Fall of the Roman Republic (Six Lives)
	The Makers of Rome (Nine Lives)
	Plutarch on Sparta
	The Rise and Fall of Athens (Nine Greek Lives)
Polybius	**The Rise of the Roman Empire**
Procopius	**The Secret History**
Propertius	**The Poems**
Quintus Curtius Rufus	**The History of Alexander**
Sallust	**The Jugurthine War/The Conspiracy of Cataline**
Seneca	**Four Tragedies/Octavia**
	Letters from a Stoic
Sophocles	**Electra/Women of Trachis/Philoctetes/Ajax**
	The Theban Plays
Suetonius	**The Twelve Caesars**
Tacitus	**The Agricola/The Germania**
	The Annals of Imperial Rome
	The Histories
Terence	**The Comedies (The Girl from Andros/The Self-Tormentor/The Eunuch/Phormio/The Mother-in-Law/The Brothers)**
Thucydides	**History of the Peloponnesian War**
Virgil	**The Aeneid**
	The Eclogues
	The Georgics
Xenophon	**Conversations of Socrates**
	A History of My Times
	The Persian Expedition

READ MORE IN PENGUIN

A CHOICE OF CLASSICS

READ MORE IN PENGUIN

A CHOICE OF CLASSICS

Francis Bacon	**The Essays**
Aphra Behn	**Love-Letters between a Nobleman and His Sister**
	Oroonoko, The Rover and Other Works
George Berkeley	**Principles of Human Knowledge/Three Dialogues between Hylas and Philonous**
James Boswell	**The Life of Samuel Johnson**
Sir Thomas Browne	**The Major Works**
John Bunyan	**The Pilgrim's Progress**
Edmund Burke	**Reflections on the Revolution in France**
Frances Burney	**Evelina**
Margaret Cavendish	**The Blazing World and Other Writings**
William Cobbett	**Rural Rides**
William Congreve	**Comedies**
Thomas de Quincey	**Confessions of an English Opium Eater**
	Recollections of the Lakes and the Lake Poets
Daniel Defoe	**A Journal of the Plague Year**
	Moll Flanders
	Robinson Crusoe
	Roxana
	A Tour Through the Whole Island of Great Britain
Henry Fielding	**Amelia**
	Jonathan Wild
	Joseph Andrews
	The Journal of a Voyage to Lisbon
	Tom Jones
John Gay	**The Beggar's Opera**
Oliver Goldsmith	**The Vicar of Wakefield**
Lady Gregory	**Selected Writings**

READ MORE IN PENGUIN

A CHOICE OF CLASSICS

William Hazlitt	**Selected Writings**
George Herbert	**The Complete English Poems**
Thomas Hobbes	**Leviathan**
Samuel Johnson/	
James Boswell	**A Journey to the Western Islands of Scotland** and **The Journal of a Tour of the Hebrides**
Charles Lamb	**Selected Prose**
George Meredith	**The Egoist**
Thomas Middleton	**Five Plays**
John Milton	**Paradise Lost**
Samuel Richardson	**Clarissa**
	Pamela
Earl of Rochester	**Complete Works**
Richard Brinsley	
Sheridan	**The School for Scandal and Other Plays**
Sir Philip Sidney	**Selected Poems**
Christopher Smart	**Selected Poems**
Adam Smith	**The Wealth of Nations** (Books I–III)
Tobias Smollett	**The Adventures of Ferdinand Count Fathom**
	Humphrey Clinker
	Roderick Random
Laurence Sterne	**The Life and Opinions of Tristram Shandy**
	A Sentimental Journey Through France and Italy
Jonathan Swift	**Gulliver's Travels**
	Selected Poems
Thomas Traherne	**Selected Poems and Prose**
Henry Vaughan	**Complete Poems**

READ MORE IN PENGUIN

A CHOICE OF CLASSICS

Adomnan of Iona	**Life of St Columba**
St Anselm	**The Prayers and Meditations**
St Augustine	**Confessions**
	The City of God
Bede	**Ecclesiastical History of the English People**
Geoffrey Chaucer	**The Canterbury Tales**
	Love Visions
	Troilus and Criseyde
Marie de France	**The Lais of Marie de France**
Jean Froissart	**The Chronicles**
Geoffrey of Monmouth	**The History of the Kings of Britain**
Gerald of Wales	**History and Topography of Ireland**
	The Journey through Wales and The Description of Wales
Gregory of Tours	**The History of the Franks**
Robert Henryson	**The Testament of Cresseid and Other Poems**
Walter Hilton	**The Ladder of Perfection**
St Ignatius	**Personal Writings**
Julian of Norwich	**Revelations of Divine Love**
Thomas à Kempis	**The Imitation of Christ**
William Langland	**Piers the Ploughman**
Sir John Mandeville	**The Travels of Sir John Mandeville**
Marguerite de Navarre	**The Heptameron**
Christine de Pisan	**The Treasure of the City of Ladies**
Chrétien de Troyes	**Arthurian Romances**
Marco Polo	**The Travels**
Richard Rolle	**The Fire of Love**
François Villon	**Selected Poems**